OMNIPOTENCE

Book 1: Odyssey

Geoff Gaywood

This is a work of fiction. Names, characters, businesses, places, events and incidents are either the products of the author's imagination or used in a fictitious manner. Any resemblance to actual persons, living or dead, or actual events is purely coincidental.

Matador
9 Priory Business Park,
Wistow Road, Kibworth Beauchamp,
Leicestershire. LE8 0RX
Tel: 0116 279 2299
Email: books@troubador.co.uk
Web: www.troubador.co.uk/matador
Twitter: @matadorbooks

ISBN 978 1785899 188

British Library Cataloguing in Publication Data.
A catalogue record for this book is available from the British Library.

Printed and bound by CPI Group (UK) Ltd, Croydon, CR0 4YY
Typeset in 11pt Minion Pro by Troubador Publishing Ltd, Leicester, UK

Matador is an imprint of Troubador Publishing Ltd

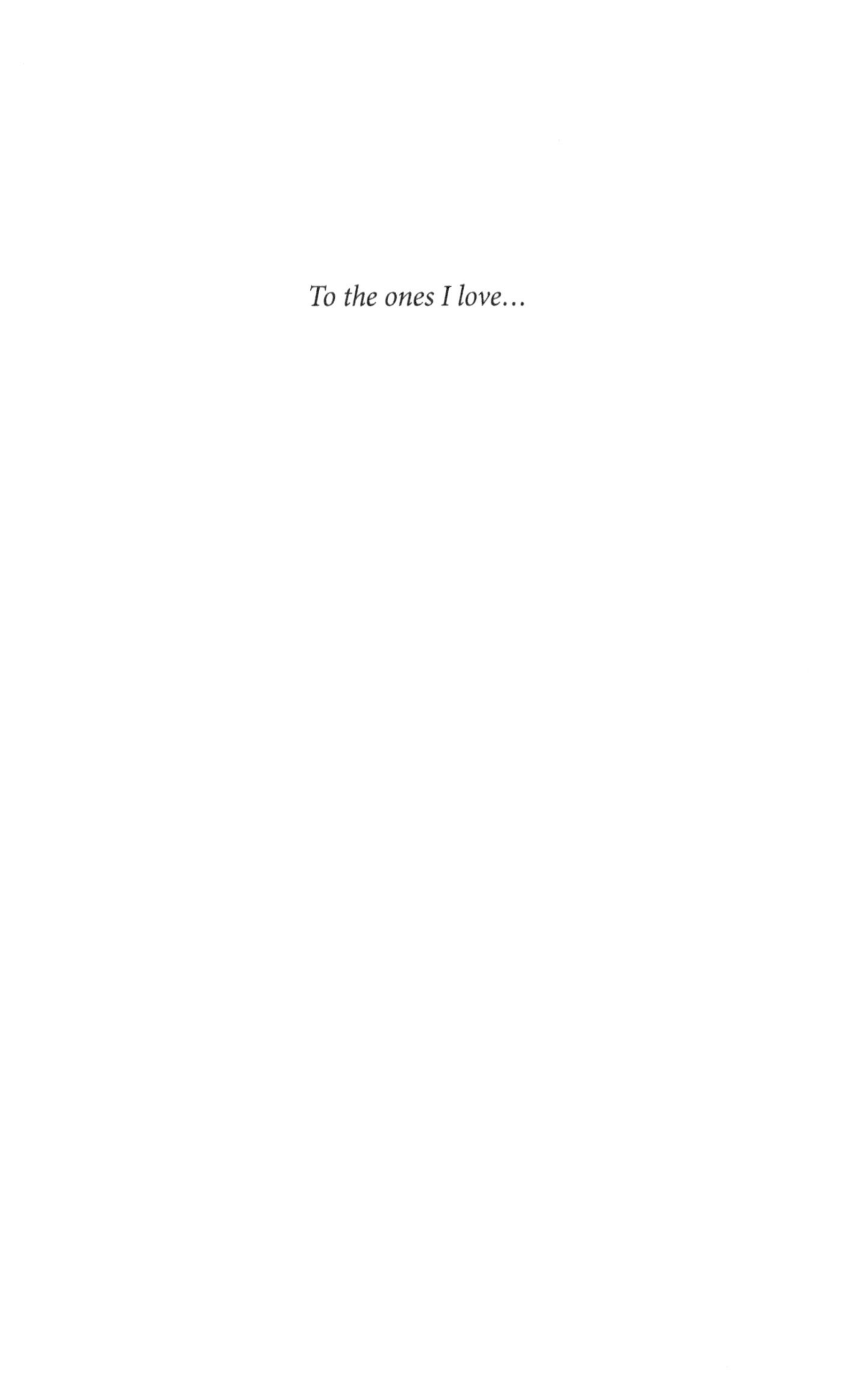

To the ones I love…

Contents

1
A Hole in the Sky

Arlette raised her head off her sweaty wrists and blurrily surveyed the expanse of soft white sand before her.

"Henri, where the hell's my piña colada?"

There was a grunt from the direction of the brightly painted bar just across the beach, then a shadow fell across her upper body.

"Your phone 'as been buzzin'," said Henri.

She rolled over and smiled up at him.

"Come down here and smother me with that sublime black body of yours."

He dropped onto one knee, carefully balanced the glasses on the sand under the shade, and pulled her up into his arms as though she were practically weightless. He caressed her face with such tenderness that she could have purred with pleasure, and she opened her eyes to soak up his great brown eyes with their huge, silky lashes. There followed a long, languid kiss that left her limp and breathing deeply.

He laid her down on the sand, sat up and pulled her phone from his trunks.

"You 'ad three calls," he announced, "all from the same ... from Washington."

"I know," said Arlette quietly. "I'd have let them through if I had wanted to" – she pointed at the finely textured little black disk of her earphone – "but I'm not receptive right now – to phone calls."

Henri grinned. 'A powerhouse, this woman,' he thought to himself. 'Tender, almost vulnerable one minute, utterly and unquestionably in command the next.'

"We're going to enjoy the rest of our day together – to the full," said Arlette with exaggerated lust.

At 8.00 a.m. the following morning, the breakfasters on the terrace of the Acapulco Paradise hotel witnessed the soundless arrival of a craft that appeared from nowhere and hissed to a standstill on the grass before them. Arlette, dressed immaculately in the pale blue uniform of a colonel in the International Space Exploration Agency, stepped smartly across the lawn towards it. Her mouth barely moved as she responded to her incoming call. "Yes. Who? Oh." The machine almost imperceptibly engulfed her as she reached it.

Seconds later it was gone. A wave crashed on the beach.

The birds, only slightly confused, began to sing again.

Arlette sat back, tightly belted in her contoured seat, as the machine hurtled into the stratosphere. She did not glance to the left or right, but intensely studied the plush, pinkish padding above her and turned over in her mind the sole piece of data she had just been provided with – General Lee, Special Operations, 9.00 a.m.

'Why is he in Washington?' she thought. 'And why do

I have to be snatched off the beach with no notice?'

No explanation was obvious to her and, conceding to herself that she would find out soon enough, she relaxed into a comforting reverie that began with her recalling a hilarious story that Henri had recounted over dinner the previous evening. It had begun with his mother in Haiti, a chicken, a priest and some underwear. It had gone on and on, articulated in his charming fractured English, becoming more and more absurd until the tears were running down her face and her throat ached from laughing. "Oh, Henri, I do love you!" she had blurted out, and instantly regretted it.

But Henri knew exactly what she meant, which was not what she had said, and anyway he was far too savvy to allow a slip like that to spoil the mood of the evening. So he had taken her hand, pulled her graciously out of her chair, and walked her along the beach as the light of an exquisitely beautiful honey-coloured moon had danced on the sea beside them. At the end of the beach he had stood her against a palm tree, given her one of those deep, languorous kisses and then, without any hesitation or change in his almost perpetually joyful expression, he had lifted her off her feet and made love to her, there and then.

She sighed and shifted in her seat. It had irritated her intensely when he had told her later that she had "yelped like a puppy". But in the end he was just a man, a source of entertainment, social and physical, nothing to get overly sentimental about. Their relationship had sprung from a chance meeting, his perfect manners and his irresistible banter. It had barely touched the cultural or intellectual, and yet there was a tantalising mystery about him. He was somehow deep and powerful under all that polish. Arlette cleared her head.

The machine juddered, the engine note changed and then died. A door slid open.

"Good morning, Colonel Piccard," said a fresh-faced young lieutenant with an impeccable uniform and an obsequious expression. "Welcome to ISEA Washington HQ. You have twelve minutes to freshen up. General Lee will see you in his office."

Arlette 'freshened up'. She followed the young lieutenant down a corridor lit by a kaleidoscope of moving images of space equipment and events, breathing deeply and thinking to herself, 'I don't really need this. I am thirty-seven years old, have a brilliant career behind me, I've been decorated for gallantry and I'm happy with myself. I am not going to be sold some tedious mission requiring years of self-deprivation and hardship for some obscure purpose.'

She stiffened as she entered General Lee's spacious, brilliantly lit office.

He was standing with his back to her, looking at one of perhaps a dozen screens of ongoing space operations. He was a tall, elegant Han Chinese, perhaps fifty, with a great mop of very black hair, wearing a heavily decorated uniform.

"Good morning, Colonel," he said brightly. "I am so sorry to snatch you away from your well-deserved leave. We'll have you back in Acapulco later today. Please sit down."

Arlette sat.

The General glanced at a file on his monitor, frowned,

and then came and sat with her, an expression of good-natured attention on his face as though he was about to be sold something he actually wanted.

"What was it about Acapulco that attracted you?" he asked.

Arlette surveyed this innocuous question with some suspicion – he most certainly knew where she had been in the previous three months, but she answered honestly.

"I love the place and felt there would be no one there who might recognise me and chase me around," she said simply, "and it worked."

"Oh good," said the General, and, after a pause, "I notice you are not wearing your Crimson Star."

Arlette raised her eyebrows. "I haven't got round to it, General. It's rather – prominent – and I'm not overly fond of ceremonial trinketry."

The General's face hardened. He rose and walked back to his monitor.

Rather testily, he said, "Colonel Piccard, you have recently been awarded the most prestigious decoration with which this great global institution can honour its heroes. There are no other living recipients. It says on the record that you showed exceptional courage in the face of almost certain disaster, that you personally intervened medically to save the lives of two severely injured crew-mates, that you showed extraordinary ingenuity and presence of mind to resolve complex technical problems in conditions of extreme personal danger and that you were instrumental in saving the Dalian space station and nineteen of its twenty-four crew members."

Arlette looked at the floor.

"You will wear your Crimson Star out of respect for this institution and your five dead crew-mates, and you will not allow your personal vanity to detract from your responsibilities as an example of the qualities we aspire to."

"Yes, General," said Arlette in the most deferential tone she could muster.

General Lee returned to the chair next to her with the same good-natured expression back on his face.

"Colonel Piccard," he said, "you are of course well aware of the progressive deterioration in Earth's climate, and the mission of the ISEA to address the issue of potential alternative habitats."

Arlette nodded.

"You are to take command of a very important mission," he said calmly.

"Where to?" asked Arlette rather guardedly.

"To a solar system in the Omega 16 sector of the galaxy which contains two rocky planets harbouring conditions considered to be in the range of human habitation."

Arlette started to laugh. "Is this a cosmology test, General? Omega 16 is at least 10,000 light years away. It is far beyond our technical capabilities to..."

"No it isn't," said the General, "We've done it."

Arlette stared at him in utter disbelief. This had to be some joke, or some kind of virtual exercise.

"But we can't travel faster than the speed of light..." It was a helplessly redundant comment.

"No, we can't," agreed the General.

A pause.

"Then you have a shortcut?" said Arlette, her eyes widening slowly as realisation crept up on her.

"Yes," said the General.

There was a long silence.

"How did you do it?" asked Arlette, adjusting herself to a dimension of theoretical thought where she had often played before, but that she had never considered could have approached the realms of reality in her lifetime or the conceivable future.

"We created what is euphemistically called a wormhole, although that is hardly an appropriate term for a conduit large and stable enough to enable a spaceship to pass from one area of the universe to another."

Arlette considered this carefully. "Never mind the complexity of positioning and orientating such a monumental contrivance, you would need an astronomical amount of energy to do that, equivalent to..." She thought hard for a second or two. "Equivalent to the mass of a sizable star," she said, smiling incredulously.

"No, not if you can focus the energy to do just what you want to do and avoid the wasteful pyrotechnics. A small planet, or a large satellite would do," said the General as if he was also considering an interesting theoretical possibility.

Arlette stiffened sharply.

"A moon?"

"Yes," said General Lee, as though he were getting close to conceding a game of 'I spy'.

"Which one?" demanded Arlette.

"Proteus," said General Lee quietly.

Arlette was outraged.

"YOU'VE BLOWN UP ONE OF NEPTUNE'S MOONS TO MAKE A HOLE IN THE SKY? FUCK MY BOOTS! HAS NO ONE NOTICED?"

"It's been one of my trickier diplomatic missions to convince national governments to suspend academic observations of Neptune," said the General with some feeling. "But after all we are pursuing an objective here that has their unconditional support."

"Like what?" demanded Arlette.

"The identification of a long-term home for the human race once this planet becomes uninhabitable due to climate change." said General Lee with some obvious impatience.

Arlette was breathing deeply. "What about the amateur astronomers?" she asked. "The guys combing the sky for something new? How did you keep them quiet?"

The General stiffened slightly. "That is being dealt with on a national level," he said with slightly flaky nonchalance.

Arlette arched her eyebrows.

"There have been no wet operations, if that is what you are alluding to," he added.

She let it go.

"So there is a direct passage to a planetary system 10,000 light years away hidden behind Neptune?" she observed. "Cool!"

"We have brought about a severe and targeted localised distortion of space–time, or LDST, which has resolved itself into a stable intragalactic shortcut between two defined coordinates. Obviously it is not hidden behind Neptune any more because Neptune is following a defined orbital path, which, I am happy to say, has not shown any significant deviation since the, er … transformation of Proteus," said the General, in what sounded very much like 'the official version'.

“So it’s just hanging outside there? Is it detectable?”

“Of course it is if you know what you are looking for, but, if you don’t; not easily, no.”

“So,” Arlette continued with her inquisition, “how did you know whether you had identified a suitable planet?”

The General took a deep breath. “We knew that it was a suitable environment 10,000 years ago, because we could analyse the radiation which reached us directly. Of course we had to send a robot there to check in more detail, and to test the stability of the shortcut. The mission was successful. It returned most of the data we needed.”

“But how could you monitor and control a device 10,000 light years away?” asked Arlette, still grappling with the enormity of this apparent accomplishment, which she could not get her head around with any astrophysical theory she was aware of.

“We used the shortcut as a conduit for communications. We positioned repeater satellites at the mouth of each end of the shortcut to bounce the signals to and from wherever the robot was in Omega 16.” The General shrugged. It was obvious.

“So, you want me to go there?” Arlette was beginning to sense the biggest sinking feeling she had ever experienced.

“Yes, we want you to command a mission to Omega 16, assess the suitability of the two candidate rocky planets for human habitation, set up bases that are secure and can be expanded on subsequent missions, and bring your crew and ship safely back to Earth to report.” General Lee was wearing his good-natured expression again.

“How long will it take?” asked Arlette, returning to her normal, clipped tone of communication.

"Thirty days' familiarisation and set-up, 320 days operational." And before Arlette could articulate her next question, he added, "Your ship is approaching completion at the lunar construction platform. Virtual training starts at the Shanghai facility next Thursday. The only task you need to focus on in the meantime is crew selection. You can take the recommendations and profiles back with you on the shuttle device to Acapulco. Any further questions?"

"Yes. Do I get to vote on this?"

General Lee looked her straight in the eyes, wearily.

"You are without doubt the right candidate for this job, and you are about to become the greatest navigational explorer in the history of our civilisation. You will have every resource you require."

He sat back and smiled. That was that, as far as he was concerned.

Arlette rose slowly to her feet.

"OK," she said.

2
Wild Oats

"Colonel Piccard, please remove your jacket."

Arlette slipped off her jacket and handed it over.

The young lieutenant handed her a replacement and a spare in a plastic sack. There was an addition to the medal bar, a broad scarlet band with five gold stars on it. Arlette thought it gross, but she buttoned her lip. She had agreed to wear it and it was of no further consequence.

A few minutes later she was buckling herself into the shuttle, and as the whine of the machine's engines rose for take-off, she had the entire structure of the crew of her new command displayed above her holographically.

There was not a single rookie. All had had spaceflight experience and had fulfilled their roles with distinction. All were trained in spaceflight practice and had shown aptitude to perform under stressed conditions. Their professional specialisations were carefully selected:

Administrators	4
Agricultural Engineers	6

Biologists	4
Botanists	3
Cooks	8
Commander	1
Cosmologists	6
Entertainment Managers	2
Fitness Instructors	8
General Physicians	4
Instrument Engineers	8
IT Engineers	16
Maintenance Engineers	12
Mathematicians	2
Military contingent	30
Navigational Analysts	8
Nutrition Physicians	2
Paramedics	6
Physicists	2
Pilots	4
Propulsion Engineers	8
Psychiatrists	2
Psychologists	8
Total	153
Women	81
Men	72

4-shift configuration, 1G induced gravity

Arlette was being offered two alternative nominees for each role. She moved swiftly through the lists, applying her own knowledge of many of the candidates. By the time the shuttle touched down in Acapulco, she had 129 of the crew selected and had sent 36 messages asking for advice from colleagues on the remainder. She would settle the list at breakfast tomorrow and notify Command HQ. Then she would switch off until she was picked up for relocation to Shanghai next Wednesday.

As the door of the shuttle slid open and the scents of hibiscus and sea water wafted in, Arlette was thinking of a swim, a cocktail and a lounge in the late afternoon sun before she called Henri.

She slipped on her newly decorated jacket, stepped onto the grass, and walked back across the lawn which she had crossed almost exactly eight hours earlier with the same elegant, confident stride.

A little while later her supple body hit the tepid surface of the pool, rousing her enough to slide her hands gracefully and unhurriedly through the water. She swam for barely fifteen minutes, eased herself out, shook her long, dark hair and raised her hand to the waiter as she settled into the nearest lounger.

"Si, Señora?"

The waiter was an absurdly handsome young man who looked as if he had just stepped off a film set. She regarded him with the appreciation of a sculptor for a nice block of marble.

"Mmmm – Mai Tai," she said, eyes hooded. Then, opening them wide, "Please."

"Si, Señora" he said, and slid his eyes a little too slowly over her body before turning away.

Arlette savoured this harmless little flirtation and briefly fantasised about doing something quite disgraceful with him behind the bar.

Then a hideous thought struck her – 'Holy fuck, no sex

for a year!' Almost panic-stricken, she wondered how she could have accepted this command without the slightest thought of her personal well-being. She could have asked the General … No, she couldn't.

Oh, really? Would it not have been entirely appropriate to discuss the management of the sexual needs of the crew over this extended period? Perhaps not at this stage; perhaps indeed this was an issue to be discussed calmly and professionally with her psychological staff. Yes, yes, relax, all in good time. But none of the crew were in any permanent relationship with any other crew members as far as she could tell from their personal files, and they were all of reproductive age. There was going to be an awful lot of clandestine sex, and, if she was not extremely careful, not-so-clandestine sex, which could put crew discipline seriously at risk. Phew!

She sipped her Mai Tai.

This would all be managed proactively with the informed and open support of her specialist crew. Everybody would fully understand the issues and risks up front and would conduct themselves with the utmost responsibility and restraint. This issue would have been addressed before in other extended missions, and there was no need to re-invent any wheels. OK, now switch off and enjoy!

A shadow fell across her face.

"Arlette, ma belle, 'ow could you deprive me of a single minute of your irresistible personage?" He pronounced the final word 'personnarge', and it sounded like profiteroles and cream. She half opened her eyes and gazed up at his gentle face, atop his rather splendid torso.

"Henri, you soulless brute, I am still recovering from your assault on my person last night, which may well have damaged several of my vital organs as well as my self-esteem."

"Ah," said Henri, dropping to his knees and bringing his lovely smiling face right up to hers. "I 'ave come to restore your self-esteem by returning your knickers, which you left hanging on a palm tree..."

She slapped his face with all the force she could muster, and then immediately regretted it. She pulled his head against her breast and said softly, "Oh you pig, you lovely, adorable pig."

Henri grunted and stroked his cheek. "Alors, ma belle, can I tempt you to a romantic dinner...?"

"Absolutely not. I want to go dancing until dawn. I want to lie on the beach and watch the sun rise. I want hot fresh croissants and coffee right there. I want to be utterly spoiled and pampered and then, and only then, made love to."

"Mais, comme tu veux, ma belle," said Henri with his lovely smile.

And indeed it was so. She spent the next few days in hedonistic revelry, enjoying every sensation and experience permitted by the law, and some which probably were not, and she paid due respect to whoever was supposedly the custodian of wanton personal behaviour.

Henri obliged her tirelessly with charm, wit, sympathy, lovely surprises and sex in the most unexpected places. As Wednesday drew closer, she started to prepare herself mentally to impose the self-discipline on herself which she knew would be central to her command, and on Tuesday night at 10 p.m. she kissed Henri on the cheek, wished him goodnight, goodbye and good luck, and left him standing there, looking utterly perplexed.

The shuttle arrived at 4 a.m. the next morning. By 5.00 she was boarding a military jet that landed in Shanghai just over two and a half hours later. She was met secretly, but with full military honours, escorted to dinner with some of the great, if not the good, of the Chinese national administration, and then to her quarters to meet her immediate personal staff. She retired early, and as her time difference correction medication hit her and her consciousness faded, said to herself, "OK, Omega 16, watch out – here I come."

3

The Team Comes Together

Arlette woke at 6.00 a.m., rose, brushed her teeth, grimaced at herself in the mirror, switched on her phone, selected a news channel, grabbed a bottle of water and skipped onto the trainer for a warm-up. She worked herself hard for thirty minutes with half an eye on the breaking news on a floor-to-ceiling screen. A murderous drought in Turkey, where soldiers were shooting starving civilians, over two thousand anticyclone fatalities in Japan and another nuclear power station disaster, and a complete collapse of control in the Indian food riots. Arlette stopped and stared at the pictures of devastation and misery. She shrugged. It was going to get worse, she knew; much worse. She stretched, stripped and slid into the shower while her incoming messages were relayed to her over the audio.

There were messages of welcome from most of her closest staff and many of the members of her new crew, to which she responded warmly but briefly, a status briefing from General Lee, a hate message which would have to be referred to security but to which she did not listen once she had detected the tone, half a dozen messages from friends who assumed she was still in Acapulco, and a story from Henri who had no idea where she was but had assumed that it would do her good to be made to laugh.

It did.

Arlette felt the warm water stream over her body like the caressing lips of a lover and closed her eyes. She let her fantasies roam a little and then asked herself out loud, "Are you happy, Arlette?" She decided she was. She liked her persona, she liked her body, and she liked the way she was engaging with the new people she was meeting. She reminded herself to make no snap judgements where none were necessary and not to overdo it with the humility. This was fairly low-level stuff for the first few days – familiarisation and data-gathering. Establishing a modus operandi with her senior staff members would only start in three days' time; situation training was a further two days off.

She walked into the dryer and twirled herself around while the warm air jets coaxed the last drops of water off her body. Finally she attended to her personal toilette and slipped into the silky smooth pale blue jumpsuit which was to be her daily working outfit. There were little pinholes on the chest where the Crimson Star had been removed overnight on her instructions. 'If there were any members of the crew who have not already been told about my damned medal already', she thought, 'they will find out on the grapevine. I am not going to flaunt it, regardless of General Lee's admonition. This is my show and it will be conducted my way.'

She switched off all communication systems, sat on

her bed and looked out over the Yangtze. The morning mist was beginning to clear, a huge watery sun was hanging just above the horizon and China was busy on the river just as it had been for thousands of years. Always the great societal divisions but always great respect for learning and hard work. Egos, jealousies, feuds and competitions – yes, but love and commitment for the great human endeavour could always be invoked. She felt a wave of affection for humanity flood over her and a surge of thrill for what she was about to embark on.

'Arlette baby, this is your destiny – let's go and grab it,' she thought, rising slowly to her feet.

She was joined at breakfast by her three personal assistants: Chang Chao, Chinese, Staff Officer for personal and security issues; Julia Rogers, English, Press and Diplomatic Liaison Officer; and Marcel Rousseau, French, Technical Liaison Officer. The conversation moved quickly and informally through their respective areas of responsibility and an easy, open communication style took hold. Security and the possible significance of the hate message brought the three of them sharply into unison.

"Commander," (she would have to get used to that) said Chang, "an unresolved security issue can destroy a mission like this with more finality than a serious technical failure. You must understand that there can be no shortcuts or compromises." Everyone agreed with him. "We will identify the originator of this message, the nature of the threat, and eliminate it," he said simply.

Arlette recalled General Lee's comments about 'no wet

operations' with distaste, but when it came to the safety of her mission and her crew she knew that she could and would not argue against whatever steps the security authorities might decide were necessary. She toyed briefly with the idea of insisting on being informed if any 'extreme' measures were to be taken, but realised that she would be far less qualified to make those judgements than in the case of the countless routine but critical technical decisions that she would be delegating to her crew members. She looked at Chang carefully for a minute and then said, "I am counting on you to do so."

Chang nodded.

As if to break any tension that might be building up, Julia intervened. "This is currently a secret mission," she stated, "but the tide of speculation is going to start rising any time now. A huge spaceship is nearing completion on the moon. It has obviously been financed for a specific purpose. There are waves of social unrest every time we have another extreme meteorological event. The key political leaders backing this project have agreed to maintain secrecy only up to the point where we decide we have a 'Go'. Once that happens we will be goldfish in a bowl."

Arlette winced at the thought.

Marcel interjected in his lightly accented Gallic drawl. "It could be earlier," he said. "Our illustrious new commander is a global celebrity after all the publicity surrounding her incredible bravery in saving the Dalian and its crew. The whole planet wants to know where she is. Quite a few people know she is in Shanghai and, even though everyone is sworn to secrecy, leaks will happen and questions will be asked."

"Well, Julia, you will be manning the stone wall," said Arlette.

"Mmmm," said Julia. "It's comforting to think that I have only my dignity to lose. Journalists will be intrusive, deceptive, seductive and abusive and will make up what they can't find out. We will come under tremendous pressure, I warn you."

"I can take it as long as they are seductive." It was Marcel again. He was ignored.

Arlette changed the subject. "Do we have any radically new technology to get our heads around, Marcel?"

"Nothing of mission-critical importance. Almost all the new technology is in the targeted mass transformation that has created the wormhole, and the detection and orientation required to align the ship to enable it to pass through. Since the wormhole is indeed a shortcut, the total distance to be covered is only a few tens of billions of kilometres. Therefore we don't need to get anywhere close to the speed of light to accomplish the mission. Our tried and tested anti-matter reactor motors will do the job nicely." He paused.

"However, there is a new feature which will contribute enormously to crew comfort and efficiency. The Ukrainians have done a brilliant job with the targeted mass transformation technology to develop an induced gravitational field – it's produced in the tubular rings around the fore and aft of the ship – and as a result we shall have artificial gravity, exactly 1G in fact, throughout the crewed areas of the ship. You can imagine what this will do for our comfort, health, fitness levels, fresh food options and mobility." There was a murmur of appreciation around the table.

Arlette sat back and considered this. With one exception, all her previous spaceflights had been made in zero gravity, which profoundly changed every aspect of your thoughts and actions. The exception had been IP243, a space station which had had its crew quarters in a huge rotating ring. It had failed spectacularly when a shuttle rocket had misfired and hit the space station, leaving the crew to re-invent weightless mode activities in a particularly unsuitable environment. But the induced gravity on this mission was going to enable every crew member to behave in ways unrestrained by their environment. Their emotions and all their other personal characteristics would be much more visible. Gone would be the splendid isolation that a commander on a weightless mission could invoke inside his own life-support cocoon. She would be constantly visible, her fears and failings under scrutiny, like the captain of an ocean liner. She knew that her courage would not let her down when facing danger on her own. She was not so sure how good she would be when she had to inspire many others to perform at the same level, simultaneously. She nursed a terrible foreboding of some sort of catastrophe that would reveal her inadequacies, and she shuddered.

Meanwhile Marcel went on. "When the ship reaches its destination in Omega 16 we shall of course be orbiting bodies of which we have imprecise knowledge, so there will be a fair amount of original navigation work to be done, but we will not be in another universe unless something has gone terribly wrong, so special relativity will be entirely adequate."

Arlette grinned. She liked Marcel. It was such a pleasure to have someone around who could reduce the technical enormity of the mission to such engaging simplicity. "OK, everyone, we need to go and have a look at the simulator and start to get a feel for our new baby. Let's go."

4
Into Virtual Reality

Chang guided them down to the monorail terminal inside the crew quarters building and pointed out the security features. They would not be going to any other part of the building and they would be monitored constantly. The monorail car was driverless, noiseless and anonymous. It whisked them briefly out into the sunshine, from where they had a fleeting view of the Yangtze, and back into a huge, monolithic building that looked like a purpose-built factory of some kind. The car flashed through three brightly lit stations before arriving in a huge hangar.

"Here we are," said Marcel, "and there is a full-size mock-up of the command centre of IP262."

A squat tower stood before them, covered with matt black plates and topped with a shallow dome. There were no visible windows of any kind.

"IP262? Is that the best they can do for a name?" Arlette had expected something a little less prosaic. "You will get to name her," said Marcel, "once you get to know her. Come and have a look at the model."

They gathered around a scale model of the ship, some twenty metres long and so complete in detail that it looked as though it could move off at any minute. "This is one-tenth full size," said Marcel. "It is designed with multiple high-impact skins to avoid any damage being done by stray cosmic matter that gets through its extremely potent laser-guided defence system. The large tubular rings fore and aft are the gravitation field generators I mentioned before. They are also heavily protected. The long tail houses the anti-matter propulsion units – you really don't want to be anywhere near the stuff that comes out of there – it will go through anything and leave a very unpleasant mess behind.

"Amidships are the two excursion vehicles which will travel piggy-back with us, the launch and retrieval bays, the exploration hardware and the military operation centre. Behind that are the laboratories and foreign matter storage areas. Right in the front of the craft is the farmyard. Vegetable food is grown hydroponically, and animal proteins with a full range of textures and flavours are produced in sterile conditions. Immediately behind the farmyard are the crew quarters and recreation areas – very extensive and comprehensive."

"Are there no windows?" asked Julia, with obvious disappointment.

"There are direct observation ports around the vehicle launch and retrieval areas and there are windows on the command deck, although they are always covered when the ship is moving at operational speeds," said Marcel. "However, there are cameras mounted over the entire external surface of the ship and the view is projected continuously onto the inside walls, so you have an uninterrupted view of the universe around you at all times."

"Nice," said Chang.

"Pretty basic technology," said Marcel nonchalantly.

"Oh, and lifts and stairways run through the ship from aft to fore. The gravitational field is longitudinally orientated, so you are in fact in a tower with many floors, with the farmyard at the top and the engines in the basement. You'll get used to it."

Arlette stepped back and contemplated. 'What a simply awesome ship,' she thought, 'and what incredible trust has been put in me.' She felt overwhelmed by it for a brief moment, and scared, but then Marcel was calling her on into the command tower mock-up. Suppressing an impulse to turn to some figure in authority for reassurance, she breathed in, raised her eyebrows and widened her eyes, and stepped forward.

It was not what she had expected. The room inside the tower was a bowl-shaped stadium, with modules for each of the key control functions located at various levels on the periphery. The control platform itself was mounted on a stalk, and mobile so that it could move her effortlessly to any point in the room that she might select and engage directly with any one of her key controllers, one on one. The roof and walls appeared to be windows straight onto the universe outside.

She mounted her control platform, settled into her body couch, surveyed the eager faces around her, and touched 'start' on her screen. Instantly she found herself moving in a smooth arc to a position next to the launch engineer, her workspace dovetailing with his and her screen transformed to the launch sequence.

Their eyes met briefly. "Jake Thibault," he said softly and nodded, and touched his monitor with three fingers.

There was a slight tremor, but no sensation of acceleration.

"Is that it?" she asked.

"That's it," he said. "Anti-matter is a fantastic fuel because you can store a phenomenal amount of potential energy in a very small space, but the cost of producing it is so high that you must use it efficiently. For a mission of this scale, optimum efficiency is achieved with a reactor delivering a force of just one tenth of Earth's gravity. At that rate of acceleration we will reach our rendezvous with the shortcut in thirty-five days, and will be travelling at three thousand kilometres per second. Then we will fire the boosters and orientate the ship to enter the wormhole."

Jake anticipated the Commander's next question, and he went on, "We don't use the boosters at the outset because the fuel we need for them can only be replenished when we have ample water locally for electrolysis. Of course we can use them to get us out of trouble in a hurry if we need to, but higher rates of acceleration save only a few days of transit time, increase both cost and risk and make no sense when we have a manageable mission duration of less than a year."

Arlette smiled. He was so completely at ease with his task. She had a hundred questions about the technology that she would love to ask, but this was not the moment. She needed to move on and get a grasp of the scope of the operation and the roles and personalities of the key players.

She worked her way through all the positions in the command centre, sometimes returning with a further question, but gradually building her confidence in the capabilities of the ship and its crew. By the end of her first day in the simulator she was elated and felt no compunction about showing it to her personal assistants.

"Oh fuck, boys and girls, is this a gravy boat or what?!" giggled Arlette as they sat down in the monorail car to return to their quarters. Julia and Marcel threw back their heads and laughed with her. Chang smiled but did not laugh. There was something on his mind.

Before returning to her quarters Arlette took a twenty-minute swim, then she showered and changed into casual clothes. She would have a quiet dinner with her personal team, chat about impressions and people, poke a little into their personal lives, hopes and fears and then slip away early for a book or a movie.

That was the plan, anyway.

The four of them met again shortly afterwards, folding into large soft armchairs before a curved panoramic window, the lights on the river twinkling in the dusky distance. Each selected his or her favourite cocktail, sipped, sighed, and sipped again.

Julia spoke up. "Are you comfortable meeting your crew in this piecemeal, informal way?"

"Yes," came the reply. "I think it is natural among professionals to meet on the job. Perhaps a more important question is 'Are they comfortable?'"

"Hard to say", said Chang, "with such a varied bunch, but my feeling is that respect and confidence will be gained by personal interaction, not by formalities. We'll do that at the end of the week when we've knocked a few of the sharp corners off. Then you can attend to the bruised, the miffed and the worried much more effectively."

"What do you think, Marcel? Today was mostly about the flight technologists getting a first chance to show their colours, wasn't it?"

"Oh, yes," said Marcel. "There were plenty of rehearsed set pieces delivered today, naturally. But as Chang pointed out, these people must build their relationships from their professional strengths. We show them respect, we make them comfortable. We have to go through the process."

"What did you think of Sanam Ghorashian, the lead pilot?" asked Arlette, somewhat archly, keen to get some controversy going.

"Ambitious for glory, competitive to the point of combative, perfectionist – and ravishingly sexy," was Marcel's assessment.

"I'd like to see her under pressure," was Chang's comment.

"I can tell you from her personal record that she is superb under pressure," said Arlette. "What did you think, Julia?"

Julia pulled a face, and Arlette could easily imagine how she was picking her way through a number of uncomplimentary observations. Finally she said, "She is a star and not a team player."

"OK," said Arlette, "but I warn you that, despite the prevailing humility being put on show today, we have very few shrinking violets in the cast."

"I know that you like strong players who can prevail in any kind of catastrophe, Commander, but we are not going into battle on this mission. We have to get along with one another and get our jobs done, often in completely alien and stressful environments, for the best part of a year. Teamwork will be mission critical, the more so as time passes." Chang was obviously concerned.

After a pause Arlette smiled. "OK, Chang," she said brightly. "I will place special emphasis on that point when I address the whole crew next week, and please consider it your personal responsibility to monitor and champion team behaviour."

"I will," said Chang.

They moved over to the dining table where a traditional Cantonese meal was waiting for them. Chang proceeded to provide a running commentary on the origin and content of the dishes, occasionally with crude and unappetising snippets of information which nobody wanted to hear.

'Why is it that even the most cosmopolitan of Chinese delight in shocking us with the variety of things they eat?' thought Arlette.

"Chang," she said, "you seem to be very knowledgeable about Chinese cuisine. Did you ever work in a kitchen?"

"No," said Chang, "but I was the family cook because I lost my mother at an early age, and you have to be creative in a household as poor as ours was."

"Did you resent losing your mother?" asked Arlette.

"Not really," said Chang, his jaw set and an air of stocky determination about him, "but I resented my vicious, bullying father who used to bring home his drunken workmates to sneer at me and taunt me because I was passionately interested in art. I ran away from home when I was twelve and got an unofficial job in an electronics factory. I used to watch the production processes out of the corner of my eye and one day I walked into the manager's office and told him how he could improve productivity. He laughed at me, but he implemented some of my ideas. Then, a couple of months later, he sent me off to school. I'm still in touch with him, but I never saw my father again."

There was silence.

"And what is your passion now?" asked Arlette.

Chang leaned forward across the table. "To ensure the success of this mission and the safety of its commander," he said with good-natured intensity. "I think that we are all beginning to realise that we are stepping into history, creating a point of inflection. No human frailty or mechanical imperfection can be allowed to deflect us."

"Bravo Chang," said Marcel.

"And you, Marcel, what are your passions? – those which are fit for discussion, I mean."

Marcel pursed his lips. "Power," he said. "Awesome power. The first time I saw a rocket take off my whole body trembled with excitement over the release of raw energy. When I went into space I was struck by the enormity of the momentum of the moon and planets. I did my PhD on propulsion systems. I just love the idea that we, feeble little creatures that we are, can be masters of this universe; and", he added in typical Marcel fashion, "I'd love to ski the wormhole."

Smiles all round.

"Julia?"

"Oh, for me the great story is nothing until it has been told to the world, has thrilled every child, swelled every heart with pride, and driven every leader to do greater things for humanity. Yes, I'm passionate about it. What we do and what we stand for will be subject to scrutiny for generations. We are the standard bearers of our civilisation. We have to set standards of behaviour and achievement that will always be admired."

"And what about you, Commander?" Chang asked, his eyes fixed on her.

"Well…" Arlette raised her eyebrows. "I am awed not only by the technology being brought to bear, but also the intellectual capacity. It's not my nature to feel humble but from where I sit you cannot avoid it. I badly want to go to that star and decorate its planetary system with concrete evidence of human achievement, and I want to make sure that every member of the crew can feel the pride of knowing for the rest of their lives that they were brilliant when they had the opportunity to advance humanity."

There was a murmur of approval.

5
The Passion of Julia Rogers

Julia Rogers awoke the next morning at 5.30 to an urgent beeping signifying a major diplomatic alert. 'I'm not ready for this' was her first conscious thought as she stumbled to the bathroom, hastily arranged her hair and shambled back to sit on the bed.

"OK, tell me."

The beeping stopped. The huge screen flicked on to reveal the familiar sight of the ISEA international Diplomatic Ops room in Paris. The faces of three situation analysts appeared around a table.

"Morning, Julia." It was Ahmed Tadayan, a senior political analyst. Next to him sat Anastasia Petrovnik, a much-decorated Russian aero-ace, and Mirwan Kahil, a former Palestinian general.

"We've got grief in Armenia," said Ahmed. "There was a terrorist attack in Yerevan two hours ago which cost more than a hundred lives, while the country is still in the grips of an unprecedented heatwave. The Armenians blame the Azerbaijanis, the Turks claim the Armenians are provoking a conflict, the Iranians have sent in military aid, and the Russians are fuming about violations of international sovereignty. Everybody wants access to Armenian water and hydroelectric power."

The other two analysts spelled out the potential military scenarios on top of the already bewildering political complexities. It was a tinderbox. Hundreds, even thousands of years of history, crimes, grudges and hatreds were about to be unleashed once more, only to create more crimes, grudges and hatreds, and all this in the context of deteriorating weather patterns that were threatening traditional livelihoods.

"This will get worse before it gets better," concluded Ahmed. "You will need to isolate any crew members from this area with strong nationalist feelings. Good luck."

'Forty years of economic, scientific and resources collaboration between the G25 powers and no progress with tribalism,' thought Julia. 'Here we go again.' She projected the mission crew ethnic origin list onto an adjacent screen. 'Four Iranians, three Turks, an Armenian and twenty-seven Russians. Holy cow.'

Julia lay back on her pillows and pondered the state of the world. A sense of doom descended on her, that her life's dream could be snatched away by some crazed extremist who had no agenda other than hate.

Ever since she had been a little girl, growing up in northern England, she had wanted to be at the heart of a great multinational venture. She smiled to herself as she remembered sitting on her father's knee with her nose in a dusty antique book of maps of the political geography of the world in the late twentieth century. Each new page they turned produced a flood of excitement in her, and her father had stoked up her fascination by showing her around each country with live internet pictures.

She had wanted to see every country with her own eyes, to smell the smells, to speak their languages, to solve their problems, to eliminate poverty, to eradicate disease. She would fall asleep imagining herself being instrumental in some great triumph of diplomacy.

Her father was a computer scientist working on weather pattern models and specialised in severe storm dynamics, her mother a research pharmacist, developing DNA-specific medication for individuals with serious diseases. Julia had been nurtured in scientific wonder, full of optimism and confidence that every last barrier to universal human happiness would be conquered. When she was eleven she was taken to a celebration party in Trafalgar Square to mark the fiftieth anniversary of the signing of the Arab–Israeli peace treaty.

'People danced, they cried, they hugged each other,' she recalled. 'Grand old men with long beards talked about the transformation from war and poverty to peace, mutual respect, cooperation and prosperity. They praised the vision and courage of the political leaders who had signed the treaty, lamenting how their successors had rarely lived up to the same standards.'

Sadly, their concerns were proven justified and the blush of rapid economic prosperity was to fade as religious and political factional disputes erupted again in a pattern that seemed to repeat the history of millennia.

Julia Emily Rogers was born during a huge rainstorm in March 2074. A few months later the whole family, wearied by the persistent floods that afflicted the area, sorrowfully sold their charming Victorian red-brick house at a discount from its purchase price and moved to Manchester.

A vast project to divert the floodwaters of the Thames, which were becoming more prevalent and extreme as climate change progressed, into the Solent on the south coast of England had long been mooted but had failed to gain traction as rival political interests presented conflicting data, countless objections and multiple alternative suggestions, the most recent of which had been the building of a huge dyke around Greater London. The scale of these projects, and the number required to protect vulnerable parts of the country, was unfinanceable given the prospects for the economy. As a consequence there was a general exodus northwards to higher ground and a great economic renaissance in the Midlands and the north. Manchester was well on its way to becoming the new financial and business capital of the UK.

Julia thrived in this young, optimistic society. She was a voluble, intensely bright child, with curly, dark brown hair, arresting grey eyes and interested in everything and everybody around her. Her three brothers all adored her because she would engage in their interests with enthusiasm, asking naive but penetrating questions, and delighting in the extravagant imagery of their answers, based, albeit somewhat loosely, on their perceptions of the wonders of the scientific world.

She was popular at school, a tireless natural organiser, defender of the weak, and, in due course, a polished debater. What she lacked in natural inclination towards maths and physics she compensated for with blistering determination and hard work, which, her being naturally athletic, also characterised her attitude on the track and the tennis court. Puberty, teenage rebellion, boyfriends and sex – they came and went. She fell desperately in love with a dreamy, drifting youth at seventeen, and found herself pregnant. Appalled and embarrassed at the enormity of the compromised situation she found herself in, she tearfully confessed her stupidity to her parents, who treated the whole episode as a tiresome learning experience, whose obvious remedy was speedily implemented.

Shaking this off, Julia regained her inspiration and won a scholarship to Paris University, where she studied International Relations with Predictive Futurology. By that time Cognitive Transmission Technology was becoming widely available, allowing an individual to transmit her thoughts via an implanted nanochip device directly to another by microwave radiation, without the need for speech or text, and in the language of the recipient.

CTT required the communicating parties to agree, while in visual and verbal contact, to use the technology between them, and then a call could be initiated just by picturing the recipient. It required focus, clarity of thought and practice to work efficiently and all potential users had to pass stringent tests to get a licence to use it. This was primarily a measure to protect the naive from divulging sensitive information involuntarily. However, CTT was brilliantly successful with like-minded academics exploring complex theoretical issues, and extremely fast and effective between people who knew each other well and needed to work together secretly or in an emergency. The mental directory was a priceless tool for most callers, but almost all preferred to speak normally when confidentiality was not an issue, even though it was their thoughts that got transmitted, not the spoken word. A caller could not access the recipient's thoughts outside of the topic of the call, or vice versa, but most users would admit to the occasional embarrassment of sending or receiving thoughts that were not intended for transmission.

Preoccupied as she was with the sociological impact of rapid technological change, and excited by the potential of CTT, Julia moved to Oxford and wrote her PhD thesis entitled 'Mind-sharing – collective augmentation of human thought'. She argued that CTT would quickly be extended to enable individuals to selectively share whatever sectors of their minds they chose to, with single or multiple partners, and that the result would be a quantum jump in human intellectual power, as well as sensory experience. It gained her international recognition as a practical contemporary philosopher and she was courted by a plethora of prestigious international organisations.

Julia retained her slightly stocky, athletic appearance. She was trim and pretty enough, medium height, with a rather aquiline nose, square face and an intense, but not intimidating, energy radiating from her grey eyes. Most men found her unnerving, not because she used her intellect to overpower them, but rather because she suppressed it and seemed to have so much in reserve. Unfortunately her judgement of men tended to go to pieces when she found herself in an intimate situation where pheromone interaction prevailed, and she tended to get involved with jocks whose admirable self-confidence often turned out to be self-absorption and indifference to her intellect. Consequently her sex life was at times vigorous but vacuous.

Julia emerged from academia a polished and confident twenty-six-year-old with her childhood inspiration intact. She had stayed the course, prepared herself, and now, as the worst fears of climate change were beginning to be realised, she knew she must deliver.

But the political and social environment in the world as it entered the twenty-second century was no longer a progression of great cooperative international endeavours as it had been fifty years earlier. While the foundations of global cooperation in the field of macro-economics, human health, space technology and resources management had been well laid out after centuries of wasteful competitive nationalism, the increasing frequency and severity of extreme climatic events was draining the wealth of almost all nations and beginning to undermine the progress that had been made in reducing poverty and providing education and health care to all underprivileged communities.

The huge agricultural robots that had transformed the quality of life of so many farming communities degenerated into hazardous, expensive junk in cataclysmic storms and floods, leaving their surviving dependents with neither the means nor the knowledge to replace them with alternative means of food production. Even the most advanced, highly productive genetically modified crops could not stand the loss of water supplies as deserts advanced into former bread baskets. Extended heatwaves and severely cold periods and their consequences killed tens of thousands of people at all levels of society, aggravated by increasing energy supply failures and costs.

It had long been apparent that humanity needed a Plan B and the ISEA had been founded with the mandate to develop the alternative of planetary resettlement. This did not replace the huge ongoing projects in climate-change management and resource conservation, but it was very well funded by the G25 governments. The reason for this was the time-honoured instinct for self-preservation; political leaders the world over knew that, should society break down as a result of the failure of these measures, they needed to be among the first to get off the planet.

Julia had received several very attractive offers from major data houses, which saw enormous potential value in mind-sharing, but commercial exploitation of her ideas was absolutely repugnant to her, and she approached one of her senior academic colleagues for advice on joining the UN. A couple of weeks later she received an invitation for "a spot of dinner with someone in communications at ISEA".

Her host turned out to be an extremely articulate and entertaining former US Ambassador to the UK, who was retired but "doing a bit of work for the ISEA". He explained to her in compelling terms how the ISEA would be on the cusp of future international relations and told her that, if she really wanted to use her mind to transform the future of humanity, here was her opportunity. She was utterly dazzled and would have signed a contract on his napkin if he had asked her. Two days later she received a formal invitation and a plane ticket, and her path of entry into the greatest adventure in human history began.

6
Ethnicity Ubiquitous

"I will not allow this mission to be undermined by primitive tribal disputes!" Arlette banged her fist on the breakfast table emphatically. "Anyone with an agenda will have to go."

Julia had given as concise a summary of the situation in Armenia as she could, but she pulled no punches about the strength of feeling that could exist between some of the crew members, who were, after all, flag bearers of national pride, especially in the case of the smaller countries.

"Then they will have to choose between national pride and the mission. Let's have all those affected together and make their choices clear to them."

"That might just drive their inclinations underground," said Chang. "I would suggest a more subtle approach."

"Subtlety be dammed!" said Arlette. "This is a fundamental issue of loyalty and commitment. We are all bound to subordinate our personal interests and feelings to the best interests of the mission. Anyone whose position has changed as a result of a regional conflict needs to stand up and say so and take the consequences."

"I suggest one-on-ones with one of our psychologists," Chang went on. "We have eight on board. That's just a half a day's work to identify where the problems may be."

"That's already been done," Arlette fumed. "Everybody has been screened for their suitability. I don't want a reluctant crew member nursed along with soft soap. Please get all those on the list together in the command centre at 11.00. We can have the psychologists there to watch the body language, but I want to make it clear exactly what is required and to have the opportunity to look each one in the eye."

Julia was trying to imagine how a crew member would feel if, having been singled out because of their nationality, they were then asked to reconfirm their loyalty. 'It won't catch the criminally inclined,' she thought. 'Basic screening must have done that – but could the mind change in a crisis like this, when people are dying and emotions inflamed?' She decided that she would have a word in Arlette's ear before the meeting.

Virtual training proceeded as scheduled and Arlette familiarised herself with the maintenance section, talking to each engineer about his equipment responsibilities, trying to gauge the resilience of the individual and how he or she, and the associated hardware, would stand up to conditions of extreme stress. She spent a long time with the gravity generation section, doing a virtual walk through the entire plant, going over the development of the technology and quizzing the team about the procedures in case of equipment failure. All four of them were Ukrainians, who talked with passion and great pride about the inspired innovations along the way to producing the functional hardware.

Dima, the group leader, was fair and burly with stunning royal blue eyes. He touched Arlette on the forearm with each point that he made, as if he wanted her to share the affection he obviously felt for his wondrous machinery. He also touched Dasha, whom he called 'my baby girl', although she was 42, equally burly and a former test pilot, Andriy and Vlad, the other members of the group, in the same intensely personal way whenever he introduced them into his holographic presentation.

Finally he said with passion, "Comanderrr, we will never let you down!" Arlette didn't doubt it.

At 11.00 precisely Arlette entered the control centre to talk to the thirty-five crew members with an 'Armenian connection'. Julia and Chang sat below her as she positioned her body couch in the centre of the chamber, slightly above the rest, and the mission psychologists ranged themselves randomly within the audience.

"I have not had enough time to get to know each of you personally in the context of this mission," she began, "and I apologise for addressing you in this rather formal way, but as Commander I have to assess whether recent events in Armenia could have any disruptive effect on our mission. The political assessment group at ISEA HQ advises that there is a lot of history in the region that could lead to even more serious conflict, and while I have the greatest sympathy for all of you who might have family, friends and other interests in the area, I cannot allow a situation to exist where animosity between any of you could develop as a result of political conflict."

There was silence.

"Teamwork and collaboration between all members

of this crew at all times is an unquestionable prerequisite for participation in this mission. We are going to be together for the best part of a year and will find ourselves in situations, possibly stressful and dangerous situations, as yet unknown to mankind. I have to know from each one of you that I, and all the other members of this crew, have your complete loyalty and support regardless of any political event that might transpire. Is that clear and reasonable?"

A murmur of assent rumbled through the room.

"Does anyone have anything they want to say in public?" Arlette looked from one face to another. There was very little emotion that she could see, but then anyone with malicious intent would hide it, wouldn't they?

"Very well. The mission psychologists will hold one-on-ones with each one of you, starting in half an hour. I hope you understand that this is a necessary precaution to protect all of us from situations which you yourselves may not realise could arise."

Brief smiles flickered across the faces of Chang and Julia.

"I ask for your compassion," said Arlette, "for your forbearance and your tact. But above all I demand professionalism and your unquestioning loyalty to the mission. If anyone wants to talk to me privately about this matter, just call." She gestured with one finger towards her earphone. "This is a priority matter now."

The meeting dissolved. Marcel met her at the door. "Propulsion section," he said.

* * *

Just as they were about to enter the lift, Arlette held up her hand and pointed to her earphone. The CTT communication went on for several minutes, the device transmitting her thoughts directly to the other party, and theirs to her, soundlessly. Finally she nodded and turned to her colleagues. "General Lee has assigned a high-ranking international security expert to the mission," she announced, "a Colonel Bertin. He'll be here this afternoon." Julia, Marcel and Chang brightened visibly.

While Gravity had been a rather personal experience, Propulsion was grand. The team was eight strong, led a by a booming Texan as tall as a tree. He was William 'Genes' Clayton, and he exuded genial command which Arlette found a touch patronising.

"Welcome, Commander, to the skunk works," he said, proffering a huge hand which swallowed hers. "It's 'Genes' with a 'G' rather than a 'J.'"

Arlette had really not given it much thought, but now she had to ask why.

"On account of ma size, I s'pose," drawled Genes. They got down to business.

The team was introduced: four women, three men, all brimming with enthusiasm to tell her in elaborate detail just how huge and powerful their baby was, how safe it was and how much it had in reserve when required.

After the virtual tour, which included a rather charming animated presentation of the physics of the anti-matter annihilation process and the malevolence of the exhaust particle stream, Arlette got into an intense cross-examination of the disaster scenarios and recovery procedures.

To her final question, the answer from a still-grinning Genes was, “Then we all get fried, Commander, finito.”

* * *

“The new security chief is here to see you,” said Chang with an air of weariness. “Impressive guy, almost certainly CIA.”

Arlette grimaced. ‘That’s all I need,’ she thought, ‘a helping hand from tactless, diplomatically naive Uncle Sam.’

As she entered the conference room a tall, militarily erect man in a colonel’s uniform was standing with his back to her, studying a projection of the ship’s power unit, his hands linked behind his back. He turned slowly towards her.

Arlette’s eyes widened as she recognised him. Surprise, outrage, betrayal, disgust and ultimately cynicism tore through her brain.

“I am Colonel Henri Bertin,” he said evenly. “I have been assigned to your command by Mission Control because of heightened concerns about security in the current political situation.”

7
The Paragon and her Context

Arlette looked him steadily in the eye, and he looked steadily back, coolly, but without arrogance. She walked halfway around him, as though she were inspecting a new recruit, turned and walked back.

"Well, Colonel Bertin," she said at last, mouthing the words as if they were acidic, "I am very glad to see you."

The words 'bastard', 'manipulative', 'deceitful', 'betrayal' and 'humiliation' ran through her mind as she processed the situation in her head. He had been a plant sent to observe her in Acapulco, to test what? Her loyalty, her discretion? He had seduced her for professional reasons – he probably had a handbook! She looked up at him sharply for a moment.

"Please define for me exactly your orders from Mission Control."

"Yes, Commander," said Henri. "My orders are to take responsibility for all security matters, to recruit and equip a security detail from the military contingent on board, monitor the entire crew with respect to potentially divisive or dangerous behaviour, interface data continuously with Mission Control and act to prevent or contain any incident that threatens the security of the mission, with deadly force if necessary."

"Are you familiar with the personal records of the entire crew?"

"Yes, Commander."

"And have you identified any high-risk individuals?"

"We have identified certain individuals who could be personally at risk because of their nationalities, ethnic backgrounds or careers, but we know of no individuals who have any terrorist backgrounds or inclinations – they would never have got past basic screening." Henri paused. "However, political animosity and stress can trigger unexpected behaviour. A truly multinational crew like this is a great statement about the values of our civilisation, but it's a security nightmare."

"And what are your qualifications for this task, Colonel?" she asked, some needle in her voice.

"I believe I was selected because of my experience in handling similar situations. I speak Arabic and Mandarin as well as my native Haitian French and English, and I believe I have an appropriate military, intelligence and diplomatic record."

He was in such perfect control of himself that Arlette wanted to slap him to see if he would flinch, but she just nodded.

"And could you please define for me your mission objectives at the time we met in Acapulco?"

He took a deep breath and started to speak, but Arlette cut him off. She really did not want to hear it. She raised a hand. "Another time, perhaps," she said. "I need a coffee. Report to my office in thirty minutes and we will discuss your mission in detail."

"Thank you, Commander Piccard," said Henri.

* * *

Arlette Augustine Piccard was born in Lavaur, near Toulouse, France in May 2078. Her parents were both scientists at the nearby European Space Centre, her father a descendent of the early twentieth-century Belgian–Swiss physicist, balloonist and submariner, Auguste Piccard.

Arlette was an extremely precocious child, strong-willed and fearless; she would take on anyone regardless of age, sex or size and would never give up on anything she set out to do. Her intellect was apparent at an early age, and she was an infant prodigy of a pianist, a soloist with the Toulouse National Capitol orchestra at the age of six. She was an only child, a fact celebrated by her mother, who loved to say that there could never have been room for two like her. She was a frequent visitor to the nearby European Space Centre from an early age, curious about every aspect of space exploration.

When asked at age seven what she was going to do when she grew up, she said simply. "I am going to the stars," and she never doubted that she was.

At high school Arlette developed into a superb athlete and a straight-A student. Her ability to focus was legendary, and only marginally short of obsessive. She was either idolised or hated by both boys and girls, but she took it all in her stride philosophically, if not always graciously.

One term-end report pointedly commented that 'Arlette would do well to listen to others as well as herself at times.' However, her leadership abilities were obvious and she was capable of turning a rabble into an effective team to achieve just about anything that she set her mind to.

She took English and Mandarin, as did the majority of her fellow students, along with her maths and physics, and her choice of Beijing University as an undergraduate school came as no surprise. "They are leaders in space technology and accelerating away from the rest," she said simply. Then she moved to Michigan to do her PhD on the physics of multiple universes and to California for post doc in near-light-speed transportation dynamics, obtaining her pilot's licence in her spare time. But academic life frustrated her after a while and she longed to 'get out there and do it, not just talk about it'.

At twenty-six years old she had the world at her feet. She was an attractive woman, tall, slender and elegant with a faultless, athletic figure, long, lustrous dark hair, a very straight, delicate nose and coal-black eyes. Her olive skin seemed to be almost permanently tanned. She had a patrician air about her and easily commanded attention at any professional gathering, speaking with authority or not at all. She enjoyed the company of men far more than women, periodically engaging in physically intense affairs which often dissolved into natural intellectual friendships when the passion had burned itself out. She was utterly unsentimental and could never recall ever having actually been in love. Rather she judged men on their ability to entertain her with whatever combination of charm, wit, social skills, intellect or physicality they possessed, and she loved to be told stories. She was, however, brutally short with those that did not measure up to her expectations.

Arlette joined the ISEA as a trainee cosmonaut and very quickly found herself on the operational list. Physical and mental duress seemed to bring out the best in her, not just in implementing emergency procedures but in solving complex problems in highly original ways. At twenty-eight she was assigned her first mission and from then on she was on every commander's preference list.

In 2104 the ISEA was a haven for the elite, able to select the most exceptionally talented people from around the world. Founded in 2075 in a triumphal period of economic progress some twenty years after the G25 had reached an epic agreement to manage economics, natural resources and scientific research centrally, the ISEA was ostensibly the vanguard of human civilisation venturing out into the universe. Behind closed doors, however, it was the vehicle to develop an escape route for humanity from the climatic catastrophe that was inexorably enveloping the world. Originally a Sino-US–Russian–European joint venture, it had rapidly thrown off its unworkable national origins and become a powerful, independent global institution, financed in accordance with a set of G25 rules that was rarely challenged by governments eager to ensure that they remained on board.

The ISEA high command was answerable to a G25 committee that was primarily preoccupied with ensuring that there were no financing glitches, while its strategic decisions were reviewed by a very supportive scientific advisory board. It had full military autonomy beyond the orbit of the moon and its operational decisions could only be questioned by a two-thirds majority in the G25.

Consequently, it got on with the job while the academics and intellectuals of the world argued ineffectively about its activities.

Despite the grand pillars of progress that were in place for the greater good of the planet, it was politics with economics as usual on an international level. While the great powers succeeded to a large extent in avoiding large-scale military conflict, the world was plagued by technological and economic burglary on a huge scale. The standard of living of the poorest and most backward communities on the planet progressed agonisingly slowly and the wealth gap widened persistently. Regional factional disputes produced horrific consequences for local populations, which were, however, economically insignificant and were treated as such.

Economically China was by far the greatest power, slipping comfortably into the role it had occupied for most of the two previous millennia, but now completely global in reach. India was arguably more influential, not so much as a superpower, but rather because of the skill of Indian communities around the world in integrating locally to obtain positions of power and influence.

The US was prosperous but had retreated into comparative isolation after it became obvious that its global military reach was no longer affordable or effective. Europe had achieved full economic and political integration and was very efficient economically, but risk-averse and politically impotent.

With the decline in the relevance of its fossil fuel

industry, Russia had lurched from one despotic regime to the next until it was finally taken under the wing of the Chinese, who restructured it along the lines of their earlier political system. It had now become a low-cost agricultural and industrial goods production satellite for the world's sophisticated economies, although it maintained a strong presence in global space technology.

The Arabian leaders on the other hand had shown astonishing vision in responding to the changes in global power structure, investing their declining oil wealth in social infrastructure to create great centres of learning, diplomacy and international finance. Instead of allowing factional rivalries to flourish after the signing of the Arab–Israeli peace treaty, they engaged in huge projects which resonated deeply with the population, such as the transformations of the ruins of Damascus and Babylon into 'Peace Cities'. While the divisions within Islam were not resolved, they had progressed to a largely academic and intellectual competition in place of the horrific blood-letting of the first half of the twenty-first century.

Initially, Africa had shown a dramatic transformation, becoming a hive of entrepreneurial creativity, producing new global mega-companies, consumer-related technologies and billionaires with dizzying rapidity. The peoples of Africa had emerged from their docile history and took to this opportunistic life style with alacrity, charming the world with their music, their entertainment and their refreshingly original approach to creating fun in every aspect of life. However, the remorseless encroachment of the Sahara southwards drove such large numbers of refugees into central and southern Africa that social order was undermined and the continent collapsed into anarchy.

While Arlette viewed the cultural diversity in the world with fascination, she had grave misgivings about its affordability. History seemed to her to have been a succession of very similar learning experiences, repeated over and over again, with, apparently, very little permanently absorbed in the process. She viewed planet Earth as something of a lost cause, but she was quite determined that the new habitat of mankind would be a working Utopia. She knew how to get the best out of people. All that was needed then was to surround herself with the best of them and point them in the right direction. And now, the tools to do so had been placed in her hands.

8

The Grilling

Functional familiarisation progressed smoothly for the next five days. As the crew settled into their roles and began to interact operationally, their self-confidence blossomed and informal but disciplined professionalism emerged as the natural modus operandi.

With the subsequent commencement of operational mode simulation, the tempo picked up and stress levels were increased. Once all standard procedures had been practised and honed to perfection, random system failures were introduced and the tenacity of the crew tested to the point of 'certain catastrophe'. Arlette was, however, conscious of two serious deficiencies in the training process; firstly insufficient time to test responses at the point of prolonged physical exhaustion, and secondly that responses to loss of induced gravity could not be simulated virtually – they had to get off the planet to do that.

She informed Mission Control that she would be decamping to the lunar base four days early because, she said, "She was growing tired of being treated to flawless performances of procedures already practised to the nth degree and wanted to see how they would behave when seriously unexpected shit hits the fan."

While acknowledging that her crew had been extraordinarily well prepared, she was uneasy that not a single one of them had broken down under the induced stress of disaster scenarios. It was all just a bit too polished.

Her request to Mission Control was approved. Arlette immediately called for a total crew conference to announce her decision. She addressed her central command in the control room, and the rest of the crew at their virtual stations via the ubiquitous projection system.

"Crew members, I have some announcements," she began. "Firstly let me say how proud I am of all of you for your flawless performance in the pre-flight testing we have undertaken so far. Mission Control and I have done our very best to drive you to your limits in the situational tests we have devised, and we have failed to detect any significant weaknesses. However, we have assumed so far that you will always be operating in 1G. In the event that our ship is seriously damaged, we may well lose that luxury and, since we are currently well within the safety limits of our schedule, I have decided that we will conclude our pre-flight testing programme in zero gravity. We leave for Lunar Base in two days."

A spontaneous shout of excitement arose in the control centre and ran through the entire crew. It was followed by a short burst of applause.

Arlette smiled. She went on: "I have been informed that IP262 has completed pre-mission testing and is in lunar orbit awaiting our arrival. Duplicates of all the gear and personal effects that you have with you here are already on board and in your allocated cabins. All you need to take with you are your phones and your professionalism."

Smiles broadened.

"You will be airlifted to the Wenchang Launch Centre, which is less than an hour's flight from here, and then shuttled directly to the ship. Since the shuttles only have a capacity of ninety passengers, there will be two successive flights. Dimitri Kazarov will captain the first flight and Sanam Ghorashian the second. You are both very familiar with the hardware – please select your crews and coordinate with pre-flight testing command."

A few heads turned almost imperceptibly towards the two pilots selected. Neither showed any visible response.

"The name of our home for the next 336 days will be Prometheus. Those of you whose early spaceflight mentors had a quirky interest in ancient Greek mythology, as mine did, may recall that Prometheus was the creator of humanity, and its defender against the jealous wrath of the Gods, whose omnipotence he challenged. In other words, just my kind of guy."

There was a ripple of laughter, and more applause as Arlette stepped down and slipped away to her office. She called in Julia Rogers.

"We'll need to do a presscon at Wenchang," she said.

"Yeah," said Julia. "Mission Control wants to keep it as low-key as possible. Routine mission. Absolutely no politicians. The press won't like it a bit."

"Well, give them as little notice as possible and we'll dumb it out."

"You can't say you don't know where you're going,

Commander. General Lee will cover with a story about testing the interstellar capabilities of IP262 for further human exploration. We'll use the new induced gravitation technology as a smoke screen. Just pray that nobody asks what happened to Proteus."

"What if they do?"

Julia sighed. "You raise your eyebrows and refer the question to General Lee," she said. "Don't worry. If the questioning gets really sticky there will be an unscheduled fuel emergency and we'll have to clear the site."

"They won't buy that!" Arlette looked at her archly.

"Oh yes they will. Do you think we can't organise some pyrotechnics and a nice blaze? This is China, you know!"

Arlette's jaw dropped momentarily. Then she widened her eyes and said, "Alright Julia, it's your show. I'll just take the ticker-tape parade when we get back."

"That's the spirit, Commander," said Julia quietly.

* * *

Dinner the following day was a sombre affair. The four of them discussed the latest outrage on the Armenian border, which had seen the destruction of an entire village and all eight hundred of its inhabitants. All parties in the conflict were accusing the others. They discussed the typhoon that was wreaking havoc in Japan but was not expected to cause any serious disturbance in their own airspace, and they talked about the drought now beginning to cause fatalities among farming communities in North America.

And, as usual, they talked about personnel. But there

was very little to remark on. Everyone had been on their best professional behaviour, and if there had been one or two looks, perhaps a little jealousy, nothing to cause concern had been detected.

"Are you telling me, Julia, that there's been no fallout from the Armenian situation at all?" asked Arlette incredulously.

"Nothing that I've noticed, or more importantly, that any of the psychologists have picked up," replied Julia. "It's far too early, and everybody knows that if they show any questionable behaviour they will be off the mission and replaced immediately. Things will pick up as soon as we leave lunar orbit." She smiled brightly.

Nobody mentioned that this would be their last dinner on Earth for at least a year, but they all thought about it, and not without trepidation.

When Arlette got back to her quarters she stood for a long time looking out over the Yangtze, breathing slowly.

* * *

There was something of a holiday atmosphere at the Wenchang Launch Centre when all the crew had arrived. They were herded into the rather grand conference centre for a formal welcome, of a type that most of them had already experienced on earlier missions. However, to Arlette's intense embarrassment, a huge portrait of her appeared on the screen as the lights went down and the station commander asked all present to stand and show their respect for the heroine of the Dalian incident.

Arlette sat, damp-eyed, with her lips buttoned and her

jaws clenched as the noise rose and everybody began to stamp on the floor. She remained perfectly still, her eyes fixed on a point just below the screen, as the noise subsided. The station commander made a pretty little speech of welcome to the crew of IP262, then wished them "good luck and happy landings". The tension was gone and the crew were dismissed to prepare for extra-terrestrial travel.

Julia tapped her on the shoulder from behind. "Let's go and talk to General Lee," she said.

Arlette took a quick break and joined the General and Julia in the press room, still mercifully empty.

"What's your take on their mood?" she asked after a peremptory handshake.

"Impatient and critical of the rate of progress." came his curt reply.

"Wouldn't it be easier if we just let it out?"

"Easier for who?" demanded the General. "The pressure we take in the short term is a small price to pay for the space we will then have to make the difficult decisions if we have to. Once you are in Omega 16 we will start to let out some good news, but not before. Is it clear that you will answer only questions related to our simplified mission objectives, crew readiness and hardware, and refer the rest to me?"

"Yes, General," said Arlette, relieved that she had remembered to get her Crimson Star sewed back on before she left Shanghai.

The doors of the press room opened and the press streamed in, took their assigned seats and studied the three figures seated behind the table before them. Two Chinese 'moderators' sat on either side of them, glowering like bouncers.

Arlette turned to Julia and suddenly asked behind her hand, "How's your Mandarin?"

"Not as good as yours but enough to stay in touch," came the answer.

The TV lights came on. One of the moderators stood, raised his hand for silence, and said in clipped English, "Ladies and gentlemen of the press, we have twenty minutes to answer your questions. Please be brief." He pointed to a woman in the front row.

"Commander Piccard, was your record of gallantry the reason for your selection to command this mission?"

Arlette hardly had time to raise her eyebrows before the General leaned forward with a genial smile and said, "The development and selection of commanders at ISEA is a process that takes many years, and requires potential candidates to prove themselves in a wide variety of analytical, technical and human skills. Commander Piccard has met all those standards."

Another journalist was pointed out.

"Commander Piccard, what is the objective of your mission?"

Arlette glanced at the General, who gave her a calm smile and an almost imperceptible nod.

"IP262 is designed for interstellar planetary exploration," said Arlette. "We shall be testing the capability of the ship to deliver exploration teams to potentially habitable planets outside our solar system."

"What planets?" someone shouted. The moderator stood up, caught the eye of one of his colleagues at the back of the room, and moved his index finger fractionally to the right. There was a brief scuffle and the perpetrator was removed.

"This mission will test the ship's capabilities in deep space," went on Arlette, unperturbed. "We need more knowledge before we can send a ship to land on a planet outside our solar system. Don't forget that our closest neighbouring star, Alpha Centauri, is four light years away."

The moderator pointed.

"Will you be testing human hibernation technologies on this mission?"

"No," said Arlette, and, grasping the opportunity, she added, "but we will be testing induced gravity, which will give us the capability to sustain normal healthy life for extended periods. The work that is being done on human induced hibernation does not require it to be conducted in a spaceship."

The moderator pointed again.

"General, please clarify for us why international governments are spending billions on this programme, while conditions are allowed to deteriorate on Earth, immeasurably increasing the deprivation of the poor."

General Lee put on his concerned expression. "The purpose of the ISEA", he intoned, "is to develop the capability of man to expand his reach into our galaxy, to increase his available habitat and the overall potential of his civilisation. Our agency does not conduct climate control research or operations."

"But isn't this just a bolthole for the rich and powerful?" insisted the questioner. The moderator glowered at him.

"Personal wealth and political influence are not criteria for interstellar explorers," said the General with finality.

A chorus of questions erupted from the floor. The moderator stepped in front of the speakers and raised a hand. "The crew have a heavy schedule. We shall terminate this press conference if order is not maintained. Three more questions." He pointed.

"The crew list includes members from all five countries involved in the Armenian conflict. How are you going to deal with the inevitable antagonism? Do you have a police force on board, arms, detention cells?"

Julia leant forward. "All crew members have been extensively screened and their loyalty to the mission confirmed. We have no..."

The room erupted. The moderator stood before the journalists, stone-faced. He looked at his watch and an uneasy quiet settled. Julia continued, "As you know well, the ISEA has always operated with crews chosen for their abilities, regardless of nationality, ethnicity or orientation of any kind. We have never had..."

The noise rose again and a booming voice from the back of the room called out, "We have never had such complacency, greed, indifference to suffering and political manipulation..."

Julia stood up and raised her voice. "We are deeply conscious of our responsibilities to civilisation, and the urgency of the situation. This mission will take us as far, and as fast, as our technical capabilities will allow..."

"Cretin!"

A barrage of shouts and insults followed. The moderator looked at the General, who responded with a flick of the head. The three of them rose and left the room, while the moderators remained, staring at each shouting face in turn.

9
Prometheus is Born

Two hours later the crew were filing into their shuttles mounted on the huge transport planes that would take them to the upper stratosphere. From there they would progress into Earth orbit on their own rocket motors. It was the moment when these rockets engaged, the awesome brute strength of chemical explosive force, that never failed to impress even the most hardened space traveller.

Julia sat next to Arlette. "Not my most gratifying presscon," she said with a sigh.

"Well, next time you'll have the advantage of the communication time gap to cool things down between questions," volunteered Arlette.

"It'll be more of the same until we announce that we are leaving the solar system, I'm afraid."

"Yes, but that will be a moment to savour! All will be forgotten in their thirst for information about the wormhole."

"I think General Lee will be hogging that one," said

Julia, "but they'll rapidly lose interest in him once they know what we're up to. For the time being I'm more concerned about keeping the lid on ethnic hatred."

The plane took off and the passengers busied themselves with their mail and functional admin. All dressed in their pale blue uniforms, they looked, and to some extent behaved, like school kids on a Sunday outing. A half hour later Sanam Ghorashian entered the passenger cabin of the shuttle and addressed the crew members as she strode up and down the aisle, a wisp of black hair falling provocatively over her cheek.

"We have 15 minutes before we disengage from the mother craft and fire the escape velocity rockets," she announced in her haughty Oxbridge tone. The passengers were immediately divided into those who paid attention and those who found something else to occupy themselves, which corresponded roughly with their gender.

"From then on we shall be weightless or approaching weightlessness, so you will remain tethered in your seats until we have docked with IP262. When you use the washrooms please use the tethering conduits. This shuttle is not designed for weightless activities and serious injury could occur during manoeuvres, which can occur at any time. Your in-seat communication modules provide a comprehensive range of services. In-flight time will be 22 hours and 14 minutes. Enjoy."

She turned and headed back into the cockpit, without having made eye contact with anyone.

"Hey, Sanam, thanks for the warmth and sincerity," muttered Julia.

Arlette stretched back in her seat and opened up video

contact with her chief propulsion engineer. "Hey, Genes, why is it that we still have to spend a whole day to get to the moon? Can't you guys build something a bit hotter?"

"Nice one, Commander," drawled Genes. "If you guys would let me get my hands on that induced gravity technology so that I could control the G-forces on your puny little bodies, I might just give you a ride you won't forget in a hurry."

"Yes … OK", replied Arlette as she caught up with his thinking, "but that's a lot of energy and hardware for a pretty modest economic return."

"Hell, lady, you don't get much new space technology for popcorn."

They grinned at each other momentarily before their screens faded.

"Brace for ignition!"

There was a roar and a jolt. The shuttle lifted its nose and shot into space, pinning its passengers in their seats. 'Point of no return,' thought Arlette.

The journey was long and boring, and most slept at best intermittently in zero gravity for the first time in a while. Breakfast was a pretty mediocre affair of warmed-up packaged nutrients, and queueing for the washrooms while floating about on a tether made everybody irritable. However, the mood picked up when they entered lunar orbit and there was a cheer when IP262 was sighted, floating majestically above the horizon.

"Hello, my Prometheus," breathed Arlette. "You are indeed a Titan."

The shuttle approached gingerly, in little jerks as the final course corrections were made. There was the tiniest of bumps and then the clamour of machinery as the airlocks engaged and locked.

"Welcome to IP262. Please keep your tethers hooked up as you disembark, but remember that induced gravity will begin to affect you immediately," the pilot said, and signed off.

Euphoria gripped the crew as they entered their new ship. It was airy and spacious. It was tastefully decorated. The main spaces seemed to be open to the universe by virtue of the external cameras projecting the view onto the internal walls. There were little touches like vases of flowers in corners and paintings on the walls. There were internal maps posted at intervals. There was light everywhere and soft, pleasant music.

"Please make your way to your allotted cabins," said a voice. "You will find them on levels 3, 4 and 5." The lifts began to hum and the crew to explore their new quarters. If this was how extra-terrestrial life was to be, it had plenty of takers.

Henri Bertin barely glanced at his quarters before heading up to the monitoring centre. The eye scanner granted him immediate access, but the room was empty. He switched through the entire range of monitoring cameras, but in most cases received a 'clearance restricted' message. "How can I detect malevolent activity", he fumed quietly to himself, "if I have no eyes and ears; and who does have clearance?" He called Arlette and got an icy reception.

"Colonel Bertin, we have an automated surveillance system in place that scans the whole ship continuously and will alert you, and me, in the event of any subversive activities," she said flatly. "We do not engage in clandestine snooping into the private affairs of the crew on this ship. The IT department can show you the criteria which trigger the reports. You'll have to work on those criteria if you believe it necessary for the security of the mission."

End of conversation.

"Merde!" said Henri to himself. "Automated surveillance my arse! If I need to know, I need to know. Do I need to apologise for doing my job?" He called again. "We need to discuss this in the interests of..."

She cut him short. "Check out the criteria first," was all she said.

The second shuttle arrived half an dhour later, and, a few minutes after the new arrivals had settled into their cabins, the central communication system came to life.

"This is IP262 administration. Will all crew members please access their in-room terminals within the next thirty minutes and link their phones. You will then have your detailed schedules and shift rosters to hand. Please synchronise all devices to Central European Time. Your cabin lighting system will adjust to your shift schedule automatically, but you can select external view at any time. The ablutions are set to normal gravity use. In the event of a loss of gravitation they will switch automatically to weightless mode. Will all section leaders contact their opposite numbers in the ground crew by 15.00 and arrange handover. Ground crew are to prepare for departure at 16.00. Commander Piccard will address you at 17.00. Thank you."

Arlette breezed into her spacious quarters, checked that all her clothes and personal effects were in place and that the support systems were all working, showered and changed.

Seconds later the door buzzer went. She glanced at the screen – it was Henri. She let him in, maintaining her distance and an air of professional humility.

"I'd like you to approve some changes in the automatic surveillance criteria," he began. "I really need this to provide effective security – please."

Arlette took the piece of paper he held out to her and scanned it. She looked up at him as if studying him for the first time. "I won't have the ethnic screen," she said. "Is the rest absolutely necessary?"

"It is," he said, "but the automated surveillance system remains in place as a first defence of personal privacy. This just makes the suspect profile better suited to the potential threats we have on board Prometheus."

"Then get it done" said Arlette, handing back the piece of paper.

Henri nodded and turned to leave. Then he had second thoughts and turned back.

"I just want to say that I deeply regret having offended you, that I am honoured to be under your command on this mission, and that what happened to me in Acapulco was a joy, not a duty."

Arlette pursed her lips. "I hear you," she said. "Keep your distance."

Henri nodded and left.

Arlette turned and studied the star-scape on the wall for a moment, then called in Chang, Julia and Marcel. "So, what questions are being asked?" she enquired.

"Crew members want to know if their personal time is going to be monitored," said Chang.

Arlette felt a little chill in her stomach.

"We need clarity on the rights of the crew to external communications," said Julia.

"The crew want to know how much freedom of movement they have," said Marcel.

"Anything else?"

"It's pretty mundane at present. Crew members are generally surprised at the quality of life on board. They like the feeling of private space they have, which is very much enhanced by the projection of the external view on the walls, and they like the scale of the leisure facilities, unheard of on earlier ships. We'll learn more in the next week or so, but I think you should address the privacy and communication points this afternoon. Can I draft something for you?"

"No thanks, Chang," said Arlette. "I'm clear on the answers and I would rather that they sounded spontaneous."

At 17.00 she was ready, seated at the desk on her control platform, eyes resting on the prompt screen before her.

"Fellow Prometheus crew members," she said, "welcome on board. According to Greek legend, Prometheus was a Titan – a giant – who bravely stood up for mankind in the face of the depravity of the Gods. Our role on this mission is to extend the bounds of human civilisation, bringing with us the values that have sustained us so far.

"Whatever we find in the part of the galaxy that man will be entering for the first time, we shall treat with respect and humility, bringing only the very best we have to offer.

"To that end we must have discipline and mutual respect within this ship."

Arlette tried to soften her expression as she addressed the next topic.

"Some issues have been raised regarding personal freedoms. Obviously there must be limits in the interests of the security of the mission, but although we have the technical capability to monitor everything that occurs on this ship, those files will not be seen by human eyes. They will be scanned by our security software, but only for signs of obvious malevolence in the interests of us all. This applies to your personal activities, your internal communications, and your freedom to move around the ship. External communications will be subject to more rigorous vetting, again electronically only, because our rules preclude transmission of mission-sensitive information to third parties. The rules are all clearly stated in the standing orders on your in-room terminals.

"We have three days of arduous training ahead, almost all of it to be conducted in the context of a failure in the ship's gravitation system. This will affect everything we do on the ship and we must be satisfied that we can operate effectively in these conditions."

She now smiled.

"We are about to embark on the greatest adventure in the history of mankind. I am very proud to be a member of this crew and I have faith that you will all play your parts such that each succeeding generation will look up to you with wonder and admiration. Thank you."

Arlette's face faded from the screen and was replaced by the newly minted Prometheus logo: a pair of hands cradling flames.

10
Underway

The remainder of the pre-launch training and preparation was completed in an atmosphere of suppressed excitement. Incoming world news coverage was delivered in an edited form, largely devoid of contention. Crew members were familiarised with every functioning component of the ship by means of clips showing the successful test processes.

A popular form of entertainment was the video footage of the induced gravity system failure tests, particularly those taking place while crew members were in the canteen or in the pool, since no warnings were given. While the antics of crew members suddenly confronted with airborne food, particularly soup, were viewed as slapstick despite some nasty burns, the implications for swimmers finding themselves in, rather than on, a few hundred tons of water were more serious and resulted in several emergency rescue missions and subsequently the institution of 'life savers' in the pool area.

Hannah Cohen, the medical director, was not at all amused by these incidents. A tall, statuesque, prematurely greying woman and, at forty-six, the oldest member of the crew, she had seen a number of very able space personnel lose their lives as a result of exuberant behaviour. Hannah managed to combine an apparently effortless intellectual grasp of scientific medical complexity with a commanding managerial presence and, although she had no children of her own, an unfailing motherly touch. Her multiplicity of talents had been recognised early on and she had become the youngest medical director in US history before being virtually drafted into the ISEA by the then US President. Her long-term partner, Jafar, was a Palestinian she had met in medical school who now lived in Beirut. He was an established international journalist, and, as Hannah's career had blossomed, his life had become increasingly peripatetic. They were well used to long separations and brief reunions, but always managed to stay in contact. Hannah was able to perpetuate this tradition by means of the special communication channel available to her as the ranking medical officer on board Prometheus. She was, as a result, one of the best informed of all crew members.

"A collapsed lung, a fractured skull and two ulna fractures, one compounded," Hannah was telling Jafar. "That's today's output of training accidents. That woman really does push reality training to the limit."

"Why would she take that kind of risk with such a highly trained professional group?" Jafar wanted to know.

"She tells me she has to know how individual crew members will react when confronted with a real disaster, and that includes the medical team."

"Well, they wouldn't be on the crew list if they hadn't been through all that," observed Jafar.

"Yes but she's leery of virtual exercises. She says she likes to see a bit of blood on the carpet. Of course she still has back-ups available for every crew member; she can replace them right up to the time we launch. But I think it's also part of her process of adjusting to absolute command. She wants it known that she will not flinch from the tough calls."

"And how do you feel, Hannah-le?"

"Excited. I'm focused on the immediate. Actually I'm glad to have the medical team busy with these incidents. But I miss you, Jafar. I can't just jump on a plane when I need your warmth any more. I have to be professional 24/7 and I will have no intimate life for a year. It's a heavy price to pay, even for the adventure of a lifetime. Do you miss me?"

Jafar smiled his big, warm smile at the appealing image of his lady love on the screen before him. She was giving him her vulnerable look although he knew that she had almost infinite reserves of courage and forbearance.

"Yes, Hannah-le, I miss you, just as I have missed you every day for most of my adult life. But I also tell myself every day that you will only be mine as long as you are free, so missing you is not such a burden. Oh, and do you remember little Aini, the girl in the flat below who was so terribly burned and lost both her arms and legs? Well, I saw her riding a bike yesterday, completely kitted out with neurologically controlled prosthetic arms and legs, shrieking and giggling like all the other children. These are the moments that compensate me for life's other deficiencies."

"Deficiencies?!" shot back Hannah. "Is the lack of

carnal relations for a whole year with the woman of your dreams just a 'deficiency'?"

Jafar sighed.

"Alright, Hannah-le, my door is locked and I can do anything I like in front of this screen." Jafar began to unbutton his shirt. "Take your top off and show me your pretty little titties."

"No! You can't mollify me with video sex. I just want to know that you're aching for me."

"Yes, about fourteen times a day."

"Good," said Hannah with a pout. "What else is going on in the world?"

"Well, the average temperature is now supposed to be four degrees hotter than it was 100 years ago," reported Jafar. "It's unbelievably hot here now in Beirut and the drains stink. Milk is unobtainable and half the time there's no fruit in the shops because the low-temperature storage systems fail. I just got back from Armenia. I was taken out to see the remains of a Russian relief convoy. Apparently the Iranians assumed it was carrying weapons and just opened fire. The corpses of twenty-three nurses were just lying there in the dust with all their supplies and equipment burning around them. Pretty girls in the flower of their youth, their lives and good intentions blown away in a couple of minutes of insanity. I talked to the Iranian commander and he just shrugged and claimed that it was all a Russian trick. It's the utter heartlessness of these people that disgusts me. Nobody cares. It's not as though they are driven by some deep-rooted conviction. It's just the violence of survival. Did you hear about the 400 inmates in a Siberian prison that were burned alive when a cloud of methane released from the melting tundra ignited? Jonny Tarbuck was there for AP. He said the whole prison looked like a fast-food production line. All these roasted bodies in their cubicles."

"Please, Jafar! Isn't there anything edifying in the news?" asked Hannah.

"Not that I can see," said Jafar. "The climate management conference in Hong Kong collapsed in chaos. The Chinese wanted to run aggressive large-scale trials of new aerial seeding compounds to induce rainfall, and some barmy American academic vetoed it on the basis that it was 'ungodly'. The only outfit that seems to be getting anything done is your lot at the ISEA."

"Well, Jafar darling, the next time we talk will be when we are on our way to our rendezvous with…"

"With what?" Jafar wanted to know.

"With … destiny," said Hannah after some thought. I'll tell you about it when we get there."

* * *

The launch itself was spectacular only in that the rocket motors were fired to get the ship out of lunar orbit and onto its planned trajectory, whereupon the anti-matter propulsion system took over the slow but relentless acceleration of the ship.

Life on board Prometheus began to take on the semblance of routine. Shifts changed, command and control alternated, minor irritations arose between some individuals, sometimes due to technical glitches but more often the result of clashes in personal style.

Colonel Henri Bertin and his SWAT team, now ten strong, scanned the output of the newly modified automated surveillance system for signs of nefarious intent and found nothing.

But in another part of the ship, a sector now carefully sealed off and sanitised of all observation devices, a quite different mood prevailed. One of the section leaders was scanning the confidential crew records, data he had no right to see. He was looking for certain behavioural patterns, and he was finding them. He looked at his watch. The afternoon shift would be coming off duty in ten minutes. Time to move.

Joining the jostling queue for the evening meal he picked out five individuals with whom he was to come into close proximity during the next ten minutes or so. None would feel the tiny prick in their skin as his hand clapped his good-natured greeting on them. But none would ever be the same again.

* * *

Back in the crew quarters, Marcel leaned forward for the eye scan that would open the door to his quarters when the door to his left half opened, revealing part of a scowling face. "Hey, how are your IT skills?" it demanded shrilly.

"Not bad, Sanam," said Marcel, his face cocked to one side. "Are you having some grief with the internal system?"

"Damn right! It needs modification."

"Oh really? What kind of modification?"

"It needs some manners," said Sanam simply. "Come in."

Marcel went in.

To his amazement the walls of the room were hung with tapestries, and a large arch of scarlet fabric was mounted above the head of the bed. It looked quite extraordinarily exotic in the otherwise bland decorative scheme of the ship. "Well, you have certainly stamped your personality on your little corner of Prometheus," he said.

Sanam scowled again.

"Just what is the problem?" He looked quizzically at the monitor with its frozen image of Sanam in her splendid setting.

"That!" She pointed at the monitor. "I am being spied on in my personal space."

"How did you get hold of that data stream?" asked Marcel, with some interest.

"Never mind!" snapped Sanam. "I want it stopped."

"Yes, but the data is only being electronically monitored. Nobody is going to see it unless the scanning system picks up something..."

"I want it stopped!" yelled Sanam.

"Give me a reason why," said Marcel.

"Because I may want to have company in my room."

"Same applies," said Marcel. "You can do what you like with whoever you like. As long as it's not subversive, no one will ever know."

"Marcel, please."

"OK, I can put a block on it, but the system will record personnel movements around the ship, so if you have a frequent visitor, it will show up."

"I don't care! I just don't want to be videoed in my bed."

"OK, I'll put a block on it, and that will be on record, but you'll have your privacy."

"Thank you, Marcel," she said sweetly.

As he left his room an hour later he passed three women coming the other way. "Good grief, a girlie party," he thought.

When he got to Arlette's quarters Genes was already there, spread out over a sofa. Arlette sat in an armchair, sipping fruit juice.

"Hey, Marcel, Genes and I were just discussing the reliability of the induced gravity system. He doesn't think it will hold up."

"Anything you noticed during the system failure tests?" asked Marcel.

"Naw," drawled Genes. "Fact is I was impressed how fast they brought it up. Ah just think the generators are under-designed. They are operating too close to capacity for my liking. Not enough slack in the system."

"Come on, Genes, we can't put Texas-style overcapacity into everything. They did their sums and delivered the goods," said Marcel.

"If we come out of the ass-end of that wormhole with the gravity system still operating, I'll be mighty surprised," said Genes gravely. "That's the kind of stress that will test the system, not flippin' them switches up and down," he added.

"Got any suggestions to beef it up, Genes?" asked Arlette.

"Yeah. Let me do some more thinking about that."

"What do think about the team, the Ukrainians?"

"As good a bunch of guys as you'll find anywhere," said

Genes. "That's not the issue. It's the hardware that bothers me."

The conversation drifted on to people. "You happy with all the other players so far, Genes?" asked Arlette casually.

"Too soon to say," came the reply. "That CIA guy, Bertin, is making no friends. They're always the same. Come across evil. Loyalties and agenda is anyone's guess, methods can be as messy as he chooses."

"Aren't you letting your imagination run riot? How do you know he's CIA?" Arlette looked concerned.

"CIA, KGB, Mossad, whatever." said Genes. "Unaccountable and unconcerned. Who's going to ask the questions if the wrong guy disappears?"

"He's answerable to me," said Arlette, somewhat hopefully.

"Hey, I don't doubt it, and I'm sure you have no reason not to trust him."

Arlette looked away. She felt uncomfortable and Genes could see it. He dropped the subject.

"Hey, Marcel, you're the master of all things technical. Where do you see our challenges?" he asked.

"I'm about where you are," replied Marcel. "A severe localised distortion of space–time sounds to me like the kind of place where things might break, even though the explorer probes got through the wormhole and back without apparent damage. Time spent now on enhancing the robustness of our systems is well spent in my view. Why don't we get together tomorrow at 10.00 and define some specifics?"

Genes was on his feet.

"You bet," he said, "Let's call in Dima from Gravity and Gerry from Hull Integrity as well."

He turned. "G'night, Commander, Marcel," and he was gone.

Arlette turned as the door closed behind him. "He gives me a very solid feeling," she said, as if to no one in particular. "Sure," said Marcel, "but you'll get to feel the same about all your section leaders. There is immense depth of knowledge and experience on this ship. Genes is good but not unique."

His French intonation was just evident in the way he said this, and it made Arlette smile.

"Alright," she said. "What do you think of Bertin?"

"I'm more sanguine than Genes. He has a job to do. It requires knowledge that most of us do not need and should not have. I have no doubt that he is amply qualified and appropriately experienced. He asks questions and gives no answers, and that's OK with me. I don't find the opinion of non-security people of any relevance on security issues."

Arlette nodded. "Yes, but what do you think of him as a man?"

Marcel considered this question carefully. "Strong, courageous, cunning. If I had to make a quick decision, I'd trust him with my life."

"Thank you, Marcel." The smile on Arlette's face was unexpected. "And you, where are you personally?"

It was an odd question. Marcel considered his commander carefully. A strong woman with a broad range of competences, who had quickly gained the confidence and respect of the crew, but somehow still not at ease with her authority. Not surprising given this was her first major command? She was used to standing out in small groups, but had not yet assumed the commanding self-confidence of a major leader. You could not fault the content of what she was doing, but the style was still a little uncertain, a little too open to push-back.

"I am supremely confident of our ability to deliver technically on this mission," he began, leaning forward and smiling at her, "and I have developed a huge admiration for you and the way you have moved into your role. I am personally excited about you as a leader, and I am very proud of being on your team."

He gave her a long, appreciative look that took in all of her, including her implicit sexuality, and he was, for a moment, deeply conscious of it. She felt it too, a little glow that was respectful and in context, but nevertheless appreciative of her holistically. She smiled broadly.

"I have noticed you biting your lip on several occasions, holding back on comments you think might be disruptive," he went on. "I think the time has now come when you have the standing to express your views freely. A command like yours is lawfully authoritarian. I want to see your strength and I'm happy to go and pick up the pieces if necessary."

Arlette looked at Marcel and nodded almost imperceptibly, holding his gaze for a while.

"Thank you," she said again.

11
Pandora Strikes

Some twenty-two hours later, four men and a woman were seated in a sealed room with the section leader who had approached them individually at dinner and invited them in to see what he had described to them as 'an unusual martial arts movie'. It began with a sequence of kick-boxing clips in which the victors became increasingly vicious in their assaults, finally administering lethal blows to the windpipes of their opponents.

There was no apparent reaction from any of the viewers.

The next clips included a series of gruesome torture scenes in which the victims were horribly abused and finally thrown onto a heap of bodies, apparently dead. The final sequence showed a series of visually explicit beheadings carried out by swordsmen who apparently took pleasure in what they were doing.

When the movie had ended, the section leader strode to the front of the group and, engaging each one with intensive eye contact, withdrew a sword from its sheath.

“Are you ready to kill for me?” he growled.

There was a shout of assent.

* * *

When Marcel returned to his quarters it was obvious from the commotion next door that Sanam had company, multiple company. He entered his room, checked his mail and switched on the external view. Mars was clearly visible and he zoomed in to take a closer look at the planet, particularly the delicate, fleeting polar cap.

Sanam’s door opened and slammed. Several women poured out, giggling. Finally Marcel opened his door a crack and looked down the corridor at the departing revellers. Two women were standing there, their arms around each other, engaged in a passionate kiss.

Marcel closed his door noiselessly. “Hey ho,” he said.

* * *

Dimitri Kazarov had had a tedious day simulating landing mishaps in the excursion vehicle with Sanam Ghorashian. She was a perfectionist, intent on forecasting and controlling every conceivable option. He was a seat-of-the-pants man, with lightning reactions and deep intuition. They had been programming contrived piloting challenges into the EV control system to test each other.

“What the hell is this?” yelled Sanam as the EV simulation once more inexplicably lost its directional control system and plummeted into the ground.

"Struck by a large flying animal," said Dimitri with a grin.

"Idiot!" yelled Sanam, staring at the data field before her "It weighs forty tons and is flying at 200 kph! This is mindless!"

"I am not an idiot and we are here to understand the limits of the system we are going to fly," said Dimitri as calmly as he could.

"Look," said Sanam with venom, "I am a scientist and a pilot and not to be trifled with by some deluded Russian sci-fi freak. We do this with credible scenarios or not at all."

"Your arrogance in deciding what is and what is not a credible scenario on a planet where we know nothing more than its size, temperature profile and atmospheric composition is intolerable! Perhaps you should stick to flying shuttles between well-defined coordinates, like the over-trained and spoiled Persian princess you are..."

"Oh," Sanam glowered, "how you Russians love to tell everyone what to do! How inventive you are in contriving suffering for others! How brutally you..."

The door of the simulator was wrenched open and Henri Bertin marched in with eyes like ice.

"Stop this activity immediately and return to your quarters," he said, physically stepping between the two of them.

Dimitri rose, turned, spat on the floor and left. The look on Sanam's face was one of unbridled hatred.

"Please, Major Ghorashian, you are better than that," said Henri. She left without a word.

Some time later Dimitri was queueing to collect his

evening meal when one of his convivial colleagues shoved him aside and whispered in his ear. Dimitri grinned and nodded. An hour later he was seated in a small group about to watch an 'unusual' movie.

It wasn't what he expected, and his curiosity began to turn to revulsion, not so much at what he was seeing, but in terms of the demonic pleasure it seemed to be giving to the rest of the small audience. He rose from his seat, a wave of nausea came over him and he reached out to steady himself. The movie stopped and he was suddenly conscious that all eyes were on him. There was a little flash from a blade before him and then a sharp pain in his chest. He felt his warm blood spilling down his body and heard a cacophony of shouts in his ears. Then he slid to the ground and his consciousness ebbed away.

Major Kazarov failed to report for duty on the main flight deck the following morning and did not respond to calls or prompts. A quick inspection showed that he had not filed an activity report for the previous day or slept in his room. After all section leaders on the ship were ordered to carry out local searches, he was found sitting in the pilot's seat of the EV simulator, holding a piece of paper in his hand. On it was printed the word 'PANDORA'. He had been dead for at least eight hours.

Henri Bertin sat with his two-man detection team in his office, reviewing the video records of the last twenty-four hours. It was quite clear that the video monitoring system had been hacked and numerous records deleted. Nowhere was there any evidence of where Kazarov went after he left the EV simulator or how his body had been delivered back there.

He called the IT section head and requested back-up on the lost records. There was an embarrassed silence, followed by a rather nervous response. Henri's heart sank. "No chance?"

"No, sir."

The three men looked at each other. Was it possible that, with all the analytical sophistication on this ship, they would have no surveillance data to identify a murderer right in their midst?

* * *

Henri was in the Commander's office, and she had just asked him the question he had asked himself ten minutes earlier.

She was livid, and he felt the whole weight of her anger and disgust without her uttering a single harsh word. He apologised without false humility for failing to detect the vulnerability of the video monitoring system and told her that IT was working on backing up all surveillance data.

Then she asked the question he was dreading. "Well, Colonel Bertin, what do you suggest was the motive for the murder of a key member of my operations team?"

Henri frowned. "Well, the only motive we know of is ethnic hatred. We know of a very ugly exchange between Major Ghorashian and Kazarov, but with seriously compromised surveillance records we do not know where she was or who she spoke to after that incident. If that was the motive, she had very significant back-up, because she is not known for her IT skills, not at the level required to hack into an encrypted system."

"So?"

"I have asked Intelligence for comprehensive research into the backgrounds of these two and for any leads on how they may have interacted in the past."

"Wasn't that done already?"

"Yes, but now it will all be repeated in the light of this incident." It was a pretty long shot, and Henri knew it.

"Is that all?" Arlette's voice reeked of contempt.

"No, there was a message in Kazarov's hand – it just said 'PANDORA.'"

Arlette stiffened and the blood drained from her face. "Do you know who Pandora was?" she asked icily.

"She was the girl who couldn't resist opening her box of treasures, and let out all the evil into the world."

"Good, good!" Arlette was sneering. "And who sent her, and why?"

"It's not really my area..."

"Oh, I think you might have to do a bit of homework, Colonel Bertin! Pandora was sent by Jupiter, the King of the Gods, to unleash misery on man, because he was so angry that Prometheus had championed mankind and undermined their authority! Do you see any connection?!"

Henri did. "Merde!" he said.

"Yes! Loads of it! Now, go and do your homework and explain to me why an apparently ethnically motivated murder would be qualified with a thinly veiled threat to the entire mission!"

Henri rose and left.

12
Bad Salad

"Tell me about this spat you had with Kazarov, Major Ghorashian." Arlette was watching her rather nervous visitor carefully.

"Oh, I was irritated with his intuitive approach to crisis simulation and let off some steam. He fired back. Neither of us allowed the Armenian crisis to get in the way, as I am sure you have seen from the video record. I am saddened and terribly shocked that he is dead, but I cannot seriously believe that our disagreement had anything to do with it."

"Did you have any interaction with Kazarov before this mission?" asked Arlette.

"I never worked with him before, but we met seven years ago at an astronauts' ball in Houston. I thought him terribly arrogant and told him so. He was not polite to me either and we had, well, quite a loud altercation."

"Anything physical?" asked Arlette.

Sanam glared at her.

"No; I mean, did you hit each other?"

Sanam laughed. "Yes, I slapped him. He deserved it.

But we never spoke again until we met in Shanghai for this mission."

"Anything else I should know?"

"No," replied Sanam. "Our interaction on this mission has been completely professional. I am genuinely sorry to lose a valued team-mate."

At 10.00 a.m. Arlette made an announcement to the crew of Prometheus.

"Good morning, fellow crew members. It is with profound regret that I have to announce the untimely death of Major Dimitri Kazarov from heart failure. His condition was undetected until his body was discovered this morning. A post-mortem examination has been carried out. To all of you who knew him, as I did, he was a man of great professional skill, integrity and humility. He will be greatly missed as a valuable member of this crew. His next of kin have been informed and have given their permission for his body to be consigned to permanent orbit around the sun. The ceremony will take place tomorrow at 11.00 a.m. Thank you."

'Well,' thought Henri, 'those who don't know any more need not know any more, and those that do are going to keep it quiet.' He stood up and gazed at the universe for a moment, contemplating how little he really knew. Then Julia strode in.

"So, what's your explanation?" she demanded.

"Feelings run deep when there's ethnic conflict," said Henri with a shrug.

"You know that's bullshit, Colonel Bertin!" said Julia. "Ethnic conflict my arse! A highly decorated Iranian pilot has a sophisticated back-up team on board to murder a colleague because he's Russian and she dislikes what the Russians are doing in Armenia? Please!"

"Has the Commander talked to you?" asked Henri warily.

"Of course she has! And of course she has told me about the Pandora note. I am one of her closest personal advisors and this is not a cops and robbers exercise – it suggests extremely sinister intent by somebody or something that we have not identified."

"Alright Julia," said Henri. "You have security clearance; let's do this together. Kazarov was one of four pilots on board. What does his death do to the mission?"

"Nothing decisive," Julia responded. "But it tells us just one thing. Someone on board has an agenda and the capacity to kill and to use sophisticated methods to avoid detection. If he, or she, can do this once, he can murder again or cause some other form of mayhem."

"So why would he show his hand now with an act that draws our attention to him, but is not decisive?"

"He wouldn't," said Julia, "not if he's as sophisticated as he must be to have avoided detection. Something must have forced his hand. Perhaps Kazarov discovered him, or just got in the way somehow."

"Well, Julia, that leaves us with a malevolent presence on board which could disrupt the mission. Is it trying to get us to turn back, and if so, why?"

"Possibly. We don't know whether Mission Control received any threats before the mission left. Perhaps they did but decided to press on because of the political urgency. If so, they will have some idea of the level of the threat. What have they told you so far?"

"Assume ethnic conflict and deal with it," said Henri, "while our investigations continue."

"I don't like that," said Julia. "It sounds like politically looking the other way."

"No, you are underestimating the intelligence community. To me it sounds like 'we know who they are and we're going to eliminate them.'" Henri was deadly serious.

"So, that would leave us chickens up here to deal with a ruthless murderer on board, who can hack into our security systems and God knows what else!"

"Careful who you're calling a chicken. That's my job you're talking about."

"Well, Colonel Bertin, I most sincerely hope you are up to it!" said Julia.

"I am," said Henri, "but you had better be prepared for a bit more spilt blood."

Julia stared at him. "OK," she said.

* * *

"Jafar, we've had a murder on board!" Hannah was visibly shaken as she made video contact.

"Tell me," said Jafar calmly, as both of them adjusted to the transmission delay.

"One of the pilots, a Russian, was delivered to me for autopsy yesterday. He had been found dead in the simulator, stabbed cleanly through the heart. Nobody seems to know by whom or why, but I've been instructed to report heart failure."

"Stabbed with what?" Jafar asked.

"Clearly a very sharp blade," said Hannah. "There was no contusion on the surface. Who would have such a thing on board and why?"

"Anterior or posterior entry?"

"Anterior. Why?"

"Because it means that the murderer was probably a colleague who he had no reason to fear," said Jafar.

"Well, that could be anyone," said Hannah. "Bertin is baffled, I can see that. He mentioned the possibility of an ethnic dispute over the Armenian crisis but he doesn't really believe it."

"Well, given he's a Russian, I would bet it's over some Mafia-related dispute," said Jafar.

"What interest could the Mafia have in a mission like this?" Hannah's brow was deeply furrowed.

"Power. Influence. Revenge. Who knows? Let's hope that the score is settled now."

"Yes, let's hope so," said Hannah uncertainly. Then, as an afterthought, "Does the Mafia have much influence on international affairs?"

"Huge," said Jafar. "They are into everything related to human misery. Drugs, the black market, protection rackets, political murder. There's always money to be made when there's social upheaval. The entire city council of Shenzhen was assassinated last week, apparently because of their generous welfare policy. The press suspects the Mafia, and there was an article in the Jerusalem Post yesterday to the effect that the Mafia has become the best run international organisation of all time."

Hannah frowned. "As if we didn't already have enough to worry about on this mission."

"Don't fret, Hanna-le," said Jafar. "You are probably safer there than here, but do be careful. You are in the midst of a very big deal. Your intuition about people is usually excellent. Don't ignore it."

* * *

Within three weeks of the death of Major Kazarov, a clandestine squad of nineteen crew members had been formed who could be transformed into malevolent automatons with blind obedience to their leader upon his command, but their demeanour during periods of duty and recreation was unremarkable, because they remembered nothing when not under his control. There were no ideologues, no religious or political convictions. It was not necessary or relevant, since the changes in their brains that were receptive to specific triggers were caused by a viral infection, not by psychological manipulation.

They were trained in martial arts and the use of assault weaponry, and fed with a stream of visual violence, for which it seems that they had an insatiable appetite. The entrance to their training quarters was through an unmarked door in one of many similar corridors, but in this case the records of the nearest monitoring camera were programmed to revert to showing an empty corridor automatically by the opening and closing of the door.

The design strength of the squad was to be twenty-four plus their leader. That meant five more 'infections' would be required, and, shortly afterwards, five new recruits would need to be tested. This process was not particularly arduous – a chance meeting, a slap on the back or a bit of friendly joshing, a 24-hour incubation period, and then an 'initiation'. The candidates had been chosen based on their profiles, and particularly their DNA, which would make them susceptible to the virus that would be injected into them.

One such candidate, Brekhna Khan, a towering, warrior-like woman and a maintenance engineer, found herself to be the subject of just such attention as she was helping herself to a plate of salad in the canteen. A squeeze on the arm from one of her crew-mates, for whom she had developed quite a fondness, took her by surprise. She turned sharply and found herself practically in his arms as he said, "Hi, Brekhna!"

However, perhaps because she was left-handed, the direction of her turn was exactly the reverse of what he had expected, and the micro-syringe in his palm slipped away and disappeared into one of several large bowls of salad behind her. Cursing soundlessly through his grin, he just had to hope that the object in question would not be noticed before it was flushed away with the garbage. Apparently unperturbed, both he and Brekhna made their way onwards and enjoyed a boisterous conversation over their meal together.

Three coincidences conspired to make these events rather more significant than they were already. The first was that Brekhna was wearing a bangle under her uniform sleeve which had deflected the syringe needle, so that the contents had discharged themselves harmlessly into the material of her jacket. The second was that Julia Rogers arrived at the salad bar just in time to take the last spoonful from the bowl into which the micro-syringe had fallen, and the third was that she was in the company of Henri Bertin.

Three minutes later, as she was just about to put a forkful of salad into her mouth, Henri reached out and took it from her. "I don't think I'd eat that if I were you," he said, looking quizzically at the contents of the fork. "Who could possibly be using something like that on this ship?"

They stared at each other for a long moment.

"If I let my imagination loose on this, it goes open-ended," said Julia.

Henri nodded slowly. "I think I'll take it up to the farmyard," he said. "They have analytical equipment there that should give us an idea of what was in there."

"Perhaps you should check the crew medical records first – you don't want to go too large if it turns out to be someone's personal medication." The look on Julia's face as she was talking said volumes about how her mind was racing, but she kept her comments low-key. She said, "I seem to have gone off my food. Shall we go to the farmyard together?"

They got up without a word, and Henri was already speaking soundlessly by CTT to Medical Records as they left the room. He grunted. "MR has nothing," he said to Julia perfunctorily.

They were joined in the lift by Genes Clayton. "Well," he drawled, looking them up and down with a big grin. "An unlikely couple if ever I saw one. Does PR need security or does Security need PR?"

"Perhaps it's a bit of both, Genes," said Julia. He was gone with a wave at the next stop.

As the doors of the lift opened at the top section of

the ship, they were met by Helmut Schindler, the chief biochemist. “Welcome to the farmyard!” he boomed. “We don’t get many distinguished visitors up here.” His offer of a quick tour was waved away with a brief smile. Henri glanced around. “We have some confidential business,” he said in a low voice.

Schindler guided them into his office, and Henri produced a napkin from his pocket, which he opened to show him the micro-syringe. “Could you please tell us what this contains?”

Schindler stared at the object before him with obvious distaste, then lifted it gingerly into a glass dish with a pair of tweezers. He was going to ask Henri where he had got it, but decided he didn’t want to know. “I expect you have already realised that this is an item not used in normal medical practice,” he said. “It’s used to deliver very small quantities of materials which are potentially very toxic. It is also used by the criminal classes – clandestinely,” he added.

“I want to know what it contained,” said Henri levelly, “and I want no one else to know of its existence besides us three.” He did not elaborate.

Schindler nodded slowly. “I’m not equipped for forensic work,” he said, “and the syringe has been mostly discharged, but I can probably classify the contents for you. If you need more detail I can do a molecular scan and transmit the data back to home-base for further analysis.”

“No, do the scan first and let me have the data. How long will the analysis take?”

“The molecular scan can be done in half an hour. The analysis will take four to six hours. Less if I could get my whole team on it.”

"No!" said Henri sharply. "It has to remain between just us three. I'll wait here for the results of the scan, then you can do the analysis."

Schindler raised his eyebrows quizzically and then thought better of it. He sighed. "It's going to be a long night," he said. He took the dish and left.

Henri made a call to one of his military detail. "Brady, you are to report to Dr Schindler's office in the farmyard in thirty minutes, armed and ready to stand guard at the doctor's lab."

Brady arrived twenty minutes later. He was ordered to wait outside Schindler's office.

Schindler returned a few minutes later and handed Henri a data stick. "I can't tell anything from the data on there as it stands, but I'll give you a call as soon as I have finished my analysis."

Henri nodded and opened the door to leave. "Brady, accompany Dr Schindler to his lab and ensure that no one interferes with his work, and call Koh for back-up if you need to."

The two of them maintained a studied silence as they descended in the lift and headed for Henri's office. "So, now what do you think that micro-syringe was doing in the salad bowl?" asked Julia as Henri closed the door behind her.

"It had been used, or mostly used, possibly without the agreement or knowledge of the recipient. That means we have a victim somewhere, either in the kitchen or perhaps in the meal queue. If the intention was malevolent, we will know pretty soon. If not then the implications are much more complex, because it may mean that the intention was to disable someone or" – he turned the thought over in his mind – "influence somebody."

Julia studied him. "What would be the motive for such a pre-meditated act – and it would have to have been planned for that micro-syringe to have been on board in the first place – during this mission? It could hardly be just to settle an old score; the perpetrator would know that the fallout would be to throw the sustainability of the mission into question. I think that we have a conspiracy here, and my intuition tells me that there is a link with Pandora."

"Well, who would want to disrupt the mission?" mused Henri.

"Oh, you know that better than I do! Political enemies! Big business interests! Most of the world does not share our ideological goals unless there is something in it for them!" Her indignation was boiling over.

"Whoa, Julia, we have only found an unidentified bit of medical detritus. It probably just contains insulin. We need Schindler's data before we can take any sort of direction."

"I think Dr Schindler would have taken a different tack if he had thought it was insulin, or was it that he was so impressed that it was our CIA man who had brought it to him?" She looked at him with a rather crooked smile, but Henri remained dead serious.

"No, I think he probably knows a lot about the nefarious uses of micro-syringes," was his reply.

"And do you?" she asked.

He shrugged and she got up to leave. "Julia..."

"Yes?"

"Be careful. I'll call you as soon as I have news from Schindler."

She leaned towards him across his desk, her face inches from his. "Keep me well and truly in the loop, big man," she said with real authority. He grinned, sat back, arched his eyebrows and gave her an appreciative look-over. Julia frowned, turned on her heel, and left.

Four hours later Henri was woken from a little reverie by his phone alarm. He yawned, stretched and checked his phone. Nothing yet. He called Brady.

There was no reply. He frowned. A breach of discipline was unexpected and worrisome. He called Dr Schindler. No reply. Henri stood up and stared at the wall in front of him. Then he called Koh. "Had any contact with Brady?"

"No, sir," came the reply.

"Wake Sergeant Kropnik and get to my office immediately, in combat readiness!"

His men were there in four minutes. "Brady was left on guard duty with Dr Schindler at 21.05," barked Henri, "and he failed to answer a call from me just now." Both men looked incredulous.

"Let's go!"

Dr Schindler's office was deserted. It was eerily quiet and the laboratory lights were off. Henri waved his men in to search with infra-red vision. It took barely two minutes, and then a whisper from Kropnik: "Man down!"

"Check for any other presence!" Henri himself was scanning every detail of the laboratory.

"It's clear!" whispered Kropnik. Henri switched on the lights.

Dr Schindler was lying face down in a pool of blood.

A blade of some kind had entered his back just below the shoulder blade and passed through his chest. There was no pulse. As Henri rolled him over a piece of paper dropped from one hand. With growing trepidation Henri turned it over and saw just what he had dreaded – the word 'PANDORA'.

Brady was nowhere to be found.

13
Uneasily to the Threshold

The discussion between Henri and Arlette that ensued early the following morning was 'difficult'. As Henri described the events leading up to the discovery of Dr Schindler's body, Arlette sat stone-faced at her desk, processing the input with profound unease. Finally she sighed and spoke soundlessly and anonymously by CTT through her earphone. Chang appeared barely two minutes later.

"Colonel Bertin, bring Chang up to speed and then report jointly to Mission Control and tell them I want their instructions by return – that's what, ten, say twelve hours? Call me as soon as you have completed your report and I will deliver my confidential views to them then. We are approaching our rendezvous with the LDST staging point and I am scheduled to address the crew at 10.00 hours tomorrow. Oh, and Chang, drop back here when we're done with Mission Control." Her eyes did not meet Henri's as they left.

* * *

"Any response to the molecular scan from your home-base analytical team yet?" Julia asked.

"No," came Henri's curt reply, "but they were understandably disappointed that we were unable to provide any direction from our own on-board analysis. Analysing data fields is a lot more complex than when you have the actual chemical compound in your hands. I don't expect anything back this side of the wormhole."

"Do you think we should proceed with the transfer in the light of this uncertainty?" Julia had little doubt that the answer would be affirmative.

"We heard this evening that Mission Control and the Commander are resolved that the mission is not to be deflected by isolated security issues. Whether we are this side of the wormhole or the other side is, in their view, just a technicality. We have to establish control and complete the mission. Sending the cavalry to our rescue is not an option."

A little grin passed across Julia's face. The imagery seemed very quaint and very 'Henri'. However, the pressure on him to get quick results was now further intensified. "So, we've got two bodies and an absentee. Where do you suppose Brady is?" she asked.

"I see two possibilities," said Henri. "He's either a victim whose body has been removed because it incriminates the murderer in some way, or he is part of the plot and is in hiding."

"So where's the video evidence?" asked Julia incredulously. "It hasn't been hacked again?"

Henri rolled his eyes. "According to our video monitoring records, Dr Schindler was never in his lab after we left last night, and Brady never left his post."

"This is intolerable, Henri. The system is useless. It's hopelessly compromised." Julia's face was flushed with anger.

Henri scowled. "They're trying to re-programme it completely," he said, "but the opposition is ahead of the game. It was never designed to be a criminal investigation system."

"Great! So we don't know whether Brady is friend or foe? But how could a trained soldier, one of your trusted military detail, be on another side? Are our screening processes compromised as well? What the hell is going on?" She stared at Henri, her eyes flashing, and for an awful moment she wondered whether he was himself some kind of enemy agent, intent on destroying the mission and her most priceless dream with it. That seemed unlikely given his willingness to share critical information with her, but she made a mental note that she would never trust him entirely.

* * *

"Good morning, fellow crew members," announced Arlette. "In just under thirty-six hours we shall be arriving at our LDST staging point and the pilots will be carrying out manoeuvres for the transfer to Omega 16. We shall be carrying out twenty hours of pre-transfer checks before the ship is locked down and transfer commences. Each of you will be familiar with the processes involved, but we will all be aware that this will be the first time in the history of our civilisation that humankind will enter another solar system. I will speak to you all again just before transfer, but in the meantime I ask you all to be absolutely meticulous in your preparation for this momentous event. Good luck."

No mention of the sudden disappearance of Dr Schindler and Brady. No apparent concerns about the success of the mission or the safety of the crew. Just pure Arlette Piccard focused resolve. Julia and Henri looked at each other, raised their eyebrows and shrugged, in almost perfect unison. It was an unspoken acknowledgement of the Commander's coldly remorseless dedication to the mission.

The crew was led to understand that Dr Schindler and Brady had been taken ill and put in isolation, but no details were released. Neither of them were involved in the transfer process, which preoccupied most of the rest of the crew, and few questions were asked.

Working in total secrecy, the home-base analysis team assessing the molecular scan that had been sent by Henri Bertin had reached a preliminary conclusion that the substance in the micro-syringe was not a chemical toxin but a virus or a mixture of viruses. What properties this virus might have would be unknown until it had been synthesised, assessed and tested in a live animal context. It was going to be weeks, not days, before they would have an answer.

Henri announced these findings the following morning at a grim-faced command meeting chaired by Arlette. Julia, Marcel and Chang sat in silence. Finally Arlette said, "Marcel, we must override the privacy rules and transform our video monitoring system into a robust and comprehensive surveillance capability. Get it done." Marcel nodded. She turned to Henri. "How do you explain Brady's disappearance?"

"I think he may be hidden somewhere in the annulus between the ship's hull and the operational quarters – either dead or alive," said Henri slowly. "We have no video monitoring cameras in there and it would not have been difficult to force an entrance to that area. Building on that theory, it could be that more micro-syringes or other materials are being stored there."

"Have you conducted a search?"

"We have conducted a comprehensive search of the interior of the ship, but we cannot access many sectors of the annulus without burning through the inner skin."

"How long do you need to conduct a thorough search?"

"Two weeks," said Henri.

"Two weeks?!"

"Yes. It has to be systematic from top to tail, and I have to be able to maintain a security capability at all times. Assuming we have a malevolent agency on board, we have to assume that they will make it difficult for us as soon as it is known that we are burning holes in the ship and searching the inaccessible areas."

"And supposing he is hidden somewhere else?" enquired Arlette.

"It's possible we have missed him," replied Henri, "but I doubt it. We are continuing to explore all possibilities. However, I cannot leave security uncertainty in such a large area of the ship. If there is a malevolent agency on board with the intention of disrupting the mission, then it will be using a clandestine base somewhere, and the only possible location is in the annulus of the ship."

"Very well," said Arlette. "You can take any action you

deem necessary once we have cleared the transfer. Marcel will be responsible for ensuring the physical integrity of the ship while you are carrying out your work. How do you read the preliminary conclusion of the home-base analysis of the micro-syringe contents?"

"An unidentified virus is a serious threat while it remains unidentified and we must be very vigilant," said Henri. "I have alerted the medical centre to be prepared to isolate patients immediately if unfamiliar symptoms are presented. Since we haven't seen anything unusual since the death of Major Kazarov, which was clearly related because of the Pandora message, it does not look as though we have any immediate prospect of an epidemic arising from this micro-syringe. Of course, we are now completely dependent on home-base to identify the virus and recommend treatment. I'll feel a lot better when we get their final report."

"OK. Chang, how do you rate the threat?"

Chang leaned forward and engaged the meeting. "One of the identified risks of a mission which is to land on unexplored territory is the possibility of alien infections. We have an excellent capacity to deal with that threat on board, despite the loss of Dr Schindler," he said, "and anything that originated on our home planet should not pose too serious a threat. The only problem we have is that we don't have a biological sample. I support Colonel Bertin's analysis and his proposed action, and we are fortunate that he had the foresight to get a molecular scan sent off to home-base as promptly as he did, but we do urgently need the surveillance system revamp."

Arlette leaned back in her chair. "It is our destiny and

our duty to be the first human beings to pass through a wormhole into an otherwise inaccessible part of our galaxy," she said. "Every member of the crew has been vetted and found to have the skills and attitudes necessary for a successful mission of this kind. If we have any bad apples on board, we must outsmart and contain them. With the exception of Colonel Bertin and his team we all now need to focus on the forthcoming transition. Thank you."

As they filed out Marcel said, "Can we please meet in my office right away. The section heads are already waiting and I would like to go through the transition process with all of you one more time. Obviously none of the previous discussion is to be shared with them."

"Do you have any specific concerns about them?" asked Julia, somewhat surprised. Marcel herded them into his office and closed the door.

"Look," he said, "the only people on board with access to the kind of resources required to hack into our surveillance systems and sustain an effective hiding place on board are the section heads. If there is a conspiracy going on, I'd bet heavily that one of them knows a lot more about it than we do."

"Agreed," said Henri. "Please watch the body language, yours and theirs, if the welfare and whereabouts of Schindler and Brady come up. Cohen, the medical director, will handle any questions about them that arise."

They filed into the adjacent conference room, and the eight waiting section heads scrambled to their feet.

"Good morning," said Marcel with an expansive smile. "Since we are about to embark on the most exciting adventure in history so far, I thought we could all share our thoughts on what we shall be doing for the next thirty days and what we expect to see and feel. Yev, would you please give us the basics."

Yevgeny Kusnetsov, Chief Scientist, rose to his feet with an air of professorial dignity, presentation remote in his hand, and grinned broadly. "As you all know, we have reached the threshold of the LDST, which is our acronym for localised distortion of space–time. It originated from here," he said, directing his pointer at a photo of an irregular, pock-marked lump of rock on the screen.

Julia looked, consciously soaking up the rich tones of his Russian-accented English.

"This was Proteus, a geologically inactive chunk of fifty thousand trillion tons of rock, ice and methane, which had been doing very little for our solar system until it was converted by the ISEA into an LDST. Now it looks more like this." A diagram of a curved, almost kinked, blueish tube with flared ends appeared, nestling in a background of stars. "Of course this is just a projection of what the math tells us it's like. A gravity wave picture looks like this." The picture showed a shimmer of light around a black dot, just off to one side of the tube. "Don't worry about the black dot; it just tells us the gravitational field is rather intense as we pass it at the midpoint of the LDST." He chuckled. No one else did.

"As a result of our slow but steady acceleration since we left lunar orbit, we are now travelling at about 3,000 km/second, or just one hundredth of the speed of light. However, we shall be in for the most extreme roller-coaster ride in history, because we are going into geodesic free fall through the centre of the LDST, allowing our momentum to carry us through to the other side. This will not cause you too much discomfort since we will all be in our ergo-couches and will not feel more than 5G at any part of the ride. Any questions so far?"

"Yes" – it was Hannah Cohen. "Please remind us non-physics geeks what geodesic free fall is, and what we can expect to happen to our bodies when we pass through the midpoint. Won't we suffer from the sudden reversal of the direction of a very intense gravitational field?"

Kusnetsov smiled. For a moment he was tempted to ask one of the engineers to explain how general relativity works, but he'd been there before and had been made to run the gauntlet for treating his colleagues like first-year students, particularly the women.

"Geodesic free fall is the path taken by a body travelling at a constant velocity following the curvature of space–time," he began. "An object of large mass like a star or a planet bends the space–time around it, just like a bowling ball sitting on a trampoline. If you roll a marble towards the edge of the bowling ball at just the right speed and direction, it will follow a curved path around the bowling ball and then continue across the trampoline, somewhat deflected from its original path. The path it follows around the bowling ball is called a geodesic – that is the path of equilibrium given the initial speed and direction of the marble, its mass and the mass of the bowling ball. If you are sitting in a spaceship going past a very massive object like a moon, and you do not fire your boosters to change speed and direction, you will follow a geodesic and will be in a natural equilibrium with your surroundings. In other words both you and your spaceship will be weightless."

Kusnetsov paused and looked at Hannah for assurance. She nodded.

"As we go through the wormhole we will be moving on a geodesic that is very strongly influenced by the singularity that controls it. You are right that we will be subject to very high rates of acceleration as we approach it. However, so will Prometheus and everything in it, so nothing will be pushing you on or holding you back. You will remain comfortably weightless throughout. And, yes, this applies when we pass the midpoint. We will all decelerate together and feel nothing. The only time you're going to be anything other than weightless is when we fire the boosters to align the ship for entry, and again to slow us up on the other side. That will be controlled to a maximum of 5G, which is when you will need to be in your ergo-couches."

"How come we'll be weightless? Will local gravity not be maintained?" Freddy Jones, Farmyard Director, looked worried. "And won't the orientation of the ship have to change?"

"Yes, I beg your pardon. The ship will be weightless – we will be subject only to the induced gravity that we choose to have on board. We'll go in head first. The ship's orientation will change only when we spin her through 180 degrees and fire the boosters to slow her down on the other side. But on-board gravity will be maintained during that process as well."

"How long is this going to take, and what will we see?" asked Julia.

"We'll burn the boosters for four hours at each end" came the reply. "The rest of the ride will take ten days. As for what we'll see, well, we'll be travelling at 26 per cent of the speed of light at our fastest point, but we all know that light will still be reaching us at the regular 300,000 km/second, so what we will see is red shift from those stars that we are travelling away from and blue shift from those we are travelling towards. I think it's likely to be rather colourful. Yes, Genes?"

"We don't need to bump into anything at 26 per cent of the speed of light, and we don't have brakes," came the drawl from the back of the room. "How can we be sure that something or someone won't be coming the wrong way?"

"Nice one, Genes." Kusnetsov was still smiling. "The communications satellites at each end continually monitor anything that goes in and out. They also carry quite an impressive military capability and can knock out just about any extraneous object that might wander into our path. Anything as big as an asteroid on a potentially threatening course would have been picked up long ago and would have caused a mission re-schedule. Any other questions?"

There were none. Marcel rose to his feet. "Thanks, Yev. You all have your specific responsibilities in the context of the transition. Otherwise it will be business as usual except during the burns. Keep me informed of any equipment anomalies – we don't need any avoidable surprises for the next couple of weeks. Thank you."

In a couple of minutes Marcel was back in his office with Julia, Chang and Henri, and the door closed behind them. "Wow, that was painless!" said Julia. "Did anyone pick up anything untoward?" There was silence.

Finally Henri said, "Yes." They all turned to him. "The whole thing was about the basics of the transition, stuff they've all heard before. The only time that a question could have been asked about Schindler and Brady was when Marcel asked 'Any other questions?'"

"And?" said Marcel.

"All eyes were then on you, Marcel, clear and attentive, with one exception."

Julia turned her head slightly to one side. "Who?"

"Genes."

"It's hardly conclusive," said Chang. "Aren't you trying a bit too hard to find something?"

"Yes, I am trying hard," shot back Henri, "but if you had been watching as closely as I was at that moment, you would have seen that he was the odd one out."

"OK, just supposing you are right that Genes has an agenda we don't know about, what should we do that we're not doing already?" Chang apparently had a certain respect for Henri's intuition.

"I'm just going to monitor his movements very thoroughly," said Henri. "I'm going to make sure that I can account for his whereabouts every minute of the day, and I want you all to watch him carefully whenever you are working with him."

"OK," said Marcel. "Anything else?"

Julia and Chang sat quietly considering the implications. They both looked up at each other at the same instant and frowned. The meeting broke up.

14
Into the Wormhole

Hannah Cohen and Freddy Jones found themselves sharing a lift as they returned to their stations, both of them staring rather intensely at the floor. Freddy looked up and gave her a thin smile. "Are you scared?" he asked. "I am."

"Yes, I am," she admitted with a sigh. "I thought about it when I was asked to do the mission, but then the challenge and excitement of working in alien conditions sort of carried me over the dam wall. Now this seems like a moment of truth and I really don't know if human beings can survive this transition. I feel a bit out of it with all these gung-ho scientist and engineer types, and I miss my partner, his calmness and his wisdom." She gave him a long, sad look.

"Come up and have a coffee," said Freddy. "Let's chat."

They went into Freddy's office and sat in big, soft chairs that almost swallowed them up. They talked about their childhoods – his in Wales, hers in Israel – so different in their environment, but so similar in being the only children of devoted parents. She listened to his stories of boyhood adventures and magical moments, told in an irresistible Welsh lilt, and her smile grew broader and broader. She talked of Hanukkah lights, of bearded uncles who told her fantastic stories, of her riotous military service and the pain of leaving home to study abroad. It was cathartic and just what they both needed. Finally they talked about the mission.

"We are soldiers, Hannah; we are here to do our duty for mankind. We chose to accept and no one tried to hide the risks," said Freddy, not with total conviction.

"Yes, I know, and I wouldn't change it. I see the anxiety in the eyes of my staff and I put on my most assured look of confidence and authority. I can convince myself when I'm doing my job. It's not so easy when I'm alone."

"Yes, that's just leadership 1A. We will go down fighting if we have to, we are well trained to. I don't think about it much. I try to put my anxiety in the context that it is a natural consequence of breaking new ground. We must expect the unexpected, and it is the unexpected that requires the presence of us intelligent human beings. All very logical, but I need a hug sometimes."

They both laughed, got up and embraced. "Thanks, Freddy," said Hannah and she turned to go.

"What do you think of Commander Piccard?" He seemed to want to prolong their conversation.

Hannah turned and looked at him, her head on one side. "I think she has been well chosen for her role. She's analytical, courageous, even ruthless, and she believes in herself and in mankind. At the beginning I didn't think she had the weight for the job, but now I see her exercising her authority with much more conviction. I would stand and fight with her if needs be. How do you see her?"

Freddy blew out his cheeks. "Sometimes I think she needs a good cry, or perhaps a good fuck. I would like to think that she has the depth to engage with real people, not just professional robots, but I haven't seen it."

Hannah laughed. "I think you are being too cruel. It's her first command. She's naturally concerned about maintaining distance. You are totally at home with your people in your farmyard, just as I am comfortable with my medical staff. She has a large crew, many of whom have vital skills she could not possibly have. She can't be a mother to them as well!"

"Yeah, maybe I need a mother," said Freddy with a grin.

"Count me out!" said Hannah, still smiling, and left.

With the transmission time now at four and a half hours each way, Hannah's communications with Jafar had become reports rather than conversations and a lot of natural intimacy was lost. This time the news that Hannah was about to deliver was so serious that she was glad to not have to face Jafar's immediate response.

"Well, Jafar my darling," she began, "I have pretty momentous news for you. Firstly, Helmut Schindler, our chief biochemist, has been murdered in a fashion very similar to Kazarov, the Russian pilot, only he has been stabbed through the heart from behind. Colonel Bertin had found a discarded micro-syringe and Schindler was analysing its contents when he was murdered. He's under tremendous pressure and keeps grilling me about what it could have contained, but it's disappeared so I have no idea. Also a soldier, one of our more senior men, has gone missing while supposedly guarding Schindler.

"I had a good chat with Freddy Jones, who runs the farmyard. He thinks the Commander is overwrought and needs a good fuck – how like a man! I think she needs a friend and perhaps it should be me. I'm looking for the right opportunity to get closer to her. I like her. She's incredibly courageous and she uses her authority very sparingly and effectively, and completely without arrogance. She's furious that there's another security crisis now, at what turns out to be a very delicate stage of our mission. Everyone in the command team is very tense, but she refuses to be distracted. She says it's Bertin's problem, and her mission will continue as planned.

"That, my darling, I can now tell you, is to traverse to a solar system which houses a habitable planet by means of an artificially induced wormhole."

Hannah paused, as if taking in the enormity of what she had just said for the first time.

"Although it has remained a strictly guarded secret until now, this has already been done safely by an unmanned vehicle. We will of course be the first humans to do it, but the scientists on board are telling us that we won't feel a thing."

Hannah allowed a grin to spread across her face.

"I'm terribly excited about it, Jafar, and I think everybody on board feels that we are just so lucky to have been chosen for this mission." Then, with a look of real concern on her face, "I do hope you understand that this had to be kept a secret, Jafar, and you won't hear about it in the news until we come out the other side. Just wish me luck and think of me going faster and further than anyone has ever gone before. I love you!"

When Jafar received this message some five hours later he just stared at the ebullient image on the screen before him and felt a lump in his throat. "Good luck, little Hannah-le," he whispered. Then he delivered a loving and supportive response, which, he mused, would reach her perhaps some days later, or perhaps not …

He stopped the machine and weighed his next words carefully.

"The news here is not so positive," he began. "There has been a missile attack on a meeting in San Francisco called to address the failure of the Hong Kong climate control conference. The Chinese President, the Japanese Prime Minister and twenty other senior politicians were killed, together with more than fifty leading scientists. Apparently the missile was launched off-shore, probably from a submarine, and no one knows who did it or why. According to our man on the spot, there was widespread looting of the damaged buildings and the police just shot the looters on the spot. It was absolute chaos. Global stock markets have crashed, the press is blaming everybody from aliens to religious extremists, and there have been riots against the establishment around the world."

The message was paused there, then continued a day later.

"I'm in Dhaka now. The city is completely under water and 85 per cent of the country is flooded. The floating corpses of people and animals are everywhere. No one knows the death toll. A man came up to me and pushed two little children into my arms and then ran away. I took them back to the hotel to feed them but they wouldn't let me take them inside and I had to give the doorman a huge bribe to let me in the back door with them."

At this point two dark, scared little faces appeared on the screen behind Jafar.

"I've tried to find one of the relief agencies to take them but they are completely overwhelmed by the scale of this flood, even though it happens almost every year. I'll never be allowed to take them back to Beirut – the city is overrun with refugees already – so I'm going to stay here until I get this sorted out. The agency is no help, of course." He sighed.

"However," he brightened up, "your cousin Hepsibah's daughter Sally has given birth to healthy triplets in Berlin, so you'll have an attentive audience for your stories of the fantastic when you get back. I love you very much."

His face on the screen looked immensely tired and sad as he signed off.

* * *

"This is Prometheus command. Booster rocket firing will commence in thirty minutes. All crew are to secure their stations and execute lock-down procedures. Electronic sign-off must be completed by 10.20 hours."

Click.

Arun Dar stepped out of the body dryer, inspected his long, slender body, and slipped into his pilot's uniform. The son of a general in the Pakistani army, Arun had always assumed that his place would be in the front rank of anything he chose to do. He had played both football and tennis at international level while cruising through his degree in astrophysics, and had cultivated the studied humility of an accomplished sports star. He truly worshipped his patrician mother and treated the girls who flocked after him with the greatest politeness and respect. Despite this immaculately polished exterior, Arun was a ruthless competitor, and, once provoked beyond a certain point, quite wild.

On the flight deck Arun slipped into his ergo-couch, and grinned at his co-pilot, Sanam Ghorashian. She looked across at him and maintained a totally neutral expression. She thought him impossibly handsome, naturally elegant, quietly competent and somehow devoid of the typical bravado bullshit that she so much hated in male pilots. This was the first time that they would fly operationally together, and she wasn't at all sorry that Kazarov was gone. They went through their checklist procedure almost at a whisper. Finally Sanam announced, "Ready to commence booster ignition."

There was thirty seconds' silence. "Commence booster ignition sequence," commanded the Flight Director. A low rumble could be heard from the back of the ship as it jerked forward, pinning them into their couches. Sanam was all business, checking the attitude and trajectory of the ship, its acceleration rate and velocity, engine performance and fuel burn constantly, looking for any signs of anomaly from the programmed flight performance. She retained total concentration for her 120-minute stint at the controls, then turned to her co-pilot. "It's all yours, Arun, and she's right on the button."

"Copy that, Sanam."

She turned and watched him, his long fingers moving across the controls as though he was playing a musical instrument. She watched his eyes as they searched the data screens, absorbing, calculating, confirming, with never the hint of a frown of concentration touching his smooth brow. She looked at his silky, coffee-coloured skin, his glossy black hair and his delicate, sculptured chin and she thought, 'This is a man I would like to be close to.'

Arun could see that her face was turned towards him in his peripheral vision, and it sharpened all his sensibilities. A flicker of a smile passed his lips and he moved his head as he went about his task in the slightly self-conscious way people do when they know they are being watched. There was some sort of pheromone interaction going on; he could feel it.

As Prometheus reached the mouth of the wormhole she was dead centre and travelling at 3,200 km/second. The boosters were shut off and the blackness of the universe outside became tinged with blue. Arun turned towards Sanam and gave her a winning smile. "Now, my beauty," he said, addressing no one in particular, "let us see what the Gods have hidden from us." Sanam narrowed her eyes and briefly cast him as a God in her mind. 'You won't be hiding anything from me,' she thought.

* * *

Shinji Yamamoto had called his entire team of fifteen IT engineers together in one meeting. Once they had settled he wasted no time in getting to the point. "Our video monitoring system is being hacked and manipulated in real time. We are going to clean up the system and upgrade the encryption. Billy and Ahmed will do the re-programming but I want each of you to carry out visual inspections of the video installations to check for tampering and bugging. Here is a list of the sectors each of you is to inspect." He leaned forward and elaborately pressed the 'send' command on his phone. "I want to be notified the moment any anomalies are found."

"Are there going to be any changes to the automated data review processes?" Shelley Matthews wanted to know.

"The rules have not changed, Shelley. Data confidentiality can only be overridden in an emergency which threatens the integrity of the mission."

"Uh-uh," said Shelley. "Bertin is getting access. Please clarify."

"Colonel Bertin is the sole individual on the ship who has the authority to decide if there is a threat to the mission. He is not accountable to me…"

"No, I bet he isn't. I just wanna know whether our rights to privacy are being abused."

"Don't be absurd, Shelley." Yamamoto was getting irritated. "Everyone's privacy is protected until such time as they have been shown to have broken the ISEA code of practice."

"Oooh, what are you getting up to, Shelley, that would surprise us? Naughty, naughty."

"Shut up, Ben!" Shelley was getting flushed. "Here we are, the vanguard of humanity, and we're subject to the same old 'Big Brother needs to know' bullshit."

"If there is any abuse of privacy, I'll be the first one to tell you about it and punitive steps will be taken to correct it. For the time being, however, the ship's command has every right to have reliable information on who is doing what and where in the operational sphere and it's our job to deliver it." Yamamoto lifted both hands to signal the end of the discussion.

Five minutes later he was on the phone to Henri Bertin. "Yes, we had one very vocal opponent in Shelley Matthews, but she's always argumentative on privacy issues. She doesn't fit the behaviour profile you gave me. Three of the others did." He provided the names and sectors to which they had been assigned.

"Thanks, Shinji," said Henri. "Let's put them on the close watch list."

* * *

Henri selected two of his security detail to assist him in carrying out a systematic search of the annulus of the ship. They began with the farmyard sector at the nose, burning through the inner skin of the ship and installing access doors at strategic locations. It was tough and unpleasant work. The thick insulation on the other side of the inner shell responded to the heat of the blowtorches by producing pungent fumes. It was very cold inside the annulus and insulated protective clothing was required to search the area, which was unlit, included a lot of infrastructural machinery, and had not been designed to allow easy movement. By the end of the first day of work Henri was more convinced than ever that the annulus of the ship provided almost unlimited opportunities for hiding places for a group of insurgents. It would not have been difficult to construct quarters in there which could be secured and linked up to the ship's utilities.

'How many are there,' he wondered, 'and how much do they know about the workings of the ship?' He badly needed some reliable intelligence, or just a lucky break. But the hacking of the IT monitoring system was a sophisticated operation which had to have had insider help. He shuddered when he thought how vulnerable the crew was against a ruthless internal enemy.

* * *

By the third day since entering the wormhole, the tail of the ship had adopted a suffused red glow, while the nose seemed to be bathed with soft violet. Prometheus had broken all known records for the velocity of a man-made object. The crew went about their business with a slightly crazed air reminiscent of The Flying Dutchman. While the physicist's predictions were borne out that they would feel no discomfort despite their phenomenal velocity and escalating rate of acceleration, the crew were constantly eyeing the diagram of the ship's progress towards the point of inflection on their monitors, as though they did not truly believe that they could bypass such an extreme cosmological anomaly without catastrophic consequences.

However, Prometheus continued on its course with serene stability. There was no detectable buffeting and no damage to the outer skin reported by the monitoring devices. One hour prior to passing the point of inflection, Sanam and Arun yielded the piloting controls to their team-mates – Deputy Commander Conradi, who had stepped in to replace Major Kazarov, and Tim Cochran, an American who was, to Sanam, the epitome of the 'bullshit bravado air-ace type'.

"Arun, come and watch the inflection point fly-by with me," said Sanam as they stepped out of their ergo-couches.

"Ah, Sanam, if I do that I shall miss it, because I shall be unable to take my eyes off you." He seemed to have adopted a Bollywood accent for this line, leaving an air of oriental ambiguity.

"Well, Arun, you'll just have to make a special effort in the interests of science, won't you?" and she took his hand quite firmly and led him out of the control centre. Their conversation on the way up to the crew quarter's level was animated and loaded with innuendo. He, playing the wide-eyed innocent, she the boss, having everything her way, as usual. As she closed the door of her room behind him he stood there for a long minute, genuinely amazed by its lavish and exotic furnishings. Sanam stood behind him and felt her heart pounding. 'Play it cool' she said to herself.

* * *

At the other end of the ship, the two members of the Induced Gravity team who were on duty were settled back in their ergo-couches, when a well-known, friendly face entered. "Hi there! Have you come to share the fly-by with us? What's the matter?!"

There were two muffled cracks, then silence. The visitor moved quietly, crossing the induced gravity control room with a canvas bag, and entered the plant room. He was in there for barely ten minutes, then passed back by the two staring bodies in their ergo-couches, and left.

* * *

Meanwhile things were getting steamy in Sanam's room. The teasing innuendo was still going on while they discussed everything from philosophy through sociology to cosmology, but she was touching him with little gestures; his arm, his hand, his face. Finally he exploded, lifting her into the air and cradling her as he kissed her with trembling passion. Sanam just complied, arching her back and thrusting up her breasts. She smiled, eyes half closed, as he laid her on the bed, stripped off her clothes and then his. She looked at the slender, elegant body before her, put her arms around his neck, her legs around his waist, and pulled herself effortlessly onto him.

At that precise moment they heard a distant 'pop' somewhere in the ship. The lights flickered, and Sanam and Arun, entwined as they were, drifted away from the floor, weightless. Neither gave a moment's thought to the cause of this astonishing physical freedom that had been bestowed on them, and, as all creation lay before them, they engaged in the most exquisite sensation that either, or in fact anyone, had ever experienced.

They went on, greedily drinking in the sublime pleasure of it as the stars before them began to flash by at an incredible pace, transforming their view into a kaleidoscopic rainbow. A brief shadow flashed over them and then the process reversed and a completely alien window on the universe began to form from the chaos.

Exhausted, Sanam and Arun slid apart in mid-air, just holding on to each other by their fingertips, watching the galaxy in all its splendour rush by.

15
Assault

Arlette's mind raced as the restraint belts of her ergo-couch were automatically activated. She called the Induced Gravity section head. "Dima, what's happened?"

"We've lost the main generator in the lower ring," came the anguished reply. "I can't get a response from my crew down there in the control room and the video link doesn't seem to be working. I'm on my way right now."

Her blood ran cold at the mention of video problems. She mentally redialled. "Henri, I've..."

He cut across her, his voice calm and precise, without a trace of his usual Haitian accent. "Lock the control centre down. Put on your weightless gear. Prepare for possible armed assault. You will have military protection within two minutes."

"Dima reports a video link problem with the lower IG control room," said Arlette breathlessly. "Is it...?"

"Yes, the monitoring system is being compromised. Act as instructed." It was clear from Henri's voice that he was on the move.

Arlette initiated the lock-down sequence and shouted

out instructions. The other occupants of the control centre acted with varying degrees of effectiveness, some almost immediately into the weightless mobility outfits and scrambling for what little cover there was, others drifting about helplessly and calling for help.

There was a deafening explosion as the steel lower access door was blown out of its frame. It arced into the control centre, hitting the roof with a crash and a shower of debris before careening around the room, arbitrarily taking out electronic equipment with showers of sparks. Five men in fatigues and masks raced in, their magnetic boots clattering on the floor as they spread out and, on a shout of "Pandora!", opened fire indiscriminately on the helpless floating figures, screaming abuse as they did so.

One man, the apparent leader, made his way to the centre of the room and held up a sword above his head. "Cease fire! Give me the scumbag Piccard, or I'll kill every one of you!"

No one moved. He pointed the sword at the helpless, floating figure of Jake Thibault, desperately trying to paddle his way back down to his station, and a burst of automatic fire followed. Arterial blood spurted from wounds in his body as it performed a macabre dance of death within the curling threads of crimson around it.

Without any warning a single shot rang out from the observation platform, high above. The man with the sword wavered and slumped, the back of his scull removed in an ugly puff of red vapour, and the sword drifted away from his hand. Henri Bertin's voice boomed out over the loudspeaker system. "You are surrounded by snipers on all sides! Throw away your weapons!"

The response was a snarling pandemonium of screams and automatic fire as each of the insurgents lurched towards the remaining crew members, firing indiscriminately. They were stopped in their tracks by sniper fire before they had taken more than two or three steps, their quivering bodies waving like willow trees in the wind, their feet anchored to the floor where they stood by their magnetic boots.

"Be prepared for a second wave!" boomed the voice of Henri. Nothing stirred except for the muffled sound of the security militia scrambling to take new positions outside the control centre walls, then silence. Again the clatter of magnetic boots, this time those of the paramedics streaming in and up the walls, methodically sorting the living wounded from the dead.

Henri Bertin appeared briefly at the remains of the lower access door. He was on the earphone. "Shinji, what is the state of the monitoring system?"

"We have no breaches at present," came the answer, "and no movement in any of the connection corridors. I'll let you know immediately if there is any change in status."

"OK," breathed Henri, puffing out his cheeks with relief. "Now tell me where these guys came from."

"They came up through the emergency stairwells from level 2, that's all I have. The cameras on levels 1 and 2 were knocked out at the same time as the induced gravity generator blew."

Henri turned this over in his mind. 'Levels 1 and 2 – Propulsion and Fuel Storage. Why didn't I follow my hunch and start the search at the bottom?'

He beckoned to two of his militia, entered the control

centre and headed for the practically headless figure who had been wielding a sword just a few minutes earlier. There was just enough left of his face to recognise him. It was Brady.

* * *

Induced gravity was restored some two hours later.

Dima Koval sat before the Command Group, his head in his hands. His eyes were red, his lips pursed and he was breathing heavily.

"Dima, please tell us what happened with the lower generator." Arlette's voice was soft. She was shocked, she was grieving, and she let it show.

"Hah!" said Dima. "It was shorted out by an explosive charge, quite a small one, just enough to knock out the system. We just had to replace a couple of components. It's working fine now, but..."

"Take it easy," said Arlette quietly.

"I have two dead comrades!" he blurted out, his chin quivering with anguish.

"Yeah," said Arlette, "we have all lost comrades. We are on a mission where loss of life is a possibility we have to manage. In this case the cause must be thoroughly understood so that it can be contained. Was there a security breech prior to the explosion?"

Dima stared at his hands. He shrugged. "I don't know," he said. "I have to suppose that someone entered the control room who had the authority to do so, killed my people and set the charge. I have no records. The security door was intact."

Arlette looked up at Henri, who sat with his head bowed, listening intently. He did not react.

"OK, and the system is now working normally?"

"Yes, but I don't have enough people to run it reliably, let alone protect it."

"OK," said Arlette again. "Take two engineers from the maintenance team. Philip Schneider will be expecting you."

Dima rose unsteadily from his seat. "And what about protection?" he demanded, looking accusingly at Henri.

"Entrance to your section will be restricted to your team and the command team only, as of now," said Henri flatly. Dima left.

"Right!" said Arlette. "We have lost five valuable people, not counting the five assailants, on top of the loss of Kazarov and Schindler. Why?"

"I am expecting that the post-mortems on the five dead assailants will give us a lead. They were all first-class people, with no record of criminality or instability. Their crazed behaviour in the control centre was too bizarre, too out of character to have been natural. They were under some kind of influence and I'm sure it has something to do with that micro-syringe." Henri looked steadily at Arlette.

"Theories, theories, Colonel Bertin, and not enough facts," she said firmly, but not unkindly. "What do you suppose was the motivation behind this attack?"

"Clearly to kill you, Commander," said Chang, who had been in the control centre at the time, "and that suggests they were trying to take control of the mission."

"I agree," said Henri quietly. Everyone looked at him. "The Pandora jibe in both the murders was an obvious reference to your stated objectives for the Prometheus mission. I have no doubt they would have killed you if they could have."

"And why?" Arlette asked. "I may have ruffled a few feathers in my career, but I don't think I've made enemies on this scale."

"It's not personal, Commander," interjected Julia. "There has to be another agenda here. Control of this mission could have political or even criminal implications. They could have blown us up by now if they had simply wanted to stop us. We must assume that the protagonists are trying to use us, not to destroy us. To sustain this mission requires the compliance of most of those on board. You could not do it with a skeleton crew."

There was silence. No one disagreed.

"So, what about this man Brady? He was clearly the leader, but you don't seem to think his death marks the end of it? Who else is in this?"

Henri sighed. "I'd just be guessing if I went any further," he said, "but I am sure that all five of them were being manipulated by someone on board. The communication time lapse alone makes it impossible to control this kind of activity from Earth. We have to find out who he/she/they are and neutralise them. It is as it was before – a police action – except that we should soon have much more to go on."

"Colonel Bertin, all the other four assailants were, as far as we knew, loyal and reliable members of this crew until yesterday. How do we know how many more could be influenced to carry out this kind of attack?" Arlette was beginning to get angry.

"I'm expecting data from Mission Control and from

the post-mortems at any time. The next part of this discussion has to be based on facts, not speculation." Henri got up.

"Sit down, Colonel Bertin!" shouted Arlette. "The loyal members of this crew will all know of this attack by now and will be wanting an explanation. Their concerns can't wait until all this testing is complete. I have to talk to them now! So let's get busy with a holding story."

Julia took this as her cue. "I'll write a script for you, Commander," she said. "I propose that the story will be as follows: a terrorist attack occurred yesterday afternoon, prefaced by the temporary disablement of the gravity system, taking the lives of two members of the Induced Gravity team and three members of the control centre staff – I will of course detail their names and service records. The Prometheus security team engaged immediately and neutralised the terrorists, and we are grateful to them that our losses were not even more severe. We have been working with home-base security to ensure that this threat has now been eliminated. Our hearts go out to the families of our lost crew-mates etc. etc. The funerals will be held tomorrow at 10.00 hours.

"Despite these tragic events, our capacity to complete our mission, and our resolve to do so, will not be affected. Then I'll reconfirm our mission rationale and objectives, work in a bit about our historic transition through the wormhole, and end with a glowing reference to the exploration of new worlds which lie before us. OK?"

"Fine," said Marcel, "and I'll release my report on the new science of wormhole transition about an hour later, just to keep everybody distracted and upbeat."

Arlette nodded, her face grim, and waved the meeting closed.

* * *

"Colonel Bertin!" Hannah's voice was breathless. "I've just received the results of the initial examination on the five assailants from our clinical pathologist." Henri waited. "They were all infected by a virus of some kind. It is not something we recognise, but it has some similarities to the meningitis virus."

"Send me the report in a form I can transmit to home-base right away," said Henri, "including any hunches you have. All they have at present is a molecular scan which may not even be relevant. Oh, and cultivate some of that stuff for further tests once we receive a response."

"Right" said Hannah.

As he waited for the response from home-base, Henri began a search of the ship's annulus at level 1. He had decided not to contact the section leader, but within a few minutes of the commencement of a burn to open up the hull to inspection, Genes Clayton arrived on the scene. "What the hell are you doing?" he demanded.

"Inspecting the inner hull for traces of use by the assailants," said Henri, looking straight at Genes with a bland expression on his face.

"Whoa!" said Genes. "Come and look at the operating layout before you charge in there. A burn in the wrong place could have very unpleasant consequences." Henri and his two-man militia were shepherded into Genes' office, where he promptly began to project a series of three-dimensional plans on the screen. Genes was in his element, detailing the location of the most sensitive parts of the fuel storage and transport systems and describing the function of each component in colourful language. "Here, here and here" he said, circling the areas with his laser pointer," we have toxic particles nastier than a hornet up your ass, and here, here, and all over this area we have an explosion risk so delicate that it would vaporise you on a flea's fart."

"I'm aware of the general layout and the nature of the equipment," said Henri, "and we don't need to disturb any of it once we're in the annulus."

"I'm mighty glad to hear it," said Genes, and Henri wondered whether his apparent relief might be genuine, and, if so, what the implications were.

It took the team sixteen hours to search the area and they found nothing. Genes seemed to be neither pleased nor surprised. "I reckon I'd have heard a bunch of terrorists holed up in my patch," was all he said.

Alerted by a signal that a message had arrived from home-base, Henri charged into his office, closed the door, flicked on his computer and downloaded the video. General Lee made a short introduction, then handed over to a presentation by the high-security pathology team. He needn't have bothered; the message was very short.

Summarising the data, the chief pathologist, a Dr Garfunkel, said, "We have found a structure in the molecular scan of the contents of the micro-syringe that almost certainly corresponds to the virus detected in the bodies of the assailants. The reaction of test animals to similar viruses which we have synthesised from our data shows that pathological behaviour is induced on infection by this type of virus in some, but not all cases. On further investigation we have learned that certain subjects have a genetic predisposition to this type of response. While we have more work to do on how this pathological behaviour is triggered in those affected, we are fairly certain that this virus can be used by someone, who also has access to the crew's genetic data, to manipulate susceptible members and cause them to commit acts of violence. Fortunately you will have live samples of the virus in the samples withdrawn from the bodies of the assailants, so your pathology department can use standard procedures to produce a vaccine promptly."

Henri sat back in his chair and stared at the screen. "Holy fuck!" he whispered.

16
The Wayward 19

At the hastily summoned command meeting Henri replayed the video. The reaction in general was one of relief; questions were still unanswered but the containment task was becoming better focused.

"So what is your next step, Colonel Bertin?" asked Arlette.

"The most obvious course of action would be to notify everyone that there's a viral infection going around and that we want to contain it by taking blood samples from all crew members. We'd know pretty soon how many other potential aggressors we have and who they are, either because we detect the virus in their blood, or because they refuse to give samples on some pretext." Henri looked around, eyebrows raised.

"What are you going to do with them once you've identified them?" asked Julia.

"Isolate them and question them one-on-one as to how the infection came about and what they know about the triggers," said Henri.

"Do you really think they're going to tell you, given the sophistication of this conspiracy? What are you going to do if they don't cooperate? Waterboard them?" Julia had her arms crossed, a slightly amused, quizzical expression on her face.

"If I'm confronted with non-cooperation, I'll keep them isolated until they can be persuaded otherwise," said Henri; "by whatever means I deem necessary," he added, emphatically.

"Alright," said Arlette. "I'll call Hannah and get her to prepare an announcement, but tell me: how are you going to identify the organisers, and how are you going to prevent them from infecting others right after this series of tests is completed?"

"I don't have an answer to the first question yet, Commander," replied Henri, "but I am confident that I can prevent any more infections when I know who the targets may be, and we'll know that as soon as we receive the genetic data from home-base. Once we have neutralised the potential assailants I think we can force the organisers to show their hands."

* * *

The following morning Henri called Arlette. "I have the list," he said. "There are 24 names on it, including all of the five dead assailants. Hannah's team is working on a vaccine. We should be ready to inoculate against further infection by tomorrow morning but we don't know whether the vaccine will prevent those already infected from responding violently if they are triggered."

Arlette drew in her breath. "How do we defend ourselves if all the remaining nineteen targets have already been infected and decide to attack us again?"

"We are monitoring all the suspects as we speak," said Henri, "and we will prevent them from assembling by force if necessary. We'll detain them one by one at the clinic if they test positive when reporting for their vaccinations."

Arlette thought this over. She was still in shock over the brutality of the attack in the control centre, but it made sense to deal with each suspect individually and well away from his home territory. "Alright," she said, "but you had better make damn sure that you are in place to pick off any aggressor before there's any repeat of the carnage in the control centre."

* * *

Hannah's announcement was made in a motherly tone.

"Dear crew-mates," she began, "I'm afraid we have a rather virulent infection going around. The symptoms are flu-like with severe headache and muscular weakness, and in view of the importance of having all the crew members in peak condition for the critical tasks ahead, we have decided that we need to take immediate steps to prevent any further cases. A vaccine has been developed and tested and we are ready to treat you all. I will notify each one of you of the time of your appointment at the clinic, and I promise that the treatment will be painless. Thank you." The last comments were made with a smile on her face.

Meanwhile a maintenance team was busy making rooms around the clinic secure for detention, and four militiamen took up positions as orderlies, their weapons stowed out of sight. "Be prepared to use force immediately if any of the patients becomes aggressive," Henri instructed them, "and be especially alert when a patient is announced as Mr or Ms."

Henri met with the command team and Hannah for dinner in Arlette's quarters. They were poring over the appointment schedule and especially the position of the nineteen on it. "Well, you've managed to get them all in on the first day," said Julia with relief. "How do you expect it to go with patients who are infected, know it and expect to be triggered – in other words those likely to be highly suspicious of the vaccination process?"

"I see three probable responses," said Henri: "no shows, sudden aggression, or acquiescence. In case one we will send a couple of militiamen to 'remind the patient of their appointment' – in fact to arrest them as inconspicuously as possible. That's why there's always a good half hour between the appointments of the nineteen. In case two we will restrain and detain immediately. It's case three where we have to be extremely careful. The patient may be playing for time or blissfully unaware. In these cases we need to monitor them for a period of time after the vaccination – can we do that, Hannah?"

"We can do half an hour," she replied, "and we'll put them into a room that is continuously monitored. But we don't expect any visible clinical reaction to the vaccine – it will have to be a case of monitoring suspicious behaviours."

"I don't think that's good enough," opined Julia. "If I were the agency who could control this group I would instruct them to avoid responses one and two – they are just lose–lose. Either you attack while you still have control over them, or you bide your time and assess the impact of the vaccine. You don't take a course of action which exposes them to being detected and taken out one by one."

"I have to agree with you, Julia," said Henri. Arlette, Chang and Marcel were nodding. "The surprise attack failed – I doubt that they'll try that again, especially considering that they can assume that we know a lot more than we did before. They'd need to lull us into a false sense of security first. They want us to assume that the vaccine had worked 100 per cent, and they probably have the means to check that."

"So where the hell is this clandestine group of miscreants operating?" demanded Arlette. "It's intolerable that we have an active fifth column on this ship and we don't know where they are! Why haven't you found them?"

Henri looked pained. "Let's be frank here," he said. "If this had been some opportunistic little operation, set up on a whim, we'd have found them long ago. It's much worse than that. Their base had to have been engineered into the ship when it was built in such a way that it occupies space that we wouldn't or couldn't search."

"Like what?"

"A secure storage area, a fuel tank, a motor, a large piece of equipment of some kind. We cannot just burn holes in things to see if they really are what they're supposed to be."

"Then we must redouble our surveillance capabilities and monitor every part of the ship," said Arlette.

"Yes, that's an ongoing priority for IT," said Henri, "and I'm hoping that the vaccination exercise will cause one of these operatives to blow his cover."

The focus of the discussion turned back to the vaccination programme.

"Hannah, what are the probabilities that the vaccine will disable the virus in those already infected?"

"Oh, the vaccine contains an antibody that will knock out the active virus in the patients, Commander, but it may be that it has chronically modified the brain function. We are researching this as we speak, but it will take a long time to get an answer using synthetic tissue. We would not really know unless we could work with the brain of one of those who had been infected."

"Well, let's do that!" Henri interjected. "Let's just take out one or two of the Wayward 19 and do further tests on them."

Hannah looked shocked. "We couldn't do that without the patient's approval; it would contravene..."

Henri cut across her. "Commander, I think we have to consider all measures to regain control of this very threatening situation."

Arlette looked at Julia, but it was Chang who spoke. "We have identified the Wayward 19, as you call them, from their genetic profiles and we shall know quite soon which of them have been infected, or if anyone else has, from blood tests. Let's not raise the suspicions of our adversary here by making people disappear on some improbable pretext. We can recall a few patients in a couple of days for further tests if need be, but for now let them think that we are confident that we have dealt with the threat. We can't afford to exclude valuable crew members from the ship's operations. We have already lost too many."

"I'm not proposing wholesale elimination!" protested

Henri. “But if we'd known in advance about the intentions of the five assailants, wouldn't we have taken them out before they could perpetrate those grotesque murders in the control centre?”

“That's hypothetical, Colonel Bertin; we can never know people's actions in advance. In the meantime we are going to adhere to the standards of civilised people dealing with others who have an externally induced mental dysfunction. How can we retain the respect and confidence of our crew otherwise? We know who they are and we have the tools in our hands to deal with them. We can review this again after completion of the vaccination programme.”

Arlette stood up and prepared to leave the table. Her colleagues followed but Hannah excused herself. “Big day tomorrow,” she said.

17
An Unwelcome Discovery

It was indeed a big day, which began in the early hours of the morning with the reorientation of the ship and a four-hour booster burn to slow her down and adjust her course. Sanam and Arun were again on pilot duty together, apparently enjoying their supposed distinction of being human civilisation's first hyper-velocity weightless lovers. Without impugning their professional discipline, they managed to communicate, by facial expression, thoughts that only the two of them could share. When their duty shift was completed, and Prometheus was on course for its first planetary rendezvous outside the solar system, they retired with smoking eyes to Sanam's quarters and indulged their lust once more before the unfamiliar star-scape. There was a moment when Sanam briefly considered what it would take to disable the induced gravity system for their personal pleasure, but the telepathic communication between them was so refined that Arun had lifted her off her feet at the same instant and subjected her to a sensation almost as sublime as before.

The vaccination programme had been underway for some ninety minutes when Ginger Clark reported for her appointment. The receptionist checked the name but did not look up from her screen as she announced, "Ms Ginger Clark, IT department, booth 3." Two orderlies fell in beside her as she approached the booth and she stiffened slightly, then stopped, looking around her. Then the cheery voice of Dr Leonards called out, "Come on in, Ginger," and she went on in, cautiously.

Dr Leonards asked her briefly about her medical history, which he knew already, and whether she had had any recent flu symptoms. "Absolutely not," came the reply.

"Good," said Dr Leonards. "Let's make sure you stay that way. I'll take a blood sample first so that we have before-and-after records of your condition..."

"No," said Ginger.

"We have to do this, Ginger," went on Dr Leonards. "When we are using a newly developed vaccine. We have to test for any possible allergic reaction before..."

"No," said Ginger, and stood up.

Almost immediately she found herself seated again, her arms held down on the table by the two orderlies while Dr Leonards deftly pricked her finger and extracted a drop of blood. Ginger screamed. She writhed and kicked, a venomous expression on her face. "Now then, Ginger, this will calm you down," said the doctor, giving her a hefty injection. Gingers eye's widened, then closed slowly. She slumped forward.

"Right," said Dr Leonards, "we may have to do that proactively with our more highly strung patients." He dropped the blood sample onto a tiny transparent pad, which he slipped into a machine. He looked at the screen briefly. "Hmm, positive. There we are!" Unknowingly, the slumped body received her vaccination.

"She didn't like seeing her own blood," said one of the orderlies. "She stared at it like a crazy thing!"

Dr Leonards called Hannah Cohen and reported the incident, adding that the sight of blood had apparently triggered Ginger's outburst. Hannah promptly directed that the rest of the nineteen should be told that they were going to receive the vaccine, but should be heavily sedated first and then vaccinated.

When Ginger awoke several hours later she was told that she had fainted at the sight of the needle. She remembered nothing. As the day wore on, this process would be repeated another eighteen times, but no infections were detected outside of the selected group.

The command team met over dinner again with Hannah and reviewed the day's events.

"Smart to apply pre-emptive sedation," said Arlette with satisfaction, "What else did we learn?"

"Bill Leonards described Ginger Clark's response as crazed; an extreme hysterical reaction. It's not clear to me whether it was a response to being restrained or, as Bill thinks, to the sight of blood."

"For an induced trigger, blood would seem more practical," observed Henri, "but a violent reaction to restraint is also a useful trait in a soldier. I think we should conclude that we have nineteen potential terrorists on board, that we know who they are, and that they can probably be triggered by some kind of violent signal."

"Don't tell me that you want to take them all out,"

said Arlette. “We just don’t have the manpower to replace them”.

“No,” replied Henri. “I have a better idea.”

“Go on, amaze me.”

“I think we should test each one of them to see which triggers work, if they still do after the vaccination, and then re-recruit them for our own purposes.”

There was a long silence.

Finally Arlette asked, “How are you going to test them for triggers?”

“Have the psychology team work with them,” said Henri. “We have identified a disorder and we know its cause. Never mind who infected them and why; that’s peripheral now. We can have the triggers and their consequences identified and then decide how we are going to manage them.”

Everyone looked at Hannah.

“Yes, that’s within the scope of the psychology team,” she said slowly, “but if we want to explore the full range of responses, we’ll need an armed presence.”

“Easily arranged,” countered Henri.

“No, not the same people we used as orderlies in the clinic. Their faces alone might trigger a reaction. We need new people.”

“OK,” said Henri. “At least I can now be fairly confident that no other members of my team are infected, so I can supply six new faces.”

“Alright, I think we had better get going. I really don’t feel comfortable knowing we have nineteen potential psychopaths around.” She rose to leave. “I’ll get this started right away.”

At the other end of the table Arlette was staring ahead, her brow furrowed. "What?!" she said out loud, obviously on the receiving end of a CTT call. "Are you sure?"

Apparently the answer was affirmative.

She looked around the table at her companions, and decided that all of them should hear the news immediately.

"Navigation has just informed me", she said, "that, while they were doing a detailed sweep of the Omega 16 solar system, they detected a space–time anomaly. There is, apparently, an entrance to another wormhole on the orbit of gas giant 16-5."

There was silence around the table.

"Holy cow," said Marcel finally. "Where does it lead to?"

Arlette swallowed. "They are telling me that the outlet is not in the Milky Way; that the connection is to Andromeda."

All eyes were on Arlette. "To another galaxy?" Marcel's voice was thin, almost reedy. A dozen questions flashed through his mind, none of which could be answered. "Someone else got here first, from an utterly alien civilisation?"

"Whoa Marcel! Let's take this one step at a time. We don't know whether anyone else has been to Omega 16, or whether they intend to come, or what their intentions are when they get here," said Arlette, "but we can expect to get some insight as we progress our explorations. Would you, Chang and Julia please debrief Navigation fully on their data, and then propose some strategic options. I have instructed them to keep the lid on this until I am ready to make an announcement."

As Henri left the room, he mused on how much more important control of the Wayward 19 might turn out to be.

Hannah's team of eight psychologists and two psychiatrists were deployed in shifts to interview and test the nineteen suspects. It did not take them longer than their first three assessments to find out that all were transformed into a state of violent frenzy by the sight of blood and the words 'death', 'kill' and 'Pandora'. It took a little longer before it was learned that the sight of a sword blade inspired absolute obedience to the sword bearer. These findings were borne out in each successive assessment.

As Henri and Hannah sat discussing these results, the significance of the sword that Brady had carried, which Henri now placed on the table before them, suddenly struck both of them almost simultaneously. "Kazarov and Schindler!" exclaimed Hannah. "It was a sword they were killed with! They were ritual murders!"

Henri was nodding. "Words as triggers would be too easily manipulated. Even pathological murderers need to know who's giving the orders. But now we have it!"

"Perhaps it's not the only one?" said Hannah, eyebrows raised.

"Hmm, seems to me it could quickly become the 'must have' accessory of the season on Prometheus," mused Henri. "I know a couple of guys in maintenance who would just love to take a shot at making some copies. Do you think there's anything mystical about this particular sword, or do you think a half-decent copy would work?"

Hannah smiled. "I'm not much into mystical," she said,

"and unless that sword contains some kind of electronic device that can trigger a response in people infected by the virus, I'd say that a good copy would do just fine. How could those terrorists have known one sword from another? It looks pretty plain to me."

Henri picked it up and examined it closely. 'No dummy, this Hannah Cohen,' he thought. "There could be something inside the handle – we'll check it out."

There was just one problem – two of the twelve maintenance engineers on board were members of the Wayward 19. "I'd appreciate it, Hannah, if you could keep Columbo and Kinross under sedation while I get this job done," said Henri.

Hannah sighed. "Alright, I will," she said.

* * *

"I'm in it up to my ears, Jafar!" Hannah was telling him. "The substance that Helmut Schindler was analysing when he was murdered is a virus which modifies the response of genetically disposed individuals and allows them to be manipulated to perpetrate the most horribly violent crimes. Now I'm a party to a forced vaccination programme and psychological experiments to determine the triggers. Twelve people have been killed, seven of them murdered by whoever is controlling this conspiracy."

Hannah frowned. "I'm also now a de facto member of the command team and working closely with Henri Bertin to help get this under control. He's a very attractive and intelligent man but with a militaristic inclination to have all suspects summarily eliminated. Fortunately Julia

Rogers maintains a pragmatically balanced humanistic view and has the capacity to laugh at him when he gets too frightening.

"Commander Piccard? Well, she just manages the debate and keeps her options open. She seems to enjoy the confrontation but she never hesitates to make the tough choices. She's very alone, though, and I think she needs to offload sometimes. I have a feeling she's looking for a soulmate and I may find myself slipping into that role. Marcel Rousseau and Chang are just typical hard-baked operatives. Rousseau has an irritating habit of looking for sexual innuendo in just about everything but I must admit he is funny. Chang is just tough and inscrutable.

"What's happened to those two Bangladeshi children? Did you find a home for them? Will you come to Berlin with me to see my niece and her new triplets? I love you."

* * *

Marcel, Chang and Julia were sitting in the Navigation presentation room with Cobus Vermeulen, the head of the Navigation section, looking at a floor-to-ceiling projection of the Omega 16 planetary system. "Planet 16-3 is at 185 million kilometres from Omega 16 and 16-4 is at 265 million," said Cobus. They both have a habitable temperature range and atmosphere, but there's more CO2 and methane on 16-4 so 16-3 looks like an easier habitat for us humans. Now, we're heading for an inspection orbit around 16-3 here," Cobus pointed, "at which point 16-5 will be here" – he pointed again – "our LDST entrance is in the orbit of 16-6 and will be here, and the new discovery

– LDST 2 – will be there. I just hope that nothing nasty creeps out of there while we're busy on 16-3," he concluded.

The three visitors saw his point. Their escape route, should it be required, would be in full view of whoever might be observing them from some vastly distant world down that weird tube. "How sure can you be that LDST 2 is functional?" asked Marcel. "Perhaps it was used aeons ago and just hung around."

"'Fraid not," said Cobus. "There's a communication satellite just there" – he pointed at the mouth of LDST 2 – "it's spewing out data to someone, and certainly not in a form that we can recognise."

"Well, how do you know it's linked to the Andromeda galaxy?" asked Chang.

"That's the easy bit," said Cobus. "Andromeda has a very distinctive radiation profile, and what we are getting out of LDST 2 matches it exactly. What baffles me is why someone there would want to visit someone here. They just have to wait four and a half billion years and they'll be here anyway; our galaxies are on a collision course, as you know." Cobus got a wan smile for that one from Marcel, inscrutability from Chang and a thoughtful gaze from Julia. Not much fun, these guys, he thought.

"Have you detected any other activity, in the LDST or in the Omega 16 solar system?" ventured Julia.

"No," came the response. "There are no other artificial objects around, just the usual complement of rogue asteroids and stuff."

"How do you know whether anything is in orbit around one of the planets which we can't see?"

"Oh, we would pick up anything like that automatically.

We couldn't see anything that had landed on a moon or something of course, but that's not a feasible option for an intergalactic spaceship … as far as we know," Cobus added, giving the prospect some more thought.

"How much warning would we get if something was coming down LDST 2?" Chang wanted to know.

"We would have to set up a satellite receptor located at the entrance in order to receive any signal coming down the tube. We may want to do that in the interests of our own security, but if we do we would probably want to knock out the communications satellite that is already there on the assumption that it is armed, just as ours is." He paused and looked around at the uncomfortable faces of his visitors.

"That done, we really do not know how much longer an intergalactic wormhole is than an intragalactic one. We can put a laser beam down the tube until it hits something and is reflected back. So I'd say we'd get anything from ten to fifty days' notice of a new arrival."

"Thanks, Cobus," said Marcel. "Please let me know immediately if the status of LDST 2 changes."

He called Arlette and gave her a brief report. "Get back here, and call Bertin and fill him in," she said.

The three of them hurried back to command quarters. Henri was already there when they arrived.

"Right," said Arlette as they settled down around the table. "We are apparently not the only race prepared to come a long way to look at Omega 16. What action do you propose we take … Chang?"

Chang leant forward in his customary fashion, his fingers tightly entwined.

"The only data we have about these unwelcome visitors is that they almost certainly emanate from Andromeda, they have the capacity to create and utilise a wormhole on a vastly larger scale than we can, and they have a satellite here in Omega 16 which has almost certainly detected our arrival and can probably monitor our activities. I would conclude that this civilisation is probably more technically advanced than ours. The most likely reason for their presence is the same as ours, although I am baffled as to why they can't find a perfectly good alternative rocky planet in their own galaxy." Chang sat back and surveyed his colleagues.

"Well, I'll give you a theory," said Marcel. "If they are at least as advanced as we are, they will be aware that our galaxies are on an eventual collision course. Perhaps they want to secure a strategic foothold. However," he added, "does it matter? We find ourselves in a space accessible to aliens whose motives we can only guess at. We may be exposed already to weaponry vastly superior to ours. Can we really afford to sit and wait to see if they offer the hand of friendship?"

"I think not," said Henri. "Our primary responsibility is for the safety of this ship and its crew. If we were to be pre-emptively attacked we would be wiped out. I propose that we take out their satellite and put one of ours in place to monitor any activity in LDST 2."

"Well!" said Julia. "That's a great way to make friends and influence people. How do we expect them to react if we attack them first?"

"They won't know," said Henri. "We'll use a laser beam to disable their satellite, not a missile. That way they won't get any data on the cause of its destruction. It could be just a chance meteor strike."

"You can't be sure that you'll take it out instantly, that they won't have the means to trace the origin of the attack," said Julia. "It's a risk."

"I'm afraid it's a bigger risk to proceed with our exploration plans under the noses of an alien civilisation that seems to have an interest in the same chunks of real estate that we do. We damage some of their hardware – well, we could always excuse ourselves for that if it turns out that they have peaceful intentions," Henri said, sitting back and folding his arms. Marcel and Chang were nodding in agreement.

Arlette frowned. "I'm afraid we have no choice," she said. "I'll report our intentions to home-base and await their confirmation."

"That will take at least twenty-two hours. I don't think we can afford that amount of exposure. We need to act immediately to ensure the security of the ship." Henri was adamant.

"Prepare the satellite and one of the laser batteries, Colonel Bertin," said Arlette. "I'll give it some more thought while you do."

Henri made the calls.

18
Fire Red 1

On his way to the vehicle launch area Henri dropped in on Benny Tromper in Maintenance. “Hey, Benny, how are my Samurai swords coming along?”

“The swords will be works of art,” beamed Benny. “It’s the transmitter inside that’s giving IT a bit of a headache.”

“Oh?”

“Yeah, it’s a very complex combination of frequencies, Shinji says, and he’s battling to duplicate it. Still, my swords will nicely dispatch a villain or two without the need for any electronics,” he said with evident satisfaction. “By the way, do you know anything about Columbo and Kinross? The clinic’s telling me that they’re concerned about their reaction to the vaccine and they’re keeping them under observation. I’m short-handed now and I need them back asap. Can you apply some pressure for me?”

Henri shook his head. “I think they really do need to be careful about any potential health issues considering the scale of the manpower losses we’ve sustained.” He turned to leave.

"Bullshit," said Benny, grinning.

"Sorry?"

"I said 'bullshit,'" said Benny again. "Don't imagine that we can't see the connection between this vaccination programme and the terrorist attack, Colonel. The sooner you share the truth with us, the better we're all going to feel. Think about it."

Henri held his gaze, then he winked and grinned. "I know I can count on your loyalty, Benny, and you should know that you can count on the leadership to protect the lives and welfare of all loyal crew members. We've had some knocks, but we're ahead now. Trust me," he said, and left.

The launch area, a brightly lit hanger, was a hive of activity. A communication satellite was standing on an assembly platform while technicians swarmed over it. "How's it going, Jianxing?" said Henri to the Group Leader.

"It big surprise to be putting a satellite into the 16-4 vicinity," said Jianxing. Henri knew that this was a question, not a statement, but he nodded and waited for an answer.

"We didn't expect to be using Andromeda radiation coordinates," said Jianxing in the same vein.

"Well, Jianxing, surprises are to be expected when you're in a new part of the galaxy. How long do you need to get the satellite ready for launch?"

"'bout two hour," said Jianxing.

"OK." Henri took the stairs to the defence platform.

As he passed through the triple security check and strode into the complex of situation rooms, Henri acknowledged salutes from all those who passed him.

Now reduced to twenty-eight men and women after the loss of Brady and one of the Wayward 19, the unit was on full alert footing and activity was intense. He made his way briskly to the office of Major Charles Connolly, the unit commander.

"Hi, Chuck!"

"Colonel!"

"You are to destroy a satellite of unknown composition and you're to bring maximum beam strength to bear on the order. Here are the coordinates of your target, Red 1. No test-sighting. Don't count on a second shot – there might be some push-back."

"Colonel!"

"How long do you need to be on full readiness?"

"Twenty-four minutes, sir!"

"OK, get to it. My order will be 'Fire Red 1', delivered by earphone."

"Yes, sir!"

Henri was in a sombre mood when he reported to his commander that preparations to replace the alien satellite with their own would be completed within two hours.

Arlette announced that her recommendation to Mission Control had been to pre-emptively destroy the satellite but that she had decided to wait for their response before acting.

"Even if we are to assume that the alien satellite is armed and could inflict significant damage on us, it is clearly not programmed to react like that or it would have done so already. Therefore we can conclude that it will wait for instructions and we can assume that those instructions will take longer to arrive than our own response from

Mission Control. Stand down the laser attack and satellite launch teams for twenty hours."

"OK, Commander," said Henri.

On his way back to his office his thoughts drifted to Admiral Yamamoto and his reputed fears that he had awakened a sleeping giant when he attacked Pearl Harbor, 174 years earlier. He tried to imagine how he would react if he were on the receiving end of a message that one of his satellites had been knocked out by an alien agency. His conclusion was that he would act with restraint while he tried to determine the other party's intentions. 'And how would we do that?' he wondered. 'Send a reconnaissance mission? Armed? Manned?' He didn't know, but he could not put his trust in an entity whose motivation and intentions he could not know. He clenched his jaw, got up and went to find Julia.

As he walked, Henri called his key lieutenants for updates on the activities and whereabouts of the Wayward 19. Seven of them were being detained in the clinic in what was effectively house arrest. All the other twelve were engaged in normal activities in their sections, no two of them together. Henri began to formulate how he would use his knowledge to test whether he could control them, one at a time, with the knowledge about triggers that he now had, but he really needed Shinji to come up with a copy of the transmission device in the sword handle first.

He gave him a call.

"Damn difficult," said Shinji. "Can't use standard components. We're working manually on circuitry. Damn difficult," he said again.

“Can you give me an idea, please?” asked Henri as sympathetically as he could.

“Twenty-four hours”, came the response.

Julia was in her quarters, working on her word processor. She flipped open the door as Henri arrived without leaving her desk, and gave him a broad smile as she studied his worried face.

“Come in! Henri, what’s bugging you?” she asked as he stood there, towering over her.

“There are some ethical issues I’d like to discuss with you,” he said at last.

Julia leaned back, and her chair-back moved with her to the point where she was almost looking vertically upwards into his face. ‘He really is very attractive,’ she thought, ‘especially when he’s looking a little vulnerable.’

Henri looked around for a chair. There were only a couple of sofas in the corner of her quarters, and a large bed. He sat on the bed and looked around, taking in the tasteful blend of pastel colours that decorated the walls, ceiling and floor. The external view projection was on, making the room an observation platform for the universe outside, but the only internal decoration was the electronic family photo album on her desk.

Julia paddled her chair towards him. “Ethics? Ooh, am I a lucky little philosopher to get to discuss virtuous behaviours with a toughie from the CIA?”

“Be serious, Julia; we are the vanguard of human civilisation out here and we don’t want to be the harbingers of its destruction. We’ve taken a tactical decision about destroying that alien satellite, but I’m not comfortable that this is only about short-term tactics.”

"Hmm. What's your educational background?" asked Julia.

"Physics and Military Science."

"OK, but you know something of classical philosophy?"

"It wasn't my strong point," said Henri.

"Do you remember Nietzsche?"

Henri looked worried. "Don't test me," he said.

"Well, Nietzsche took issue with religion, particularly Christianity, which had shaped the values of western society for 1,500 years. He believed that it was very much the responsibility of the powerful and influential to champion the creativity of the human race and do great things, not that virtue was about being nice to someone so that they would be nice to you. In my view he was right on the button. That is the way political democracy works. Those who seek power do so by making deals with sectorial interests and then doing what they intended to do for what they perceive is the greater good. They don't pander to the weak and ignorant. The super-rich, tired of their toys, devote huge resources to great deeds, like eliminating disease. This is virtue. It's not about placating others. It's about doing great things for mankind even if it costs. That's your job, Henri. Go and do it."

Henri looked at her, smiled a wan smile and nodded. He was about to get up but Julia was out of her chair and standing close up to him. She put her hands gently on his shoulders, smiled and said simply, "These are broad enough." Henri held her against him for an instant and felt the softness of her breasts against his face, then both let go and the moment was past.

When the response was received from Mission

Control, it was unequivocal. The command team watched a short video from General Lee assessing the situation and confirming the view that the alien satellite should be promptly destroyed and replaced by one of theirs to monitor any activity in LDST 2. Additionally, a probe carrying a basic exploratory capacity was to be prepared and launched down LDST 2. Both the satellite and the probe would be equipped to emit a suitably conciliatory message to Andromeda, which Mission Control would prepare with the SETI Institute. He further recommended that an asteroid should be captured and held in an appropriate orbit, so that in the event a potential intruder should be detected in LDST 2 with an estimated arrival time prior to the departure of Prometheus from Omega 16, it could be launched into LDST 2 to prevent the intruder from reaching the sector.

The message concluded with a brief summary of environmental and political news, none of it good. Global CO2 emissions had fallen another 1 per cent but atmospheric content had continued to rise, apparently due to ongoing deforestation and fires. More seriously, methane emissions from Siberia, where the tundra was melting, were now a major component in the increase in the greenhouse gas effect, and it was feared that some very large methane concentrations in the oceans would shortly reach the critical temperature where they too would be released. Gangsterism in the US was now so widespread that large parts of some states were declared no-go areas where the law was unenforceable. A similar situation prevailed in southern Africa, where an estimated three million refugees were commandeering vessels of any size to try to cross the Indian Ocean to Australia. The death rate was almost 50 per cent.

Back on Prometheus, Arlette looked at each of her command team in turn and detected no concerns with General Lee's directive. "Right," she said. "Colonel Bertin, bring all available laser firepower to bear on the alien satellite, destroy it and replace it with one of ours. Marcel, have a probe prepared for launch as soon as possible, and get Navigation to select a suitable asteroid, farm it and position it for use in LDST 2 if necessary. Let's get this done and proceed with our mission."

Henri turned to look at the screen, now blank. "Fire Red 1," he said soundlessly into his earphone. Then he turned back to the group. "Marcel, could we talk to Navigation together? I'd like to be comfortable with the mass and structure of the asteroid we select."

"Sure," said Marcel, and the two men got up and left.

The destruction of the LDST 2 communication satellite was not as clean as Henri had hoped. Despite the intense radiation being poured on it from four laser sources on Prometheus simultaneously, it emitted a burst of communication for several seconds before expiring. Cobus Vermeulen made this point as Henri and Marcel joined him. "I think you guys have gotta assume that our green-skinned friends back in Andromeda will be hearing some rude things about us in due course," he said.

"All the more reason why we need to have a sizable chunk of real estate to send down the tube in case they're coming to pay us a visit," said Henri.

Cobus nodded. "There's nothing coming through this part of the Omega 16 system for a good while, but there's a big asteroid belt between 16-5 and 16-6," he said. "We can get a drone out there to select a nice one for us and send it back. I'll get it launched within twenty-four hours."

"Whoa!" said Henri. "Let's talk mass and composition first. No point in sending a snowball down there."

"We won't have much choice on the composition," said Cobus; "that'll be pretty consistent in the asteroid belt. As for mass, I'd say anything upwards of ten million tons would be fine. Nothing could withstand an impact with a mass like that, never mind that it would probably evaporate."

"But that's tiny," cut in Marcel, "barely a hundred metres cube. Supposing they miss each other?"

Cobus rolled his eyes. "They'll both be on the same geodesic," he said. "Provided the impact takes place after they've each gone a couple of million K's into the tube, it'll be green alien soup in there."

"What's the practical mass limit on our capability to corral an asteroid?" asked Henri.

"A hundred million tons, give or take," was Cobus' response.

"Get us one of those then, please," said Marcel.

Cobus nodded. "Asseblief," he muttered.

Down at the launch area of the Military Operations Centre, work was almost complete on the replacement communications satellite when Henri and Marcel arrived. "We have an additional request from Mission Control," announced Marcel. "We need to launch a probe with the capacity to survey the solar system at the other end of LDST 2, and we need broad-frequency-range transmitters/receivers on board both to communicate."

"You nuts?" said Jianxing. "Who you gonna talk to?"

"The same entity that was communicating with the satellite you are replacing," replied Marcel.

"Well, then you're gonna need a pretty smart decoder as well," said Jianxing, "because we ain't never seen anything like de way it talks."

"Just send Mission Control copies of everything you've heard from it and leave it to them to figure that out."

"OK," said Jianxing. "Give me twenty minutes and we'll be ready to launch de satellite." He turned and cupped a hand to his mouth, "Hey, Carlos! Load a 436 and a dish to match, pointin' south." Then he turned back. "You got any more screwy requests?" he asked.

"Not that I can think of right now," said Marcel with a frown.

Henri and Marcel stayed on to watch the launch. The satellite was moved into an airlock on its trolley and reappeared outside on the launch platform a few minutes later. There was a brief pre-flight check, a ten-second countdown, then a little puff of flame and it disappeared almost instantly. They turned to watch its progress along its programmed flightpath for a few minutes, then Henri got up. "I've got to talk to Benny," he said, and left.

19
The Test

Back at the maintenance department, Benny Tromper was admiring his handiwork. Five swords lay before him on his workbench, almost perfect replicas of the original curved sabre taken from Brady after he was cut down by sniper fire in the control centre. As Henri entered, Benny turned to him, beaming with pride. "These should give you Yankees something to think about!" he said.

Henri was perplexed. "I'm no Yankee," he said, rather deliberately allowing a trace of his Haitian accent to creep in.

"Well, I'm almost certain that this one was a Confederacy weapon in the American Civil War," said Benny, picking up Brady's sword.

"An antique? How the hell was that smuggled on board?" said Henri, addressing no one in particular.

"Search me," said Benny. "But see that mark? My database says that's a Confederacy military sabre."

"Well, I'll have to think about that one," said Henri slowly. "Did Shinji finish with the transmitters?"

"He's made them but he's still testing their emission profiles. Shouldn't be a problem – they just fit in here, see?" Benny snapped open the handle of one of the swords on the table, and showed Henri the compartment inside. "I'm done," he said.

"OK," said Henri. "Get all six shipped down to Chuck Connolly on the defence platform as soon as they're complete, please." He turned to go, then stopped. "Thanks Benny, that's beautiful work," he said, putting a hand on the other man's shoulder.

As the door closed behind him, Henri called Chuck Connolly on his earphone. "Six fine US cavalry swords will be delivered to you shortly. Please store them securely in my office, then send a detail to the clinic to fetch Aldo Barreto and take him back to the defence platform."

"Aldo Barreto? He's our man in the Wayward 19. You want him back here?"

"You bet," said Henri, "and under close supervision."

Aldo Barreto was a tall, powerfully built man, sporting a bushy black beard. He had been a commando in the Brazilian army before training as a pilot, where he had excelled in aerial combat. He was recruited by the ISEA as a pilot and then, after several missions, transferred to space defence.

He was now confused and angry. He wanted to know why he was being kept a prisoner and subjected to the injection of drugs and to humiliating tests without his agreement and without explanation. He was sorry he had lost his temper on a few occasions in the clinic, but felt that his behaviour had not been unreasonable in the circumstances. Now, here he was, under arrest in the defence platform, being treated like a traitor by his colleagues.

Back in his office, Henri read through the summary of a clinical psychology report on the behaviour of Barreto, Aldo when subjected to visual and verbal stimuli.

Visual stimulation

Weaponry (video): intense interest, desire to handle, raised pulse

Military action (video): as above, intense desire to participate (restraint applied)

Sadism (video): manic response, shouting, uncontrolled and reckless physical action (restraint applied)

Spilled blood: pupil dilation, fast respiration and rapid pulse, whining and salivation

Verbal stimulation

The words 'kill', 'death', 'Pandora', 'attack' induce manic violent behaviour following any of above visual stimuli.

No symbols or words were identified that caused these behaviours to cease. The patient had to be heavily sedated in all cases.

"Right," said Henri to himself, "let's see if we can control this SOB with Brady's sabre." He examined the weapon carefully, noting that the transmitter inside the handle was activated by pushing the finger-guard forward with his thumb. "Chuck," he mouthed into his earphone, "get yourself and two men down to Barreto's cell and have his feet manacled to the floor. You can leave his hands free. I'll see you there in five minutes." He slid the sabre back into the scabbard that Benny Tromper had made for it, a good replica of the type used by the Confederate cavalry, according to Benny.

As Henri entered the cell where Barreto was being held, the man leapt to his feet and saluted, stumbling and almost toppling over as the manacles on his feet tightened. Henri returned the salute and motioned him to sit. He laid the sword on the table in front of him, still in its scabbard. Barreto showed no particular interest in it, but started with a vociferous protest about his treatment. Henri lifted a hand to silence him. "Lieutenant Barreto, you have shown a disturbing response to the vaccination you were given, to the point where you have become a potential security risk. It is in your interest as well as ours that we fully understand this response and correct it before you are re-assigned to active duty. Is that clear?"

"Yessir," said Barreto, after a brief pause.

"Good. Now, does this disturb you?" Henri picked up a water glass and smashed it on the table in front of him, then drew a shard across the back of his hand. A few droplets of crimson appeared on his dark skin. Barreto jumped with surprise and stared at the blood, his eyes wide, nostrils flared, jaw clenched. He looked up at Henri, a silent question in his eyes. Without taking his eyes off him, Henri reached for the scabbard and slowly withdrew the sabre, holding the blade vertically in front of Barreto's face. Barreto trembled, his eyes on the blade.

"Ready," he said in a strange, lingering voice.

Henri pushed forward the finger-guard. "Attack!" he shouted in his face. Barreto leapt up, lunging for the man seated closest to him, grabbing his leg as he fell and sinking his teeth into it. The man yelped with pain and clubbed Barreto repeatedly over the head with his weapon. Blood began to spread over the floor from his gashed leg, and from Barreto's feet, as the manacles tore into his ankles.

"Cease!" shouted Henri, activating the sabre's transmitter once more.

Barreto stopped, turned and gazed intently at the sabre held above him, blood dribbling from his mouth.

"Stand down!" shouted Henri a little more calmly, activating the transmitter again. Barreto's tense body gradually slackened. He began to moan.

Henri rose from his chair. "Have him cleaned up, Chuck," he said, "and get Kinross brought down here."

Within an hour Kinross had been collected from the clinic, manacled and subjected to the same harrowing test, with two important differences. Firstly, his tormentor was Chuck Connolly, not Henri, and secondly Chuck was using one of the swords that Benny had made, not the original. The results, however, were practically the same. At their debriefing in Henri's office afterwards, they carefully reviewed their experiences, and explored options for further tests. After some troubling thoughts Henri approved a slightly modified process to be used on one more of the Wayward 19, to test a wider range of commands.

At the command meeting held after the completion of the testing, Hannah Cohen was spitting fire. "I want an explanation for all these injuries!" she demanded. "Three of those men will not walk properly for at least three weeks," she railed, "and possibly never again. What you submitted them to was bestial!"

Henri sat stone-faced.

"Well, Colonel Bertin?" said Arlette.

"I can say with confidence that anyone around this

table can now control the Wayward 19. Provided that we all follow appropriate precautions, they no longer represent a threat to this mission. I apologise for the pain that has been inflicted on them, but in a situation as serious as this, with twelve crew members already lost and 10 per cent of the remaining crew representing a lethal threat, I could not cut any corners in containing their potentially malevolent activities."

"But you repeated tests that the clinic had already carried out without doing any harm to any of them," persisted Hannah.

"Not so," said Henri. "The critical part of this was controlling the activation and de-activation of these behaviours with the transmitters in the sword handles. Now we have a reliable mechanical on/off switch. The psychological data was vital, but we must be able to manage these people practically. They are all important crew members; we need their skills and their loyalty."

"They'd be more use without their limps!" said Hannah ruefully.

It wasn't the reaction she intended, but everybody laughed.

Henri looked around at his colleagues as if to say, "Did I survive?"

His eyes caught Julia's. Her head was slightly on one side. Something in her gaze was rather warm.

20
Stargazers and Dreamers

Henri's search for a concealed base used by the five control centre assailants remained fruitless, and while Prometheus' video surveillance system had become substantially more reliable, it still revealed nothing remarkable. Any concerns over the control centre massacre and vaccination programme began to subside as the distraction of deep space started to play an ever-increasing part in the crew's lives.

Having launched a hurriedly prepared probe into the mouth of LDST 2, and established a communication link as it began to accelerate away to an unknown fate in the Andromeda galaxy, Prometheus began to settle into its slingshot manoeuvre around the colourful gas giant Omega 16-6.

The huge planet, with its complex patterned blue and orange surface, its vast ring system and nine visible moons, was a mesmerising sight, and provided new and extraordinary discoveries almost hourly. By the time Prometheus had completed the manoeuvre and settled on its course to rendezvous with rocky planet 16-3, communal stargazing had become a way of life.

Many crew members shunned the entertainment centre with its almost inexhaustible spread of movies and documentaries, educational and vocational programmes, music making, culinary and sporting activities, for watching the galaxy unfold before them through the ship's high-powered telescope. Few failed to notice that, from their perspective in the Omega 16 solar system, the Milky Way galaxy had assumed an obloid shape, traced through with interconnected star systems astonishingly reminiscent of the neurons in a human brain. Not an original observation by any means, but not easily dismissed when you saw it almost every hour of the day. Numerous groups formed to discuss this concept and attempt to investigate its feasibility. None reached any definitive conclusion, other than that you could not rule out that such a constellation of charged matter could function as a brain, and with a vastly larger capacity than that of any human.

Nor were such discussions limited to the lower ranks on board. Arlette spent an evening with Marcel, Julia, Hannah and Genes hotly debating the concept.

"Oh, you're an incurable romantic, Julia," Arlette was saying. "A pictorial similarity of an area in space with the neuron structure in a brain can be nothing more than coincidental. It's no better than trying to read the future with tea leaves."

"Well, you're a faithless automaton," Julia retorted. "How can you even begin to summarise what is going on between the particles and fields in the centre of a galaxy, which contains incalculably more matter and complexity, lots of which we still do not fully understand, than a brain?"

"Julia, Julia, dear," interrupted Hannah in a mildly patronising tone. "Brains work on a microscopic scale with incredibly delicate signals and chemical structures. There is just no comparison with the brutality of stars and their interactions."

"I don't have a problem with the potential intellectual output of galactic systems," said Genes. "Hell, their complexity never ceases to amaze us. We are constantly making new discoveries about interactive systems you just couldn't make up, they're so weird. And I agree with Julia, our understanding of universal physics is still a joke. We don't know the half of all those particles out there. Who are we to decide that they can't interact to form a brain? It's just intellectual arrogance."

"Well," said Marcel, "if our galaxy has a brain, I'd sure as hell like to know what it's doing with it. Our own planet is descending into chaos, and, modesty apart, we do have a pretty impressive civilisation. Why wouldn't an omnipotent force intervene and sort out global warming?"

"Oh, please Marcel, not that old chestnut! If our galaxy has a brain, it should be acting in the interests of the greater good of the galaxy, not its weak and failing components."

"Good grief, Julia, you've got Nietzsche on the brain. I just don't buy it that a civilisation as developed as ours can be considered expendable – we've found no trace of anything like it in our galaxy or elsewhere and we've been looking hard for a long time now. Personally I won't be hanging around waiting for divine intervention, but if our civilisation is a weak and failing component, what are we doing in this spaceship? We are fighters, we are survivors, we are really important." Marcel had gone slightly pink in the cheeks.

"That's an interesting idea, Julia," said Arlette. "Just how would you define the greater good of the galaxy?"

"Survival, power, growth," said Julia.

"What sort of power? Power within the galaxy or outside it?"

"Both. If you want to maintain your internal power, you have to be able to defeat your external competitors," responded Julia.

"Like Andromeda?"

"Definitely. Our galaxies are heading for a collision, aren't they? If I were the omnipotent brain of the Milky Way, I'd be seriously worried about Andromeda, especially if it's carrying out incursions into my territory." Julia was wearing an expression of mock defiance.

"Oh, come on," said Marcel, grinning. "Intergalactic conflict should have got past gunboat diplomacy by now. It will be all about … mmm, how about malign sub-atomic particle species development?"

Everybody was smiling except Genes. "Whatever the means," he said, "Julia's right. The story is always the same. It's about power. And whether they're using thought destruction rays or wooden swords, that's just a detail. Ah actually find it hard to believe that no one, or no thing, is thinking about applying the vast resources of this galaxy to defend its greater interests against a threat that's been known for aeons. We're gonna be victims of our own arrogance if we don't wake up and realise that there's a lotta brain power out there. We need to get smart and get on-side."

Genes' comments brought a strange silence to the group. They were all suddenly conscious of the vastness and unfathomable complexity of the universe which surrounded them, so cleverly projected onto the walls and ceiling of their dining room. Now, here they were for the first time in human history, knowingly in the vicinity of an alien intelligence.

"Well," said Arlette into the silence, "perhaps it is our destiny to find out whether there is such a power, and just how relevant to it our concept of morality is."

"Here's to that!" said Genes. "By the way, Commander, where did this excellent schnapps come from? It tastes like one of those grand old central European brews."

"Oh, really?" said Arlette. "Does anyone recognise it?"

"Undoubtedly French," said Marcel, gazing rather affectionately into his glass and sniffing. "A hint of the noble 'Prune.'"

"Sorry to disappoint you hooch Aficionados, but it's the latest innovation from Freddy Jones at the farmyard. Apparently it's made from fermented vitamin supplements. He found they had a mouldy batch and decided to do something useful with it." The party broke up shortly afterwards.

Arlette was as economical with the facts as usual in her announcement to the crew about LDST 2. She announced the discovery of the wormhole, and the exciting prospect of a connection with Andromeda, but did not mention the destruction of the alien satellite, nor the corralling of an asteroid as a pre-emptive defence measure. There was general agreement in the command team that the less time the crew spent speculating about the significance of the alien satellite and the wisdom of destroying it, the better. She did, however, announce the successful deployment of the Prometheus probe sent to explore LDST 2 and of the satellite to monitor communications activity in it.

In the canteen, however, the words 'we are not alone' pervaded almost all discussions. While the response, to the effect that 'statistically we always knew that', was what everyone said, it was not what all of them felt. The unexpectedness of the discovery, and its proximity to their own planned activities, was deeply unnerving to some. The statement from the Navigation department regarding the absence of any detectable alien presence in the Omega 16 solar system was also hardly reassuring, particularly during the 16-6 fly-by. No one seeing the scale of the planet and the number and variety of its moons could pretend that it would not be possible to hide an alien spaceship there, or in the vicinity of the other gas giant, planet 16-5, for that matter.

Discussion groups were set up by the psychology section to deal with these concerns, and while these did help to counter the general feeling of unease, there was a lingering mood of insecurity which tainted the euphoria of discovery. The emphasis of command attention now turned towards rocky planet 16-3, which was growing visibly from the spec that had appeared after the slingshot manoeuvre. The ship's telescope revealed a planet remarkably similar to Earth, bathed in a predominantly blue hue, with oceans, clouds and land masses, and with every day that passed the telescopic images improved in detail until it became clear that there was indeed life on 16-3.

As Prometheus approached its rendezvous with 16-3, anxiety declined and excitement mounted. It was a time of intense activity on board, for most of the crew had to prepare to respond to conditions and situations never encountered before, and they devoured all the relevant data that poured in from the ship's sensors.

Sanam watched the beautiful planet steadily growing in her external view projection as she dressed for the task of piloting Prometheus into orbit around 16-3. Her co-pilot would be Tim Cochran – not her preferred choice. She detested his seat-of-the-pants style while secretly respecting his reaction speed and intuition. She would leave it to him to line up the ship's approach, then she would take over and refine its entry into a stable planetary orbit. It would be a truly historic moment and she relished it.

"Good morning, Tim," she said as she mounted the flight deck. He was in the process of taking over from Arun and apparently unhappy with booster fuel levels. "Look," Arun was saying. "We've had to take off a lot of speed and we've had two large moons to contend with. Also, one of the solar panels has been operating below par. You've got enough juice to get in and we'll have loads of time to recharge once we're in orbit."

"Hi, Sanam," said Tim, turning around briefly. "Your man here has barely left us a sniff in the tank."

"My man?" said Sanam, looking over Arun appreciatively as if for the first time. He stood there, intent on pursuing the debate about fuel levels, but the power and beauty of the woman captured him again, just as it had before. Finally, and without taking his eyes off her, he said over his shoulder, "Tim, Sanam will apply her usual grace and skill to bring the ship into an orbit of utmost perfection, with barely a touch on the booster button", and he smiled a glorious smile at her. Tim Cochran snorted.

A couple of hours later, as Sanam completed her checks and took over control, the trajectory of Prometheus was almost perfect. She made minor corrections to the attitude of the ship, issued a general warning to the crew to prepare for deceleration, and fired the boosters. Her touch was, as ever, perfect. She cut the power, checked her orbit data, and, with a large grin on her face, announced, "Prometheus is in stable orbit. Welcome, everyone, to planet Omega 16-3."

21
Planet Omega 16-3

The process of detailed mapping of the surface was now begun by the Navigation department. This meant that the ship's telescope was not accessible to other crew members, and they had to content themselves with the external view projection where they were working or relaxing. One detail, however, escaped no one's attention – the dark side of the planet was completely devoid of any lights. Whatever the state of development of animal life on Omega 16-3, it did not include an advanced civilisation. This was, of course, no surprise to the command team of Prometheus, since the pre-flight probe had confirmed it, but it did set the thoughts of the rest of the crew onto another track: the subject of monsters in general, and in particular the type of monsters that had inhabited Earth prior to the arrival of mammals. These fears were not alleviated when Arlette announced the selection of a landing site.

"Navigation has completed its initial survey of the surface of planet Omega 16-3", she said, "and selected a landing site for our first mission onto the surface. The length of a day is forty-two hours on average, the planet takes just under 600 days to orbit Omega 16, gravity is 1.2G, atmospheric pressure is typically 1.1 bar, and the northern hemisphere is currently in late summer. We have chosen a northerly site so as to take advantage of the longer days, and the average daytime temperatures will be a very pleasant 24 degrees. However, temperatures do drop to about 4 degrees at night. The location of the site is on a promontory on the eastern end of a continental land mass. We have chosen this in order to more easily control any animal life that may show an interest in us. The surveys conducted so far show herds of quite large animals moving around on the surface, and we shall want to disturb them as little as possible. The vegetation appears similar in type and scale to our own. I know you are all tired of the name Omega 16-3, and we will give our new planet a more appropriate name once we know a bit more about it. I'll take any suggestions you may have into consideration. The first mission to land an exploratory team will depart in two days. It will be crewed mostly by our militia and a construction team, and its task will be to set up a base camp. I will keep you all informed as exploration progresses."

The command team dinner that evening was a positively festive affair and included all the section heads.

Inevitably the discussion centred more on the forthcoming exploration than on-board issues. Freddy Jones set off the first real argument when he said how much he was looking forward to tucking into his first dinosaur steak, after all the bland protein composites his department had been serving up for the last few months.

"How could you be so irresponsible, Freddy?!"

shrieked Hannah. “Our digestive systems have no chance of coping with extra-terrestrial meat, let alone the bacteria and viruses that will be present! Yuk!”

“Oh, nonsense, Hannah. The roasting will take care of all that, and we have perfectly edible dinosaurs on Earth – crocodiles to start with, not to mention all the excellent birds that have descended from them.”

“Commander, I absolutely insist that no extra-terrestrial animal products are eaten before they have been examined in our path labs,” said Hannah firmly.

“What about fish?” asked Henri. “We're next to the water and there should be plenty around.”

“Well, let's start with the water,” said Hannah. “You may not touch it until it has been analysed for poisons and bacteria. I'll give one of your men a test kit and train him how to work it. If it's OK, you'll be able to use it after it's been distilled. You can then try small fish after they've been cleaned and boiled.”

“Boiled?” asked Shinji Yamamoto with a look of horror. “If we are the vanguard of civilisation, how could we do something so barbarous?”

“Oh, don't try and play the ethnic card with me,” said Hannah, ignoring the grins on the faces around her. “I like my sashimi as much as anyone, but we must not underestimate the potential risks of impulsive behaviour, which, I can tell you from painful experience, is not uncommon among soldiers.”

“Good thing you weren't around when our ancestors came down from the trees, Hannah,” said Marcel.

“Oh don't you start! I've said my bit.” She folded her arms and stared straight ahead.

Arlette intervened. "Freddy, what do you make of the pictures you've seen of the animal life down there?"

"It's actually pretty primitive, from what I've seen. They're quite large but don't move like the quadrupeds we know, or the bipeds for that matter. What's more, they don't seem to form random herds – they are more structured, like insects."

"Insects?!" cried Julia in alarm. "Oh God!"

"Aw shucks!" said Genes. "I was just coming to terms with dinosaur steaks and boiled fish, now we're on to cockroach fritters."

"Could be very good," said Shinji, "nice and crunchy!" Chang nodded in agreement, rather too eagerly.

Cobus Vermeulen had said nothing so far, but he had seen substantially more detailed footage than anyone else and now he opened up. "Freddy is right. Most of the creatures I've seen resemble insects, but some of them are really big. Many are carnivorous; I have seen them feeding on the carcasses of other animals. And there are plenty that are airborne. There are variations from one part of the planet to another and from one type of vegetation to the next. It's a well-developed ecosystem, but it seems to lack the variety we have on Earth. I've seen nothing that could be mammalian, or reptilian for that matter."

"Why would that be?" Arlette asked him. "This planet is about the same age as ours. Why would the product of evolution be different?"

"Well, one explanation could be that their history of catastrophic events could be different. Animal life on Earth had to keep adapting to changes which favoured the emergence of different species. Perhaps Omega 16-3 has had a quieter life."

"I think Cobus is right on the ball," said Freddy, "although I don't get the absence of amphibians. It doesn't make sense. There's plenty of water around. Not as much as on Earth, but plenty to breed life."

"Amphibians were only transitory on Earth," said Marcel. "When they crawled out of the sea they turned into something else. Maybe the first amphibians became insects here and just stayed like that."

"Something else I've noticed," went on Cobus. "The moons. They're both practically devoid of craters. That could mean that there were no asteroid strikes of any significance in the history of the planet."

"OK. So where did the water come from?" Julia wanted to know. Cobus spread his hands, palms upwards and shrugged. "The pre-life phase of the planet's history?"

"Whatever the origin of the life forms we are about to meet," said Henri, "we are going to have to deal with what is here. Our job is to establish a secure base for colonisation by our own species. Our track record on Earth has been to wipe out everything that got in our way. Are we likely to be any different here?"

"God, I hope so," said Julia.

"That's the second time you've invoked God tonight, Julia. I'm not so sure ethics has a lot to say when we are colonising a planet to save our civilisation," said Marcel.

"Well, Marcel, it might surprise you but I agree," she replied. "However, we all know that the impact of changing one part of an ecological balance can have dire consequences for other parts. So let's think it through before we spray the planet with DDT. My ethics have nothing to do with religion. They are just about getting it right to ensure success."

"OK, OK, let's deal with the immediate issues," said Henri. "Something tells me that we are going to have to establish our presence on this planet with a certain amount of force. We will need to protect ourselves, our territory and our crops if necessary. As civilisation expands here, it will deny habitat to the indigenous species. To Julia's point, the success of the mission is paramount. We will try and avoid the mistakes we made on Earth, but we will prevail with force if necessary."

"So you want a hunting licence, Colonel Bertin?" asked Arlette.

Henri leaned back, folded his arms, and looked at her askance. He was getting tired of being the only one in the group whom she insisted on addressing by his formal title. It made him, and most of the others, uncomfortable, not least because it drew attention to earlier events that were none of their business.

"You are welcome to call me Henri, Commander," he said with a condescending smile, "and yes, we shall be armed and must be authorised to use our weapons as and when the need arises."

Arlette surveyed the others for signs of disagreement and saw none. "Very well – Henri," she said, a little hint of triumph in her eye.

For the next two days the ship was a hive of activity, not only in the bay where the preparation for the launch of the excursion vehicle Lander 1 was going on, but almost every working component was inspected and tested. Shutdown of the induced gravity system for maintenance added to the generally festive mood as preparations were not as rigorous as they should have been, and there were a lot of unsecured items floating around which easily became the subject of improvised games.

Sanam and Arun, free of the duty roster as they now were, retired to Sanam's quarters and carried out the most comprehensive exploration of weightless sex that they could devise. They were not alone in this sort of activity. Sanam had made no secret of her historic wormhole tryst among her girlfriends, so that a significant portion of the crew knew by now that here was an experience not to be missed if at all possible. A quite remarkable relaxation of the normal professional distance between crew members developed very quickly, resulting in numerous hastily forged new relationships.

Arlette detected a noticeable decline in the responsiveness of the ship's leaders to her calls. She had been trying to reach Julia for nearly two hours when she finally got a rather dreamy "Hello?" response from her instead of the usual crisp "Commander?!"

"I want to discuss the excursion roster with you, Julia."

"Oh," said Julia. It wasn't quite the response Arlette was looking for.

"So, do you think you could tear yourself away from whatever it is that currently has your attention, and drop by my office?"

There was a strange noise over the earphone that Arlette did not recognise, but then the system was designed to translate thoughts into words, not other emotions. Still, it did sound remarkably like a giggle.

"I'll be there in fifteen minutes," said Julia, "about [giggle]."

Julia floated into Arlette's office twenty-five minutes later, freshly primped, and secured herself. "Sorry, Commander" she said. "I had a bit of difficulty with the zero-gravity shower. It leaked all over the place."

"Perhaps it was set up for someone taller?" suggested Arlette, rather unkindly.

Julia flushed. It was really very sloppy of her to be unprepared for a dig like that. She knew that Arlette was extremely perceptive, despite her cool demeanour. "Er, I don't know. I'll get it adjusted," she said, looking around.

"Well," said Arlette, examining her screen with a wan smile, "I'm glad you've been extending your weightless navigation skills. Can we please discuss this excursion roster that Bertin has put together?" She looked up at Julia and in an instant she knew. 'God, she's been fucking that faithless bastard,' she said to herself, and her face hardened.

Julia picked up a tablet, flicked to the roster, and regained her composure. "I think you should be on the first excursion," she said. "I know it sounds a bit like a re-take on Christopher Columbus, but you have to do the historic moments. It's your duty and your destiny."

"I want this to be truly a team accomplishment," said Arlette. "I have no time for ceremony and you know it."

"Yes, but you cannot downplay the arrival of the first humans on an alien planet. You can be as modest as you like with your crew. They know you and they respect you. But you will disappoint them and let yourself down if you don't step up to this moment." Julia meant it. She was amazed that Henri's roster showed Arlette visiting on the third landing only, but she did not want to raise his name again.

"Bertin is concerned with safety and security," said Arlette, reading her mind. "He doesn't want to risk the Commander's arrival being just a muddy accident."

"Bullshit!" said Julia. "The excursion vehicle is as robust as anything we have on this mission. It can land anywhere – on water if necessary – and it can easily move to another landing site if we don't like the first one we've chosen. You have to take the first step onto that planet, just as soon as it's been declared safe to do so."

"OK, so who should be the next one out?"

"Bertin, of course," was Julia's prompt reply. "He must immediately secure the landing site with his militia. Only then can we allow the botanists and biologists to start looking around."

"OK. Any other suggestions?"

"Yes," said Julia. "I don't think Ghorashian is the right choice of pilot. She's showy and an individualist. Tim Cochran is much more of a pilots' pilot. I'd trust him to get us out of an unexpected situation any time. The rest of them, well, they're maintenance people with a job to do assembling the base."

"Right. You will be my deputy while I am on the ground."

Julia looked at her wide-eyed.

"Yes, I've seen the quality of your judgement, Julia. There aren't going to be any technical issues of great complexity, and you know how to use other people's input intelligently. I will notify the command team shortly and then we'll all have a chat about how it will be handled."

It was pretty clear to Julia that the discussion was over. As she reached to release her restraint there was a brief public announcement from Marcel. "Induced gravity will be restored in three minutes. Please restrain yourselves and all floating objects."

Both women remained where they were, avoiding eye contact, like strangers in a lift.

Henri Bertin floated above his bed, loosely wrapped in a towel and deep in thought. Was it due to a fundamental trait of his, he wondered, that he only got involved with powerful women? It would have started with his Haitian mother, who had left her home and his drunken, brutal father, and entered the US on a forged Cuban passport, determined that her son would have a better life than his forebears. She had secured his registration, but when she returned to Haiti, Henri's father was dead from a knife wound he received in a brawl.

Then began a relationship of total mutual commitment between the two of them. Henri excelled at school and at sport. He won a scholarship to study Physics in the US, then he went to a Military Academy and graduated with distinction, adding fluency in Arabic and Mandarin to his native French and English. The only woman he cared for deeply was his mother and she treated him firmly, insisting that his duty to his country of birth was to be above all else.

Henri slipped in and out of affairs, meeting no one that remotely met the standards of courage and integrity he perceived in his mother. He was recruited into the CIA and given substantial international exposure, latterly in the ISEA. He was on the panel which selected Arlette as the prospective commander of IP262 and was given the task of vetting her. General Lee had told him at the time, "We all know she is a courageous and highly intelligent woman, but we have to get into her private life and identify any character weaknesses there may be. This is a momentous mission she has been selected for and you must be quite ruthless in probing her."

Henri had done the job he had been charged with. He had presented himself as a Haitian diplomat on vacation and completely charmed her at several 'chance' encounters. After their acquaintance had lasted almost a week and he had made no move other than socially, she had boiled over and presented herself at his hotel room door one evening in a stunning backless dress with a very short skirt. When he opened the door, she walked right in and closed it behind her, looking him over haughtily. He walked up to her and smiled, and ran his finger down her cheek to the corner of her mouth. He could feel her tremble slightly and he put his arms around her, pulling her against his body. The two of them held each other's gaze for a minute, then everything suddenly got very urgent, hands were on flesh and clothes were coming off everywhere.

In the week that followed, Henri came to realise that the boot was really on the other foot, and that he was her plaything. She could be tender, even cute, but she was always in control, not just of herself but of him as well. Henri felt a feeling inside that he had never felt for a woman before. It was a yearning to possess her, not just physically but emotionally and intellectually as well, and it affected him deeply.

Then he thought of Julia, and he smiled to himself. She

was different. There was no arrogance in her but a rather naughty playfulness. She teased him very effectively, one minute challenging him to the point of offence, the next effortlessly restoring his dignity for him with an elegant compromise. But in one way she was exactly the same as Arlette: she took what she wanted, particularly when it happened to be him. She had pulled exactly the same trick on him, but without the sexy dress. Walking into his quarters without hesitation and giving him a sort of 'now let's see what you can do' look-over. He wondered for a moment if she would have done it if she had known about Arlette, then concluded that yes, certainly, it would probably have made no difference. But he was working with these two women at the highest level. One of them was exercising her intellect and her authority, the other her intellect and her warmth. He respected them both, deeply, and, if he was honest with himself, he loved them both. While Arlette was organisationally and emotionally inaccessible, Julia was there, nudging him playfully in public and flaunting herself in front of him in private whenever she felt like it. 'Fucking like Helen of Troy with her arse on fire,' he had read somewhere. Yes, that was Julia, bless her.

Marcel's announcement jolted him out of his reverie. He scrambled into his tunic and checked with the launch deck. "Commander, Lander 1 is ready for inspection," he announced by earphone. Arlette shut down her information system and headed down to the excursion platform, collecting Marcel on the way. Lander 1 was docked to the side of the ship, her cargo loaded and ready for her thirty passengers.

It was the first time that Arlette had really looked at the vehicle that would take her to the surface of an unknown planet and she was somewhat taken aback by the sleek elegance of the ship.

"Where is the booster unit to generate the fuel for the return trip?" she asked Marcel.

"It will be launched a couple of hours ahead so that we have it in place on the ground, ready to be attached to a local water supply. It only takes eight hours for the electrolysis unit to generate enough fuel to refill the booster tanks on the lander," Marcel told her. It also gives us a 360 on the landing site so that we have detailed terrain data in advance."

"Good. What's the weather like down there?"

"Calm, clear, no precipitation forecast for the next forty-eight hours, 20 degrees when we land four hours after sunrise." Marcel motioned her forward. "Come and have a look."

They stepped through the airlock into the lander. It was similar in layout, but much smaller than the lunar shuttle, and the thirty-two ergo-couches were quite closely packed, arranged radially around a central tunnel containing a circular stairway. "It's just a short trip," Marcel explained. "The lander flies to the target area after atmosphere entry, then the parachutes are deployed and she swings round to land on her tail. The internal motors are only used briefly to control touchdown. You exit down the central staircase."

'It's always simple with Marcel,' thought Arlette. "OK. Where's the gear to construct the base camp?"

"It's all stowed in the rear section, or what becomes the bottom section when she's on the ground," said

Marcel. "The construction materials are lowered to the ground when the cargo bay doors are opened. It's all pneumatic, driven off the lander's batteries. The whole structure can move around on tracks, blows up within a couple of minutes, and maintains a constant temperature and a slight positive pressure so that you don't ingest any irritants like pollen or rocket exhaust. All the basics are already in place. You just press 'inflate', enter and live."

"OK," said Arlette. "When is departure scheduled?"

"Just under three hours from now. You'll see the landing site 360 on your screen, then please make your way down here and we'll get you boarded." Marcel smiled and saluted his commander. She touched a finger to her forehead in response.

* * *

"What is this?" enquired Chuck Connolly of his commanding officer, pointing to a prominent object in the package of gear delivered to all members of the landing militia.

"That, Major, is a spade," replied Henri.

"I see," said Chuck. "And what, in this age of intergalactic travel, will we be needing spades for?"

"Digging trenches," relied Henri.

"Might we not have some slightly more sophisticated equipment for that task?" persisted Chuck in the same vein. "And what is the purpose of these trenches?"

"No, the lander is already on its maximum payload, and we shall use trenches as our first line of defence in the absence of any other appropriate cover," said Henri.

"You expect these bugs to shoot at us?" enquired Chuck.

"No, but I'm not going to rule out spitting venom, articulated stings, prehensile claws or any other variation of insect paraphernalia that they might have. We have a very basic job of defence to do here, against a possible adversary that we do not know. We're not going to get caught without the basics. I think it is inevitable that we will get some visitors."

"Why so?" asked Chuck.

"Because the night is nineteen hours long and our camp will be illuminated. I don't know of any insect that is not attracted by light, do you?"

"Will we be authorised to shoot on sight?" Chuck wanted to know.

"I may decide to give that order, but it will not apply until I do," replied Henri. "Of course we'll all be equipped with night vision so I would hope we'll see them first."

"Not if we're between them and the light source," pointed our Chuck.

"Exactly," said Henri. "Now you see my point about the trenches."

* * *

Lander 1 departed on schedule to make landfall at its selected target site four hours after sunrise. As the craft began to cool from its atmospheric entry, the landscape below came into its full glory, illuminated by the early morning sun. Rivers, lakes, mountains and forests all appeared below them, remarkably Earth-like except for one predominant factor: there were no signs of civilisation, no infrastructure of any kind. In the cockpit Tim Cochran saw the promontory he was to land on ahead of him, checked his position, then stalled the craft and deployed the huge parachutes. Lander 1 steadied in the vertical position, sinking rapidly towards the ground. The lander's engines burst into life and the descent slowed to a crawl. She landed with the gentlest of bumps, the landing gear flexing and grumbling below them. Then it was quiet. "Lander 1 is down and on target," announced Tim, and a huge cheer rose from the passenger section.

"Please remain seated!" said Tim. "We need to do an atmosphere test before we open the doors." Unfamiliar scents greeted them as in the air in the lander was gradually exchanged with that from outside. "Remember that gravity here is 1.2G, so moving will be a bit more of an effort, but that we have 24 per cent oxygen in the atmosphere, which will compensate somewhat. Enjoy your stay on Omega 16-3!"

Arlette clambered into the stairway and started down the steps, surrounded on all sides by smiling faces. Her heart started to pound as she caught the first glimpse of alien soil below her, and she jumped the last two steps and felt the earth give a little below her feet. She breathed deeply, taking in the huge green expanse before her, crowned in the distance with snow-capped mountains, with the ocean calmly lapping on a beach a few hundred metres behind her. She sank to her knees and touched her lips to the soil, then rose to her feet and announced, "We have come in peace. We bring you the wonderment of our human civilisation, and we offer our knowledge and our skills with true humility to advance this beautiful planet and all its inhabitants. We shall call you Ceres, out of respect for the bountiful land we see around us." Clapping could be heard from the lander cabin above. Arlette turned and shouted upwards, "Come and join me; it's beautiful out here!"

22
Footfall on Ceres

Henri Bertin was the first to congratulate the commander, and he did so with a kiss on the cheek and a whispered "Bravo". He then produced a small folding table from his pack, on which he set a magnum of champagne and thirty-four beakers. Arlette found herself rather incongruously handing a beaker of champagne to each crew member as they set foot on Ceres, and shaking their hands. The whole party gathered around her in a circle, and, following Henri's lead, raised their drinks and shouted "Ceres!" This event, recorded by the lander's cameras and beamed to Earth, where it was shown worldwide, was to cause celebration in some quarters, and great grief in others.

The festive atmosphere quickly turned practical. Henri's ten-man militia was dispatched to reconnoitre and secure an area 500 metres in radius from the base camp, which was being erected at a safe distance from the lander. They waded ankle-deep through leafy, clover-like plants, sending up sprays of hopping insects before them, but apart from a flat, slow-moving snake-like creature with armoured scales, they saw nothing to concern them. A network of night cameras and motion sensors was set up on the perimeter, and when they returned to the base camp on the completion of their task, they were ebullient.

"It's clean!" said Chuck Connolly as he approached Arlette and Henri with a big smile on his face. "Ground's firm and pretty flat, no pernicious wildlife detected, nearest tree cover is about 2,000 metres from our boundary. We'll get the surveillance network connected and then we should have excellent supervision and control of the base area, day and night."

Henri nodded. "The boosters landed about 3 km east of base camp; I saw them as we were landing. They are mounted on a motorised carrier. Take three men and go and fetch them."

"Yessir!" said Chuck. He delegated the job of connecting and testing the surveillance network, then took a long swig from his water bottle. As he did so the air pumps under the inflatable base camp started to whine and the whole structure began to rise and take shape. The militiamen stood and watched it, grinning, while the maintenance team scrambled around, coaxing the expanding monster into shape. It righted itself with a pop, to cheers from the onlookers.

Henri turned to the remnants of the militia. "I want a trench from here in the direction of those trees to thirty metres short of the perimeter, then fifty metres on either side. Get to it!"

"Colonel, we can't complete that before dusk just with spades," pointed out the lieutenant in charge, somewhat miffed to be left with a manual task.

"I'm calling down some mechanised equipment right now," said Henri. "You should have it within four hours. In the meantime, mark it out and get digging!" Henri turned and strode back to find Arlette, who was inspecting her newly erected office. "I'm calling down the Phase 2 hardware now," he told her. "I need a personnel carrier and digging equipment as well as all the infrastructure components for the base. We need to consolidate here as rapidly as possible."

"OK with me," said Arlette, testing out her inflated chair/desk unit and turning to take a call. "Hi Julia!" she mouthed into her earphone. "Thank you. Yes, we've had an excellent start. Henri…" – she looked round at him briefly and smiled – "is just calling down the Phase 2 equipment drop."

Henri turned and left, activating his earphone as he did. "Hi Marcel!"

"Well, Henri, I noticed you've been softening up Jeanne d'Arc with the old surprise champies trick!"

"Yeah," said Henri, "it worked a treat. She was almost misty-eyed; almost."

"Well, congratulations," said Marcel. "It all looked really good on the news clip. Ceres was a nice surprise. A lot more appropriate for this planet than the lifeless asteroid in our own solar system. She's good with mythology. And she came across really thrilled with her new planet without overdoing the humility thing. But I guess you are busy. What do you need?"

"We're ready for Phase 2. We need the whole infrastructure package right away. We're secure enough here now but we'll be more vulnerable after dark. There's no reason to think that we can't sustain our presence on the planet, so we need to consolidate as fast as possible. In addition we need a personnel carrier, a cargo truck and a trenching machine."

"OK. No heavy armament?"

"No," said Henri. "I have no read on what sort of arms we might need. We might get a better feel from Chuck when he gets back with the booster unit, but for the time being we'll concentrate on consolidating the base."

"OK," said Marcel again. "I'll have three cargo landers off to you within the hour. Where do you want me to land them?"

"Fifteen hundred metres west of base. It's absolutely flat there and there are no credible threats in the area."

"It's on its way, Colonel. Good luck!"

* * *

Chuck Connolly's progress slowed as his detail reached the tree line. The trees were of a relatively primitive type, stubby palms and conifers, ten metres high at most, and the ground was thick with ferns and prickly underbrush. They had hardly penetrated the forest twenty metres when there was a yelp from one of his men. "I've been stung!"

"Put on your protective face masks!" called Chuck. "Cover all exposed skin!" He walked over to the injured man, who had by now developed an ugly welt on his cheek. "Taken your antihistamine?" he asked.

"Just did, sir," said the man.

"OK, men, we've got just under 500 metres to go to get to the booster unit," said Chuck, "then we'll be able to ride back on the carrier. Let's get this done!" It was hot, the shade of the trees was intermittent at best, and the insects were all over them, flying, running and crawling. The four men settled into a steady rhythm as they tramped onwards, confident that their ordeal would soon be over.

"It's just up ahead!" called Chuck, the gleaming white of the booster unit tanks just visible through the trees. "Damn, damn!" They halted. The carrier was lying at an absurd angle, one set of transporter tracks high in the air with the broken trunks of two large trees thrust through them, and sitting astride the tanks, apparently asleep in the sun, was a huge, black, fur-covered arachnid, the size of a small truck.

Chuck reported the facts to his CO by earphone. "Proceed with caution, do not use firearms," responded Henri. "Use marker rockets to get it to leave."

The men took cover behind tree trunks as Chuck prepared his launcher. "Ready – three, two, one, fire!" The rocket streaked just over the top of the creature, billowing orange smoke in its wake. The spider shot to its feet, numerous eyes on stalks scanning the intruders, the hair on top raised bolt upright. Then it spat, globs of yellow liquid hitting the men with astonishing force, accuracy and rapidity. "Stay under cover!" shouted Chuck, "and don't touch that stuff!"

"It's gone under my mask!" moaned one of the men. "It's burning me! It's burning! Aaaah!" The other three watched their comrade in horror as he dropped, screaming in pain, to his knees, and his body began to convulse. Another volley of yellow globs spattered onto him, and his screams rose in intensity.

"We're going to take it out!" yelled Chuck. "Fire after me if you get a clean shot but don't hit the tanks!" He took aim and fired a single shot just below the moving forest of eyes. The spider leapt off the tanks and hit the ground, running straight for Chuck. "Fire now!" he roared and automatic fire ripped into the spider from three sides. It rolled into a grotesque ball, legs flailing, crashed into a tree, and lay trembling. "Koh, guard the spider! Kharkov, go and help Spencer! I'm going to check the booster unit."

When he returned a few minutes later, his three companions met him halfway. "Spencer's dead," said Kharkov.

"The spider's stopped moving," said Koh.

"The booster unit is OK," said Chuck quietly, and they walked back to where Spencer lay under a tree, his head propped up on his pack, mask removed and shirt ripped open. The flesh of his neck, face and chest was scarlet and covered with angry, bleeding blisters; his eyes, full of terror, were still open. Chuck knelt and closed them with the fingers of his gloved hand, then reported the grim news to his CO.

"Colonel, we have a fatality," he said. "Spencer has been killed by poison the spider spat at him. It got under his mask and caused his skin to break into open blisters. He died within a couple of minutes."

There was a long silence.

"Merde!" said Henri under his breath. "Where's the spider now?"

"It attacked us and we opened up with automatic fire. It appears to be dead."

"OK. Do you have video of the attack?"

"Yeah, you should have that on your system already. I'm just walking over to the spider now so that you'll have full coverage from my helmet camera."

The three men walked warily around the spider's body, weapons poised.

"OK, I've got it," said Henri. "You weren't exaggerating about its size! Can you turn it over?"

"We aren't going to touch it, Colonel," said Chuck. "We can use the winch that's on the carrier to do that, but we'll get the booster unit righted and ready to roll first."

"Copy that," said Henri. "I'll be watching you. Get Koh to remove his helmet camera and leave it focused on the spider so that we can keep an eye on it while you're working."

The three of them turned their attention to the carrier and its cargo of tanks and electrolysis equipment. Chuck Connolly walked slowly around the stricken vehicle, examining the damage. As far as he could see the tracks were still intact although badly distorted by the impact with the trees. The problem they had to resolve was to get it off the tree trunks without inflicting further damage.

"Any suggestions, Colonel?" enquired Chuck as he completed his inspection tour.

"I'm just having the carrier design specs checked," responded Henri, "but I propose you loop the winch cable around a strong tree trunk and then attach the hook to the top of the tripod structure that supports the main 'chute housing on top of the tanks. The winch is on a gimbal, so it will adjust itself automatically to the direction it needs to pull in."

"Got it," said Chuck. "That tripod had to support the

weight of the carrier when the 'chutes deployed. It has to be strong enough to pull the lander over."

"Yeah, yeah, it's OK," confirmed Henri. "Proceed."

The winch cable was run out to its full extent, looped around a tree trunk and the hook returned to the carrier. Kharkov was dispatched to shin up the tripod and fasten the hook to the top.

"Well," said Chuck to his CO, "it was a truly screwy idea to put the booster unit down in a forest in the first place, but at least it's provided us with a source of anchor points to solve the problem we created for ourselves."

"That's your job, soldier," was Henri's response.

"Stand well clear of the cable!" yelled Chuck to his detail, and started the winch motor. He watched intently as the cable took up the slack and then bit hard into the bowl of the tree it was wound around. The tracks groaned and squeaked as they were dragged off the broken tree trunks but they were lifted clear without incident. Chuck cut the motor and the three men crowded round to inspect the tracks and driving gear.

"Nothing serious," was Chuck's comment. "I'm going to start the motors and see if we can get her to move forward."

The carrier's tracks began to churn into the earth, and the cable tore into its anchor point, but the great craft inched forward. Chuck walked behind it, remote controller in hand. Progress was painfully slow, but the winch cable held and the carrier eventually moved clear of the broken tree trunks that had impaled it. He stopped the motors and activated the winch, lowering it slowly back on to an even keel. There was a little cheer, and then they set about the sad task of consigning Spencer to a body bag and loading him onto the carrier. Strangely the corpse had not attracted any insect life, despite having lain in the open air for the past hour. Chuck took notice of this fact, and concluded with a shudder that the spider's toxin was probably potent enough to keep all wildlife away.

They returned to where the body of the spider lay, grotesquely propped against the tree on its head where it had come to rest, its long legs splayed in the air, huge yellow fangs prominent below its eyes. Pale blue fluid seeped out of multiple wounds in its body. It stank hideously.

The three men eyed the creature tensely, clenching their weapons.

"Aaah, it's moving!" shrieked Koh, and delivered a quick volley of shots into the creature. A slimy black bug, the size of a dinner plate, slid down the belly of the spider and scooted over the ground between them. All three jumped aside, yelling in surprise.

"Ugh!" said Connolly. "Some kind of parasite in the spider's fur! Let's get out of here."

The little party scrambled onto the carrier and it lurched back into the forest as fast as its battery-powered motors would allow. Koh and Kharkov sat at the back, their weapons trained on the spider's corpse, grimacing and unable to get the sour smell of it out of their nostrils.

For the crew members back at the base camp, the sight of the carrier slowly emerging from the trees, its tall white fuel tanks shining in the sunlight, was an immense relief. Here was their ticket back to the comfort and security of Prometheus; without this booster unit, and its capacity to turn water into rocket fuel, Lander 1 was stranded, no more than a temporary, immobile shelter.

For Arlette and Henri, however, it was a sombre affair, and the slow pace of the vehicle as it made its way towards them was reminiscent of a hearse. Together they walked out to meet it, each in turn thanking the three men for completing their task and commiserating with them over the loss of their comrade. They just nodded in return, still deeply shaken by the horror of their encounter.

The carrier was brought to rest next to Lander 1, ready to be linked up to a water supply. Then Koh and Kharkov carried the body bag containing Spencer back to the base and handed it over to the duty doctor.

The findings of the autopsy surprised no one. Spencer had died of respiratory failure brought about by a central nervous system toxin not dissimilar to those found in the venom of poisonous snakes on Earth. The nature of the irritant that had caused Spencer's skin to blister and puncture so quickly could not be immediately established, but the combination was clearly lethal to mankind, and probably to most of the other creatures on Ceres.

On hearing the news, Arlette retired to her office with Henri and called a video command meeting with Marcel, Julia and Chang, who had watched the spider attack in real time on Prometheus as it unfolded. Arlette read out the autopsy report in full and asked her colleagues for comment.

Chang was the first to respond. "We are very distressed by the death of Spencer and concerned that the animal life we see on Ceres could prove to be dangerous to humans," he said. "We have been examining our scans and have found nothing to contradict our original findings that mammals and reptiles seem to be absent. There is life in the seas but we don't see shoals of fish. What we do see frequently on land is groups of six-legged creatures somewhat like scorpions, but about the size of an elephant, and large, tightly packed herds of ant-like creatures, individually about as big as a large dog. Both these species are obviously carnivorous given the carcasses lying around in their vicinity. We think they are feeding on the herbivorous life, of which there is a huge variety of running and hopping creatures of all sizes. On top of that there are numerous species of very large flying creatures somewhat like wasps and beetles, but also elephantine in size. We think they are also carnivores." He sat back and turned to Julia, who was clearly anxious to get in on the debate.

"Commander," said Julia. "We don't rate this as a particularly serious threat in the context of planetary exploration. We will obviously have to keep the herbivores out when we start to develop agriculture, and provided we can do that successfully, the carnivores should have no interest in us. What we need to avoid is surprises of the kind that cost Spencer his life. The toxins developed by these creatures have got to be pretty potent given the size of the prey."

"Surprises are kind of inevitable in exploration," said Henri, "but I think we can improve our kit and discipline to protect our people a lot better."

"Marcel, do you think we are adequately equipped at present?" asked Arlette.

"Well" he said slowly, his head on one side, "it was always going to be a process of learning from experience. I am mortified that we lost Spencer but it was a terrible price we had to pay not to be arrogant about our supposed superiority. I would have made the same decision as Henri in trying to scare the spider off, but we have to remember that its reaction was not unreasonable given that we are much smaller creatures than it was, and it has never experienced anything like a bullet and so had no fear. It was just chasing some impudent little interlopers off its territory. If we learn to think in the right context about these creatures, properly protect ourselves from stings and venoms, and always carry arms, we should be fine."

"Assuming these creatures have the kind of instincts we'd expect," chipped in Julia, "they will stick to the diet they are used to. They may see us as interlopers, but not as food."

"Isn't that begging the question?" asked Chang. "We are all assuming that these creatures have similarities to the insects we know on Earth. It's pretty far-fetched to assume that there is any shared ancestry, isn't it?"

"Yes, but not impossible," said Marcel, "but that's not really the issue. Here is an ecosystem populated with creatures with very limited intellect, interested in surviving and procreating, and not impacted by any kind of civilisation. If that's all it is, it should not be hard to predict behaviour. They won't be mindlessly aggressive unless we threaten them, or their young, or their territory. Oh, and by the way," he went on, "your Phase 2 packages will be arriving in eight minutes."

Arlette, sensing that Chang was about to challenge Marcel into a lengthy discussion of how shared ancestry could have come about, grabbed the opportunity to close the session.

23
Phase Two

"Well, Henri," said Arlette, "hadn't you better get your boys running around after parachutes?"

Henri grinned. He sensed a hint of a thaw in their relations and he gave her a shamelessly appreciative head-to-toe look. Arlette saw it and savoured it. She rose, inhaled and looked down her nose at him. "Off you go, then." Henri remained seated.

"We're eight hours into twenty-three hours of daylight," said Henri. "I'd like to discuss our priorities for the rest of the day."

"That, Henri, will very much depend on the successful recovery of the Phase 2 supplies, won't it?" She was still looking down her nose at him.

"We can assume…"

Arlette interrupted. "No, we can't assume anything until they are safely on base."

Henri rose to his full, considerable height and let one of his stunning smiles loose on her.

"OK, Commander, I'll be back shortly," he said.

She watched him leave, her eyes lingering for a moment on his elegant butt. "A bottle of champagne from nowhere, the cunning bastard," she said to herself with a grin.

The three Phase 2 parachute clusters were already visible as Henri walked out into the sunshine. "Chuck?" he called out.

Chuck Connolly came trotting up to him.

"I want three armed men on each package. They're coming down on the west of the base where it's flat and treeless, but we're taking no chances. Everyone is to be fully kitted and masked."

"Yessir!" said Chuck. He trotted off, then stopped and turned. "There's a touch of a breeze now. What if we get a water touchdown?"

"You swim!" came the reply. "All the packages are designed to float. The water's OK, just rather strongly saline. You take a cable out, hook it up and get it done."

"Yessir!"

A few minutes later the three details were heading out, cheered on by the rest of the base crew. The first two packages landed just a few hundred metres from the perimeter, but the third one drifted just off the shoreline before it landed with a huge splash in the sea, accompanied by a groan from the spectators. After a few seconds it rose to the surface and righted itself, water streaming off the bright orange casing that enwrapped it.

The three-man detail assigned to recover the package could be seen laying their weapons and helmets aside and running into the water, one with a cable around his waist. There followed a great deal of excitement and arm waving, but they soon applied themselves and, goggles flashing in the sun, made the hundred metres or so to the package, hauled themselves up onto it and secured the cable. Sensing that they were being watched as they hauled the cable back in, they all waved vigorously to their distant spectators as if their little exploit fully deserved recognition. The carrier came to rest about twenty metres away from dry land as its tracks crunched into the pebbles on the sea bed. Somewhat to Henri's surprise, the three happy passengers did not promptly engage the carrier's motors but jumped into the water and frolicked around, shrieking and whooping. After a while they seemingly tired of this unscheduled recreation, and the whine of the motors could be heard as the craft inched its way onto dry land.

In twenty minutes they were back at the base alongside the other two carriers and their bright orange cargoes. Kropnik, who had led the detail, advanced towards Henri with a furtive smile. "Colonel" he said, proffering a kit bag whose contents were clearly moving, "I bring you a gift from the seas of Ceres."

Henri eyed the soldier cautiously and peeped inside. What he saw would have been a very familiar sight in another context, but even on Ceres it was unmistakable. It was a large, dark green lobster.

While the maintenance crew unloaded the cargo on the three newly arrived carriers, the lobster was taken off to the first aid room and cautiously examined by both the duty doctor and his biologist colleague Matt Kirby. Henri dropped in twenty minutes later. "Well?" he said.

"Without having the luxury of comparing this animal's

DNA with that of its apparent relative on Earth, I would say that this creature is undeniably what we would call, back on the coast of Maine, a very fine lobster," said Kirby.

Henri sensed an opportunity here but asked the doctor, "Did you find anything toxic or biochemically dangerous in the flesh?"

"Nope," said the doctor. "I agree with Matt. I'm not going to recommend it as sashimi right now, but properly boiled with lemon butter sauce on the side, I think it will make someone a fine dinner."

"Thank you," said Henri with a smile. "I have an appropriate recipient in mind, but I'm going to ask my guys to collect another sixteen so that the whole team can have a treat. Could you please supervise them and ensure that everything they catch is edible?"

"Will do," was the laconic reply.

Henri went straight to the kitchen, where he produced the lobster. "This one's for the Commander, but I'm asking my guys to collect another sixteen so that the whole crew can have a bit of a break from cultivated protein today," said Henri. "Can you handle that?"

"Colonel, it will be a real pleasure," said the cook, his eyes sparkling.

The unloading of the infrastructure packages generated an intense level of activity. Power was soon available from the nuclear generator, water from the desalinator, and drainage and a waste disposal plant were installed. Within four hours wall panels were erected around the flimsy inflatable structure of the camp, water and sanitation made available and basic furniture installed. The militia, instilled with new confidence with the arrival of their personnel carrier, truck and mechanical digger, took to strengthening their defences in earnest.

With nine hours of daylight still left, Henri announced that dinner would be served on trestle tables in the shade of Lander 1. It took almost an hour to get the entire base crew washed up and seated, then Arlette got to her feet and silence spread around the tables.

"Please stand and spend a minute in remembrance of Lieutenant Derek Spencer, who lost his life today defending us. He was a man of courage and humility, and an example to us all. He will be buried here tomorrow with full military honours."

Absolute silence reigned.

Then Arlette spoke again. "If I could bring myself to believe in a deity, today would be the day I would thank Him for granting me the privilege of standing here now. But we are here because of the fabulous ingenuity of the human race and the skill and dedication of every member of the Prometheus crew. Look around you at this beautiful planet, and savour this great moment in history. You are the first of the Ceresians and your accomplishments will never be forgotten. And now, enjoy your dinner. Colonel Bertin tells me we are having a surprise!"

She turned just as Henri, who had crept up behind her, slipped a plate before her, and, with a flourish, whipped off the cover. Arlette gasped and looked around. Clapping and cheering broke out. "The SOB has done it again!" she said under her breath.

The lobster was indeed superb, although the rest of the meal was only as good as could be expected given the limitations on the types of food that could be brought with them in the lander. The cook, who was the last to take his seat, was roundly cheered when he arrived. He waved them away, then got rather shakily to his feet. "If you can find me some edible plants and fruit, I can do much better," he said, and sat down. A few minutes later he jumped up again. "Just a minute," he said, and hurried back to the kitchen, only to return clutching two bottles of a dubious pink liquid. "A Freddy Jones special!" he announced.

Henri promptly took charge of the bottles, administering a small amount to everyone present. He raised his little beaker and said, "To the first of the Ceresians!" and drained it. Most of his colleagues did likewise. Arlette sniffed it, grimaced, and took a sip.

"I think I'll stick with champagne," she said to the cook with a smile.

At the end of the meal Henri held a brief consultation with Arlette and then addressed the group. "We have plenty more to do with the seven hours of daylight remaining," he said, but it's time some of you got some rest. In particular our militia, who will be manning our defences during the hours of darkness. Will the following please now go and get some sleep." He read out a list of names, then followed it with the rest and shift times of the whole crew. "This information is on your phones. We will be out of sync with the length of day and night time that you're used to from now on, and we have to learn to cope with the forty-two-hour day on Ceres. I know everybody is excited and prepared to work until they drop, but we need to get some structure into our working day now."

Those assigned to their rest period left, while others set off to complete their remaining tasks or just wandered around within the perimeter, taking a closer look at their surroundings. As Omega 16 dipped towards the horizon, and a second moon joined the one that had been visible for most of the day, a small party gathered where they had dined earlier and watched the stars come out in their new, unfamiliar patterns. It was just after this group, who had spent the last hour of twilight exchanging childhood stories with each other, had retired, and the first militia night watch had come on duty, that the buzzing started.

At first it sounded like distant traffic noise. Then it became more like the sound of light aircraft, intermittently flying aerobatics, but a long way off. It went on and on, varying in intensity, but never completely quiet.

Henri had returned from an inspection of the base defences as Omega 16 began to set. He was pleased with the network of trenches that had been excavated and the raised gun emplacements just inside the perimeter. Five men on sentry duty at a time wasn't much, but the surveillance system was working well and providing complete visual coverage of the surroundings. It would continue to do so with infra-red imagery after dark. After completing a brief report for the command team, he decided to go and give Arlette a verbal version. It wasn't a hard decision, he thought with a grin as he approached her door. He called her silently on her earphone rather than knocking, in case she had decided to get some sleep. She hadn't. She was pleased to see him, to share some of her thoughts with him. He entered her quarters, closed the door silently behind him, and turned.

Arlette was sitting in a large chair, looking at him in the dim light. "Hello," she said softly.

He squatted before her, one hand on the arm of her chair. "How are you?" he said, equally softly.

"I think," she said, leaning towards him, "I think..."

Just then there was a chatter of automatic fire and a sound like a helicopter passing immediately above them. Henri jumped to his feet and left the wide-eyed Arlette without a word.

"It's down, it's down, just beyond the western perimeter!" was the first thing he heard as he connected into the military intercom.

"What is?" he demanded.

"The big flying thing! It was coming straight at us!" It was Chuck Connolly, not at his most coherent.

"A machine?"

"No, a bug! A ginormous bug!"

"Where is it now?"

"It's on the ground, just beyond the western perimeter," cut in Kropnik, his voice calmer. "I have it in my sights."

"Yes, I see it," said Henri as his surveillance system monitor sprang to life. "Wow! It must be the size of an elephant and I don't like the look of those horns!"

"Shall I finish it off?" Kropnik wanted to know.

Before Henri could answer, a whine overhead announced the arrival of two large wasp-like creatures, apparently in pursuit of the giant horned beetle. They circled the stricken creature a couple of times and then dived onto it, clearly intent on killing it.

This could have been an interesting spectacle for the crowd of onlookers which was now gathering in front of the base, but seconds later the rumble that had been growing in intensity for some minutes became a screaming cacophony and the sky filled with over-sized flying insects of all descriptions.

"Connolly! Kropnik! Get your arses back here, now!" yelled Henri. "Guard militia, return to base immediately!"

As he scrambled out of his emplacement, Kropnik was confronted with a dog-sized moth that came lumbering up to him out of the darkness. Instinctively he opened fire and dropped the creature in its tracks.

"Stop shooting, you morons!" a female voice among the onlookers shouted.

"Easy for you!" yelled Kropnik as he raced between the bizarre creatures that were now dropping to the ground all around him. "Ugh!"

There was a crash and a scream as something went through a lighted window in the base.

"Benny, kill the lights. All of them!" barked Henri through his earphone.

A few seconds later the base was plunged into total darkness. The thumping of flying bodies into the floodlights stopped and the frenzied motion of the new arrivals on the ground slowed. Henri hustled the remaining spectators indoors and checked his men. "Koh! Where are you?"

"He's with me!" said a breathless voice. "I think he's been stung. I'm bringing him in."

Koh was indeed in a bad way. His eyes were rolling and he was pouring with sweat. His tunic was hurriedly cut off him, revealing a huge red swelling on his back – a sting had gone right through his jacket, leaving a blueish hole in his flesh. The doctor pumped antihistamine into him and hooked him up to life support.

"Out!" he said to the anxious onlookers.

The spectators of the 'insecticide', as someone put it, gathered in the conference room and called on Henri to explain what had happened. He pointed out that it was the task of the militia to guard the base and they had reacted to what they had perceived as a very real threat from the huge horned beetle which appeared to be about to attack them.

"Can you be more specific about the signs of aggression exhibited by this beetle?" someone asked.

"Are we to be surprised that an artificial light source arouses the curiosity of wildlife on this, or any other planet?" asked another.

"Can we expect your men to open fire on any creature they come across which does not comply with your expectations? Isn't that likely to increase the risk of attack?" This one was from Shelley Mathews, always provocative, but brilliant in her IT role. Her voice was clearly recognisable as the one who had called Kropnik a moron for opening fire.

Henri held up a hand. "Shelley, the militia is here to ensure your safety. We've lost Derek Spencer doing just that and we've come close to losing Koh. I don't think..."

There was a rumble of disapproval. "Could we have a little more thought and a little less brute force, Colonel?" called out Benny Tromper. "We actually antagonised the wildlife here when we really should be finding ways to get on with them. Please."

Henri realised he could not tough this one out. "Alright," he said, "we'll go out of our way to avoid confrontation in future. I think your points are well made." The tone of the muttering became softer, enabling Henri to engage with several individuals about their personal perceptions and views. After about ten minutes good humour reappeared and the group began to disperse.

Chastened from his grilling, Henri went off to inspect the base for damage. He found little to worry about, and he called his men together. "Change of strategy," he announced. "I don't want any of you exposed to as-yet unknown risks from the local fauna. We will upgrade the surveillance hardware and carry out brief patrols hourly, which we will motorise as soon as we can. Unless we see that the integrity of the base is at risk, we will not interfere with the wildlife. I will upgrade your weaponry but the killing of some animals may well attract lots of others. We have to learn to live with them. Today was day one. The floodlights will only be used in an emergency. Any questions?"

"How's Koh?" asked Connolly.

"He's still alive but in intensive care," said Henri. "The doctor thinks he'll live but it will be close. Anything else? Right – Major Connolly will organise the patrols."

Henri went to his office and sat for a few minutes, contemplating his first day on Ceres. The loss of Spencer, and Koh's delicate state of health, played on his mind for a while, but then he forced himself to think of the fantastic accomplishment that was behind them, and the limitless possibilities now open, and he smiled a wistful smile.

Despite his intense fatigue he decided to check on Arlette before he turned in. He made his way back to her quarters and pushed open the door without a sound. Arlette was in her chair, her face lit only by the light of the phone on her lap, her head on one side, eyes closed. He looked at her for a minute or two, then closed the door again and left.

Arlette watched him go from one slightly opened eye and suddenly she felt terribly alone. She thought about how her view of life had changed as this mission had progressed. The relentless demands of command had turned her into a governing machine. On former missions she had led by sheer exuberance and force of personality, with a close personal relationship with every one of her crew-mates. Now, here she was, managing everything. Her interactions with others had lost their intimacy. She sought opinions, she built consensus, she made decisions and they were disseminated. The weight of the responsibility she had was leaving no room for the light-hearted glee with which she used to do her job. This was nobody's fault; it was simply the reality of the level she had now reached in her career. She could not take a day off from being the commander. She had competent people to delegate to, but the key decisions were all hers.

And what of her private life? It no longer existed. She didn't have a sex life, which was hard and unhealthy, and she had very little personal intimacy with anyone. She could have enjoyed Henri's company, but the happy times she had spent with him in Acapulco had been a sham. She did not want to remember the intimacy she had shared with him and she could hardly remember anything tender before that. She liked Hannah but they weren't really close, and she liked and admired Julia but she was obviously helping herself to Henri's charms, totally unaware of the pain it was causing. The only other man that she had felt any attraction for was Genes, and he was not showing any personal interest in her. She could hardly proposition him – supposing he turned her down? There would be nowhere to hide! 'What I need is some new blood,' she thought. 'Perhaps I should ask General Lee to send some eligible males on a relief ship.' She sighed, and then, lightening up, 'Global fame, incredible adventure, and total command not good enough for you, Arlette Piccard?' she thought to herself and a grin spread over her face.

* * *

The first video of the landing and the subsequent encounters with the indigenous wildlife caused a sensation when it reached Earth. Arlette and Henri became instant global celebrities. For Henri this resulted in scrutiny that was professionally undesirable, and he was dismayed to learn later that he had become known as 'General Ceres'. Arlette was promptly drafted onto numerous candidacy lists for high office; after all, while Earthbound leaders obfuscated and made promises that no one believed, here was someone who had really done something with the potential to solve human misery on a vast scale. Pictures appeared of boundless pristine landscapes, untouched by any form of civilisation. Stories about giant spiders and huge flying beetles were dismissed as amusing at best and propaganda at worst. The perceived emphasis was on champagne and lobsters, and everyone wanted to know when they were going to be part of it.

The day after the pictures were released, however, the monsoons struck India with unprecedented violence, drowning tens of thousands and making several million people homeless, while huge grass and forest fires raged around the Amazon basin, in the west of the USA, in Southern Africa and the South East of Australia. Entirely unrelated, but even more distressing, were ongoing volcanic eruptions in Chile and Indonesia which pumped so much ash into the atmosphere that crops failed over large swathes of vital agricultural land. The President of China flew to Washington to discuss with his US colleague their response in the face of new data, yet to be released, indicating that the planet would continue to warm for at least fifty more years. Their joint communique referred to more grand projects to divert water to areas afflicted with worsening droughts, but failed to answer persistent questions as to how they were to be financed given the ongoing decline in the global economy. Riots protesting the sky-rocketing cost of food and the shrinking labour market broke out in numerous European cities and across Latin America, while Central Africa suffered yet another viral epidemic which the pharmaceutical companies had neither the will nor the resources to address.

Organised crime was prospering, however. Homelessness, joblessness, hunger and hopelessness were all stoking the market for hard drugs and fast credit, and with it an escalation in related theft and violence. But the organisations that were reaping the benefits of this huge and growing income were already looking ahead and starting to recruit ambitious people with totally different skill sets. Their view was that nothing could be done about global warming or the destruction of civilised society that was accompanying it. They could, however, offer a different solution for those who perceived that the ultimate winners would be those clever and ruthless enough to exploit the failure of governments and big business for their own advantage.

Three days after the first landing on Ceres, the two most powerful criminals on Earth, one Chinese and one American, met at a secret location in Bangkok to discuss progress. Joe Favaloro was from Chicago, a political science graduate and a martial arts specialist, who had shown neither fear nor remorse in the course of his violent ascent to the pinnacle of his huge organisation. He was now forty-three years old, a towering man with a penetrating gaze. He neither drank nor smoked, he talked little and listened carefully, frequently making notes on his phone. His opposite number was the reverse in almost every respect. Chan Lu Fat, alias 'The Joker', began his career in the Casinos of Macao. He was a round-faced, corpulent man, always cracking jokes but watching every move of those around him with the utmost cynicism. A glance to one of his aides and a nod in someone's direction would inevitably result in an execution, and he had a wide range of contacts within politics and legitimate business who would never cross him.

The two men dealt briefly with territorial and sectorial disputes, delegating their resolution to their appropriate henchmen. People would die in the execution of these decisions, but that was of no concern in this company. The discussion then led on to progress in politics; who had been bought, who needed to be bought, and who was becoming an irritant in need of removal. They quickly agreed that the recently elected President of Indonesia was an obstacle to business, and responsibility for the hit was allocated. Over fresh cups of green tea the discussion turned to Project Greenfield.

"Scorpion made big fuck-up of assassination," said Chan with a sour frown that engulfed his entire face in wrinkles. "I gave you best secret tool and he made big fuck-up." Favaloro waited for more. "What you gonna do now?"

"We lost five guys," said Favaloro drily. "We've got nineteen more as well as Scorpion. We'll get her when she's back in the ship and Bertin's down on the planet chasing bugs."

"They watching those nineteen," said Chan. "They know 'em. How they going to hit the bitch when they know 'em?"

"Relax," said Favaloro "They think their vaccine knocked out the effect of the virus. Everyone is cool right now. They are all doing their jobs like normal. Security on board has gotten sloppy. We'll get her with the next hit."

"Spider not sure," said Chan. "He say the Doctor Cohen pretty sharp. She suspicious but she ain't got the tools to check. Bertin's also sharp. He got a sword and two of our guys."

"Yeah, but we've still got seventeen running free and no one suspects Scorpion," said Favaloro. "Be patient and he'll do his job when the opportunity is right. We rushed it last time. We rushed it because you wanted action."

Chan frowned his ugly frown. "We ain't got much time. Those guys are getting wiser all the time and they still looking for answers."

"Well, let Spider talk to Scorpion and wise him up!" said Favaloro with exasperation. "Spider can get information much more easily than Scorpion can. It will reduce the risk."

"No ways!" snapped Chan. "Spider is backstop if Scorpion fails. No communication between Spider and Scorpion!"

"OK." Favaloro raised his hands, palms out. "Then you've got to let Scorpion choose his time, be patient."

The business done, the two men went on to discuss the evening's entertainment. "You ain't gonna believe what these Thai girls do!" said Chan, his ugly frown transformed into a weird grin.

24
The Safari

The remainder of the first long night on Ceres was relatively uneventful. Half an hour after the lights had been doused nothing remained of the invaders except the grotesque carcass of the great horned beetle. The guards sat in the control room, monitoring the surveillance system, but saw practically no movement, although the fateful buzzing from afar persisted.

By the time the sky began to lighten, most of the crew were up and about, keen to get on with the job of adapting the base to their surroundings. It was still far too cold to sit outside, so the conference room was converted to a breakfast/recreation area. When Henri arrived, copious unsolicited advice was offered on improvements of all kinds. One of the better ideas originated from the cook, who, between tirelessly delivering hot breakfasts, and with much gesticulation, suggested that they recover the parachutes from the Phase 2 drops and use them to make everything from blinds to tablecloths. This idea was later taken up with such inventive enthusiasm, and on such a scale that, before the day was out, the base had become colloquially known as 'The Orange House', a name that stuck long after the last traces of parachute fabric had eventually been replaced.

Arlette had entered the makeshift breakfast room shortly after the cook had made his theatrical contribution, had taken a seat opposite Henri, and the two of them had quickly got down to business. "I'll need better armament and more exploratory capability," he told her. "We also need more foodstuff to tide us over until such time as we can reliably forage locally."

"What do we need to adapt the base for an effective night-time black-out?" Arlette asked.

Henri told her about the planned use of parachute material. "I think there are benefits in having the crew down here busy on a project like this," he said. "It gives them ownership and encourages them to be inventive. I've commandeered some sewing machines and I think you'll be surprised and delighted with the results." He emphasised the words 'and delighted' with a smile that told her that he really did want to delight her. She laughed. His English was reverting to its native Haitian charm now and then and it made her feel less alone. She knew she had to be careful, but right now she was enjoying the warmth he radiated.

"OK," said Arlette. "What other equipment are you calling down?"

Henri gave her a list. An extension for the kitchen, a laundry, entertainment equipment, gardening and fishing equipment, food and seeds – it was all pretty mundane stuff. Armament and transportation to carry out extensive, safe exploration was, however, the most pressing need. They had to be able to feed themselves reliably and cost-effectively as soon as possible. Henri wanted to put the biologist and botanist expertise at his disposal to work, and he wanted to get Arlette out of her office and into an exploration truck, and he told her so. She laughed again. The place was buzzing. They were moving forward. She was happy.

The Phase 3 drop arrived three hours after sunrise, and this time all three packages landed with pinpoint accuracy just beyond the perimeter. The appearance of the orange parachutes in the cloudless blue sky was greeted with whoops of delight from the whole company. When the packages had been recovered and opened, something of a Christmas party atmosphere gripped the base, with everyone craning their necks to see what goodies had descended from the sky for them. It seemed there was something for everyone, but the most popular toys were the gardening tools, the fishing nets and the sewing machines. They were dragged out of their packaging and put to work almost immediately.

"Chuck, I want one of those anti-tank launchers mounted on the escort truck right away," said Henri as the military equipment was rolled off its carrier. "We're going to do a four-hour inspection tour to the east of the camp and I'll need a driver and a three-man detail on that truck to take care of any surprises."

"Yessir!" Chuck Connolly was pleased with the prospect that their next encounter with indigenous wildlife would most probably be on their own terms, but he was cautious about exposing his men. He thought long and hard about how to protect the occupants in the back of the truck and decided to include a screen that could be fitted quickly if necessary. An hour later the personnel carrier and its escort were equipped and provisioned, and their batteries fully charged. Henri handed the driver an approximate route pencilled onto a high-resolution orbital photo and went to fetch Arlette.

The personnel carrier could carry sixteen passengers in addition to the driver and an armed guard, but Henri had selected just six others for this initial foray. The objective was the location of potential food sources, so he logically included a botanist, a biologist, a doctor and a cook, but he also included the pilot and co-pilot of Lander 1, since they had very little to do at the base. As the little party pulled away, Henri stood and gave an impromptu intro, rather like a ranger on a Safari. It was of course very much focused on safety and security, but he couldn't resist adding a stern "and no fraternising with the natives!" at the end. He sat down and leaned over to whisper in Arlette's ear. "When we get around this wooded area, we should be able to see quite a sizable river. Could you please name it for us?"

"What would you like to call it?" she asked him.

"What about the Blue Loire?"

"Too blatantly nationalistic. What's the largest river in Haiti?"

"The Artibonite – they'll never buy it."

"Well, let's wait and see if it has some distinctive characteristics we can hang a name on."

The view as they rounded the wood was glorious. The land sloped away to a broad, green valley and, beyond it, stretches of the river, reaching towards the distant mountains, flashed in the sun. Progress was, however, slow and it was getting hot. The red earth was rutted and strewn with rocks and thick with coarse cactus-like plants that were surprisingly resistant to their progress. Henri got up and went forward to the driver. "Make for that wooded area over there. It looks a bit flatter."

The trees, when they reached them, were much taller and leafier than those they had seen closer to the camp, and much richer in variety. The passengers stared into the gloomy interior as they began to make their way down the edge of the woodland, but nothing seemed to be moving and the complete absence of birds and the eerie silence made the place seem sinister.

"Look at that fruit!" called out the cook, and following his pointing finger they could just make out what looked very much like a Christmas tree, decorated with red and orange packages, about seventy metres into the wood.

"OK," said Henri to the driver, "let's go and take a look." The personnel carrier and its escort ploughed in through the undergrowth, raising clouds of flying insects. "Chuck," said Henri into the intercom, "double-check that your men have goggles on and no skin exposed."

The tree was weighed down with fruit the size of footballs and the air was laden with their sickly scent. "Chuck, have a man retrieve a couple of fruits and deliver them here," said Henri, "and keep him covered at all times." One of the detail jumped down, drew his knife and approached the tree. He selected a couple of fruits and removed them carefully, then turned and walked towards the personnel carrier, one under each arm.

"Spider at two o'clock!" shouted Chuck.

The man bolted around the carrier and leapt into the open door. The spider climbed slowly down from its vantage point in a neighbouring tree and crouched on the ground watching them, its limbs moving it very slowly forward, like a fox stalking a rabbit. It was about half as large as the one that had killed Spencer.

"OK," said Henri. "Let's get out of here."

The engines whined and the two vehicles began to turn in a tight arc and head back the way they had come. The spider, however, was not appeased. It charged the personnel carrier, spitting yellow phlegm, then leapt onto the roof, dashing its fangs against the bulletproof observation hatches.

"Keep going!" shouted Henri and the personnel carrier ploughed on and out into the open ground, followed by the escort truck, with Chuck, grimly trying to keep the anti-tank missile targeted on the spider, bouncing around behind.

"Halt!" said Henri. They halted. The spider stayed put for a minute or two, then it stepped delicately off the roof of the personnel carrier, now smeared with yellow phlegm, and made its way slowly back to the trees.

"Bottle of water, anyone?" asked the cook, and everyone laughed with relief.

Once it got underway again, the little convoy continued to hug the tree line as it made its way down towards the valley. The orange football tree became a more familiar sight, but it was the cook's sharp eyes again that spotted crimson berries in a low bush just at the edge of the trees. This time the fruit was easily accessible and the passengers swarmed out of the people carrier to take a closer look.

It was all the doctor could do to prevent them from being tasted on the spot. "Don't forget that many of the wild berries on Earth are toxic to humans!" he said in a loud voice. "We will not be tasting anything we find before it is checked for poisons and pathogens!"

They had barely driven another 150 metres when there were four or five shouts from within the cabin and arms pointing at various fruit-laden trees and bushes in a shallow dip just within the tree line. This time they took a much more extended break while the soldiers collected samples of everything that looked edible.

Henri was checking the last passenger up the steps of the personnel carrier when he heard a low rumble that seemed to be coming from within the forest. Chuck had heard it too, and had instinctively swung his weapon around to the direction from which it was coming. Then they heard a different, much more immediate sound. Something very large was crashing through the trees and they could see the tree tops moving around violently as it progressed. It was not coming directly towards them but down the slope of the land in the direction of the river. Henri waved his arm and pointed, then jumped into the personnel carrier and they moved off in the same direction. As they watched through the trees they caught glimpses of a huge, yellow, eight-legged creature with massive clawed arms that were tearing small trees and bushes from its path as it ran. At its rear end five or six pointed tails were flailing around. Then, as they watched, it staggered and its outline blurred, almost as if it was melting. Its yellow colour deepened to a rippling red-brown. Henri blinked and re-focused his binoculars.

"Mon Dieu!" he said. "It's being eaten alive by ants!"

The personnel carrier came to a halt and the passengers could see the drama taking place quite clearly some fifty metres into the forest. The huge creature, eight or nine metres in length and about four metres high, had lost parts of most of its legs and was grabbing and crushing its predators with its claws, while striking out and stabbing them with its pointed tails. Its attackers were the size of large dogs, some of them engaged in direct conflict with their prey while others were simply dismantling it and carrying off chunks of its flesh. As each one departed, or was killed, another was there to take its place. After about five minutes of this relentless carnage, the prey stopped moving altogether and its predators continued to systematically dismantle its lifeless body.

"Well," said Henri, "I think we have all seen enough of that. Let's move on."

As the vehicle began to move, Tim Cochran turned around to the cook sitting behind him. "Wasn't that awesome, Giuliano?" he asked enthusiastically.

"Ye-es," replied the cook with some reserve. "I didn't mind the huge scorpion thing but those big ants are very frightening. There were millions of them. Imagine what it would be like to be hunted by them – you could never escape!"

Tim's instinctive attitude was to be gung-ho about taking them on, but he saw the trepidation in the cook's face and felt sorry for him. "We're not going to let them get you, Giuliano," he said with a hearty smile, shaking the cook's forearm, "and I'll tell you how. First of all, we won't allow any large animal, hunted or otherwise, to get close to the base where it might attract the ant-things. Second of all, Cobus Vermeulen is setting up a wildlife tracking system that will enable us to know just where they are, so we can take pre-emptive action if necessary. Nothing will be allowed to get near our cook, I promise!" and he gave Giuliano's forearm another shake.

The cook smiled weakly. "How are we going to stop large animals from getting close to the base?" he asked. "We weren't too successful last night."

"Well, we won't be making the mistake of lighting up the base at night again, so we won't be attracting nocturnal visitors," said Tim, adding enthusiastically, "and if anything does cross our electronic boundary, they'll be blown to bits by Colonel Bertin's new anti-tank weapons! See?"

The cook gave Tim another weak smile. It crossed his mind that fragments of freshly blown-up animal might be quite attractive to a swarm of carnivorous ants, but he turned his gaze outside.

The ground was becoming softer and darker now, and covered with low, leafy plants rather than the coarse bush higher up the slope. The forest began to melt away as well and it became apparent that they were on a flood plain, splashed with colour by numerous flowering plants and shrubs. The cook, ever vigilant for edible opportunities, requested a halt for a herb and vegetable hunt, and, as the party disembarked, they could hear the trickle of water in streams not far away.

Mpho Mathe, the biologist in the landing party, was bitterly disappointed with the wildlife she had seen so far on Ceres. "It makes no sense that on a planet as well endowed as this one evidently is, that there is so little variety of species. Not only have we seen no mammals or reptiles, but everything we have seen appears to be invertebrate, despite the huge size of some of them."

Botanist Carla Da Silva was also perplexed. "I can't get over the similarities with the vegetation on Earth. Almost everything I have seen looks like a variety of something familiar. Look at this." She scooped up a pretty little purple-flowered plant with her trowel and freed its roots of earth. "It's a bulb, in fact it's a tulip, near as damn it."

"Yes, you're right." Mpho leaned over a broad-leafed plant and pointed. "See this pretty little orange insect with the triangular body?" She photographed it. "It's just a modified spider. There have been creatures like this on Earth for hundreds of millions of years." The two women continued their tour of the area, both hoping to find some form of life that they could classify as utterly alien. They were disappointed.

They shared their views with Arlette and the doctor when they returned to the personnel carrier.

"You know, from what we have seen, and more importantly have not seen, you could almost believe that life on this planet started from a microcosm of Earth life some 300 to 400 million years ago," said Mpho.

"I could buy that from the evidence," added Carla with a shrug. "But it would suggest that this planet was utterly lifeless when this package arrived, and it then proceeded to evolve in a very Earth-like environment. But it is frankly incredible that nothing distinctly original evolved over that period of time. On Earth, the dinosaurs came and went, among others."

"Yes," said Mpho, "that is bizarre, because it suggests these huge oceans made only a transient contribution to the evolution of life on this planet at best. We'll probably need a fossil record to get an explanation."

Arlette pondered this for a while. "Well, the explanation may be astronomical, you know," she said.

The doctor nodded. "I was just reaching the same conclusion," he said. There must have been some selective extinctions, and the fact that the insects survived suggests they were radiation related."

"Meaning what?" asked Mpho.

"An extended period of gamma ray emissions from Omega 16? We don't know anything about the history of the star – it could have doused Ceres with radiation and killed every other living thing for all we know," he concluded

"And we don't know anything about Ceres either," said Arlette. "Perhaps the water arrived quite recently in a comet shower. And supposing your microcosm from Earth took the 200-million-year scenic route before it arrived?"

"Yes, Commander," said Carla, "there will be an explanation, but Mpho is right – the only place we'll find it will be in the fossil record."

"Well," said Arlette with a turn of her head, "sorry, but the sunhat and trowel stuff will have to wait a while because it won't help us to feed ourselves. In the meantime we have what we have to supply the proteins, fats and carbohydrates we need to survive.

"Carbs, and vegetable fats and proteins will be no problem," responded Carla. "There are plenty of candidates around, and I don't doubt that they'll respond to cultivation. Animal fats and proteins may prove to be a little more difficult."

"Oh, I'm optimistic about that," cut in Mpho. "We haven't seen much topographical variety yet. If we extrapolate from the animals we have seen so far, we can expect to find some sizable Blattodea or similar in marshy areas."

"Blattodea?"

"Yes, the ancestors of the cockroach family," said Mpho with a faint grin. "They're considered a delicacy in some parts of the world, lightly fried..."

"Er, I'm sticking to lobsters, thank you," said Arlette. "You'll have to find us something that doesn't require a huge leap of faith and can be farmed."

"Commander, we have two possible routes to follow." Mpho was engaging her seriously now. "Either we take back some of the local plants to Earth and breed cattle that can feed on them, then bring a breeding herd back here, or we fence off colonies of local fauna in their natural environment and adjust to the meat products they can deliver. We were lucky with the lobsters; we may be lucky again."

"I can't think why we wouldn't take option one," said the doctor. "It's much less risky."

"I don't agree," said Mpho. "An imported species would be prone to diseases and parasites to which it would have no resistance. Option two requires more upfront adjustment but is inherently more sustainable."

Arlette nodded, but she very much hoped that the upfront adjustments would be as easy as they had been with last night's dinner. And, preferably, delivered by a handsome man with a penchant for charming gestures.

Henri arrived and produced his map with the proposed route scribbled onto it. "We're done here as far as collecting samples is concerned," he said. "I want to get down to the river and see what it has to offer before we head over here" – he ran his finger over a yellow-coloured area – "and back up here to the base."

"Looks good," said Arlette.

The convoy moved off again further down into the valley. As the ground became more marshy they were obliged to make a detour onto a low ridge covered with dense bushes that obscured their view, but it finally delivered them onto a rocky platform bordering a bend in the river they had being trying so hard to get a sight of.

The vista was quite beautiful, the more so since it was totally unexpected. The river had cut through a shallow top layer of red-brown gravel and lay in a bed of pale grey quartz, sprinkled liberally with white pebbles. The bend below them had eroded the surrounding land to such an extent that it had become a circular lagoon, surrounding a central island only narrowly connected to the land by an isthmus of emerald green. The water was crystal clear and sparkling from the sunlight reflecting on the quartz below, and wallowing in the lagoon were five large animals.

Delight lit up the faces of the first human visitors, and most especially that of Mpho, who clapped her hands and exclaimed, "At last! Something really original – a Ceresian hippo!" They all looked. There was no mistaking that these creatures had insect origins – the six spindly legs, a separated head, chest and body, floppy wing-like appendages on their backs, and droopy, rather stubby antennae. But they were ponderous, slow-moving creatures and they were fat.

Henri turned to Arlette. "Well?"

"We'll call it Pearl River," she said, "and the Pearl River Lagoon."

Mpho was already slithering down the slope towards the water. As her feet clattered onto the narrow white pebble beach, the great beasts turned to stare at her, then, one by one, they submerged and swam lazily off into the deeper water of the lagoon, using their floppy wings for propulsion. Mpho sat down on the pebbles and waited. Within a few minutes the animals swam back to the shore and hauled themselves out of the water. They turned to stare at Mpho once more, then began to graze on the vegetation. The arrival of the rest of the party failed to generate much interest, and when the armed detail approached within a few metres of them, they just stared rather balefully at them for a several minutes, before ambling back to the water.

"What do you make of them, Mpho?" enquired Carla.

"It seems that they have an easy life here. Abundant food and no predators. Pretty meaty, too. By far the best candidates we've seen for farming."

The party returned to their vehicles, completed their photography of the panorama, and prepared to leave. "The next stop will be our last for today," announced Henri. "I want to see why this area of land looks so different on the orbital photos," he said, holding up the map and pointing to the yellow patch. "Then we'll head directly back to base."

The journey along the river bank was bumpy and

uncomfortable for everyone. They saw several more groups of Ceresian hippos, which showed no more interest in them than those at the Pearl River Lagoon, but no other sizable animals. Then the river began to widen out, still gliding over its glorious pearl carpet, the land became more even, the vegetation more grass-like, and the earth darker. Soon they found themselves in an undulating prairie, waist high in tall grassy plants, heavy with seeds of all shapes and sizes.

"Whoa!" cried Carla. "Pay dirt!" and she was out of the personnel carrier with a satchel full of sample bags.

The rest of the group watched her jumping from one plant to the next with a stream of enthusiastic chatter addressed to no one in particular. Within twenty minutes she was back, her satchel bulging. "Cereals!" she announced. "Lots! At least five varieties!" The rest of the party did their best to show interest, but there had been nothing else to see for a while but grasses, and some were beginning to get fidgety.

"I think we'll wrap it up there?" said Henri, his eyebrows raised at Arlette. She gave him a nod, and the little convoy began to make its way slowly up the rocky hill in the direction of the base.

25
La Cucina Ceresana

It was just after midday, Ceresian time, when the convoy arrived back. The rest of the crew dropped what they were doing and crowded around as the door of the personnel carrier opened and the passengers emerged. For a short while all was a confusion of shouted questions, groans and laughter until Arlette put up her hand for silence. "Give us half an hour," she said, "and we'll give you all a pre-lunch presentation. We'll be able to answer all your questions and let you see the clips we took."

The three scientists in the party took the hint and went off to prepare, leaving the pilots to treat the onlookers to some impromptu titbits of the morning's adventure.

"Anyone with arachnophobia should take the next shuttle home," announced Sanam. "It was so ghastly that I'm not going to sleep for a week. Huge quivering hairy legs, a forest of evil eyes on stalks, ugly yellow fangs and yellow glop coming out of everywhere. Ugh!"

"The army ants were impressive," chimed in Tim. "They were incredibly fast – I would imagine they could run down any creature we've seen so far – and they knew just how to get around the giant scorpion's armour. We'll have to be careful not to provoke those guys!"

Giuliano Benedetti the cook hurried off to his kitchen to see whether the newly arrived fishing nets had delivered anything of interest. He clapped his hands with pleasure at what he saw. There, in the bath he had commandeered the previous day for the unexpected arrival of the lobsters, were ten crabs, each about 20 cm in diameter. He selected one, boiled it, and carefully dissected it, tasting small quantities of the flesh from each sector. Pleased with the results, he prepared to boil the rest, then remembered that he needed the doctor's approval to serve any local food. He hurried over to the clinic and delivered a live crab in a saucepan, lifting the lid with a flourish and smacking his lips. The doctor inspected the crab and grinned. "Give me half an hour," he said.

The cook returned to his kitchen and went to check on the other arrivals on the lander that morning. There were two temperature-controlled boxes. One was an incubator which contained twenty-four carefully cushioned hens' eggs. The timer showed that they had already been at incubation temperature for eighteen days. In just two or three days he would have the first chick ever hatched on another planet, and soon thereafter eggs and poultry on the menu. In the other box he found vegetable seedlings, hydroponically grown on Prometheus and now ready for planting on Ceres. He surveyed his little domain, now so full of culinary promise, and felt elated. Then he burst into a very personal rendition of 'Bella figlia dell' amore' at the top of his voice, and everyone within earshot exchanged smiles and nods with their companions. A happy cook was very good news.

The presentation was introduced by Arlette. She traced the morning's journey on an orbital map marked with crosses and hastily assigned place names. The rocky slope was now Cactus Hill, the site of the first fruit tree became Pumpkin Tree Grove, and the area where they had seen an abundance of fruit trees and bushes was named Dale of Plenty. The spider attack and the killing of the giant scorpion were shown in slo-mo and discussed in considerable depth. There was no doubt that all of these creatures were potentially lethal to humans and that armed guards would be mandated for all activities outside the base perimeter.

"Do we assume that these spiders are forest dwellers?" Benny Tromper wanted to know. "Are they likely to attack us here?"

Mpho was on her feet. "We haven't seen them on the surveillance videos and we conclude that the aggressive behaviour we have seen is the result of us having disturbed them in their habitat. We believe they have a preference for forested areas, and avoid the open. We wouldn't expect to see them here because of the open space between our base and the forest."

"What prospects do we have of saving the life of a spitting spider victim?" asked Chuck Connolly.

"An antidote to the neurotoxin that killed Spencer is being produced on Prometheus and will arrive in a few days, and everyone will be issued with a shot to be used in an emergency," said the doctor. "But on no account may anybody enter a forested area with their eyes or any skin exposed."

"The pack of predators that killed the multi-tailed scorpion thing looked really dangerous. Do they pose a direct threat to us; I mean, might they invade us?" The question came from one of the maintenance engineers.

Mpho again. "We saw both these animals when we did our original scans from orbit. The giant scorpions seem to be solitary animals, but we saw their predators moving around in columns. I would guess that they are tactical predators. They probably chased the giant scorpion into the forest knowing that it could not move as fast there as they could. I don't think they'd invade us unless we left something outside to attract them." This produced an uncomfortable murmur in the audience.

Henri got to his feet. "We are able to track all significant animal movements from Prometheus," he announced, "and part of our job is to monitor that data and ensure that we are not taken by surprise. But", he added, "you must observe the standing orders for activities outside the base to the letter."

There was rather a long silence.

"Are the Ceresian hippos likely to be edible?" A question from another maintenance engineer.

The doctor responded. "Probably yes. They are apparently herbivores and rather docile. I can't promise that they'll taste like chicken but I think there's a good possibility that their meat will have a mild flavour."

The questions flooded in.

"Carla, did you find us any vegetables?"

"Yes," she said. "We have samples of fruit and vegetables which are currently being tested for toxins. When that's complete I'll invite you all to come and taste them and we'll decide which ones to harvest. I'm pretty sure that we have some acceptable cereal seeds, so we can expect to have fresh bread and pasta fairly soon."

This news was received with boisterous approval, a mood which persisted so that when the cook entered to announce that lunch would feature 'pasta alla granchio Ceresiana', he got an unexpectedly enthusiastic response. In fact his crab meat sauce was a masterpiece of ingenuity, concocted with a blend of indigenous herbs he had first tasted just an hour earlier.

The process of expanding knowledge of the environment, both in geographical scale and botanical and biological detail, continued under the direction of an impromptu Colonisation Committee, chaired by Arlette. Its objectives were initially security and survival, but developed into systematic food collection from an area some five square kilometres in extent. This included indigenous fruit, herbs, vegetables and cereals, the hapless Ceresian hippo, or Cerippo, which turned out to be excellent when barbecued, and a secretive rabbit-sized jumping beetle, which tasted not unlike bacon when fried, dubbed the Cerepig.

The first crew rotation was due to take place after completion of ten Ceresian days on the surface. Half of the initial arrivals would return to Prometheus, including Arlette and Henri, and would be replaced by seventeen new arrivals, with Marcel in charge and Chang taking over responsibility for security. In the pre-dawn of the day of their departure Arlette and Henri sat together over a rare cup of coffee and discussed the status of their mission.

"Astonishing, the conversion of hardened space-travellers into farmers within a couple of weeks," Arlette was saying. "All I hear about is food, and Benedetti is the undisputed hero of the mission!"

"Oh? What about the football?" asked Henri.

"Yes, of course." Arlette grinned. "Mixed football. One of my more productive innovations, don't you think?"

"Actually yes. A wonderful vent for aggression, including yours, I noticed."

"Are you referring to Benny's broken leg? He just fell badly, that's all," said Arlette defensively. "Football is about maintaining possession within the limits of the rules. He challenged me, I gave him a lawful barge and he fell over. Tant pis."

Henri grinned. The evening seven-a-side football game had become a regular event, now sporting three teams, some of whose members were training quite hard. Arlette had appointed herself captain of the Conquerors, which aptly described their attitude. Benny Tromper's team, the Magicians, were technically more skilful but were currently being outclassed by the sheer audacity of the Conquerors. Henri suspected that things would change in Arlette's absence.

"How do you see things developing socially?" he asked.

"It's command and control for the time being," said Arlette. "The commander on the ground has to listen to the input, define the programme and ensure that it's implemented. He or she has to have complete authority. For the rest, well there has to be tangible progress day by day, and people need to enjoy being here. I would like to leave a self-sufficient colony behind, but it will have to be composed of people who want to stay and build themselves a long-term home on Ceres."

"How about you?"

"Me?" cried Arlette. "I'm no farmer! I'm a space navigator. I'd rather take Prometheus to Omega 16-4 or another solar system than stay here."

"Well, either could be a lot more comfortable than being on Earth, from what we hear," said Henri. "How long do you plan to stay here? Do you have orders to quit at a certain point?"

Arlette studied him. It was an impertinence asking about her orders. On the other hand, he was right about the prospect of going back to Earth, which seemed to be slipping inexorably into social and political chaos, and she needed a strong, dependable ally. "Mission Control is responsive to my input," she said finally. "If I recommend an extended stay to secure the position of the human race here, I'm sure they will agree. They can build another ship and hire another crew. They don't need me back there."

"Do you ever think about Acapulco?" It came straight out of the blue.

Arlette's instincts were to cut him off, but she knew he wanted to get it off his chest, and perhaps that would make things easier.

"Not much," she said. "We were two adults, each with our own motivations. I was honest about mine. You weren't honest about yours. End of story."

"I was sent to do a job without ever having met you," said Henri. "I could not have done that job if I had been upfront with you. Of course I understand your anger at being deceived, but if you think I can just shrug off that experience, you are wrong. You hit a place I didn't know I had. It hurt – it still does."

"Oh dear!" said Arlette "Poor wounded soldier."

"Yes," said Henri stiffly, "I'm not ashamed to admit it."

"Well, Henri Bertin, you'll just have to put it down to collateral damage in the course of duty," she said.

Arlette shocked herself with the severity of this brush-off. It was not that she felt the need to be cruel to him, it was rather that she could not see a way to restore parity or intimacy in a situation where she was indisputably in command. It was a pleasure to look at his handsome face and fine figure, and remember the wonderfully controlled lust he had lavished on her, but how could that be resurrected in this context? She pursed her lips and continued.

"Now, where were we? Oh yes – the length of our mission. Having confirmed that we have a habitable planet, it is now our job to prepare it for immigrants. That means more than just being able to feed ourselves. We have to be able to build permanent structures from local materials. That means exploration for mineral resources, mining – industry. We know how to do these things, and we have to get on with it."

"Industry?" Henri was incredulous. "Isn't that a bit ambitious after two weeks on the planet? Where are we going to get the equipment?"

"Oh, you wouldn't believe the stuff we have on Prometheus. Portable nuclear power plants and motors of every size and description, construction kits, drilling equipment, furnaces and God knows what – and lots of very resourceful engineers. But our next task is back on Prometheus. We have to map the planet's mineral resources. In fact Marcel has been busy with that since we landed."

Henri felt completely upstaged. "But that will take years," he protested. "How much of that can we accomplish without additional help and equipment?"

"Oh, once the mineral resource mapping is done we have to demonstrate feasibility and then come up with a development plan. We already know that we have fresh water and the basic minerals for bricks, cement and glass within a workable distance from here. There's also lots of copper. We'll define what we can do with what we have, then order what we need on Prometheus II."

"It sounds to me as though we are not going back," said Henri.

"Of course we are going back!" retorted Arlette. "Once we have exhausted everything we've brought with us on Prometheus, what is the point of keeping her here? She becomes a ferry for both human and technical resources."

Henri saw it now. The powers that be on Earth would already be looking at maps of the resources on Ceres and dividing them up between them. The first proud settlers would soon be swept aside and the wrangling over wealth and power would begin. "Don't you think we might do a little better with this pristine planet than just import the way we do things on Earth?" he asked.

"Henri, just remember how this expedition was financed," replied Arlette. "The ISEA was tasked by the G25 with finding a new home for the human race once Earth becomes uninhabitable. We are scientists and navigators, not politicians. It's the politicians' job to apply the experience of several thousand years of civilisation to creating a viable new society on this planet. Ultimately Ceres will have a population of billions. It will have to be rigorously organised by visionary people. Idealism is fine for dreamers but it's not a practical basis for government."

"Don't you feel an emotional need to be part of it?" asked Henri, somewhat aghast at her detachment.

"Oh yes. But my part was getting here and planting my lips on the earth. Navigators are known for navigating, not their admin skills. I want to do my job here in an exemplary fashion, and then explore some other part of the cosmos."

"Are we going to Omega 16-4?" he asked.

"Yes, if we can. But our exploration will have to be fairly basic. We'll have used most of our equipment on Ceres. I want to have a look at that in more detail when we get back to Prometheus."

Some four hours later the returnees were entering the cabin of Lander 1. Stowed in the hold were a number of animal carcasses, including a spitting spider, a Cerippo and a Cerepig, as well as a large variety of vegetation samples, on their way for examination in the farmyard labs on Prometheus. While some members of the crew were happy to be getting back to the comforts of their personal quarters, most were sorry to be leaving the close camaraderie that had developed in and around the Orange House. As the travellers secured themselves, the atmosphere became akin to returning to school after summer camp. Stories of encounters with Ceresian wildlife began to take on embryonic embellishments that were the potential stuff of legends, and Giuliano Benedetti the cook, who remained behind, was on his way to global fame.

The spectators of the launch of Lander 1 were treated to a magnificent display of raw power rocketry out of all proportion to the puny scale and capabilities of anything left behind on the ground. As the ship lifted off and began to accelerate away, they all felt acutely aware of their vulnerability and dependence on the mother ship, and of the huge gulf between the capacity of advanced human civilisation and their own tentative foothold on planet Ceres. That this little settlement would lead to a solution of the enormously complex issues facing civilisation on Earth did not seem plausible.

26
Mayhem on Prometheus

An hour and a half later Lander 1 had docked with Prometheus and Arlette and Henri were being joined by Marcel, Chang and Julia for a debrief. As the other three were already familiar with the events that had taken place on the surface, Arlette began by talking about the current state of mind of those on the ground.

"We have a can-do pioneer spirit which I think is appropriate for this stage of the development of the settlement, but we are still in the basic adjustment phase," she said. "We have not spoken about whether some members of the crew will remain on Ceres for the long term, nor have I given much thought to selecting who might be invited to stay – I think it is too early. The weather has been very mild so far, but we will have to substantially upgrade the structure of the base prior to the arrival of winter, and that means developing sources of local construction materials. I've seen the mineralogy data, so I think it is now up to you to make a resource plan. The harvesting and agricultural activities are quite satisfactory at this stage – I assume that we'll be successful in growing staples from our own seed bank in Ceresian soil. The chicken farm is progressing nicely and Benedetti is doing wonderful things with local materials – he seems to have everybody working for him. What we need now is a set of projects with defined goals. There's a little too much entrepreneurial activity going on. Henri?"

"The security situation is a learning curve," said Henri. "Harvesting in woodland areas has to be conducted with extreme caution because of the spitting spiders. We operate a total black-out at night because the light attracts unwanted visitors, some of them large enough to do serious structural damage to the base. The giant scorpions and their predators haven't shown any interest in us, but we leave no organic waste outside. The perimeter surveillance system is working OK, but our site was well chosen and we've seen very little interest from native species. However, we take a heavily armed escort on all expeditions with the capability of stopping elephant-sized wildlife. We don't have any of the Wayward 19 on Ceres and we've detected no anti-social behaviour. How's it been here, Chang?"

Chang seemed surprised by the question. "Very quiet," he said. "We have no reason to believe that the vaccination programme was not completely successful. None of the Wayward 19 as you call them have stepped out of line in any way. They have been integrated back into their units and have been productive members of the crew."

"Integrated back into their units?" Henri was uneasy.

"Yes. We know who they are and we can quickly detain them if there's a need."

Henri thought briefly about the sabres that Benny

Tromper had made for him, and how easy it had been to manipulate Barreto with one, but he said nothing.

"Julia," said Arlette. "How do you assess the state of mind of the crew? How much information are they getting on events on Earth?"

Julia frowned. "In an agreement between myself and Mission Control, we are receiving edited news highlights for distribution to the crew. They have, as you know, no internet access other than the ISEA database, and we have agreed that there is no merit in circulating disturbing news about events on Earth. However, we have not implemented censorship on private communications between crew members and their families and friends on Earth, so we think a lot of them are quite well informed. That could put our credibility at risk."

"I don't think so," responded Arlette. "I haven't been asked to comment on any developments on Earth, and if I am, I will refer them to you as the expert. In my view honesty is the best policy. Chang, Henri – any views?"

"Could we censor private communications if we wanted to?" queried Chang.

"Absolutely," replied Julia. "We control the comms server. People would notice, of course. It would be a very crude instrument. I wouldn't want to use it unless there was something dire going on that would undermine the ability of the crew to function. Henri?"

"I agree that censorship would be a mistake," said Henri. "Everybody on this mission is here because they wanted to be part of a new start for humanity rather than trying to influence things on Earth. What we have of real value is our unity of purpose. We don't want the crew starting to mistrust the leadership. You remember how anxious we were about the Armenian episode? Feelings were undoubtedly high but loyalty to the mission came through unscathed. We have a lot behind us now to enhance that."

"OK with that, Marcel?" asked Julia.

"Absolutely," he replied. "The worse the news from Earth, the greater the relevance of what we are doing here. We need to have our noses in the dirt every hour of the day to ensure our survival. From what I have seen and heard, nobody disagrees with that."

"Alright. Is the next landing party good to go?"

"We've had a minor change," said Marcel. "Genes Clayton has decided to send one of his engineers rather than go himself. I'm a bit surprised but he says he has some concerns about the propulsion unit that he'd like to get resolved. He's hoping to be in the next party."

"A pity," said Arlette thoughtfully. "He's a very creative thinker and he'd be useful down there. Still, we can't afford to have any uncertainties about the power unit so I suppose it will have to be next time around."

Lander 2, the second of the booster-assisted shuttles that had piggy-backed Prometheus since the commencement of the mission, closed its airlock and cast off from the mother ship less than an hour later. Almost everyone on Prometheus watched the manoeuvre, listened to the countdown as she took up position alongside, and saw the flash of the engines before she shrank rapidly into the distance and dipped down towards Ceres.

Arlette returned to her quarters, deep in thought, with Henri beside her. She ushered him into her office. "You look worried," she said.

"I'll be a lot happier once I have the Wayward 19 under direct supervision," said Henri.

"OK, I understand, but will you please hang around for a few minutes while I talk to Genes. I want to hear from him about the problems we have with the propulsion unit."

"Sure," said Henri.

Genes Clayton arrived ten minutes later. He stood in the open doorway, a big smile on his face. "Welcome back, Commander. I can see that the bucolic way of life suits you!" As he stepped forward he produced a sword from behind his back and levelled it at Henri, just as four armed and masked men appeared behind him.

"Pandora!" he yelled.

A short volley of fire ripped across Henri's chest. He slumped on top of Arlette, forcing her to the floor. "Calling Julia!" he whispered in her ear as he covered her body with his.

"Hold!" said Genes sharply, pushing the motionless body of Henri off Arlette with his foot. He bent over her to rip off her earphone, but she bit savagely into his wrist and fought back until she was overpowered.

"Bind her, gag her and restrain her in the bathroom!" he ordered.

* * *

Julia was talking to Hannah Cohen when Henri's CTT call came through. She stiffened and rose to her feet. "Yes," she mouthed, then, "Hannah, we have a crisis. Genes Clayton is the terrorist leader. He has the Commander a prisoner in her quarters. Henri is badly hurt; he may be dying."

Hannah stared at her, trying to process this input, but Julia was already on her earphone to Chuck Connolly. His instructions to her were clear and immediate.

"Hannah, where will we be secure until Chuck gets here?" Julia asked. Hannah grabbed her hand and they sprinted along the corridor to one of the secure rooms used for psychiatric detentions. A few minutes later Chuck arrived with four militiamen. "Come," was all he said.

Their route back to the defence platform took a path completely unknown to Julia, and had obviously been created for the specific purpose of moving the military around Prometheus clandestinely. She made this comment to Chuck Connolly and he gave her a wry smile. "Colonel Bertin knows what he's at," was all he said.

Kropnik was at the security hatch as they emerged into the defence platform. "They're on the move," he said grimly as they hurried to the control centre.

"What do you know about Henri?" shot back Julia.

"The shots that took him down were not fatal. He was wearing bulletproof protection and nobody bothered to take off his earphone right away, so we know what happened. But we've lost the earphone and the video surveillance now."

The location of each of the Wayward 19 was shown as an orange dot on the three-dimensional map of the spaceship. They were formed into four groups, obviously now fully coordinated. "How come you can see where they are?" asked Julia, obviously relieved.

"The doctors gave them each a little present when they were being vaccinated," was the reply.

Their smiles faded as the familiar drawl of Genes Clayton came over the public address system.

"Crew members of IP262, this is Commander Clayton," he said. "There has been a change in the leadership of our mission. Commander Piccard has stepped down and Colonel Bertin has lost his life resisting arrest. I am now in command. All crew members are to return to their quarters immediately at this time and await instructions. Our militia is wearing orange armbands. You must follow their instructions or the consequences may be severe. Further announcements will follow in due course."

A few moments later a call came through to the defence platform control centre. The statement from Genes Clayton was as follows: "You will lay down your arms and surrender to my militia immediately. Failure to do so will result in the execution of Commander Piccard and random members of the crew that I will select. Their deaths will be entirely your responsibility and will continue until you comply." He did not wait for a response.

Julia, Hannah and the two soldiers sat and faced each other around a square table.

"OK, we have a hostage crisis and we are dealing with known killers," began Julia. "Rules one, two and three are negotiate, negotiate and negotiate. We have a defined leader whose motives and objectives we don't know. We have to explore those to make any progress. What are our military options?"

"We have a surviving military contingent of twenty-six, of which ten are currently on Ceres," said Chuck. "Numerically then we are at a slight disadvantage. But we know where our enemies are and they will find out pretty quickly that our men are not to be found. They will have to assume that we are all in the defence platform."

"In fact that is not the case," put in Kropnik. "We have an advantage in that we can move around outside the inner shell, and between the floors, to most parts of the ship undetected, we have sighting holes our snipers can use, and we have arms caches in strategic locations."

"Yes," added Chuck. "They are vulnerable to our ambush capability while they remain in groups of four or five as they are now."

Julia supressed the elation she felt at Henri's foresight. "Shouldn't we assume that they will start murdering people as soon as we start shooting?" she asked.

"I think so, yes," said Chuck. "We must have the time to be as well positioned as possible before we strike in order to minimise collateral casualties, but we will have to shoot to kill. Given what we know of their fanatical behaviour, there is no credible scenario for disarming them."

Julia glanced at Hannah, who sat, stony-faced, beside her. Hannah looked her sternly in the eyes and, almost imperceptibly, nodded.

Julia stared at the table. "This could cost the lives of both the Commander and Colonel Bertin," she said to no one in particular.

"I promise you that our first shots will take out the guards in the Commander's quarters," said Chuck solemnly.

"You have spyholes into her quarters!?"

"Absolutely. We have three men above the ceiling... – he turned to look at the control screen – "... there now.

It was our number one priority. And I can confirm that Colonel Bertin is alive, if not entirely well."

"Right!" said Julia. "How much time do you need to get into optimum position?"

"Thirty minutes," said Chuck.

"Good. Get going."

Julia picked up a pad of paper and began to scribble notes on it. She turned to Hannah. "We have to wait," she said. "We can't contact him. We haven't acknowledged receipt of his ultimatum. He has to call again." She went on with her notes. Hannah bit her lip and fidgeted.

When the phone went they both jumped. "This is Julia Rogers."

"You have five minutes to disarm the door and surrender," said Genes.

"I can be helpful if you could explain to me what you are trying to achieve."

"The only help I require is that you disarm the door and save me the trouble of using explosives to do it."

"Well, I would hardly do that without some assurance about the safety of the rest of the crew. Just tell me what you want to achieve."

There was silence, then "Four minutes," said Genes and the line went dead.

With just half a minute of his ultimatum to spare, the phone went again.

"Are you ready to surrender now?" asked Genes, in a voice somewhat more tense than his usual mellifluous tone.

"We can talk about the terms of surrender once you have told me what you want to achieve. Until you do that

I have no incentive whatsoever to cooperate with you. I might as well wait for you to blow open the door and kill me."

"There are no terms of surrender. It's unconditional," shot back Genes.

"In that case, there is no surrender," said Julia calmly and put the phone down.

She turned to Jesse Mobutu, the sole remaining soldier in the defence platform. "Why would he hesitate to blow up the door?" she asked him.

"Because he probably knows that I will blow away anyone who comes within ten metres of it," he said with a grin, pointing at a sniper's port in the middle of the door.

"Could he have any heavier weapons, anti-tank missiles for instance?"

"Not likely," said Jesse. "We have control of the armoury. Nothing has gone."

"But he does have explosives. We know that from the control centre attack."

"Yes, and automatic weapons, probably all stolen by Brady before the attack, but nothing else."

"OK," said Julia. "Keep a sharp eye open for any activity out there."

She sat back in her chair and snapped her fingers. The deadline came and went. Nothing on the screen indicated any change in the position of the four hostile groups.

The phone went again. "I have explosives in place. Are you ready to talk?" It was a change in position and a trace of a smile crossed Julia's face.

"Yes, I'm ready to discuss terms. Please tell me what your objectives are."

"We are not discussing my objectives, we are discussing surrender!" yelled Genes.

"OK," she said quietly. "What happens to Piccard and Bertin when we surrender?"

"They… Bertin's dead, I told you!"

"Alright. In that case, please bring his body and place it in front of the door of the defence platform."

"No, I will not! You are wasting my time!" shouted Genes, but he stayed on the line.

"Actually, Genes, you are the one who is wasting time," said Julia. "I have just asked you a simple question about what you want to achieve, and for no apparent reason you have given me no answer. How can you expect me to comply with an absolutely no-win proposal from your side?"

"Bitch!"

Hannah and Julia broke into broad smiles.

"OK. Well?"

There was an inaudible but palpable sigh at the other end of the line.

"We do not want to see a perpetuation of the wasteful incompetence of political leaders on Earth. We want to see a new order in Omega 16, one that respects capability and authority."

"We?" said Julia with a touch of irony. "And who is 'We'?"

"My associates and I."

"Who are?"

"That's none of your business!"

"Well, are these national interests or business interests?"

"That's none of your fucking business!" screamed Genes.

"Oh, I think it is. We would like to know who we'll be working for. I mean, business interests we can understand, but national interests would be difficult for a cosmopolitan bunch like us."

Genes fell into the trap. "Yes, of course it's business interests," he said.

Julia switched the phone to mute and turned to Hannah. "It's the Mafia!" she said, half laughing. She switched the phone back on. "OK, what sort of a deal can we expect from you guys if we cooperate?"

"A deal?! You get to live and work, that's the deal!"

"Yes, but if we won't work or we're all dead, you won't be able to function, you and your pathological zombies."

"We know exactly how we will operate, and it's none of your business!"

"Well, Genes, as things stand I have to tell you that there is no possible deal that I can see, because you are unable to give me any assurance of the survival or welfare of a single member of this crew."

She switched off the phone. "How much longer do we need?" she asked Hannah.

"Only ten minutes," Hannah replied. "Keep going."

Julia waited for three minutes and then redialled.

"Yes?!" snapped Genes.

"Genes, I was thinking. How about you lay down your arms and I guarantee you a safe passage home?"

"You're out of your fucking mind!" he screamed.

"No, I'm not. We seem to have a bit of a Mexican stand-off here and we could do a deal such that no one would really know what happened. There was a fallout between you and Commander Piccard over some confidential issue. You lost your patience and over-reacted. No big deal after months in space. We got together, resolved the issue, and no hard feelings. Think about it," said Julia and she cut the phone off again.

As she did so, Chuck came through on her earphone. "We're ready to go on three of the groups but Genes and his team have doubled back and are headed straight for the defence platform. I need more time to get in position," he said. Julia glanced at the screen. Chuck was right.

"If he's headed here, you don't have more time," said Julia. "Pull the trigger – that may stop him – if not we'll fight it out right here."

"Permission to fire?"

"Permission to fire!"

"Yes, Ma'am!"

The carnage began. As the snipers dropped the leader of each group, from their hidden vantage points, the reaction of the remainder was mindlessly violent rage at any visible human target. It was almost instantaneously obvious that there would be no surrender and the snipers' orders in this case were to systematically kill their adversaries as fast as possible. Thirteen men were shot in a matter of seconds. Only one survived, and that was Ginger Clark.

"They're coming for the door!" yelled Jesse.

"Let them have it!" shouted Julia back to him.

"Whoa! It's a suicide bomber…"

There was a deafening explosion and the supposedly bomb-proof door arched inwards and rolled on to Jesse, crushing his legs. For a moment Genes stood in the entrance, shrouded in smoke, his ubiquitous grin in evidence one more time.

Julia snatched up the sabre that Chuck had left on the table and leapt forward like a cat, her eyes wild with fury. "Kill him!" she yelled, lunging towards Genes with the sabre. There was a sharp crack of gunfire and for a moment the grin seemed to hang in the smoke like that of the Cheshire Cat. Then it vanished and Genes' body crashed into the room. The three remaining insurgents stood immobile in the scattering smoke, staring at the sword in her hand.

Julia, trembling from head to toe, regained a vestige of her presence of mind. "Stand down," she said quietly, and sat down.

Hannah was instantly on her feet. There was a huge gash exposing shattered scull fragments along the side of Genes' head. She felt his neck for a pulse and to her amazement she found one.

"Julia, get me life support for Clayton!" she said, then, "You boys! Help me get this door off this injured man!" and the last three members of the Wayward 19 still on their feet laid down their weapons and meekly obliged.

27
Chang's Descent

"Well, Henri, it seems that your contribution to saving Prometheus from the international Mafia was to give me a black eye and bruised ribs," Arlette was saying as dinner arrived.

"That's not quite fair," snorted Julia. "The clandestine routes through the ship that Henri installed were absolutely decisive. We'd have had no chance without them."

"I concur," said Hannah, "and now I really understand the value of an independent security organisation. It's as well that no one knew of their existence."

Henri winced as he tried to control his knife with his left hand. His right arm was in a sling, made necessary by the one bullet that had actually penetrated his flesh, just above his elbow.

"Oh dear!" said Arlette, her voice dripping with irony. "Did we bang our elbow when we fell over?"

"I think, Commander, that Henri is in a great deal of pain," said Hannah. "His chest was horribly bruised by the impact of the bullets that were fired into his armoured vest at almost point-blank range."

Arlette tried to supress a snigger, and it turned into a smile. "I'm so glad to see you around this table, safe and sound," she said, her eyes glowing with pleasure. "Do we have any loose ends to tie up on this affair?"

"I'm afraid we do," said Henri in a rather weak voice. "I do not understand why the surveillance of the Wayward 19 was allowed to lapse to the extent it did while we were away on Ceres."

Arlette was suddenly serious. "Wasn't that Chang's responsibility?"

"Most definitely it was," said Henri, "and now he's in charge of security on Ceres. Has Marcel been briefed on today's events yet?"

"Actually no," said Julia. "They're all in blissful ignorance about what happened here. Marcel only landed on Ceres about ten minutes ago. They're still busy with post-flight checks at the moment."

"Did Genes' announcement not go out to Ceres then?" asked Hannah.

Julia shook her head. "No, Genes used the emergency system on Prometheus. He had no access to communications with the Orange House because he never had control of the comms centre. But perhaps he did send someone on Lander 2 an earphone message before it lost contact entering the atmosphere of Ceres."

"Mmm," said Arlette, "that is just possible in the pre-entry phase."

"In that case, our leadership on Ceres could be in severe peril," said Henri grimly.

Arlette tried to reach Marcel by earphone. He did not respond. "Henri, alert your militia leader on the surface!" she shouted.

As she did so, Hannah noticed a wince pass across Arlette's face. She walked around the table and leant over her. "Could I walk with you back to your quarters, Commander?"

Arlette looked up sharply, and saw quiet concern in Hannah's face. She nodded and smiled weakly.

They hardly exchanged a word on the short walk to her room, but once inside Hannah produced the basic tools of her trade from her bag and was all business.

"Lie on the bed, please," she said.

The examination was brief. Hannah sat on the edge of the bed and smiled down at her. "You're stressed out of your mind," she said. "Let's talk about it."

And then, quite suddenly, the tears came. They came and came, and Arlette's body shuddered and shook as she buried her head in a pillow and let out a long wail of pain. She reached out for Hannah's hand and grasped it, but it was several minutes before she regained her composure.

"Good," said Hannah. "That was long overdue. Now you can just download all the shit on your mind and we'll deal with it together."

"I don't know where to start," blurted out Arlette.

"Well, let's start with fear. There must be loads of it considering what you've been through. You are an extraordinary woman, but you've been through some terrifying experiences and it's not possible that you did not feel fear. But you have internalised it and now it's biting you. Let's get it out."

"I just can't take another traitor!" wailed Arlette. "How can I trust anybody? How can I function without trusting people? First Bertin, then Clayton and now Chang! How could they put these people into my crew? How can I do this job when I'm confronted with deceit and treachery at every turn?"

Hannah was very surprised to hear Henri's name but she collected herself quickly. "Let's start at the beginning," she said, "with Bertin."

"The bastard!" growled Arlette. "The rotten, sneaky, ruthless, deceitful bastard!" And she told Hannah the whole story. "I was practically in love with him and it was all an act to check me out! Aaah!" She clenched her fists in rage. "And now he's fucking Julia! Aaah!"

There was a silence. Arlette looked up sheepishly.

"Have you finished?" asked Hannah.

Arlette grinned through her tears.

"Was he a good fuck?" asked Hannah, grinning back.

"Very," said Arlette, "and he should have stayed that way instead of invading my professional life."

"Well, Arlette – I think I'll have to call you Arlette – it sounds as though that one was a draw. You were about to take on one of the most important commands in history and some security freak thought you ought to be checked out. Not surprising in our business, it's pretty much full-frontal nudity with our private lives, isn't it? He was your lover and now you're his commander. Perhaps you should just have it out with him and call it quits. Do you still want him?"

"No."

"Good. Just remind him who's boss and move on," said Hannah. "Now, it was not your fault that Clayton turned out to be a treacherous murderer. The jury is out on just what his motivations were. How do you feel about him personally?"

"I liked him," said Arlette. "He's highly creative with a rather attractive roguish charm. What he did was utterly appalling but I rather feel he's more misguided than evil. What do you think?"

"Well, remember I was with Julia when she negotiated with him," said Hannah. "She and I are both convinced that he was being manipulated by the Mafia, and, frankly, killing innocent people for the Mafia is evil. But, if that's the case, his motivation was pure greed and no reflection on you. I wonder if Chang is implicated as well; with the Mafia, I mean?"

"My God, yes, maybe. I think we'll know soon enough." Arlette smiled and stood up. "Thank you, Hannah. I feel much better." They hugged.

"From now on," said Hannah, "you can dump your stuff on me and we'll talk it through in complete confidence, OK?"

Arlette smiled. "You're good at what you do," she said. "It's a blessing that you're here."

* * *

The first person to exit Lander 2 after its arrival on Ceres was Chang. He greeted the onlookers warmly and asked the doctor to go and check on Marcel, who had apparently passed out in his ergo-couch during entry. He then walked briskly to the security office where Lee Bai, Chuck Connolly's replacement, greeted him respectfully.

"Take me to the communications centre immediately," he said, "and bring your weapon. We have some potential security exposure." Lee Bai complied.

Dispensing with formalities as he entered, he instructed the duty technician to disconnect all communications circuits with Prometheus except the phone in Henri's office.

"Lee Bai, you will remain here and ensure that my instructions are obeyed," he said, and walked out to commandeer Henri's office.

The doctor was baffled by Marcel's condition. The man was unconscious and totally unresponsive. It appeared that he had been heavily sedated, but by whom and for what purpose was a mystery. He decided to leave him where he was for the time being and then a thought struck him. If Marcel had been sedated by someone, that person was almost certainly one of the passengers on Lander 2. If he left him alone in the lander, Marcel would be an easy target for a second, perhaps lethal, attempt to disable him. He decided he would stay put and keep him under observation.

Now settled into what had been Henri's office, Chang recalled the message that Genes Clayton had delivered to the crew, while also on an earphone connection with Chang in Lander 2 as it approached entry into the atmosphere of Ceres. With Bertin dead and Piccard a prisoner, they had achieved their objective quite elegantly and, with no real leadership and confronted with Genes' pathological killers, capitulation would have been bloody but quick. He, Chang, of course would not be implicated in the violence. He would step naturally into the commander's role, and use Clayton and his hoodlums to do any dirty work that needed doing. He had no need to throw his weight around unnecessarily on Ceres either. He had control of the militia and control of communications, which allowed him to relay appropriate messages via Prometheus back to his Mafia bosses on Earth. He would need to dispose of Marcel Rousseau, of course, but the man was clearly very sick and would unfortunately succumb to some unidentifiable ailment in the near future. He thought briefly about conferring with Genes on progress with mopping-up operations and decided not to get involved for the time being but just to wait for the all-clear. In the meantime he prepared and sent a brief encrypted report to Chan Lu Fat.

Chang got up and walked back to the security office, and there he commandeered Lee Bai's second in command for a tour of the facility. Henri, meanwhile, was becoming increasingly alarmed about the complete loss of communications with everyone on the ground. Beginning to believe that Lander 2 might have crashed into the base and wiped it out, he called the lander itself. The line was live. He waited. Finally the voice of the doctor came on the line. "Hello? Who's calling?"

Henri enquired about the success of the landing and how the new arrivals were settling in. Everything was fine as far as the doctor knew, except that Mr Rousseau had apparently taken an overdose of tranquillisers – was he a nervous traveller? No; well his life was not in danger but the doctor would keep him under close observation. He didn't know anything about a communications problem. Yes, they had power, nothing seemed abnormal.

Henri's instincts were on high alert. He probed the doctor for an explanation of Marcel's condition until he finally acknowledged why he had decided to stay in the lander with him.

"Good move," said Henri. "Please stay with him until he is fully compos mentis, and call me on this phone if you notice anything abnormal or have any concerns."

Henri sat back and considered the options. Had Chang deliberately allowed the Wayward 19 to regroup? Were Genes and Chang in cahoots?

A call came in to his earphone. It was Shinji Yamamoto. "We just had a message go through Comms Centre to Earth from Orange House" he said.

"Where to?" asked Henri.

"I dunno. It's encrypted and the address is coded. I just know one thing," he said. "It was sent by Chang."

"Got him!" said Henri under his breath. He thought for a moment, then called Lander 2 again. It took the doctor several minutes to climb up to the cockpit and take the call. "Yes?" he said breathlessly.

"Doctor, I have good reasons to believe that Chang may have nefarious intent towards this mission. He may be dangerous and you should not trust him. Can you organise yourself some company in the lander to provide additional protection?"

"Well," said the doctor, "I wouldn't ask one of the militia because they report to Mr Chang, don't they? But perhaps I could ask the pilot and co-pilot? They have a good reason to be here, and they don't have much else to do."

Within ten minutes, Sanam and Arun, her co-pilot,

had arrived in the lander with a supply of fresh food and water. After listening carefully to the doctor, they settled into the cockpit to amuse themselves, and began to set up the navigation equipment for gaming. The doctor examined his patient periodically, but saw no change in his condition.

Twenty minutes later Chang appeared at the entrance and climbed up to where the doctor was sitting with his patient. "How's he doing?" he asked.

"Fine, stable," said the doctor.

"Good," said Chang. "You can take a break now. I'll keep an eye on him and call you if there's any change."

"I'd rather not do that," said the doctor. "In my experience this kind of condition can deteriorate very rapidly…"

"Take a break, Doctor, that's an order. Lee! Escort the doctor back to the base!"

Lee Bai clattered up the stairs to where the other two were standing. As he reached them, Chang pointed a finger at the doctor, then pointed downwards, and turned away towards the prone form of Marcel in his ergo-couch.

"Come on, Doctor," said Lee, and put a hand firmly on his shoulder. The doctor turned to protest once more, and as he did so he caught a glimpse of movement higher up the staircase.

"Well, please call me immediately if there is any change," he said and began to descend the stairs. "And by the way, I have some information I would like to share with you about some of the other crew members down here."

"What sort of information?" shot back Chang.

"Oh, behavioural," went on the doctor, moving steadily down the steps.

Chang was staring down at him. "Behavioural?"

"Yes. There are some things you should know since you are in charge down here," said the doctor.

"Who in particular?"

"I think we need to discuss that in confidence," said the doctor, "but they are people you will need to be able to rely on. We can catch up later."

"Wait!" said Chang, but the doctor was already moving out of the lander cabin and down the landing ramp.

Chang stood watching the departing figures for a moment, then shrugged, turned, and approached Marcel. He studied him for a minute or two, then put his hand carefully into his pocket and pulled out a syringe.

* * *

News of the hijacking of Prometheus spread rapidly through the criminal community on Earth. Chan Lu Fat had called Joe Favaloro to congratulate him as soon as he had received Chang's message. "Your man done good!" he said with a mouth full of cigar. "We're in business!"

"I ain't heard nothing from Clayton," said Joe cautiously.

"Well, my man Chang's on the ball," said Chen, "and he's already down on the planet, bossing. The CIA man got wiped and the bitch is tied to the toilet."

Joe allowed himself a grin. "Sounds good," he said.

Within hours both men were receiving fealty from their peers and business prospects soared.

The message received a little later by Mission Control told a very different story. While acknowledging the foresight of Colonel Bertin in setting up the secret surveillance and mobility passages, it described in glowing detail the courage of Julia Rogers and recommended that she be awarded the Crimson Star. However, it also lamented the loss of life of eighteen crew members who were not in control of their actions through no fault of their own, and the piteous performance of pre-flight security. Genes Clayton had not been infected by the virus; how could his criminal loyalties have gone undetected? There was, however, no mention of suspicions over Chang's role.

The Mafia-inspired rumours of the takeover which emerged in the media, however, were full of praise for Clayton and Chang, who, it was suggested, had finally lost patience with the despotic political manipulation of the ISEA and struck a blow for ordinary humanity. The cruelty of the odious Colonel Bertin, already responsible for the loss of so many lives aboard, had, it was suggested, reached intolerable levels. Commander Piccard, far from being the hero portrayed in recent propaganda, was no more than a CIA stooge, sent to prepare a soft landing for the political big-wigs who had so miserably failed the populations they represented. Now, hard-working citizens with initiative would be able to participate in the wealth and freedom offered by these two brave men, and turn their backs on the greed and corruption of the political establishment.

Mission Control had no choice but to go public with the news that the attempted takeover had actually been foiled, but, in the absence of any explanation of Clayton's behaviour, and reluctant to announce the death of a further eighteen crew members, was unwilling to provide any more information.

The media responded with the gravest cynicism. The mission was out of control. The hopes of tens of millions of desperate citizens, whose tax money had financed this great venture, were once more to be dashed by the utterly ruthless authorities who cared nothing for the welfare of the ordinary citizen.

Ugly demonstrations broke out across the world against any and all forms of authority. In New York the Mayor's office was attacked by a huge crowd and overwhelmed. The Mayor himself was dragged out and lynched before the National Guard was able to restore order, and more than 700 were killed in the process. A similar protest took place in Beijing, where hundreds of thousands of people took to the streets, ransacking any administrative buildings they could find. The government responded with tanks and machine guns and more than 5,000 were killed. There was a spate of attacks on government buildings in the main European capitals, with missiles launched from remote high-speed mobile carriers, which were later found abandoned. Almost a hundred government officials died as a result, as well as nearly a thousand civilians. Political leaders were aghast at this new development, because it indicated that huge financial resources were being brought to bear to bring down civil order.

* * *

Chang rolled up the sleeve of Marcel Rousseau's tunic, rubbed his arm and selected a vein. A shoe on the stair behind him creaked softly. He spun round and a hard, coffee-coloured fist hit him right on the point of his jaw. "Bad idea, Mr Chang," said Arun Dar.

Chang plunged forward and fell half onto the ergo-couch beyond Marcel's so hard that it turned in its gimbal and delivered him forcefully onto the one below. This in turn spun him even more forcefully onto the next one down. Arun watched with increasing horror as Chang's flailing body progressed ever more rapidly down through the lander cabin until it hit the bottom with a sickening thud. Arun scampered down the stairs to where Chang was lying on the rear bulkhead, eyes open, neck bent at an impossible angle. "Oh, my God!" he said.

Sanam came skipping down the stairs behind him. "What happened?"

Arun turned to her, his face contorted with anguish. "I've killed him!"

"Good," said Sanam.

* * *

The news of Chang's death was another blow to Henri. The loss of life in the process of defeating the conspiracy had been horrendous, and perhaps all but two of the casualties were innocent of deliberate malevolent intent, of whom one was now dead and the other, Genes, was in a coma. The other four survivors almost certainly knew nothing of its origins. Furthermore, there was no certainty that the crew did not include one or more other sleepers, who might turn on the leadership at an inopportune moment. It was, however, reassuring that all the arms on board had now been accounted for and were under the full control of the militia. Henri prepared a security analysis bitterly critical of the pre-mission screening programme that had failed to identify two traitors at the highest level of leadership in the crew. If this could happen on such a high-profile mission, how flawed, or even corrupt, could the rest of the ISEA be?

28
Sombre News

Marcel recovered consciousness after six hours. He remained weak for another twenty-four, but then recovered completely. Phase 3 exploration, which was to concentrate on the identification and assessment of natural resources in Ceres, then began in earnest and involved journeys long enough to require the crews to spend at least one long, cold Ceresian night inside the personnel carrier. Their encounters with the local wildlife life were, mostly, more amusing than frightening. They made a number of sightings of the giant, multiple-tailed yellow scorpions, which galloped off clumsily when they sighted the little convoy. They also had several encounters with cow-sized beetles which bumped into them during the night for no apparent reason. One popular conclusion was that the personnel carrier was being mistaken for a potential mate, and consequently they became known as Sightless, Lecherous and Obtuse Beetles, or SLOBS.

More importantly, an extensive outcrop of limestone was identified only six hours' drive from the base, and the process of calling down equipment from Prometheus to exploit it for the production of building materials began. The transporters that had been sent down with each package of equipment to enable its recovery were put to work to perform their secondary task as bulk carriers and within a week the base had begun to look like an urban building site. The limestone face of the new buildings remained perfectly in character; it was a rich orange in colour.

The total complement on the ground had now risen to fifty-five, with Lander 2 becoming a dormitory for those who could not be housed in the base. This was not a sustainable arrangement, but it provided solid motivation for the construction workers, as the majority of those on the ground had become, to get on with the job of building a permanent base as quickly as possible. That construction could not continue efficiently at night was a major frustration. The crew were conscious of the buzzing in the distance every night but still attempted to finish some tasks with the use of flashlights. These interludes became progressively longer and it was only a matter of a week or so before an ominous drone was heard one night coming in their direction. The lights were quickly shut off but the hapless beast still crashed into an unfinished wall and caused it to collapse.

Life on Prometheus went through a painful readjustment as the crew were constantly reminded of the recent loss of their fourteen former comrades by the need to find replacements and double up on duties. Nearly everyone had lost a friend and they were remembered not by their final acts of treachery but by their earlier camaraderie. Carefully edited videos of the latest outrage and the earlier control centre assault were shown to all members of the crew, and no one was in any doubt about the danger the Wayward 19 had represented, but most wondered whether it wouldn't have been possible to contain them rather than kill them. The four survivors had been integrated back into their former positions, but none of them were able to explain lucidly how they had felt when under the influence of Genes and the stimuli being delivered to their highly sensitised brains.

The sombre atmosphere was further aggravated by the boring routine of checking and rechecking equipment and systems on board, and most of the crew were now looking forward to participating in activities on Ceres, regardless of spitting spiders, long, dark nights, and predominantly manual labour.

As Chief Navigator on Prometheus, Cobus Vermeulen enjoyed the rather enviable task of conducting the detailed surveys of the surface required to select future landing sites. Cobus was a studious, modest man, an astronomer by training, and, true to his South African origins, passionate about cricket. He shared this with a handful of his Indian, Pakistani and Australian crew-mates, but sadly there were too few of them to play the game on board properly. They did, however, manage to stage a five-a-side game in the gymnasium which knocked out so many of the lights that they were obliged to curtail any further matches. Cobus was tall and well built, blond and boyishly handsome, with an innocent smile that was utterly beguiling to the opposite sex.

He was constantly finding himself surprised by his

own success. He had so impressed the staff when he visited the Large Telescope in Cape Town as a small boy that they had kept in touch with him and sponsored his studies. Emerging, to his surprise, with a first-class degree, Cobus was dispatched to California, where he quickly developed a talent for picking out extraordinary astronomical events from the cosmic background and his name began to appear frequently in academic literature. He was recruited into the ISEA, proved himself to be a natural pilot, and "fell over the Omega 16 system by accident". Nevertheless, he was amazed at being recruited for the Prometheus mission when his predictions about planets 16-3 and 16-4 were proved correct, and he accepted immediately.

The primary focus of interest for landing sites was no longer flat, secure surfaces but rather environments that could be developed to support larger populations. He was examining a promising river estuary when a warning flashed onto his screen: "Moving Object at 16-5.3".

"Damn," he said at this unwelcome distraction. He re-orientated the ship's telescope to the gas giant 16-5 and focused it on the third of its moons, now progressing across the face of the planet. He saw nothing at first, but as his eye shifted to the shadow of the moon on the planet's surface, he saw a second, much smaller, darker, shadow beside it, and it was moving. He increased the resolution to maximum. The shadow was cigar-shaped, and, as he watched, it slowly retreated back behind the moon.

Cobus sat back and bit his lip. "There's something behind that moon," he said to himself. "It's not a natural object, and it doesn't want me to see it." He thought for a minute, then pulled up the visual archives and selected 16-5.3. Of all the passes of moon 3 across the surface of 16–5 in sunlight since they had arrived, there was no similar event, nor was there any other case of movement in the radar records. "Damn," said Cobus again. He checked the radar scan. Something was definitely moving behind moon 3, and too close in to be in orbit.

He called Arlette on his earphone. "Commander, I have to report that there is an unidentified object moving close to the third moon of planet 16-5. It is not a natural body and the records show that this movement is new."

"Do you have photos?" asked Arlette.

"Only of its shadow. It's on the far side of the moon, facing the surface of the planet."

"Get me the best detail you can of the shadow and bring some stills up here in fifteen minutes," she said.

When Cobus arrived at the Commander's quarters, Henri and Julia were already there. He nodded at Arlette and Henri, then stepped up to Julia. "It's a privilege to be on this ship with you," he said. "What you did was just incredible."

"Thanks, Cobus, I rather surprised myself," said Julia.

They sat down and scrutinised the photos that Cobus had brought with him.

"I don't like the look of those knobs," said Julia. "They look like turrets."

"You're right; this is not a natural object," said Henri. "Have you detected a comms stream from it?"

"No," said Cobus, "but I've got it under close surveillance now. We'll soon find out if it's talking to someone."

"Will you have immediate intel if there's a missile launch?" queried Henri.

"Yes," said Cobus. "We'll pick up a heat signature if there's a missile coming our way, and our shielding should be effective against lasers. What concerns me is its size; it's about four times as big as we are by my estimation."

"Well," said Arlette, "it's still a long way away and hasn't shown any aggressive tendencies, so I guess we'll just monitor it for the time being."

"What do we do if it does show aggressive tendencies?" Julia wanted to know. "We don't have any armaments to take on a thing of that size!"

"You're right. Given the options of fight or flight, I'd opt for flight in the circumstances," said Arlette.

"And leave our colony on Ceres unprotected?" Julia was aghast.

"If that's the only way we live to fight another day, yes."

As they left the meeting, a thought struck Henri and he hurried after Cobus.

"Something just occurred to me, Cobus, in terms of what we might do for heavy weaponry. It would be a bit of a one-shot strategy, but I was wondering how you were getting on with..."

Cobus turned and grinned at him. "I'm already on it, Colonel," was all he said.

Some twelve hours later moon 3 dipped behind gas giant 16-5. "Well," Cobus thought to himself, "now we'll have to wait and see."

* * *

“Yes, Hannah?” Henri lifted his head as her news was delivered into his brain. “I’ll be right there.”

He hurried up to the clinic. “He’s conscious but not yet coherent,” she told him when he arrived. “He must be as strong as a horse to have come through so quickly.”

Genes was propped up in a sitting position, his head and torso in bandages. One foot was rather obtrusively manacled to the bedpost.

“Well, Genes, how are you feeling?” was all Henri could think of to say to this rather comical-looking figure.

“Ah don’t rightly know who ah’m talking to,” replied Genes weakly.

“You are talking to Colonel Henri Bertin,” said Henri, “and you have a great deal to tell me.”

“Well, Colonel,” said Genes, “Ah’m mighty pleased to meet you, but could you please tell me where I am and what I’m doing here in this hospital?”

Henri sighed. He took Hannah’s arm and they moved outside. “What are the probabilities that this is genuine amnesia?” he asked her.

“Rather high, I’m afraid,” said Hannah.

“How long is it likely to last?”

“Days, weeks or even longer.”

“How do we know if it’s genuine?”

“I’ll be able to do psychometric tests on him in due course, but not for a while – he’s too sick.”

“OK,” said Henri and they moved back inside.

“You are on the spaceship Prometheus,” he told the bandaged figure, “and we are in orbit around planet Omega 16-3. I want a full explanation for your conduct on this mission.”

Genes chuckled. "Hell, Colonel," he said. "Do I get to meet Mr Spock?"

* * *

Mission Control continued to suppress the news of Chang's death and the circumstantial evidence of his treachery. Chan Lu Fat, suspicious that he had received no follow-up message from Chang, waited forty-eight hours and then released a spate of rumours that he had been murdered by fascist agents on Prometheus. Once again, Mission Control was obliged to release more information than it wanted to and to confirm Chang's death. However, this time it also released a partial transcript of the negotiations between Genes and Julia, in which Genes admitted 'business interests' as his motivation for taking over Prometheus. The public was not impressed, nor did they give much credence to the report that Chang had died accidentally while attempting to give Marcel Rousseau a lethal injection. For the second time in twenty-four hours public sentiment erupted into wholesale violence against the authorities and destruction of property, exacerbated this time by a report that 700 women and children had been found dead in a refugee camp in India, apparently abandoned by the camp administrators because the water supply had failed.

* * *

Oblivious of the concerns on Prometheus and the crises on Earth, the pioneers on Ceres pursued their site development activities with close to manic enthusiasm. Scientists and engineers happily applied themselves both to creative improvisation and to hard manual labour, the foundations and steadily growing stone walls of the Orange House began to give the base a sense of permanence, and food production diversified and expanded to meet the needs of all. The cook, Giuliano Benedetti, spurred on by his initial successes, became the base's first true celebrity, introducing his latest creations at mealtimes in his unashamedly accented English with flourish and humour.

Marcel Rousseau proved himself an outstanding colony administrator, encouraging all forms of innovation and intelligently reading the ever-changing needs and desires of the pioneers for challenge and entertainment. While seven-a-side mixed-gender football remained unquestionably the most popular leisure activity, running and swimming, music and art all began to take root in the daily agenda. Following the initial success in exploiting the limestone deposits for the production of stone and cement, copper smelting was identified as providing the next big opportunity for expanding the scope of their activities.

This was not a role he had ever imagined would suit him. Marcel had a passion for power and speed. Born in Grenoble, in south-eastern France, he had been a wild youth; a mountaineer, sky-diver, maniacal skier, and then an avid racing driver. His parents, despairing that he would ever do anything productive, had promised him his own racing team if he would just go to university and get some kind of degree. He chose Propulsion Engineering and fell deeply in love with rocketry. He took a year off to go to

China and do clerical work just so that he could witness the testing of the huge spaceship motors that were being developed there. When he returned he announced that he was done with 'Earthbound pastimes' and would be going into space with the ISEA. He was, however, first required to spend two years in the design section, where he astonished his supervisors with his ability to conceive, articulate and implement remarkable engineering innovations. He would come up with the most bizarre ideas, talk right through all the instinctive objections, and then shrug his shoulders: "You see, it's simple." And it would be. He was immensely popular with the crew of Prometheus because he was utterly without pretensions and would wade in to help anybody with a problem to solve. At no time in his early career had he ever imagined how much satisfaction he would get from fostering the creativity of others and facilitating their success. Now he wondered how he could possibly have been so lucky as to be in a position to guide the very first human civilisation on another planet.

As time progressed, more and more of the pioneers felt that they would like to be on the list of those asked if they wanted to stay, even if they were not yet sure about it. The long, tedious and dangerous journey back to Earth, where the quality of life was steadily deteriorating, appeared less and less attractive, and how could they assume that they might be given the opportunity to return at some future date? As they travelled further afield towards the mountains and lakes to the east, the space and the scope of opportunity on Ceres appeared open-ended, the threats and discomforts manageable. Friendship and camaraderie flourished, and love affairs began.

* * *

Cobus Vermeulen was awakened by a beeping from his phone and knew immediately that it meant trouble. He switched on the personal communications system in his room and then connected into the automatic tracking system.

There it was.

A black dot was moving steadily away from gas giant 16-5 towards planet 16-4. And it was moving fast: very, very fast; possibly as fast as one twentieth of light speed. He requested an ETA from the system assuming that it would make a slingshot manoeuvre around planet 16-4 and got the answer 52.4 hours. He called Arlette on his earphone.

"Dark Shadow is on the move," he told her. "It could be here in just over two days."

"OK. Get up here in thirty minutes. We'll want to access all the relevant data you have."

The meeting was short and tense.

"Of course it's entirely possible that it's just going to investigate 16-4," Arlette was saying, "but we must assume it can see us just as well as we can see it, and that it is coming here. Henri, notify the crew that we are now on yellow alert. Cobus, how long will it be before we know whether it's coming here or not?"

"Thirty-six hours," he said.

"OK. Henri, I want a reception plan and a combat plan. Assume we'll be using Lander 1 as a lifeboat. By the way, Julia, how's Genes?"

"Making an extraordinary recovery. He's up and about

in his room but still claims he remembers nothing since his space ranger days."

"Do you believe him?"

"No. We gave him the video of his assault on the defence platform and a recording of his negotiations with me, and watched him playing them. Neither Hannah nor I believe he's genuinely amnesic."

"Alright. Have him brought up here. I want to talk to him one-on-one. Thank you!"

The meeting ended.

Genes Clayton was delivered in chains to Arlette's quarters by two armed guards. The top and sides of his head were heavily bandaged, but the only mark on his face was a black eye. The guards manacled his legs to the legs of her desk, and stood behind him, their fingers on the triggers of their weapons. "Wait outside, you two," she said. "I'll press my panic button if I need help."

The two guards looked at each other, shrugged, and left.

Arlette sat half on the desk and looked at him hard in the eyes for fifteen seconds, then she climbed down, sat in her chair, and continued to stare unblinkingly at him. Finally she said, "What turned you into a mass murderer, Genes?"

"Ah'm not…" he began.

"Don't bullshit me!" shouted Arlette before he could say any more. "Shall I show you the video or play the transcript again?"

He looked at her steadily and said nothing.

Arlette leant over her desk and engaged his eyes with hers. "Listen very carefully," she said. "You came very close to losing your life. If I decide that you continue to pose a threat to this mission I'll have you snuffed out like that!" She snapped her fingers. "However, if I decide that you could still make a useful contribution, I might be lenient, at least for a while."

Genes looked at her. He showed no emotion, but Arlette hardly expected anything else given the skilful deception he had practised before.

"But let me be absolutely clear," she went on. "You will tell me now the complete and unadulterated truth about the conspiracy you have been involved in, or I will send you back to your cell and keep you in isolation indefinitely."

She sat back and folded her arms.

"What kind of useful contribution can I make?" asked Genes.

"You are an intelligent, resourceful and creative man with a lot of practical experience. I've lost a lot of people and I can use those skills. I'm not saying that I will trust you or forgive you, I'm just saying that I might give you back part of your life if you are prepared to do everything I ask of you."

Genes swallowed. "Deal," he said hoarsely.

"Right," said Arlette. "You will start by recording a complete confession, beginning with your first involvement with organised crime. You will explain how the plot to take over the ship was planned and executed and you will name all names. You will reveal your hiding places on Prometheus and yield all materials to the security forces on board. When you have finished your confession I will review it and decide whether it is sufficiently full and complete. Once I am fully satisfied, I will commit the confession to the archives. I will not release any details to anyone on this mission other than to my closest advisors. I will, however, release some information to Mission Control if I think it is relevant to the security of the mission."

Arlette paused. "Were you really going to kill me?"

Genes looked at her sadly. "Yes," he said quietly.

"Do you still want to kill me?"

"No," he said, almost choking.

"Good. I'm going to the control centre now. There's a phone, get on with it." Arlette rose to leave. As she was in the doorway she said to the guards, "Leave him to work and let me know when he's finished."

Genes poked the phone on the desk before him into life and began to speak into it.

"I guess I have to go back to the beginning and put all this in context. My father died when I was fourteen. He was a property manager, a bailiff, on the Chicago East Side and apparently he lost his life in a shoot-out with some tenants. I was already quite tall by then, and was known around there because I had won a few maths competitions. We had a visit, my mother and I, from my father's employer. This guy said he knew we had no insurance and he wanted to help us. He said we could live in one of the firm's apartments in Houston and keep an eye on the other tenants, and the firm would pay for my schooling. My mother agreed – she really wanted me to go to college – and we moved down there. It was fine – I went to college and only then did I realise that it was the Mafia that was looking after us. I was becoming very disillusioned by that time with the failure of government to deal effectively with political and social problems, and it seemed to me that these people had a better idea about how society should be run."

Genes went on to describe how he was approached when he had been selected for the Prometheus mission, and promised total authority over the new planetary territories to implement a closely controlled meritocracy. He knew his mother, now suffering from dementia, would be well looked after and he was convinced that his views, working closely with his benefactors on Earth, would ultimately prevail over weakness, compromise and corruption. He had stuck to his commitment, partly from conviction and partly from concern over the fate of his mother, but he had observed that a certain nobility of purpose had begun to form on Prometheus, to which he felt strongly attracted. "I am now willing", he declared, "to commit myself to this cause."

29
Dark Shadow

Hannah was invited to sit in with Henri, Julia and Arlette as they listened to Genes' confession. He said he felt that benevolent dictatorship would be far more effective than democracy in the early stages of political development on the planet and that he could be a successful leader in this context. He named Joe Favaloro, Chan Lu Fat and Chang Chao as co-conspirators, together with the operatives who had helped him set up his secret quarters on Prometheus as its construction was nearing completion. He described the properties of the virus he had been given to infect those on board with a genetic disposition to pathological violence, and the initiation process he had been trained to deliver to those infected. He expressed remorse for the terrible assault in the control centre that had cost many valuable lives and for his kidnapping of the Commander and Henri Bertin. However, he claimed that he had intended to take over the ship without bloodshed on the second attempt, and that he had been deeply shocked by the slaughter of almost all of his soldiers before they had harmed anyone.

Finally he acknowledged that his motivations were lust for power and greed and that he could now see that the little colony on Ceres was developing in a wholly healthy, democratic fashion which he fully supported.

"What do you think?" asked Arlette when it was finished.

"The more the charm, the bigger the bastard," said Julia emphatically.

"Oh, Julia, is that your professional opinion or your personal experience?" tittered Hannah.

"Both!" said Julia.

Only Henri wasn't laughing. "He's a showman and an opportunist", he said, "and not to be trusted."

"I don't propose to trust him, Henri, but I do propose to use him. Ever since we lost Jake Thibault I've been uncomfortable that we don't have a motor man in the control centre who has an instinctive touch with the propulsion units. Genes knows it better than anyone and he'll be constantly under everyone's scrutiny there. If we are going to tangle with an alien spaceship, I want nothing but the very best in that job."

"Is he really that good?" queried Henri. "Aren't there younger people we can bring on?"

"Not in the face of a real and present danger from Dark Shadow," said Arlette. "His former henchmen are all dead or incarcerated, his base is blown, and he has no weapons or explosives or other equipment. I hope that's a manageable security risk."

"Yes," said Henri finally. "If you need him we will make it so."

Genes was back in Arlette's quarters an hour later.

"In your confession," Arlette was saying, "you have admitted your guilt for a host of crimes, including murder and treason. There is no immediate need for a court martial, since there is no dispute about these crimes or your culpability, and our psychiatric staff have pronounced you sane. However, given the circumstances, sentencing will be suspended at my discretion. Do you understand?"

"Yeah," said Genes.

"Do you want legal advice?"

"Er … no," said Genes.

"No?"

"No!" said Genes emphatically.

"Your future behaviour may, at my discretion, have some bearing on your sentence. You are now under house arrest, which means that you are restricted to your quarters and, when required, to the control centre. We will monitor all your activities and communications at all times. Do you understand?"

"Yeah," said Genes.

"You will be allowed in the control centre to perform the role of propulsion engineer, and that role only."

Genes' eyes widened slightly.

"In that role you will obey my commands in full and without question, and you will execute your delegated tasks in the interests of the safety of the ship to the best of your ability. Is that clear?"

"Yes, Commander, crystal clear," said Genes, a little touch of his swagger returning.

"Do you know what to expect if you do not comply?" asked Arlette finally.

"A bullet in the back of the skull, I would think," he replied with a shrug.

* * *

Cobus Vermeulen watched the approach of Dark Shadow to planet Omega 16-4 and scowled. There was no deceleration. The craft was not going to enter orbit; it was going to slingshot around it. He waited until the manoeuvre was complete and a new course set, then called Arlette.

"When can we expect them?" she asked.

"If they elect to, they could enter orbit around Ceres in sixteen hours and four minutes," replied Cobus. "Of course they may fly by."

"I'm not counting on it," said Arlette grimly. "How's your snowball doing?"

"It's in the right window," replied Cobus. "We have options."

"OK. Come and join us for a pow-wow. Oh, it might surprise you but Genes Clayton will also be there."

"Commander?"

"Yes, he's a bad man but toothless now. We are going to be using his motor skills."

"OK," said Cobus dubiously, then, "I'm on my way."

When he arrived, Henri, Julia and Genes were sitting around the table with Arlette, engaged in a discussion about signalling to an alien culture. Arlette looked up. "Cobus, we are now on red alert. Was Dark Shadow already concealed in the Omega 16 system when we arrived, or has it come through LDST 2 since then?"

"Our satellite has not signalled to us since the

installation tests were completed, so it has not detected any movement in LDST 2," said Cobus, "and therefore we have to assume that Dark Shadow was sitting somewhere, probably on moon 3 of 16-5, when we arrived.

"Why would it do that?" asked Henri.

"There could be lots of explanations, but the most obvious one is that it could be a convenient platform for exploration of the Omega 16 solar system, located close to the exit of their wormhole. I expect they are just as surprised to see us as we are to see them."

"OK," said Arlette. "Dark Shadow was not sent to deal with us, it was on an explorative mission of its own. What are they thinking now?"

"It depends on whether their mission was peacefully motivated, to explore and possibly settle, or military, to gain a foothold in another galaxy," said Henri.

"Alright, what is most likely given that they are on their way here now?"

"Military is marginally more likely," said Genes. "What would we do if we were in their position? We would say, 'OK, someone else is busy with 16-3. Let's not risk a confrontation, let's go and have a look at 16-4 – they're pretty similar planets.' It's taking quite a risk of confrontation to come straight here unless they are planning some grandiose display of friendship when they get here."

"Right. What would a grandiose display of friendship look like?" asked Arlette.

"Fireworks," said Julia.

"Pardon?"

"Fireworks. Something obviously harmless to a

civilisation at least as advanced as ours, showing a non-aggressive response."

"I've heard worse ideas," said Genes. "Do we have any?"

"Actually, yes," said Arlette. "They are intended for our return to Earth orbit, but we could spare some for this purpose. We can also turn Prometheus any colour we like using the LED circuits in the external cameras."

"That's cool!" said Julia. "Totally non-aggressive. We could go green. Even aliens know that represents photosynthesis, the basis of peaceful life on both 16-3 and 16-4."

"Well," said Arlette, "I was expecting a complex coded transmission, and we've ended up with a rotating colour display!"

"Not exactly," cut in Genes. "We are not going to go yellow!"

"Right," said Arlette. "Our guests arrive in orbit around Ceres in their 800-hundred-metre-long spaceship and we put on a colourful welcome display for them. Good. What happens next?"

"They either make a similarly harmless gesture to us, or they blow us to bits with their alien ray-guns," said Julia. "If we've concluded that they're more likely hostile than not, it seems like a bit of a risk."

"I don't see us being neutralised that easily," said Henri. "We don't have much truly offensive capability, that's true, but we do have very substantial defences. We can deal effectively with incoming missiles and laser beams. If they have something that can get round that, then our only other option is to run for it."

"Let's look at that one," said Arlette. "Supposing we pull the plug on Ceres for the time being and blast off for a look at 16-4, just as they are arriving?"

"Let's face facts," said Genes. "Their ship is hugely faster than we are. If we sail off to 16-4 we'll be a sitting duck for anything they want to throw at us. Here we have a couple of landers, the atmosphere of Ceres and Cobus' snowball to play with. If we have to fight, we're better off fighting here."

There was silence for a while. "No other ideas?" asked Arlette. No one had any.

"OK," said Arlette. "Let's look at offence. What do we do when we conclude that that they are hostile?"

"We get ourselves smartly around the other side of Ceres and hit them with the snowball," said Genes.

"I think that's about right," said Cobus, "although the window we can hit them in diminishes as our asteroid gets closer. Right now we can play games with it, but we can't turn it around."

"I think we all understand that, Cobus," said Arlette, "and obviously we need to refine its path as we get an exact fix on Dark Shadow's location."

"Yes, we know that we can do that with a high degree of accuracy with the hardware we landed on the asteroid. Now it's just three-dimensional trigonometry," said Cobus.

"Genes, are you up for this?" asked Arlette. "It's going to be your hand on the controls."

"Right up my alley, Commander," said Genes.

Dark Shadow entered orbit around Ceres, visible on the horizon but not close, and at a slightly higher altitude. The two craft notionally eyed each other, in fact assessing their opposite number's offensive capability. To the onlookers on Prometheus, Dark Shadow looked very menacing indeed. It was indeed cigar-shaped, but seemed to be bristling with spikes and towers of all descriptions. After several minutes of systematic scanning, Arlette had the light show switched on, and the external colour of Prometheus progressed slowly from blue through all the colours of the spectrum three times, finally stopping at green. There was no reaction. The process was repeated. Still no reaction. It was repeated a third time...

There was a massive crash somewhere amidships and a huge lurching jolt. Prometheus began to turn a slow cartwheel and, with its loss of orbital speed, to dip down towards Ceres.

Induced gravity failed, then pressurisation failed.

"Isolate sections 3 and 4!" yelled Arlette. Air pressure stabilised but did not recover. The crew in the control centre fought to get into their restraints as loose equipment crashed around and showers of debris hit them.

"Stabilise this tumble, Genes!" she shouted.

"I'm trying, Christ I'm trying!"

The external cameras began to pick up the ominous glow of ionising air as Prometheus plunged deeper into the atmosphere of Ceres.

There was a jolt as Genes fired one of the boosters and the cartwheel seemed to slow, but then it went into reverse and the whole structure started to groan with the heat and stress that it was never designed to withstand.

A weird screeching sound began to permeate the ship as the protective tiling on the outside overheated and began to tear off.

"We're going down! We're going down!" shouted someone across the control centre.

Arlette looked at the chaos on the control panel, clenched her fists, and in utter terror screamed:

"GOD SAVE US!!!"

But something in her head extracted some data from somewhere, for suddenly she shouted to Genes, "Left-hand booster, 70 per cent, 15.23.36, eighteen seconds!"

In among the utter confusion that prevailed, Genes recognised this as an entirely coherent instruction and executed it, although neither the boosters nor any other component of the propulsion system were ever intended for use other than in deep space. Seven seconds later, the left-hand booster fired at 70 per cent of full power for eighteen seconds. Prometheus stopped tumbling and lurched sideways on to a new path, for she was now bouncing off the atmosphere rather than ploughing into it. The screeching persisted for a while and then began to subside. The navigator lifted his head and stared at his console in disbelief. "We're going back into orbit," he said, and tears began to roll down his cheeks.

Arlette fought to regain her composure. She had cracked but by some miracle her intuition had come to her rescue. Intuition? Where had that data come from? Well, she had no time to dwell on that. Her ship was critically damaged and exposed to a merciless enemy. She had only one card to play.

"Genes! Total focus on the asteroid!" she shouted.

"We're not yet stable!" he shot back.

"Fuck stability! The asteroid!" she screamed.

Genes turned his attention to the path of the asteroid

that was approaching Ceres and carrying the direction control parasite that Cobus had landed on it many weeks ago.

All the data was there. He ran the algorithm.

"2.7 degrees. Hell, that's tight, but still within limits!" he said to himself as he concentrated his mind on the instruction that was about to be issued.

"Yeah!" he said and released it.

On the strange little frozen world hurtling through space, equipment clicked and seismic events ensued. The asteroid minutely altered its course as it approached the blue globe of Ceres and began to touch the upper limits of its atmosphere. The watchers on Prometheus saw it streak past below them, tearing an orange gash in the blue and then ripping up the dark side of the planet.

Slowly, slowly the nose of Dark Shadow appeared above the black disk of Ceres and the morning light of Omega 16 touched it for an instant.

Arlette, her fists clenched, eyes and mouth wide open, watched as the orange streak curled upwards and ever closer to the horizon of the planet. "Yes, YES, YES!!!"

The orange streak expanded into a savage ball of fire as it hit the massive ship, then retreated, tossing off fragments of the broken intruder in its wake.

Dark Shadow was gone.

30
War Games

Genes closed his eyes and exhaled. "Tim, sort this thing out please," he called across to the pilot.

Tim Cochran took control and Prometheus went through a little jig of direction and attitude corrections. A few minutes later he reported, "Prometheus is in stable orbit. Good morning, everyone!"

Arlette reeled off instructions to her lieutenants.

"Helen. Restore pressurisation to one bar and get me a catalogue of leak locations."

"Dima. Dima, are you there? Good. Are the rings OK? Good. Get me back 1G. Well, fix it."

"Benny. Damage report. Yes of course you'll have to go outside. Put all your people on it."

"Henri. Get out there and find out what hit us. Work with Benny."

"Hannah. Get the paramedics to look for survivors in and around the sealed-off sections. And give me a body count."

"Genes. Give me a propulsion system integrity report. No, stay here and delegate."

Henri Bertin did not like wearing a spacesuit. He felt clumsy and vulnerable and he hated having to delegate responsibility for on-board security, even for just an hour or so. As he emerged from the airlock he felt something akin to vertigo as he anxiously sought out the anchor for his tether and clipped it in place. He clambered up the hull of the ship to where there was a huge dent in the side, some twenty metres across, just about level with the clinic inside. Gas was leaking out from a multitude of punctures and condensing into little clouds. There was no sign of an explosion, nor of burning of any kind. Just a big, round dent. Benny caught up with him and they both hung there in space, looking for evidence of some kind.

Finally Benny said, "They've been playing billiards with us."

"Yes," said Henri. "I don't understand. They must have sophisticated weapons. Why would they hit us with a solid object?"

"That's for you to figure out," said Benny. "I need to get back inside to repair the skin and stop the leaks."

When they had got back through the airlock and taken off their spacesuits, gravity had been restored, but the air pressure was being kept low to keep losses down. Benny dispatched a team to fix the leaks and went to confer with Arlette. Henri climbed into the annulus of the ship to see if there was anything inside that might throw some light on what had hit them. There was not. He went back to his office and sat thinking for a while, partially to recover from the effort of moving around in the low-pressure atmosphere, and partially because he was looking for inspiration. Finally he got up and went to talk to Genes Clayton in the control centre.

Genes frowned. "Weird," he said, "but then it did the job, didn't it?"

"Yes, of course," said Henri. "No one could expect this kind of ship to survive if it fell into an atmosphere. But why would they carry such a primitive weapon? It had to be a catapult of some kind."

"Naw," said Genes. "I think we were hit by a space-age cannonball fired from an electromagnetic gun, and I think they probably used it because it doesn't leave a heat trace like a rocket-powered missile. It gave them an element of surprise and it was enough. Finito."

It was a reasonable explanation and Henri decided to adopt it as a credible interim theory and to concentrate on the deeper implications of the attack.

He called Cobus. "Any sign of activity in LDST 2?" he enquired.

"Nothing," said Cobus, and then, as an afterthought, "Shall I wake the satellite up and test it?"

"I think that would be wise in the circumstances" said Henri, beginning to feel uneasy.

He was not surprised when Cobus called back a few minutes later, a worried tone in his voice. "It's not responding," he said. "I can't even get it to acknowledge my call."

"In that case I think you'd better look at the signal history in that part of the sky over the last week or so. I'm afraid you may find that there's been quite a lot of activity."

"OK," said Cobus.

He was back again after a few minutes. "You were

right. There's another alien satellite there and it has been spewing out data in all directions."

"There you go," said Henri. "It was easy enough for us to knock out their satellite and replace it with ours, so we shouldn't be surprised that they – probably Dark Shadow – knocked out ours and replaced it with one of theirs again. Well, now that Dark Shadow is gone," he went on, "let's knock out theirs again and replace it with one of ours."

"OK, I'll get to it," said Cobus.

'That puts a new complexion on things,' thought Henri. 'If we could see them just before the asteroid hit them, they could see us. That probably means that back in Andromeda they will know that we survived even though Dark Shadow did not. They will also know that the asteroid strike was no fluke. They would have been tracking it as it went behind Ceres, convinced that it would go harmlessly off into space, and then, surprise, surprise, the next time they see it, it's coming straight for them! Hardly coincidental! Merde and merde!'

He felt the same feeling as he had felt when summoned before the head teacher at school in Haiti after he had written something very uncomplimentary about her on the wall of the boys' room. Were teachers really smart enough to recognise his writing? Apparently they were – he hadn't really thought that through when he did it.

Retribution was likely to be rather more severe than a whack on the wrist this time, though, he thought grimly. But was there already another Dark Shadow, or perhaps multiple Dark Shadows, in the Omega 16 system, or was Prometheus now alone? If they were alone, were they being watched?

A thought occurred to him. He called Cobus again. "Can the mission," he said.

"Colonel?"

"Abort the mission. I've changed my mind."

"But we're already in countdown. It'll..."

"Abort the mission immediately!"

"OK, Colonel, will do," replied Cobus. "Should I can the replacement satellite as well?"

"Yes," said Henri, "at least for the time being."

"Can I ask why?"

"Yes," said Henri. "My primary concern now is to know whether there are any more alien spacecraft in the Omega 16 system. If there are, we can expect them to be in communication with or via their LDST 2 satellite. I want you to keep monitoring its communications and tell me if it is exchanging any data with another entity inside the Omega 16 system, or down LDST 2, or both. We can't devise a strategy until we have that intel."

"Understood," said Cobus, "but I can tell you now that the LDST 2 satellite is quite obviously looking for Dark Shadow," he went on. "It's sending out repeat messages towards us periodically, and it's not getting a response."

"That's good news," said Henri. "Let me know immediately if there is any change."

"OK, but if you're concerned that there may be other alien craft around, should I corral another asteroid from the belt?"

"Absolutely, yes," said Henri.

Reparations to Prometheus went on around the clock. There was no serious structural damage but a lot of internal equipment had been destroyed. The most extensive repair work was to replace the protective tiles on the outside skin that had been lost or damaged by the impact and the subsequent burn through the upper atmosphere of Ceres. This was tedious and exhausting work because it had to be conducted in spacesuits, but for those involved there was one lasting impression: Prometheus was one tough spaceship.

After two days the interior of the ship had returned to normal and routine resumed. Arlette called for a strategy meeting with her aides, who now regularly included Genes, Hannah and Cobus as well as Julia, Henri and Marcel.

"Before we start," she said, "I would like us to celebrate the fact that we incurred no fatalities in the attack, although we still have two of our medical staff in a serious condition due to oxygen deprivation. I want to commend the entire crew for their courage and bravery." She did not mention Genes, but she looked at him as she said it.

"Right. Let's start with security," she said. "Henri, should we continue on yellow alert? What threats does Prometheus face now and how do you rate them?"

"Yellow alert should stay in place," replied Henri. "The satellite we put in place to monitor movements in LDST 2 has been silenced, and a new alien satellite was active there prior to our first sighting of Dark Shadow. It is almost certain that all events up to the destruction of Dark Shadow are known in Andromeda, and to any other alien ship currently in the Omega 16 system."

"There are others?" asked Julia in horror.

"We have no indication that there are any, but we cannot rule it out," said Henri. "Cobus, can you please elaborate?"

"Ja", said Cobus. "We have been looking at the signal records of the alien satellite at LDST 2 and we found that it has been in regular contact with Dark Shadow and with a source at the other end of the wormhole. Right now it is not getting a response to its calls to Dark Shadow, and it is not communicating with anything else in the Omega 16 system. That's encouraging, but it doesn't mean that there aren't any more alien ships in the system. We can find no record of communications between the satellite and Dark Shadow before it started to move either, so there could be other Dark Shadows out there, waiting for instructions."

"Is that the scenario we have to live with?" asked Marcel over the video link.

"For the time being, yes," replied Cobus, "but the risk diminishes with time if we detect no contacts between the satellite and another source in the Omega 16 system."

"So, Henri, are we still on a war footing?" asked Arlette.

"Yes," said Henri flatly. "Dark Shadow will have been tracking the incoming asteroid while in orbit around Ceres, and will have calculated that it would miss them. Even if they only had sight of it for a few seconds before it hit them, they will have assumed that the only reason that it could have changed its path would be that we had manipulated it. We have to assume that that information went back to Andromeda, and that it could only be viewed as an act of war."

"Well," said Julia, "they can hardly be surprised since they tried to blow us out of the sky first."

"Technically that's not correct, Julia," said Henri. "They actually hit us with a solid projectile of some sort which was intended to knock us out of orbit. It's a fine point, I know, but they apparently wanted the atmosphere of Ceres to destroy us."

"Why would they make that distinction?"

"Perhaps it was intended to be a legal distinction?" suggested Marcel. "If there was no missile heat-trace record, they might claim that a malfunction on Prometheus had caused it to crash into the atmosphere."

"Who's going to listen to a story like that?" Julia wanted to know. "Some intergalactic court of justice?"

"Perhaps that's not as far-fetched as it sounds," said Arlette thoughtfully, "but I accept Henri's conclusions. We must be extremely vigilant of any alien communications traffic. Cobus, make sure we have an automatic alarm system to pick up any changes in the comms pattern out there."

"Now, before we tackle the issue of how we are going to pre-empt any further aggression from these aliens," Arlette went on, "Marcel, how is the security situation on Ceres?"

"Rather quiet," he replied. "We've stopped shooting at LFIs when they approach us at night because we've learned that they do less damage when they're not full of bullets. We did come across a shameless pair of giant scorpions mating – definitely not for the faint-hearted. Oh, and Giuliano got bitten by a crab in the kitchen. That's about it," he concluded.

The others allowed themselves a chuckle.

"Alright, let's return to the issue of our survival," said Arlette. "How do we respond when we detect another alien craft in the Omega 16 system?"

"Well," said Genes, "we could always appeal for divine intervention, like last time."

"Pardon?"

"Yeah. You asked for help from the almighty and he delivered. That's my take on it anyway."

"You're not serious?"

"Well, I'm kind of curious about that instruction you gave me," went on Genes. "The craft was tumbling and spinning at the same time and its velocity was increasing. The temperature on the skin was rising and the air density was changing. That's quite a tough set of parameters to input into a sophisticated mathematical model. To do that in your head and pull out an answer which had to predict the exact attitude of the ship at a particular instant when a certain amount of power from a particular booster would correct everything and push us back into orbit, well that, lady, generates more respect in me than I never had for no deity."

All eyes turned to Arlette.

"It was just instinct," she said with a shrug. "What can I say? Something inside me just reeled it off."

There was silence. A mutter in the background on the line from Ceres sounded very much like 'Jeanne d'Arc'.

"I beg your pardon, Marcel?!" said Arlette, visibly irritated.

"I didn't say anything," said Marcel. "Must have been a crossed line."

"Well, this is not a strategy!" snapped Arlette. "Where are we going with this?"

"Let me give you a fireside space story instead," said Genes. "The Gods of Andromeda and the Milky Way know that their galaxies are going to collide and are real nervous about the outcome. Andromeda sends a boarding party to the Milky Way. The Milky Way God is really pissed but is all out of thunderbolts, so he gives a human who happens to be in the vicinity a sneaky bit of data so she can zap the Andromeda guys. Finito!"

The laughter that followed was more about Genes' terminology than his ideas.

Julia intervened. "I think we need to give the Commander some space on this," she said. "Let's come back to it. Can I call in Benny to do the damage report?"

When they did return to the topic of defence strategy, Henri set out the context once more.

"As Cobus pointed out before, we are now closely monitoring signals to and from the alien satellite at LDST 2. If it is in contact with any source within the Omega 16 system we will know we have another Dark Shadow to deal with. If the nature of the signals it is getting down LDST 2 from Andromeda changes, we can probably assume that we'll be expecting a new arrival. For as long as neither of these things occur, we can assume no immediate threat.

"We need the alien satellite to stay where it is because it is currently our only source of data. However, if we are expecting trouble from something on its way up LDST 2 we have to be prepared to act immediately. Therefore I propose to put an attack satellite up within striking distance of LDST 2, and also to corral another asteroid that we can use in the Omega 16 system or put down LDST 2 in the path of an incoming ship. We'll call it First Defence. Is that approved?" It was.

"OK," he went on. "Now let's consider our choices if we detect another alien ship within Omega 16. If it starts to move towards us or 16-4 we should assume that it intends to attack us. It is possible that it will instead move towards LDST 2 as a means of escape, in which case I propose that we let it go. Any other views?"

There were none.

"Right. So the worst-case scenario is that Dark Shadow II comes out of hiding and decides to come over and finish us off. Do we stay or do we go?"

Nobody responded.

"Let's look at the two options: one – we stay. We don't want to wait to see if he's going to respond to our friendly greeting; we pick our moment and attack him."

"But he's ten times our size!" wailed Julia. "A head-on confrontation would be suicide!"

"I didn't say anything about a head-on confrontation," replied Henri. "If there's anything you learn at military college, it's that you don't confront a superior force. You use guerrilla tactics."

"Guerrilla tactics? We hide behind convenient orbiting boulders and take pot-shots when he's not looking!?"

"Please, Julia!" said Arlette.

"No," went on Henri, "We use multiple vehicles and vary the tactics."

"Multiple vehicles?" queried Arlette, "We've only got one … No, of course we've got the two landers but they're not armed."

"We might change that," said Henri, and suddenly Arlette saw that they might.

"Of course they are very manoeuvrable," she conceded.

"Can't we use a steerable asteroid like last time?" cut in Marcel.

"Yes and no," said Henri. "Yes, we can, and no, not like last time."

"To your earlier point about guerrilla tactics," added Genes thoughtfully, "we might use multiple steerable asteroids, some as decoys, others as missiles. We could make this place full of nasty surprises for a huge ship like that."

Henri looked at Arlette, raised his eyebrows and smiled. There was an unspoken message there – something like 'when will this guy run out of creative ideas?'

"Thanks, Genes," he said. "In scenario one you would be responsible for setting up a network of steerable asteroids in various orbits around Ceres that we could use to keep Dark Shadow II wondering which day of the week it was."

Cobus was grinning all over his face. "I love it!" he said.

"OK, boys," said Arlette, "enough of the gaming, let's look at alternatives."

"Option two," said Henri. "We wait until it's clear that Dark Shadow II is on its way, and just at the point when they are committed to their course at full speed, we come around Ceres at full power going the other way, back towards LDST 1, and escape!"

"There's too much wrong with that to even comment," said Genes. Everybody seemed to agree with him.

"Henri, put together a detailed plan for option one," said Arlette.

"Commander, could I have a word?" asked Julia as the meeting broke up, and then, when they were alone, "You're not going to go soft on Genes, are you?"

"Of course not! He's a murderer and a traitor!" Arlette retorted. "I'm just using his mind."

"Good. In that case you need to watch your body language," said Julia. She did not elaborate. "But I've got something a bit more delicate to talk to you about," she went on.

"Yes?"

"Yes. I want to talk about the experience you had when you gave that critical instruction to Genes about the boosters."

Arlette looked at her cautiously. "Yes?"

"I've heard what you said to the others, but I've also watched the video, and Genes made a cogent point. We don't really have an explanation for an event that saved this ship and everyone on it, and possibly a lot more than that."

"What did you see on the video?" asked Arlette.

"I saw a look of incredulity, like you were receiving a message that was almost too good to be true," said Julia. "If you want to watch it with me in slo-mo, you'll see it as well."

Arlette looked at her for a long time. "Yes, I did get a message," she said quietly. "It just had complete ... authority. I could not have failed to repeat what I was told."

"Did the voice say anything more than the instruction you repeated to Genes?"

There was another long silence.

"Yes," she said. "It said, 'You will save us' and then the booster coordinates. That's all."

"Us? Save us?"

"Yes."

"You must have thought about it. Do you have an explanation?"

"No," said Arlette simply.

"Well, what you surely will realise is that what you have just told me would classify you as psychic."

"I suppose so."

"Have you tried to ask your 'voice' for an explanation?"

Another silence. "Yes."

"What happened?"

"I tried to ask it who it was. I felt a presence. The words 'You know that' came into my mind."

"Do you know, Commander?"

"Perhaps. I don't know."

"Are you going to tell me?"

"Don't push me any more, Julia," said Arlette.

The report on the Dark Shadow incident that reached Mission Control caused immense consternation and debate. Knocking out an unmanned satellite was one thing; destroying an intergalactic spaceship, almost certainly at the cost of a large number of alien lives, was quite another. It was an act of war on an unprecedented scale that could have unimaginable consequences for the future of the human race.

On the other hand, on what basis was the human race to concede its own Milky Way to an alien civilisation from another galaxy? What right did the Andromedans have to colonise our planets? If we were not prepared to stand on the tiger's tail, should we just accede to extinction?

The response that reached Arlette was a masterpiece of political ambiguity. 'Avoid confrontation', 'use force defensively', 'proactively defend "our" Ceresian territory', 'seek practical compromise'.

"Bullshit," said Arlette, and filed it.

However, a lot of excellent military advice was forthcoming, which resulted in significant upgrades to the performance of landers 1 and 2, and their conversion into formidable attack craft.

But it was the asteroid defence system that really impacted the morale of the crew. Genes devised a system of eight asteroids with exclusive elliptical orbits, either around Ceres or one of its moons. Each had the capability of quite astonishing changes in direction at relatively short notice, using the 'parasite' control systems that had been landed on them, and the interacting gravitational fields of Ceres and its moons. When it had been put in place and tested, there were those, particularly on Prometheus, who rather hankered after a little trial of strength with Dark Shadow II, which, they felt, was almost certainly coming.

"I talked to Arlette after the Dark Shadow incident," Hannah was telling Jafar, "and she has no doubt that it was a supernatural agency of some kind that delivered that data into her mind. She said it was a crystal-clear response to her call for help and she had received an immediate response: 'You will save us' and the coordinates. She doesn't want to tell the other members of the command team explicitly because she fears they'll think she is losing her grip. I believe her but I can't get my head around the implications.

"Apparently General Lee at ISEA went spare when told that Dark Shadow had been destroyed. What were we supposed to do, let them have a second shot at us?

"The colony is coming along fine. The atmosphere down there on Ceres is wonderful. Everybody seems to be happy to make a contribution and appreciative of what others are doing. The quality and variety of the food is astonishing and everyone seems to get such pleasure from every little achievement; you would love it."

Hannah's message left Jafar feeling extremely uneasy. He really was not able to take the idea that Prometheus and its crew were under the protection of a deity seriously and he was worried that the mental faculties of the leadership were cracking up in the wake of the bizarre events that they had experienced. He tended to share General Lee's view that the destruction of an alien spaceship was extremely bad news and wondered whether this brave little mission might not ultimately lead to the doom of mankind.

"The world press had a field day with the destruction of the alien spaceship," he announced in his response. "The saintly pioneers of Prometheus are now perceived by many as galactic buccaneers. Religious noodniks everywhere are staring up into the sky, looking for alien invaders. In Europe and India there have been huge protests calling for apologetic approaches to be made to the Andromedans. I was in Berlin yesterday and witnessed an anti-ISEA demonstration there. You can't believe how angry and frightened these people are. I interviewed a few of the protesters and many see that the only prospect of a secure future for the human race has been blown away. They are formulating a message in a mathematical code that will be sent down the wormhole to Andromeda. I wish you would discourage further engagement with the Andromedans if you possibly can."

Jafar looked away.

"There's an appalling heatwave in central Europe and the Rhine is so low it's closed to water traffic," he went on. "The price of bottled water is astronomical and you can't sit outside a restaurant without people coming up to you and begging – in Berlin!"

He smiled. "Now some good news. I have finally managed to get Shan and Shiv back from Bangladesh. We have formed a cooperative here in our block to look after them. They are really lovely boys, three and four years old, and they just absorb everything they hear and see. You would be captivated by them." He smiled again. "I miss you – please come home soon."

* * *

Colonisation on the surface of Ceres proceeded apace in the weeks after the Dark Shadow incident. The new two-storey Orange House entered its final stage of construction, and a roof was built of local wood rafters and locally made tiles, flashed with gleaming local copper sheeting. Only the windows, of optical grade plastic, were imported from the stores on Prometheus. The colonists were immensely proud of their settlement, especially now that they had fully equipped individual rooms and quite extensive areas in which to spend their leisure time during the long Ceresian nights.

Giuliano the cook continued to produce new dishes of astonishing variety and originality, and had taken under his wings a couple of maintenance engineers who felt that cooking was to be their ultimate expression of personal creativity. However, it was probably the smell of freshly baked Ceresian rye bread that attracted them most.

Several of the varieties of fruit found in the Dale of Plenty had now become staple favourites, and required restocking every few days. The militia charged with this task were always meticulous about covering their skin, and to their relief saw neither spitting spiders nor army ants for weeks on end. On their final day of duty before crew rotation, a team led by Kharkov arrived at the Dale some four hours after sunrise as usual, and drove into the centre of the grove to begin work. They were properly kitted out and masked, but felt no need to carry weapons other than the knives they used to cut the fruit off.

They approached their task with enthusiasm, and had taken to singing a novel version of the cook's favourite Rigoletto vocal quartet as they worked, replete with unconventional noises and an improvised text that was less than complimentary to the lady to which the music had originally been addressed. Just as they reached the chorus, which now ended with "... took her knickers o-off!", Kharkov turned around to see that a large spitting spider had crept between them and the truck which contained their arms.

"Keep very calm, guys, and turn around slowly," mouthed Kharkov by CTT to his colleagues. They did so. The spider rose and stiffened. "We'll split up, Bennet and Koh to the left, Zandy and Kruger to the right. Be ready to use your knives until you reach your weapons, then shoot to kill. Ready, go!"

The four of them separated and raced through the undergrowth, trying to confuse the creature as they looped around it. The spider reacted by running this way then that, spitting out yellow venom in all directions, until it selected Kharkov and charged. He ducked and weaved through the low branches, then managed to shin up a rather flimsy tree, just escaping the creature's snapping fangs. Two huge, hairy legs reached up towards him and began to pull the tree over as he hung on precariously by his hands and crossed ankles. The spider, unable to make an impression by spitting venom at Kharkov's posterior, then used a third leg to give it a sharp poke.

"Ow!" yelled Kharkov. "For God's sake, kill it!"

Koh was the first to reach the truck. He grabbed a weapon, spun around and opened fire. He did a pretty good job on the spider, but a bullet penetrated the branch that Kharkov was hanging from and it broke, dropping Kharkov, branch and all, straight on top of the frenzied animal.

Kharkov rolled himself into a ball, spun off the creature and smacked straight into a tree trunk, concussing himself.

"What a mess!" said Koh with disgust, surveying the phlegm-spattered scene. "Let's get him in the truck and go home. Leave the fruit, I've gone off it."

At the subsequent debrief the question was raised as to whether the spider's presence was a coincidence or a deliberate ambush.

Chuck Connolly was baffled. "I can't understand how you could have been so preoccupied that you didn't notice the spider creeping up on you," he said. "We were lucky that our protective clothing held up and Kharkov wasn't poisoned. In future we will always post an armed lookout."

No one mentioned Verdi.

Cobus had just returned from an enjoyable week on Ceres in copper pipe production, but was rather glad to take back from his deputy the pleasant task of confirming to the mission leadership each morning that there were no unusual communication patterns to or from the LDST 2 alien satellite in the last twenty-four hours.

He was to be disappointed. He knew the moment that he took his seat in front of his monitor that an entirely new type of chatter had begun between the alien satellite and a new source down, and possibly moving in, the wormhole. He immediately initiated the processes to launch an attack rocket and a replacement satellite, and activated a change in course of the First Defence asteroid. Then he called Arlette and reported the news to her.

31
Silver Streak

Henri and Marcel were enjoying breakfast in the early morning sunshine on the newly completed first-floor terrace of the Orange House, when Arlette approached, frowning. She told them the news, then sat down to join them. "How confident are you that we can knock it out before it clears LDST 2?" was her first question.

Marcel looked at Henri. "It depends on factors outside our control," he said. "It's a race against time. We don't know how long it's been coming up the wormhole, or how long the wormhole is, or what speed it is travelling at. If we apply our own experience, we've got plenty of time – at least twenty-four hours – to spare."

Arlette relaxed a bit. "It's just a feeling I have," she said, "that they won't allow themselves to be beaten by that asteroid collision trick a second time."

"Well, it's the best trick we have," put in Henri. "A few million tons of rock and ice moving at high speed can do more decisive damage to a large spaceship than any tactical weapon available to us here."

The discussion moved on. "Has the military hardware been installed in the landers? Are they now fully operational?" she asked.

"Yes," said Henri. "That was completed a week ago. All four pilots have been training for attack missions in them. Sanam and Tim were military pilots before they joined ISEA, as you know, and have been coaching the others."

"I gather Sanam's coaching skills go beyond fighter pilot tactics; at least with Arun, they do," said Arlette with a touch of spite in her voice.

"I don't think that's quite fair, Commander," said Marcel. "I think they have fallen in love and are not prepared to hide it. Not a bad thing for a new colony like ours. And they aren't the only ones."

"Oh?" said Arlette archly. "Are you offering cohabiting quarters now in the Orange House?"

"I haven't been asked yet," replied Marcel, "but perhaps we should be proactive about it. Better than having people creeping about at night in the black-out barefoot."

Arlette's comments were a lot closer to the mark than she knew. At about the same time, Sanam and Arun, having completed a simulated attack on Prometheus in Lander 2, were parked in orbit, weightless, and 'reviewing the data'.

"Look at me, Arun," said Sanam, removing the last of her clothes and floating across the cabin in front of him. "Aren't I a naughty girl?"

"You are the most ravishing beauty in the Milky Way!" said Arun, struggling with his safety harness.

"Well then, you should look and not touch," she said,

"It's my prerogative to touch. Now you just stay there and I'll see what I can find." She ran her hands over his body. "Oooh!" she said. "Is that nice?"

He exploded; she knew he would, and she smiled and smiled as he vented his passion on her.

When Mission Control received Arlette's report that some sort of vehicle from Andromeda was progressing up the LDST 2 wormhole towards Omega 16, General Lee had no option but to report the news to the Heads of State of the G25 immediately. This precipitated a diplomatic crisis, dividing those who were adamant that Earth must assert itself within its home galaxy, and those who pointed out that these aliens would easily determine which solar system LDST 1 was connected to, and would bring galactic conflict into Earth's back yard. A summit meeting held a few days later did nothing but deepen these divisions. The instruction to Prometheus that was hammered out after two days and nights of debate elaborated the risks in lengthy detail and required the mission commander to use all available means to avoid conflict, but not to concede Earth's right to colonise any uninhabited planet in the Omega 16 system.

When this message finally arrived it was of no practical relevance and, after discussing it with her aides, received the same response from Arlette as its similarly conflicted predecessor. She binned it.

In the three days it took to bring the First Defence asteroid from its parking orbit to the mouth of LDST 2, life on Ceres proceeded in its customary good-natured fashion, despite a protracted rainstorm that temporally halted construction work.

It was during this period, perhaps hastened by the confinement that ensued, that several budding relationships blossomed. Perhaps the most celebrated, and certainly the noisiest, was the passion that enveloped Carla Da Silva, the botanist, and Giuliano Benedetti, the cook. Upon the delivery of yet another cereal seed that he believed would take his bread-making to hitherto undreamt of heights of aromatic perfection, he declared that she was the most beautiful woman he had ever seen, that she was the mother of perfection and harmony and that he would happily lay down his life for her, all in Italian. Carla didn't know much Italian, but she got the gist alright, flung her arms around him and kissed him with all the passion she could muster. Giuliano then broke into his favourite Rigoletto aria, a sure sign to the rest of the crew that a wonderful meal was on the way, and the two of them were practically inseparable from then onwards.

Carla's colleague on the celebrated first Safari, Mpho Mathe, also much appreciated by Giuliano for her discovery of the wonderfully versatile Cerippo, was a slim, elegant woman whose passion was her profession. She was a superb talker, and her presentations on wildlife were always packed. She was probably the most envied woman in the crew, for she was a stunning beauty, her dark brown skin and fine facial features absolutely perfect. She and Marcel would talk together for hours, gently educating each other about the magic of their respective sciences. Most of the crew knew they were in love before they themselves recognised it, for it seemed to them not quite proper for intellectuals such as they were. However, when the lights were suddenly cut after the rainstorm in anticipation of the arrival of the LFIs, and they reached out to each other in the darkness and touched for the first time, there was no mistaking the nature of the magic that shot through them both. They linked hands and drew each other closer. Cheeks touched, then lips touched and a fire broke out that burned the whole, long Ceresian night.

* * *

Cobus was baffled.

His satellite had been in place at the exit of LDST 2 for almost twenty-four hours, receiving a stream of unintelligible data from whatever was moving towards it up the wormhole. The data stream had stopped, probably, he surmised, because the Andromedans had realised that their own satellite was no longer functional. Then, after what seemed like a massive disturbance somewhere down the wormhole, it started again, but now it had become two almost identical signals. Why would that be? He had to conclude that his knowledge of wormhole dynamics was far too slim to even attempt an explanation, so he called in the expertise of Yevgeny Kusnetsov, Chief Scientist.

"What do you make of this, Yev?" he asked.

Kusnetsov sat down at the monitor and began to work with the data. After a few minutes a 3-D diagram appeared on the screen. "Hah!" he said. "Your alien friends are re-engineering the LDST. It has become a two-lane highway!"

"Why would they do that?" asked Cobus.

"Who knows? Perhaps they're sending a whole fleet!"

Cobus shuddered at the thought.

When he reported to Henri, Cobus gave him just the facts and left out Kusnetsov's dire prediction.

Henri's response was immediate. "Merde! How long will it take you to get a second first defence asteroid down from the belt?"

"At least fifteen days," replied Cobus. "I'd have to get a unit up there first, select an asteroid, and then get it back here."

"OK, forget it," said Henri. "We'll just have to be lucky."

"I don't get it," said Cobus.

"Look," said Henri. "If we send our asteroid down one lane, and the alien ship comes up the other, we're out of luck, aren't we?"

"Yes, but I wouldn't want to be on that ship if they pick the wrong one," said Cobus.

"Given their apparent capabilities in wormhole engineering, I suspect they will have thought of a way round that," said Henri grimly. "Can't you split ours in two?"

"No, our parasite equipment doesn't have anything like that kind of explosive capability," replied Cobus. "It works on induction, not brute force."

"OK, I'll talk to Marcel and let you know if we come up with a plan. When will our First Defence asteroid be there?"

"In another six hours," said Cobus. "Do you want me to send it straight on down?"

"Probably yes, but I'll confirm that before it arrives."

Henri's subsequent discussion with Marcel and Arlette didn't change anything.

"They've created themselves an escape road!"

exclaimed Arlette. "I just never believed they'd let us take them out with the same trick we used before. Throw in First Defence by all means, but let's get ready for a new alien visitor."

"Let's think this through," said Marcel. "If Yev is correct, and I'm sure he is, knowing his mental capacity, then they will wait to see which side our asteroid is coming down, then change lanes and wave it past."

"Change lanes!?" Henri was incredulous. "At a significant fraction of the speed of light? I'd like to meet the driver!"

"That's neither here nor there," went on Marcel. "We don't know if or how they could do it, but I wonder if the course modification equipment we have on the First Defence asteroid would work when it's going down a wormhole?" He called Cobus.

"Naar – nice one!" said Cobus to Marcel's question. "I don't see why it should not respond but it'll be in a massively distorted electromagnetic environment, so I wouldn't like to predict the outcome."

"Well, surely that's better than just crossing our fingers?" suggested Marcel.

Cobus agreed. "I can see that we're getting a slightly stronger signal from one side than the other," he said, "so that's the side I'll put First Defence on to start with. If the stronger signal moves to the other side, I'll yank the wheel and we'll see what happens!"

"OK," said Marcel. "Keep us posted. You're go to put First Defence into LDST 2 as soon as it arrives."

Arlette and Henri were nodding.

Cobus took a break to think. First Defence did not

have an intelligent navigation system and would have to be controlled by him directly. That meant that there would be a significant communications delay between his receiving the data on the signals coming up LDST 2, and his instructions reaching First Defence.

"Well, so be it," he thought. "If they change lanes at the last minute, we won't have time to react. But would they take such a risk?" He thought not.

When he returned to his station to deliver the final course correction to First Defence, he was calm and resolved. He set up an alarm system on his phone to warn him if there was a tell-tale shift in the strength of the two signals, then called Henri.

"We're in attack mode," he reported. "I estimate that it will be no less than forty-eight hours before the alien ship and First Defence approach one another. I have a system set up to warn me if the ship changes lanes." He went off to talk to Kusnetsov again.

"Hmm, what's the mass of that asteroid of yours?" asked Kusnetsov.

"Seventy-two million tons, Yev," replied Cobus.

Kusnetsov busied himself on his computer for quite a while. Finally he looked up. "The kinetic energy of that thing at the speed it will reach when it's halfway down the tube could threaten the integrity of the LDST, you know."

Cobus didn't know. "So?"

"Well, I wouldn't want to be a spectator in the front seats."

Cobus grinned. "But we'll be watching from here," he said.

Kusnetsov shrugged. "In that case we might be in

for quite a show. Make sure we have the ship's telescope pointing in the right direction."

"Well," thought Cobus as he made his way down to the canteen, "this job does have its moments."

On her way back to her quarters for a shower, Sanam stepped into the lift to find Julia already inside. She looked decidedly unfriendly. "Have a good time up there in the lander, Major?" she enquired.

"Yes, the whole exercise went extremely well. Arun and I are very happy with..."

"Yes, I should think you are," Julia interrupted her, "and I suggest that you ensure that the internal monitor is switched off next time before you..."

"Oh my God!"

Julia got out at the next floor and left her there, biting her lip.

"This is going to be it!" thought Cobus as he sat down before his screen. The signal being picked up and relayed to him was quite constant, but now there was only one. The alien ship was progressing rapidly up the wormhole towards Omega 16, and First Defence was accelerating down towards it in exactly the opposite direction. He reported to Henri. "All steady for possible collision within the next two hours," he told him.

At almost the instant that he heard Henri reply "Copy that", his alarm went off: the signals had switched sides. Cobus was ready. He moved to activate a pre-programmed message to First Defence to change course.

As he did so something in his head caused him to hesitate, and he heard, quite clearly, 'Wait ninety-six seconds.' For some time he found he could not move his hand on the keyboard. Then he heard the word 'Now!' He pressed the key and the instruction was released.

For the next four hours the signal from the alien ship grew steadily stronger, then there was a huge burst of static. It took several minutes to clear, but then the signal resumed.

"We missed."

He put his head in his hands and breathed deeply several times, trying to cope with the disappointment.

A call from Kusnetsov came in. "Did you see that?!" he shouted. "Fantastic! Well done!"

"But we missed – the ship's still coming," said Cobus despondently.

"Oh that, yes, but didn't you see the LDST go?"

"Go? Go where?"

"It's gone, man! I told you this might happen! It destabilised and imploded! You've closed down the wormhole to Andromeda! Wait till you see the video! Awesome!"

Slowly Cobus' thoughts started to clear and he began to think of the implications. "It's just him and us now," he said slowly.

He switched his monitor over to the ship's telescope channel and watched a re-run of the event. You could see quite clearly the blue luminescent tube of LDST 2, perfectly stable one moment, then erupting with a savage flash and almost instantly disappearing. That was it. No debris, nothing. Just black space where the blue tube had been.

Except for one thing. The silver streak of an object moving very fast towards them.

Henri, Arlette and Marcel took Cobus' incoming call on the video link. They knew instantly that the news was not good. "We missed?" asked Arlette.

"Not exactly," said Cobus. "We missed the alien ship, but we hit the LDST."

"How do you know we hit the LDST? What does that matter, anyway?"

"Because it's not there any more," said Cobus, and waited for the news to sink in.

"Oh, that does change things," said Arlette, and a hint of a smile crossed her face. "Now we have only one adversary to deal with, and there's no way the cavalry can come and save him. I think we're ready, aren't we, boys?"

32
The Truth in the Parable

According to the data that Cobus was receiving from his satellite, which was now sitting in a space where the mouth of LDST 2 had previously been, the alien ship was approaching Omega 16 at a mind-bending 60 per cent of the speed of light.

"I hope he's had his brakes serviced recently," remarked Cobus to Kusnetsov as they sifted through the data.

"Probably had a bit of a following wind from the collapse of the LDST," observed Kusnetsov. "I would think they'll overshoot Omega 16."

This time he was wrong. Silver Streak, as it was now to be known, entered the Omega 16 system on a path that took it directly away from the star, adding some gravitational assistance to the on-board deceleration process. But it went as far as the outer reaches of the planetary system before it slowed sufficiently to turn and head back towards rocky planets 16-3 and 16-4, more than thirty days later.

During this long and involuntary tour of mostly empty space by the alien spacecraft, the status of the

Prometheus mission improved substantially. News of the destruction of LDST 2 was greeted with huge relief on Earth, and the doomsday prospect of imminent invasion by aliens retreated. No one paid much attention to the fact that Silver Streak was still in the vicinity of Ceres in cosmological terms. It was a very long way away, and strategically disadvantaged.

* * *

Developments on Ceres surged ahead during this long military respite. The hens began to lay, which, for Giuliano and his new soul mate Carla, was an event of galactic significance. Sanam found herself pregnant, and far from being embarrassed or inconvenienced in any way, she rejoiced publically in this historic achievement. "Weightless conception is perfection!" she crowed.

The relationship between Marcel and Mpho continued to develop as he attempted to explain to her, while she was lying quite naked on her back, the physics of the interaction between the two bodies as they passed each other in the wormhole. "This bit here is the alien spaceship" – and he gave it a squeeze – "and this bit right next to it is our friend the asteroid 'First Defence'" – and he stroked it softly – "and this bit down here is the entrance to..."

"Don't you dare!" she shrieked.

The Orange House was completed, and in one final flourish of construction enthusiasm, equipped with a freshwater swimming pool. Exploration had now reached all the way to the mountains in the east, and a permanent camp had been established in the beautiful area of lakes at their foot. There they discovered the gazelle roach, a shy, rather elegant, fast-moving creature that quickly became a dinnertime favourite.

Freddy Jones had arrived on the fourth landing party and started to transform the rather crude process of gathering whatever was available into structured agricultural production. He transplanted the fruit trees which had become popular into orchards, cleared fields for cereal planting, and started growing the vegetables that had been brought from Earth in seed form.

While those who had developed a taste for the bucolic were happy, a lot of the engineering types were becoming increasingly frustrated at the challenges of developing manufacturing. The initially generous supply of motors, pumps, furnaces and machines of all description from Prometheus was drying up. Transformation from cottage industry to industrial manufacturing seemed impossible and serious group discussions began to brainstorm these issues. They needed steel, power, heavy machinery and fuel. Specialist equipment could be brought in on subsequent missions from Earth, but the resources would have to be developed locally. The search began for deposits of coal, iron ore and other minerals, and the potential of the eastern mountains for hydroelectric power generation was assessed.

In their private debates on these issues, Arlette and her aides realised that those with practical knowledge of industrial development on Earth would constantly be pushing the colony to emulate the home they knew. Without a plan which targeted very specific development goals, and provided the skills and resources to achieve it, frustration and eventually conflict would grow.

When Arlette mentioned these issues briefly to Genes, he responded in his usual casual, off-the-cuff fashion, "Why not get into shipbuilding? We have wood, wind and the need to explore. That's how they did it in the fifteenth century."

It was a seminal idea, an activity in which almost everyone could contribute in some way, and when it was informally proposed the response was almost universal approval.

* * *

Back on Prometheus, Kusnetsov had been entertaining himself by analysing the data that the satellite had collected on the LDST just before it imploded. He invited Cobus over for a chat. "You know, I'm beginning to come to the conclusion that the instant you chose to send that instruction to the asteroid to change course was probably the greatest coincidence in the history of space travel," he told Cobus.

Cobus suddenly felt very uneasy. "Sorry?" he said.

"Yes," went on Kusnetsov, "it looks to me that you hit the diametric centre of the LDST system with your seventy-two million tons of junk, and that's what caused it to destabilise."

"But … but that was an accident!"

"Yes, I know! But an incredibly lucky one for us and incredibly unlucky for Andromeda!"

Cobus stared at him. "Oh my God," he said under his breath.

Despite his misgivings, Cobus was now a hero on

Prometheus. He had told his story many times, but always left out the bit about his ninety-six seconds' hesitation – it just didn't sound very professional. He was, however, to be undone by a presentation that Kusnetsov gave after he had finished his study on the implosion of LDST 2. Julia, always keen to improve her physics, attended, and she pricked up her ears when she heard the words 'greatest coincidence in the history of space travel'. She looked at Cobus, and Cobus looked away.

'There's something I need to know,' she said to herself, and she collared him immediately after the presentation was finished.

"Come and have a chat, Cobus," she said. "I'd like to hear the story from the horse's mouth."

Back in her office he told her about the preparation, the decisions that had been made and how they had been made. He praised Henri, Marcel and Arlette for their foresight and made himself out to be a minor operative, but he scrambled the bit about activating the instruction to the asteroid to change course. Julia, who had listened patiently, picked it up immediately.

"Take me over that bit again, Cobus," she said. "Did you send the instruction to change course immediately you picked it up that the alien ship had changed lanes?"

"Er, no, not quite," said Cobus.

"Why not?"

"I, er, I had a bit of cramp," he said.

"You had a bit of cramp, so you didn't press the key?"

"Right," said Cobus.

"And how long did your cramp last?"

"Ninety-six seconds," said Cobus.

"Ninety-six seconds? Not eighty-five seconds, or a hundred and three? How do you know?"

Cobus looked down for what seemed like a long time.

"It felt as though I was being told," he said.

Julia's tone softened. "You heard a voice in your head?"

He looked up sharply. "Yes, sort of," he said.

"Tell me exactly what it said."

"It said, 'Wait 96 seconds' and then 'now.'"

"And you obeyed it?"

"Yes," said Cobus.

"Why?"

"I couldn't move my hand and..."

"You could have used the other one."

"I didn't want to."

"Alright, Cobus," said Julia. "That must have been a very special moment for you. Have you thought about it much since?"

"Yes I have," said Cobus. "I thought I'd made a terrible mistake but now it seems like ... like it was kind of inspired."

"And where do you think this voice came from?"

Cobus just shook his head.

Julia called Arlette privately and related what she had just heard. There was silence for a while and then Arlette responded quietly, "So, it's not just me who is psychic."

"I don't think psychic is quite the right word any more," said Julia. "I think we have to recognise that two events of vital importance to us have been influenced in our favour by some external agency."

"And who or what do you suppose is that agency?" enquired Arlette.

"I don't know, but I can't get around the possibility that it is using us to undermine the alien threat."

"You believe Genes' little parable about the Gods of the Milky Way and Andromeda?"

"Not quite, but it fits," said Julia.

Arlette let her head fall back and she stared up into the pale blue sky of Ceres for a long time. Then she jumped up and started walking quickly, calling up Henri as she went. "Get together with Marcel and link up with Julia and Cobus," she said. "We have something important to discuss."

The meeting took place in the freshly furnished conference room at the Orange House, with a video link to Julia's office on Prometheus. Arlette wasted no time on other matters.

"I want to tell you about the experience I had when we were knocked out of orbit by Dark Shadow," she said. "You remember that we were tumbling and spinning out of control and Genes was trying to correct the problems with a booster thrust. A set of coordinates came into my head and I instructed him to follow them. He did so and the ship corrected its attitude and escaped back into orbit." She paused. Everyone was watching her intently.

"Well," went on Arlette, "I did not calculate those coordinates; the data just came into my head and I repeated it. I have given a lot of thought as to how that happened and have concluded that the data was put into my mind by some external agency, rather like earphone input which goes straight to our cognitive centres. One possible motivation for this would be to protect our galaxy from an external intruder, but I have no proof of that. Cobus, I believe you had a similar experience?"

Cobus looked hugely relieved. He no longer felt alone, and the concept, as Arlette had expressed it, sounded entirely reasonable.

"Well, ja," he said, "that sounds very similar to what happened to me when I saw that Silver Streak had changed lanes in LDST 2. I was going to send the instruction to First Defence to change course, but something told me to wait ninety-six seconds, so I did. Now Yev tells me that that delay almost certainly caused the LDST to implode."

Henri and Marcel looked at each other, incredulous.

"Now," said Arlette, "on the assumption that Cobus and I are not gifted with analytical capabilities far in advance of anything we ever dreamt of, I conclude that the input we received probably came from the same source, with the same motivation. Does anybody have any other ideas?"

Nobody did.

"In that case," went on Arlette, "there may be something out there with immense power and influence, and since we shall probably be confronted with aggression from Silver Streak shortly, it seems to me that we should do more than just hope we get some more fortuitous input just at the right moment. So, the question we have to address is: 'how do we do that?'"

"Supposing we assume that Genes' parable is on the right track," said Henri. "That there is, in our own primitive terms, a God of the Milky Way."

"Wow!" said Marcel, breaking the tension. "General Lee would be really impressed with our networking!"

Arlette wanted very badly to say, "Fuck General Lee!" but she resisted. "Let's continue with this," she said. "If our assumption is correct, then we can only expect help if it is consistent with the best interests of the Milky Way galaxy."

"That's a can of worms," said Marcel. "Is our colonisation of Ceres in the interests of the galaxy?"

"Clearly yes," said Julia. "We are intelligent and want to survive. We have put up a fight against an enemy of the Milky Way to defend our civilisation, which we have now extended to a planet which was uninhabited and vulnerable to assault by aliens. We are adding value to the galaxy."

"Well, fine, but I think we can assume that we're not going to get help with the washing-up."

"OK, Marcel, OK – your point is presumably that it has to be a matter of great strategic importance for the galaxy? Then I'm sure we agree," said Julia.

"Does our survival count, even if the galaxy is no longer under a direct threat because we blew away the LDST?" Marcel persisted.

"I would think so, yes" said Arlette. "We are, as far as we know, the only intelligent beings in the Omega 16 system, and consequently the only agency that can prevent the Andromedans from invading. They've shown an interest in this star system, presumably because the rocky planets are of potential value to them. Who's to say they can't create another wormhole and come back?"

A rather dark silence descended on the meeting.

"Look, the point I'm making", said Arlette, "is that we are a strategic asset in the fight with Andromeda. As long as we are willing to fight the Andromedans to hold on to Ceres, we deserve support." She looked from face to face. They were all nodding.

"Good. Then let's make damn sure we put up a good show when Silver Streak comes looking for us."

Henri and Marcel got up.

"Oh, and one final point," she went on. "I want to bring Genes into this. I know his record is despicable, but he's by far the best motor man we have, and, if we're going to tangle with Silver Streak, I'll need him again. Is that OK?" No one protested, not audibly anyway.

A few days later, back on Prometheus, Arlette summoned Genes to her office. "What's the status of the asteroid defence system?" she asked him.

"We have six asteroids in various orbits around Ceres, and one around each of the moons. Well, of course, they are in elliptical orbits, but you get my drift." Arlette nodded. "Since the bandits cannot control them, but will assume that we can, it should make them pretty twitchy about entering orbit around Ceres. So, firstly it's a deterrent."

"Why only eight?" asked Arlette. "I thought you wanted twelve?"

"Yeah, that would have been ideal, but it's all the parasite controllers we had left."

"Oh," said Arlette. "Does it still give you complete coverage?"

"Pretty good, but not complete," replied Genes. "There's a window of scope to move each one at any particular time, and at any particular time we can hit just about any spot with at least one of them. But it can be a bit tricky making the calls." This was about as close to modesty as Genes was ever going to get in his life.

"Do you have a battle plan?" Arlette asked him.

"Vaguely. I think we should play hide-and-seek around

Ceres and the moons and get the asteroids to do the dirty work for us. I still need to discuss the details with Bertin."

"OK, now there's something personal I want to discuss with you," said Arlette.

Genes' eyes twinkled. "Hey lady, I'm ready to get personal just as soon as you are."

Arlette glared at him. "Was that supposed to be a pass?" she demanded. "Are you trying to add harassment to murder and treachery on your crime sheet?"

Genes briefly considered another playful remark and then thought better of it. "No, Ma'am," he said seriously. "I've told you before that I have great respect for you."

"I'm glad to hear it. Now what I am going to tell you is known only to my core team. I'm going to let you in on it because you were in the firing line last time and will probably be there again."

Arlette repeated what she and Cobus had told the others, and their conclusions. Genes listened, nodding intermittently.

"Well," he said, "I stand by what I said before. Whoever generated those coordinates has a near perfect grasp of dynamics. I would take those orders anytime."

"Good," said Arlette. "That's the way it has to be."

33
The Battle of Ceres

Cobus looked glumly at his monitor. There was no doubt about it, Silver Streak was not on a peaceful mission to explore Omega 16-4, it was on its way to Ceres. Arlette took note of his report, then called in Julia.

"We have to be pragmatic," she said. "If Prometheus comes to grief in this battle, then our colony on Ceres becomes more important than ever. There will be later missions from Earth, I have no doubt, but it is vital that our bridgehead thrives in the meantime. I want you to go down there and replace Marcel, at least for the duration of the battle. I need his scientific brain engaged up here to make sure we win."

"But if we lose Prometheus the colony will be marooned!" protested Julia.

"Not so," said Arlette. "You have direct communication with Earth from there via our satellite at the mouth of LDST 1."

Julia thought it over. She knew she had no military skills to contribute, but she hated the idea of sitting on

Ceres, doing nothing more than keeping her fingers crossed.

Arlette read her mind. "It will tax your leadership skills to the limit to keep everybody calm and focused while all this is going on, and even more so if the outcome is bad," she said, "but I must have a leader of your calibre down there, Julia."

'I'm being soft-soaped,' thought Julia, 'but I suppose it makes sense.'

"Alright, I'll go."

It was bright and blustery when Julia walked down the ramp from the lander. Marcel came out to meet her. "I just want to bring you up to speed," he said, putting an arm on her shoulder and guiding her into the Orange House. They sat in his office, now to be hers, and discussed practical details.

"We only have one doctor down here; all the rest of the medical staff are on Prometheus," he told her. "I think we ought to organise a training programme so that he can transfer his experience to as many people here as want to get involved in case something happens to him. I suspect we are in for a rash of pregnancies."

Julia nodded.

"More immediately," he went on, "there is a lot of anxiety about being cut off if the battle goes badly for Prometheus. We do have the satellite link of course, and I think we should open it up so that people can watch current events on Earth, albeit with a twelve-hour delay. I would point out to General Lee that the morale of the colonists here is vitally important. He might want to put together a panel to respond to daily questions. That could be useful for everybody; we're almost all amateurs now. Finally," he lowered his voice, "please look after Mpho for me; she's very frightened that I won't be coming back."

Julia nodded again. "Of course I will."

The departure of Marcel and the other returnees marked the first time that there had not been a lander parked on the edge of the base. Arlette had ordered them both back to ensure that she had all available offensive capability at her disposal, but it made the place seem forlorn and abandoned. Julia decided that she would counter that immediately. "Get me a big sound system set up in the meeting hall," she told Communications, "and find me a DJ. We're going to have a party tonight."

Henri was sitting with Arlette, Marcel, Cobus, Chuck Connolly and Genes, looking at an animated 3-D projection of Ceres and its two moons, which included Prometheus and the eight attack asteroids.

"We estimate that Silver Streak will enter this orbit here." He pointed. "And Prometheus will be here, behind moon 1."

"The moons have been named Apple and Pear by the Orange House. Let's stick to that," said Arlette.

"OK, we'll be behind Apple, on this orbit." He pointed again. "We will have a fix on his position at all times because we have set up three tracking satellites to do just that, but he won't be able to see us when we shift our orbital position." He paused for a drink.

"As soon as he is in stable orbit, Genes will select the asteroid with the most favourable trajectory and alter its course to achieve impact, and he will keep doing that until we are successful. We do not intend to expose Prometheus to direct conflict with Silver Streak, nor are we going to be firing any missiles unless I decide to instruct Chuck to do so. We do have the landers armed and ready, but again they will only engage with Silver Streak as a secondary tactic."

"Why would any particular targeted asteroid attack be unsuccessful?" Arlette wanted to know.

"Two reasons," Cobus interjected. "Firstly the parasite guidance equipment could be damaged, or secondly, Silver Streak moves at the last minute. Parasite is not a smart system; it cannot home in on a target and make last-minute course corrections. Each change of course must be made by a specific instruction from the motor man."

"Isn't that a bit of an oversight?" asked Marcel.

"Not really," said Cobus. "The system was designed to steer unwelcome asteroids out of harm's way, not to attack alien spaceships."

As Silver Streak approached, the Prometheus battle team took up their positions in the control centre while the pilots waited at the launch platform. They all watched the satellite pictures as the huge ship began to manoeuvre for orbital entry. As it was doing so, three streaks of fire shot out from the middle section.

"Three alien missiles launched!" reported Cobus.

"Chuck, anti-missile defences up!" shouted Henri.

"They ain't coming here," said Genes with disgust. "They're going after our asteroids."

He was hunched over his console, punching in commands.

"Dang. Now move!" He hit the entry key.

"Asteroid six down," reported Cobus.

There was a communal groan in the control centre.

"Asteroid three down."

A long silence. Genes continued to battle with his keyboard. Finally he leant back. "Lost two, saved one," he said, "but five is on track!"

They all watched the screen as the fiery trace of asteroid five skimmed around the atmosphere of Ceres.

"Still on track!" shouted Genes, staring intently at his monitor. "Yes, yes … Dang!"

He sank back in his chair, utterly dejected. "They're getting smart," he muttered.

"Alien missile launch! Two of them!" announced Cobus.

Again Genes applied himself furiously to try to steer his asteroids out of the path of the missiles that were homing in on them. The rest of the crew in the control centre could only watch him, agonised, and hope, but it was an unfair contest.

"Asteroid seven down," announced Cobus glumly. "Asteroid one down."

Then, "Wait!" he yelled. "Incoming missile! Defence live!" Everyone heard the launch of the departing rockets as they rose to attack the intruder.

Seconds later there was a monumental crash and Prometheus juddered. A fire started somewhere in a data bank and the control centre began to fill with dark, acrid smoke. "Suits and helmets!" shouted Arlette. "Secure for loss of gravity. Sellick, kill the fire!"

Pandemonium briefly ensued as the crew snatched up their space helmets and secured themselves in their ergo-couches. A few minutes later the fire was extinguished and the smoke began to clear. Everyone turned their attention back to their monitors.

"Air pressure stable!"

"Induced gravity normal!"

"Skin integrity OK."

"Power supply OK."

There was a brief silence.

"Genes, propulsion?"

There was no answer.

"Genes?"

Genes was no longer there.

Sanam was carrying two cups of hot coffee and was thrown off her feet when the debris from the destruction of the incoming missile hit Prometheus. She crashed against a bulkhead and went down in a heap, blood streaming from a cut on her temple. "Oh, Sanam!" wailed Arun, rushing over and cradling her in his arms.

"Get off, you lump!" said Tim Cochran. "And go and get me a bandage!"

Arun stumbled off, accompanied by the other co-pilot, to find a first aid box.

When they returned, they sat around watching Tim Cochran do such an extravagant bandaging job that hardly a strand of Sanam's rich black hair was visible.

"How am I going to put on my helmet with this on my head?" Sanam wanted to know.

"Get a bigger helmet," was Tim's helpful suggestion.

"What's Genes Clayton doing in Lander 2?" Arun asked casually.

"What?"

"Genes Clayton. He was just closing the airlock when I got back. What's he doing in there?"

They all turned towards the airlock just in time to see Lander 2's boosters flash.

"My God!" said Arun. "He's stolen our ship!"

When Tim Cochran reported the theft of Lander 2 to Arlette, she cursed herself for her utter stupidity in trusting a man for even a second who she knew to be a cunning and ruthless criminal. She assumed that Genes has taken the opportunity of the fire to steal the lander to save his own miserable neck. Her anger raged through her and she could not speak for several minutes. Finally it drained away and she was able to instruct Cobus to take over as motor man.

But Cobus was already tracking asteroid four and could see that it was being controlled.

"Asteroid four is on track," he said. "It's being controlled from a vehicle – that must be one of our landers!"

"Show me!" said Arlette incredulously.

The great screen focused in on asteroid four. It was being shadowed, and the shadow was immediately identifiable as Lander 2.

"What the hell is he doing?" howled Arlette.

"I would say that he's guiding asteroid four to the target," said Cobus. Everyone was riveted to the screen.

Genes was no stranger to the lander's cabin, or its systems. Flying had always been his passion and he had trained in just about every vehicle used by the ISEA in the last twenty years. He tuned into the asteroid guidance system, did a swift pre-flight check, released the lander, turned her with the retro-rockets, and then fired the boosters.

"I will not fail," he said, not just to himself.

He picked up asteroid four on the guidance system and then checked the position and course of Silver Streak. "In the window," he breathed.

Genes made only one small course correction as asteroid four curved around Ceres before Silver Streak appeared on the horizon. He saw the flash of rockets as the great ship began to counter-manoeuvre, then his mind revealed to him the data he was certain was coming.

"2.3 degrees left in six seconds."

He complied.

"1.2 degrees down in three seconds."

He made the final correction.

Genes saw the asteroid pile into Silver Streak and the beginning of a cataclysmic explosion. Then Lander 2 was shredded into fragments by the blast.

The destruction of Silver Streak was the most fantastic spectacle that anyone on Prometheus had ever seen. The images, captured by the satellites put in orbit to track the invader, and slo-mo'd, showed the asteroid enveloping the spacecraft as its surface ice melted on impact, then the destruction of the ship as the rocky centre smashed through its body, and finally a huge explosion as the energy of the impact ignited everything combustible in it. Sadly, though, this was not all it showed. The elegant white form of Lander 2 appeared in the picture at the moment the explosion detonated, and it seemed to turn almost instantly into a cloud of white dust.

"There goes a very brave man," said Henri into the silence that followed.

34
Shaping the Future

The enquiry conducted by the leadership team that followed found no evidence that Genes had not acted entirely on his own initiative. He had understood the limitations in the scope of control of the asteroids by the parasite systems and realised that the alien ship had correctly seen this weakness. All they had to do was move out of the way when it was too late for a remote signal to change the asteroid's course any more. Genes had probably concluded that he would have to be able to steer the asteroid up to the last moment, and he had taken the only course of action open to him to achieve that end.

He was, then, a belated hero in the eyes of the Prometheus mission, and his attempts to take control of it earlier began to be seen as the sadly misguided results of his social convictions, rather than greed or the lust for power. This suited the leadership, who cared more and more about the cohesiveness of the mission, and less and less about accounting to Mission Control for their actions.

Hannah had been observing Arlette as the findings of the enquiry were delivered, and went to see her shortly afterwards.

"You miss him, don't you?" she asked.

Arlette looked at her dolefully. "Yes," she said. "Somehow I never doubted that he had greatness in him. I knew he was wild and a risk-taker, and he deserved no mercy for what he did, but he gave his life to save our mission. I can't help being deeply affected by that."

"How close did you feel to him personally," asked Hannah.

Arlette looked away. "Nothing happened," she said finally. "But it could have, in the right circumstances."

"Perhaps you shouldn't have raised the bar so high?" said Hannah. "You're strong enough to follow your own instincts. Nobody would think any the less of you. You need physical contact and human warmth, you know. You're not a zombie."

Arlette looked straight into Hannah's eyes. "Yes," she said, "you're right. I do regret it. I wish I'd let him charm me and that I'd taken him into my bed. I could have handled the consequences, but I was just too … proud. But what about you, Hannah? What are you doing for human warmth?"

Hannah laughed. "I have my Jafar back home," she said, "and we have some very private exchanges on the video. I'm OK. I feel his love and that sustains me. How do you feel about Henri these days?"

"Gosh, Hannah, you don't pull your punches, do you?" said Arlette with a grin. "You know he's fucking Julia, don't you?"

"Yes," said Hannah lightly. "I think they enjoy each other's company, intellectually and sometimes physically. Does it bother you?"

Arlette was going to say 'No' but changed her mind. "It does," she said, "because there is unfinished business between us. I'm not jealous of Julia. I'm not like her and her relationships with men seem to be just, well … playful. I think she's completely unaware about my relationship with Henri. I don't think there's any spite in her."

"But?"

"But Henri and I should have had a long talk, and we haven't," said Arlette with a shrug.

"Well, you should," said Hannah, "as soon as possible. And, if the mood takes you, you should take him to bed and then laugh with him about it afterwards. There's tension there when you interact. It would be better if it was resolved."

"Gee, thanks Hannah!" said Arlette, laughing. "I feel better already"

"Good," said Hannah. "There's something else. You're preoccupied with this Omnipotence thing, aren't you?"

"Well," shot back Arlette, "aren't you?"

"No," said Hannah. "If it's there, it's there, and it's always been there. We are going to do our best and live in accordance with our values. Don't look over your shoulder; you cannot possibly second guess what is required of you. It should be enough to know that your instincts have served you well. You must do what you must do and take this mission where you believe it should go. We all see the complicity of Mission Control and we all know we are here to do a good job for humanity. Let's continue with our internal debates, but be yourself and stop worrying about pleasing everybody."

"Do I try to please everybody?" asked Arlette.

"No," said Hannah, "but you worry about it."

* * *

Cobus Vermeulen was charged with setting up an early-warning system to detect any fresh intrusion into the Omega 16 planetary system, and he deployed an extensive array of satellites encompassing all the planets to do so. With this underway, the focus on extending the colonisation of Ceres was increased. A substantial extension to the Orange House was commenced, with the objective of housing a population of 100, and the camp in the Lake Area was expanded and fortified.

The shipbuilding programme advanced slowly at first with the construction of an eight-seat motor-assisted sailing vessel, which allowed for modest one-day excursions that were more pleasurable than practical, but design work then commenced on a much larger ship with on-board accommodation. The construction and fitting-out of this ship became a favourite activity at the base, and extensive debates went on about the design of her facilities. The jubilation at her launch was somewhat tempered by the list she adopted in the water, but this was promptly corrected with ballast. When Arlette was asked to name her, she chose Orange Queen because her sails were, inevitably, made of the same orange parachute material that had proven so versatile in other applications.

The colony was yet to face a Ceresian winter, but

satellite assessments of the weather patterns at the same latitude in the southern hemisphere of the planet indicated that frosts would be only a rarity, even at the depth of the long nights. They would remain dependent on the nuclear power plants that had been brought in Prometheus, supplemented by solar power for recharging the batteries of the vehicles, but coal deposits had been found close to the surface, so energy dependence was not a great concern.

The issue that really did concern the leadership was how to close the industrialisation gap for a population that was used to sophisticated products. They could make none of these for themselves, and to import all the equipment to manufacture a household item like a phone from its basic raw materials was completely impractical. The technology was of course available, but the manufacturing infrastructure was not.

Arlette was invited to give the opening address at the first Ceres development conference, which was attended by over 90 per cent of the colonists. Sensing the potential for social conflict, she chose her words carefully.

“We all understand, I’m sure,” she began, “that the pace of development of our settlement here is determined by what we have brought on Prometheus, what we can do ourselves, and what can, over a period of time, be delivered from Earth. Since we cannot produce or import all the things we were used to on Earth, we have to be highly selective. It’s your job to make those choices,” she went on, “but before you do, I recommend that you examine carefully our successes and failures so far. In judging them I suggest that we do not look only at material advancement, but also at their contribution to social cohesion. We are, largely I think, a happy, cosmopolitan community. If you compare that to the history of society on Earth over the last hundred years, that's already an exceptional achievement. Let's keep it that way."

She got good-natured applause. She had resisted being directive; she trusted the judgement of her own team to participate and steer the process clear of calamity.

Freddy Jones then delivered a rousing presentation on agriculture. At the end he boomed, "Unlike the industrial sector, we are able to bring all the experience and nearly all the technology accumulated on Earth and put it to work on Ceres. We are not bound here by the mistakes of the past; we can use them to our advantage. We already know we have a wonderfully fertile planet, and in our sector we can all look forward to almost endless growth and success."

The conference ploughed on through presentations and workshops on IT, medicine, construction materials, energy and a number of other topics, some stimulating, others sadly deficient, but, at the end of two long days, almost everyone had had a say in something and felt very much a useful part of the community and its future.

The topics that were not discussed were politics and leadership, and Arlette had been emphatic on that with her own team. "We have a command structure that was accepted by every member of the Prometheus crew before the mission began," she pointed out, "and I'm not prepared to risk destabilising that at this early stage by holding elections of any kind. If anybody thinks that this leadership team is not working, then they should speak out and we'll resolve it between us. Do we all agree?"

'How could anybody fail to?' thought Marcel a bit ruefully, but he did not disagree in principle.

The discussion that took place after the conference, however, had a rather different tone.

"There was a big issue in the discussion about constructing accommodation for a new shipload of immigrants from Earth," reported Henri. "It's dammed hard work cutting up blocks of stone, mixing concrete and building walls. People are prepared to do it for themselves and their colleagues, but not for a bunch of newcomers. Someone suggested payment in kind. It's going to have to be a negotiation point with Mission Control."

"That's going to be tricky," said Arlette. "Mission Control is assuming that we'll get it done. They will be sending a lot of stuff with them."

"Well," said Julia, "we cannot afford to have anyone claim that we are using slave labour, so we'll need to construct a nice little package that can be labelled 'goodies for residents' as opposed to the 'for everyone's general benefit' stuff. We absolutely do not want to create any grounds for the residents to resent the newcomers."

"OK, Julia, I see your point," said Arlette. "Please take ownership of that one."

"People also feel strongly about the skills of the newcomers," went on Julia. "They want farmers, builders, plumbers, electricians, doctors and engineers with relevant experience. They don't want any more theoretical scientists, and they certainly don't want any politicians!"

"We'll have to make that clear at the outset," said Henri. "I suggest we get the right to vet the list. We have a delicate balance up here, socially and ethnically. Mission Control must understand that."

"That should cause a lively debate back home!" chimed in Marcel. "'New settlers grab immigration policy reins! Is the tail wagging the dog?' I can see the headlines now."

"I should imagine that the number of applicants will be huge," said Arlette. "There'll be plenty of scope. We'll just need to negotiate tactfully."

"OK," said Julia, "but let's be proactive on all these points. If we let General Lee make a proposal, it will be a hell of a job to move him. Much more effective if we send him a bright little message one day saying, 'we're ready, we know what the colony needs to thrive and grow and here it is. Bang!'"

"We've still got a lot of work to do on the list," said Marcel. "The industrial group wants a Bessemer furnace and a steel mill. They say there cannot be any real progress without steel."

"Oh, good grief!" said Julia. "How retro-industrial-revolution can you get? We'll be wanting railroads and ocean liners next!"

"I sometimes wish we still had Genes around," said Henri a bit wistfully. "He had an instinct for looking at things from an unconventional angle. It would not surprise me that an engineer, charged with designing a pocket steel mill for another planet, couldn't come up with something workable."

"Doesn't that apply to just about anything we want?" asked Marcel. "Isn't it more important that we define our priorities and challenge the folks back on Earth to meet them? Isn't that what our conference was supposed to do?"

"It did," said Arlette. "It just came up with a list longer than we can manage. Wouldn't you rather have a microchip machine rather than a steel mill?"

"Not if I couldn't get any raw materials for a microchip machine. Have you any idea of the weird elements that go into those things, and what it takes to extract and refine them? At least we know we have iron ore and coal here."

"Well, we are going to have to make these choices, so we'd better sit here and decide how we are going to prioritise," said Arlette.

The meeting went on long into the night.

Arlette decided to use every member of her team to present a part of what was a first attempt at an immigration policy for Ceres to Mission Control. She began by reporting on what had been achieved so far in terms of self-sufficiency, growth and social cohesion, pointed out their concerns about industrial development and then handed over to Julia.

"Let me start by acknowledging that what I am going to say is the view from Ceres, not an attempt to take into account all the other factors that you have to consider," she began. "We are a small pioneering community which has, within a period of three months, established a viable presence on Ceres. We are limited in the rate at which we can grow by the lack of infrastructure, but we recognise the physical impossibility of correcting this in the short to medium term because of the huge amount of equipment and know-how required. For example," she went on, "we see no prospect of being able to prospect for oil and gas, or producing it if we should find it, in the foreseeable future. That means we are likely to remain dependent on the small nuclear power plants we brought with us for lighting and heating, on solar power which we use to recharge our vehicle batteries, and on coal which we can use for our expanding energy requirements. We have some avenues where we can expand, like agriculture and transport, but a large majority where we cannot do so without a very substantial airlift from Earth. These facts of life are well understood by the steadily increasing band of settlers we have here. Despite the high level of education of most of the crew, more and more are beginning to enjoy the pioneering life and find themselves able to make a meaningful contribution to the community. Discussions about returning to Earth are becoming few and far between.

"It is our conviction", she concluded, "that the most effective way to develop Ceres as a successful human society is to apply this model in numerous settlements around the planet, sited in close proximity to its major natural resources, and equipped with the hardware and know-how to exploit them specifically. We will then have motivated people in stable communities with the interest and potential to grow and trade with one another. We need, as a top priority, a team of geologists to carry out a global survey and so pave the way for the foundation of an efficient global economy."

Marcel followed her with his assessment of technology requirements. "First, second and third it's communications!" he said. "All members of this community need to avail themselves of the combined knowledge of the human race, so we must make the global internet available to all with robust transmission and reception systems. Fortunately this is not a great deal in terms of shipment volume. Then", he continued, "we must bolster our medical community with additional skills and manpower. We are in an alien environment here and very vulnerable to unknown bacteria and viruses. Moreover we will inevitably be seeing a rash of happy events within the next year." He paused.

"As for the industrialisation of this particular community, we see steel, copper and probably other metals production as likely candidates. This needs geological verification, as Julia pointed out, but with this background, our longer-term evolution is possibly into heavy engineering, driven in part by the considerable hydroelectric potential we have seen in the mountains to the east of us. We will need, therefore, some very creative engineers to transform practical experience on Earth into manageable technologies for Ceres."

"Henri?" prompted Arlette.

"Security issues are manageable at present," said Henri. "The indigenous animal life can be dangerous if you are unprepared, but they aren't a threat to the community as a whole. We also see no signs of internal instability within our community. Our concerns about ethnic conflicts related to events on Earth have pretty much evaporated. This is a happy community engaged in the healthy pursuit of their own well-being. Our biggest threats by far are the potential return of alien spaceships from Andromeda, should they manage to establish a new wormhole, and any conflicts we might import with new immigrants from Earth." He glanced at Arlette, who was mouthing "Genes" at him.

"Of course," he went on, "we have had the crisis over

the conspiracy led by Genes Clayton and backed by Chang Chao. We have no grounds to question your conclusions that this was a Mafia plot to take control of our mission and exploit the outcome for criminal purposes. The heroism of Clayton in the Battle of Ceres has gone a long way towards relieving the concerns of our community and putting the issue into the perspective of misguided political views. But, getting back to the Andromeda threat," he went on, "we now have a system of observation satellites throughout the Omega 16 planetary system which will give us ample warning of any new arrivals. The faster we get on with colonising Ceres, the better we'll be able to manage any unwelcome visitors."

Arlette then summarised briefly. "We need a limited number of new immigrants with specific skills and a lot of equipment as we have specified," she said. "New expeditions to targeted locations on Ceres need to be carefully planned and resourced according to the local opportunities and conditions. We think that's subject to a very comprehensive geological survey and at least a year away. We urge you to think very carefully about the suitability of new immigrants to the pioneering way of life which is likely to predominate here for a considerable period of time. Those who are not willing or able to participate in the basic activities which sustain and benefit the community are likely to find themselves a centre of controversy rather quickly. Thank you." She cut the link.

"Well, let's hope they're in a frame of mind to listen," said Arlette with a sigh. "By the way, which of you want to stay here and be part of the development of Ceres and which of you want to come with me to Omega 16-4?"

35
The Parting

The response from Mission Control which arrived a day later seemed to Arlette to be almost completely unrelated to the communication that had elicited it and was concerned almost exclusively with the Andromeda threat. It alluded briefly to the initial colonisation process as being successful, and made no reference to the programmes for further development, but rather focused entirely on what was perceived as the need to introduce armed spaceships to defend against future alien incursions. These spaceships were being designed and constructed as a top priority, apparently at the expense of everything else needed to develop the settlement.

Arlette, Julia and Henri glumly watched the video a second time around.

"I don't believe it!" said Julia. "How could they be so utterly insensitive and testosterone driven?"

"I'm not surprised," said Arlette with a tone of resignation. "The big-wigs don't want to find themselves under greater threat here than they were on Earth."

"Exactly," said Henri. "That's a response governed by the political leaders who want to be in control. The welfare of the ordinary citizen comes way down the list when the security of the state is in question. They are naturally going to concern themselves with that before they commit further manpower and resources. After two spectacular defeats, wouldn't you expect the Andromedans to make no mistake the third time?"

"I may be naive about the technical capabilities of an alien civilisation from another galaxy," countered Arlette, "but putting through a wormhole to another galaxy is not just an afternoon's work, whoever you are."

"Agreed," said Marcel. "We have earned ourselves a substantial degree of security, not least because the communication channel for the Andromedans has been cut off and they could not know what might be waiting for them next time they try to come into our space. If they are going to try again, it might well be to another part of the Milky Way which is not populated by prickly Earthmen."

"Exactly," said Henri again, inserting himself back into the discussion. "One of the options they would certainly have to evaluate would be the reaction we have just seen from Mission Control. The Andromedans know we have a substantial commitment to this part of the Milky Way. We have a settlement and we have fought hard and successfully to defend it. They know we have an open wormhole back to our own solar system, so we would be in a good position to improve our defences. I think Marcel is right: they'll look elsewhere for a foothold in the Milky Way next time."

"Surely Mission Control will understand that

argumentation?" put in Julia. "It's so wasteful of time and money to build a military fleet when we just need resources to keep our settlement growing. How long will it take them to do that, anyway, Henri?"

Henri looked over at Marcel. "I would think a year at least. What do you think?"

"At least!" came the response.

While Henri and Marcel engaged in an intense discussion about the possible nature of the warship that might be built, and what its capabilities would need to be, the two women went for a walk in the Ceresian sunshine.

"Are you serious about going to 16-4?" asked Julia.

"Absolutely!" came the reply. "The settlement on Ceres needs wise leadership, but that doesn't have to come from me. Marcel or you can do that job perfectly well. I need to know whether 16-4 is habitable and a potential alternative to Ceres. It makes a huge difference if we have two planets, both of them larger than Earth, which could become new homes for the human race. Surely you see that?"

"Ye-es," replied Julia cautiously, "but it's also taking you away from the mission you were charged with. It looks to me as though we are heading for a break, or at least a fundamental change, in our relationship with Mission Control, and that bears thinking through very carefully."

Arlette laughed. "Of course you are right!" she said brightly. "And I'm not someone who has a reputation for rashness, but I am not going to follow poor policies slavishly either. Mission Control has taken data we have given them and come up with an answer that all of us here think is the wrong one. It's our job to help them get it right. However, if, for reasons of local political expediency, they don't get it right, then I'm not going to implement a policy that I think is bad, not only for Ceres but also for the rest of humanity."

"You do realise that that could be considered piracy, don't you?" Julia asked, a smirk on her face.

"You really believe that?!"

"It could be seen that way if someone had a political reason to do so, Commander," said Julia. "This is a very important step you are considering and we need to air it thoroughly."

"I know, and I'm trying to do just that." Arlette reached out and held Julia's arm. "I just have you three and I need you all to be with me," she said softly.

Julia compiled a video of all four of them addressing various aspects of the alien threat, and building on the argument that the least likely choice of location for the Andromedans to attempt to gain a new foothold in the Milky Way would be Omega 16 or the Earth's solar system, where they would be sure to meet unknown but serious opposition. It reiterated the need for a certain number of skilled immigrants and selected equipment.

After several days Mission Control finally responded with a short statement to the effect that they saw little point in further developing the colony while it remained so vulnerable to attack, and that if Commander Piccard felt that the resources on Prometheus were inadequate to continue with her mission, she should return with her ship to make the case for a second trip at a later date.

"I'm surprised he didn't propose to tax us to finance the warships we don't want!" spluttered Julia after they had watched it.

"It's consensus politics," said Henri. "The G25 leaders are only concerned about how they look to their constituents."

"I don't know about you three," said Marcel, his palms face down on the table before him, "but I would rather spend the rest of my days with the woman I love doing my best for this great little community." He turned away and stared at the wall.

"Well," said Arlette. "Who's for going back to Earth and begging for development resources while our bosses are engrossed in building military ships to confront an enemy that they know nothing about and will probably never see?"

They all looked at her, and, one by one, shook their heads. "Right," she said, "let it be recorded that the leadership of the Prometheus mission elects to stay in Omega 16 and to make its best endeavours to enhance the security and prosperity of its settlement on Ceres."

They all nodded.

"I have one more question for you," said Arlette. "I am asking for your approval to take Prometheus to planet 16-4 to assess its suitability for human development."

"Why do that when we have barely begun exploration of Ceres?" asked Marcel.

"I think," said Arlette, "that whether we have one planet or two to develop in this system has a huge bearing on the potential of Omega 16 as the long-term home of the human race. Prometheus has provided the mapping data and the mineral surveys. The rest has to be done on the ground. We need to know if 16-4 is attractive and habitable."

Julia spoke first. "Yes, I want us to move forward," she said. "This is a quantum step you are proposing while the further development of Ceres will be incremental until such time as Mission Control provides fresh resources. I want to go."

Marcel shook his head slowly. "Our entire investment is in Ceres. We must nurture it at all costs. I vote to stay."

Arlette turned to Henri. He was looking at her with an expression that seemed to be somewhere between bemusement and affection, but he sounded quite decisive in his response. "I am with you, Commander," he said.

"Thank you," said Arlette quietly. "Are we then all in agreement with the appointment of Marcel as Chief Administrator of Ceres?"

Everyone smiled.

"In that case, Marcel, you and I need to agree on who will crew Prometheus and who will stay on Ceres. Let's get that done and identify any tricky cases that may require some diplomacy before we announce our decision."

Freddy Jones was the only section leader to make the decision to stay on Ceres, and some considerable arm twisting was required to get food production and preparation adequately manned on Prometheus, but within a week the choices had all been made and all concerns addressed. The announcement was made by Arlette, as succinctly as ever, and a send-off party organised. It was held two days later and coincided with the worst rainstorm they had yet encountered on Ceres.

Arlette was rather more passionate when she stood up before the group she was about to leave while the rain thundered down outside.

"I want you to know that nothing I have ever known gives me more pride than to be a member of this dynamic community on Ceres," she began. "I hope you are all conscious of the extraordinary significance of each one of you in the history of the human race. I often wonder how history will see us, but when I look around me today I see that every value that humanity stands for is represented here. We must now invest further to secure our future in the Milky Way. We shall go to planet Omega 16-4 and assess its suitability for a second human community, but you will always be the pioneers who changed history. It is our destiny and our privilege to go where no human has ever gone before, but we do so with humility and the knowledge that we bring not just the skills and knowledge of single human beings, but the very best of the thousands of years of civilisation which we represent." At that point there was a dramatic crack of thunder directly overhead. She looked up, smiled, and bowed. "You obviously get my point!" she said and stepped down to laughter and applause.

Marcel stepped up to the podium. "I can't call on the same level of authority as Commander Piccard," he began, and there was another perfectly timed clap of thunder; "well, apparently I can," he went on, to laughter, "but I want to echo those sentiments. While we lack many of the conveniences that are commonplace on Earth, we also lack the anxieties and uncertainties that are increasingly afflicting the Earthbound population. Our social cohesion, tolerance and goodwill is a pleasure to all of us. Let's continue to build a society that makes space for everyone and that will be an example for future generations. But for now let's salute the crew of the Prometheus mission who will be taking the next step to ensure that we all have an even greater future ahead of us." A rumble of approval ran around the room, and then the music started.

The departure of Lander 1 the following morning was watched by most of those who remained on Ceres, but the mood prevailing, as the craft shrank to a bright dot in the sky, was sombre. For a second time there would be no means on Ceres to take the pioneers back to the mother ship, and it reminded them all of their isolation and dependency on one another.

Back on Prometheus, the prospect of heading back into space to explore an unknown planet after a long and often tedious period in orbit energised the entire crew. Bjorn Johansson, the new leader of the propulsion section, was quick to assert himself in all aspects of the ship's operations. He was a man of few words, with a shock of yellow blond hair and a ready smile, but no one who was subjected to inquisition by his icy blue eyes doubted his intelligence and insight. He greeted Arlette with a nod and a smile, and reeled off data on booster fuel regeneration, hull integrity, gravitation system performance, satellite status and food stocks, ending with "we are in excellent shape" and a brief smile.

"Hmm, can you fly?" asked Arlette.

"Of course!" he replied. "I was a combat squadron leader and have piloted most of the ISEA vessels."

"Have you been through the motor man trial process?"

"Not yet, but I can do it before we leave and let you have the results." He smiled again and half raised his eyebrows.

Arlette nodded. "Yes, do that," she said.

Julia and Henri were talking to Cobus Vermeulen when Arlette entered. "These are the satellite photos we have of 16-4," he said. "You can see that the weather patterns are quite a lot more turbulent than they are on Ceres."

"Is that a hurricane," asked Julia, pointing at the screen.

"Yes," said Cobus. "They seem to be fairly common."

"Have you chosen a landing site?" asked Arlette.

"We have several candidates in the southern hemisphere, where it is now early summer," replied Cobus. "We'll refine them when we get into orbit."

"What's the day/night cycle?" Henri asked.

"It's only fourteen hours in total," said Cobus, "but there are three moons so the nights are usually going to be lit by at least one of them."

"Still, that's a pretty narrow operations window," went on Henri. "Let's hope we don't have to deal with the insect mentality and can work at night. Have you seen any wildlife yet?"

"Not yet," said Cobus. "We're going to have to wait until we're in orbit."

* * *

"She's back on board and spitting fire about General Lee's decision to build military ships at the expense of providing us with more immigrants and equipment," Hannah was telling Jafar. "She's taking Prometheus on a mission to explore the other rocky planet in this solar system and I really wonder how much further she may go. I have been talking to her and she's seeing her mission more as extending the presence of humanity in the Milky Way galaxy than finding a bolthole for the human race. I think she is convinced that this is the correct thing to do in the broader context, but she's anxious for reassurance that she's not appearing to be manipulated by some inscrutable alien influence. All I could do was compare her to the great explorers in history and point out that they all did what they thought they had to do, without knowing what the ultimate consequences would be.

"She's in great shape, physically and mentally, but very deeply touched by the bravery of Clayton. She had made an incredibly courageous commitment to him and her judgement was vindicated. She misses him and there's no other male around who comes up to her expectations. We have become very close and we talk about everything – love, sex, fear, jealousy – everything.

"Ceres has become really lovely now that the Orange House is finished. I think I'd like to grow old with you there. Love you, Jafar."

Jafar sighed when he got her message, and for the first time began to think that he might never see his beloved Hannah-le again. He looked at the notes he had prepared, sighed again, and threw them away. There was nothing he could tell her that wasn't about pain, death, destruction and fear. The fabric of human civilisation was coming unravelled, civil order was breaking down, and no news that put a positive spin on the future carried the slightest credibility. He talked instead about Shan and Shiv, how they were learning English and Maths, how bright and charming they both were, and the joy he had in coming home to them after a trip away. He tried to be positive about General Lee's decision, pointing out that there was still a lot of support for fresh emigration to Ceres and that his apparent militaristic preoccupations would evaporate in due course. "Be patient, my love," he concluded, "our time will come."

* * *

Prometheus was held in orbit around Ceres for another two days so as to achieve an optimum transit time, then the boosters were deployed and she headed into space for her rendezvous with planet 16-4. The damage done to the external cameras during the combat with Dark Shadow had now been repaired and the crew could once more enjoy an uninterrupted panorama of the universe outside. For a while Ceres, its blue oceans, grey-green land masses and white cloud formations, dominated the view, then attention turned to the speck that was to become planet 16-4, and, on the ship's telescope, the first views of the grey-brown planet with its distinctive three moons.

The first signs that their rendezvous with planet 16-4 would not be a smooth one occurred while they were still more than a day away from entering orbit. Cobus Vermeulen reported an exceptionally violent field of electromagnetic activity in the vicinity of two of the planet's moons as their paths crossed. "I don't get it," he said. "There seems to be some intense radiation out there but it's not coming from Omega 16."

"Haven't you seen this before from the satellite we have in place there?" queried Arlette.

"No," replied Cobus. "We've seen nothing like this and it looks as though it has knocked out our communications satellite – I can't get it to respond."

"Well, keep a close eye on it and let me know if it's a threat to the ship."

Cobus did so and it appeared to him that the disturbance, whatever it was, had subsided as Prometheus approached the nearest moon and began its preparation to enter orbit.

Nothing prepared them for the sight that greeted them as they broached the starlit horizon of the moon, for there, dead ahead of them, was the unmistakable fine blue trace of an LDST trumpet, and they were heading straight into it.

36
Omnipotence Theory

"Sanam! Get me out of this!" yelled Arlette to the pilot.

But Sanam wasn't moving, she was just nodding her head and staring at the blue trace in space as they approached it.

"Arun! Take control and get us off this course!"

Arun turned his head half towards her and then seemed to hesitate. A quizzical expression passed across his face, then his hands dropped away from the controls.

"Merde alors! What's got into you?" But before she had finished uttering the words she knew the answer.

Bjorn Johannsson had meanwhile scrambled across the control centre and yanked Sanam bodily out of her couch. He lurched forward, the left-side boosters roared into life and the ship jerked to the right in response. Almost instantaneously Arun reached out and exactly corrected the manoeuvre, then he turned towards Johannsson disapprovingly, as if challenging him to try something else.

But there was no longer anything else to try.

Prometheus was now accelerating into the wormhole to an unknown fate in the vastness of space.

Arlette watched the speed and location data flashing up on the screen before her, powerless as the point of no return came and went. Her head fell into her hands for a moment, but then her despair suddenly evaporated, to be replaced by a sense of exhilaration. She sat back and consciously controlled her breathing, then she called Cobus Vermeulen.

"Cobus, get me a fix on the location of the exit of this LDST," she said calmly.

"Ja, well," said Cobus, "I'm going to have to get into the archives and look at a lot of sky to match the profile we're getting from down the LDST. It would have been easier if you had asked me before we entered..."

"Yes, yes," said Arlette. "Just get to it." Then she left her couch and hurried to her quarters, summoning Julia and Henri along the way.

The three of them sat to watch the video record of Sanam and Arun as they piloted the ship into the LDST. They saw the surprise on their faces as the LDST came into view, heard Arlette's command to change course and saw Sanam's eyes widen for an instant before she appeared to let go of the controls. Arun was looking at her in amazement; he appeared to react to Arlette's command, turning towards her for confirmation, then his head moved forward with a look of concentration, as if he was trying to hear something, there was a moment of recognition and then his hands dropped away. A second or two later Sanam was yanked out of her seat and replaced by Bjorn Johannsson. He fired the left-hand booster without hesitation and looked confused when the manoeuvre was almost instantly reversed. He reached again for the booster control but obviously saw Arun was going to counter his move, so he looked around for help. By that time Prometheus was already entering the wormhole.

They watched the video in slo-mo three times without comment.

"Well?" said Arlette finally.

"They were being manipulated", said Henri flatly, "by an earphone message straight into the auditory cortex. We have no way of recovering that input."

"How do you know the input came through an earphone?" Julia asked.

"They were both wearing them and that's the only way I know how to get a message directly into the brain," replied Henri.

"OK. So who do you suppose is giving this input, and to what end?" persisted Julia.

Henri turned to Arlette. "Can you answer that?" he asked.

Arlette looked at him, deep in thought. Then she said, "Let's ask them."

Julia was charged with the interrogations. She welcomed Sanam warmly into her office. "Hell of a thing to find ourselves in someone else's wormhole!" she said with a big smile.

"It seems to be our destiny," replied Sanam, not looking at her.

"Are you unhappy about it?"

Sanam gave her a wistful look. "No," she said, some conditionality in her voice.

"Did you hear Commander Piccard's command? Was it clear to you what she wanted?" asked Julia.

"Yes, it was clear, but then it wasn't."

Julia waited for her to elaborate.

"Something in my head said 'Enter', just that, 'Enter', and it seemed completely right to do so."

"Was it a distinct CTT message, a voice, or just a feeling?" asked Julia carefully.

"Not as personal as a CTT message. It was a voice, a command."

"Male or female?"

"I don't know. It was … neutral."

"Why did you obey it?" asked Julia, her tone soft.

"It wasn't something external. It was part of me. There was no judgement I could make. My mind decided." Sanam shrugged.

"Did it occur to you that you had disobeyed your Commander?"

"No. I'm sure I did the right thing."

"Even if your Commander wanted you to do something else?" asked Julia.

"I suppose I assumed that she was scared of something unknown. My mind told me there was nothing to be afraid of."

"Nothing to be afraid of? That was a bit rash considering Clayton's conspiracy, wasn't it?" persisted Julia. "Didn't you think about that kind of malevolent mental manipulation? Did the voice tell you we would be safe?"

"No, not explicitly; it's just something that felt certain to me. It still does. You might just as well ask me 'do I want to be a woman?' or 'do I want to be happy?' These questions only have one answer."

"But, surely Sanam, there was a choice?"

"No, at that moment there was no choice. My brain did not perceive a choice. The choice process was inoperative. I'm sorry, I don't know how else to express it."

Julia sat back, chin in hand. "OK," she said. "But do you think in retrospect that this was your personal intuition, or was it an external input?"

Sanam stared at the ceiling for a while. "It was initially an external input, but it took charge of my intuition," she said finally.

"OK, Sanam, thank you," said Julia, and she leaned forward and squeezed her hand. "Thank you."

Arun arrived five minutes later, obviously in a great state of consternation. He sat before Julia, wringing his hands and shaking his head.

"Please," he said. "Please don't ask me to explain my actions. I can't."

"Arun, have you ever taken hallucinogenic drugs?"

He stared at her, a look of horror on his face. "Of course not! I'm a pilot!"

"Well, pot then?" asked Julia.

Arun's eyes darted left and right. He put on a slightly impish expression. "Once or twice recreationally," he said with a tilt of his head, then seriously. "But never less than a day before going on duty!"

"OK," said Julia. "Did it affect your judgement? Did you do things you would not have done otherwise?"

"Yes, but they were silly things, things that you regret the next day."

"Do you regret not changing the course of Prometheus?"

"No," replied Arun.

"No? Didn't you understand the Commander's instruction?"

"Yes, but I received another instruction."

"A CTT message? From whom?"

"No, it wasn't a CTT message. It wasn't from a person," Arun said. "Something in my head said 'Enter'. We were doing that so I did not act until Bjorn interfered. That could have been very dangerous. I corrected it immediately."

"Did you receive another instruction?" asked Julia.

"No," said Arun. "I already had my instruction. I acted accordingly."

"What was it about this instruction that made you think you could override the Commander's orders?"

"It felt like a command from the almighty," replied Arun. "I knew it was right."

"The almighty? Do you believe in God?" Julia was astonished.

"No, but that's how it felt. It was a split-second decision. You can't ask yourself questions in that situation. You do what you know is right, and safe."

"Safe?! We are going down a wormhole to God knows where! You call that safe?"

Arun thought for a moment. "Yes," he said finally. "I believe we are safe. I think … I think someone is watching over us."

"Really? Do you really believe that?"

"Yes," came the response. "And it's not a belief, it's just

a confidence that I've had since that moment." He was calm, and he was unshakable. Julia let him go.

"There's a pattern here," Julia was telling her colleagues, who now included Hannah, "and it's the same pattern as we've seen before. They are both emphatic that their input did not come from a CTT message, and quite sure that what they did was right. Was there anything in their blood, Hannah?"

"No" said Hannah. "All their reactions and their blood chemistry were normal. Whatever caused this behaviour was circumstantial."

"So, do we have a conclusion?" Arlette wanted to know.

"Yes," said Julia. "You, Commander, Cobus, Sanam, Arun, and probably Genes as well, have had your actions manipulated at a cerebral level by a power that is using that capacity to protect us from disaster. Omnipotence has a purpose for us that goes beyond our own plans."

"Right," said Arlette. "The question in my mind now is 'for what purpose are we being sent down this LDST?'"

"We might have a better chance to answer that if we knew where we were going to," said Henri. "Hasn't Cobus come up with anything yet?"

"Let me check," said Arlette, and she called Cobus. They engaged for a few minutes in soundless CTT communication, then Arlette turned back to the group. "Ladies and gentleman," she announced, "I'm told that we are on our way to a very large binary star system in the Milky Way about 50,000 light years from Earth known as Theta 7 and it contains at least two Earth-like rocky planets. Does that help?"

“The obvious conclusion is that our next task is to secure one or both of them for human habitation,” said Henri.

“But we can’t just hop from one solar system to the next, populating planets and defending them against alien invaders!” said Julia. “There are 200 billion stars in the Milky Way. It’s really difficult to believe that we could have a role to play in such vastness.” She sighed.

“Really, Julia,” put in Hannah. “There’s no need to be melodramatic. Humankind has been listening for a sign of intelligent life from somewhere else in the universe for more than a hundred years and we’ve heard nothing. The evidence, or lack of it, suggests that we are a lot more special than you think. I really don’t find it so hard to believe that we are being used by some powerful entity in our galaxy to defend it against external threats. The history of warfare on Earth is full of stories like that.”

“I don’t like the sound of that, Hannah; it suggests we are expendable,” said Julia.

“Very possibly we are, but it’s a fact that the only life we have lost in defending ourselves, and possibly this part of the Milky Way as well, against those aliens, was that of a confessed murderer.”

“Oh please, Hannah, you’re not suggesting that Omnipotence has a moral conscience as well?”

“Probably just enlightened self-interest,” said Henri. “Why would … it … put the only tool readily at its disposal – us – at risk? It doesn’t need morality.”

“I don’t like arguing this space much,” said Hannah, “but if our Omnipotence was only interested in exploiting us as a military tool, why not save Genes as well? He was a significant military asset as it turned out, if you ignored his treachery."

"Just a minute," said Arlette, "do we need to go into this morality stuff? We are accelerating down an LDST towards two more habitable planets. Might we not have a role here to apply our initiative and intelligence to, rather than just our reproductive powers?"

"My militarily incentivised Omnipotence would be saying, 'job done in Omega 16, move proven asset to deal with next potential threat'," suggested Henri.

"Oh God!" said Julia. "I can't take any more of these snowball fights with mystery alien spaceships. Supposing you're right? We get to Theta 7 and there's this alien ship bristling with armaments, waiting for us. This is not a military ship! We don't have anything more than a modest defence capability. Shouldn't we make a quick turn around and head back to Omega 16 the same way we came?"

"Perhaps we'll be a lot safer in Theta 7 than in Omega 16," suggested Hannah quietly.

"The promised land! Of course!"

"Shut up, Julia," said Arlette, "and let's apply the Omnipotence theory. What other purpose could we have that would be of benefit to the Milky Way galaxy, apart from defending it against incursions from Andromeda? Why did we go to Omega 16 in the first place?"

"Who knows?" said Hannah. "And why are we preoccupied with this question? The fact is we are going there at the behest of a vastly superior power, which has taken extraordinary care to preserve us to get us to this point, to do something which we set out to do in the first place, and love doing. What else do you want?"

There was a silence.

"There you go," said Arlette finally. "Now the collision with Andromeda is not due for about four billion years. That's plenty of time to go forth and multiply to secure the galaxy. Wouldn't we be willing to go along with that plan?"

"Absolutely!" said Henri, looking around with a scandalous grin. "When can we start?"

Follow the Omnipotence blog on http://omnipotence.co.uk/

Extrapolating into the near future of mankind

The Omnipotence Blog takes the view that the key events and decisions that will decide the future of mankind, as advancing technology brings it to the threshold of interaction with extra-terrestrial intelligent beings, are fast approaching. There is no room for fantasy. The social, philosophical and technological pre-cursors of our civilization are already in place and deeply imbedded. We will learn a lot more, but the time scale is too short for us to evolve physically or neurologically. Our instinctive behaviours will be as they are now. The pressure may come from deteriorating conditions on our own planet, or competition from outside, but our period of cosy isolation on Planet Earth is fast coming to an end – and, judging by our current political behavior, we are woefully unprepared. If you are interested in these themes, this blog is for you...

Acknowledgements

Omnipotence is the product of the inspiration and engagement of others and I am deeply grateful to

Editor–in-Chief Jo-Anne Hazel for her enthusiasm and skilful guidance, Editor Lisa Robbins for her direction and encouragement, Designer Dave Hill for his gifted visual interpretations and especially to those personally close to me who have breathed life into this story.

Use of the following images is gratefully acknowledged:

Front Cover:
Whirlpool Galaxy
http://hubblesite.org/newscenter/archive/releases/2005/12/image/a/
Out of This Whirl: the Whirlpool Galaxy (M51) and Companion Galaxy STScI-PRC2005-12a NASA, ESA, S. Beckwith (STScI), and The Hubble Heritage Team (STScI/AURA)
Earth from Space
http://earthobservatory.nasa.gov/IOTD/view.php?id=501&eocn=image&eoci=related_image

NOAA Geostationary Operational Environmental Satellite—GOES-8
Earth as seen on July 6, 2015 from a distance of one million miles by a NASA scientific camera aboard the Deep Space Climate Observatory spacecraft. Credits: NASA

Inside Front Cover:
Teleport
https://commons.wikimedia.org/wiki/File:Teleport.jpg?uselang=en-gb
Wikimedia Commons, the free media repository